GOSPEL HOUR

GOSPEL HOUR

T. R. Pearson

William Morrow and Company, Inc.
New York

Recognizing the importance of preserving what has been written, it is the policy of William Morrow and Company, Inc., and its imprints and affiliates to have the books it publishes printed on acid-free paper and we exert our best efforts to that end.

Library of Congress Cataloging-in-Publication Data

Pearson, T. R., 1956–
    Gospel hour / T. R. Pearson.
      p. cm.
    ISBN 0-688-09480-5
    I. Title.
    PS3566.E235G67   1991
    813'.54—dc20   90-43837
                                                                               CIP

Printed in the United States of America

First Edition

1 2 3 4 5 6 7 8 9 10

BOOK DESIGN BY ROBIN MAKIN

For
Zachary

I

*H*er Carl. He'd been in life a man of proclivities and she was meaning to speak of one of them, had even already discharged her customary wistful breath and was just before embarking upon her "Ah" and upon her "Carl," which served evermore as preamble to a proclivity, when she noticed how her grandbaby Delmon over by the doorscreen had assumed an unsavory posture which she elected to speak of instead and so apprised him of the perils of slouching like induced Delmon her grandbaby to elevate straightaway his lowslung parts as he laid once more his lips upon his Lorna Doone. Delmon simply did not as a rule bite his Lorna Doones but had developed instead a process of ingestion which called for him to suck on and saturate a half of his cookie until it had become exceedingly damp and pliant that he'd extract it from his mouth to ascertain it had become exceedingly both of while remaining quite utterly unbit as well, which was evermore a matter of some wonderment to Delmon though he hardly suspected himself that a soggy Lorna Doone would seem much of a marvel to anybody otherwise.

"What is it you're eating?" Delmon's grandmomma wanted to know once she'd noticed how Delmon was by turns sucking on and admiring a manner of item. "Is that a cookie here in the middle of the morning?"

And Delmon displayed for her his damp, pliant, unbit Lorna Doone, which in fact stirred appreciably his grandmomma who called for her daughter Marie to come from the kitchen and see for herself Delmon's soggy cookie that a six-and-a-half-year-old child had no business eating hardly an hour past breakfast, but Marie did not feel much inclined to come from the kitchen and see it and so merely called out to extract from Delmon assurances that he would not make a practice of eating cookies early in the day, which Delmon swore an oath about prior to resaturating his Lorna Doone that had become in the course of the proceedings unduly dehydrated and markedly unpliant.

Her Carl had known the value of a sensible diet and Delmon heard from his grandmomma a scrap of nutritional wisdom that had dropped, she let on, directly from her Carl's lips, heard it in fact two times as it seemed to his grandmomma a fairly crucial sort of a scrap. She spoke as well of the various food groups and told how it did not appear to her people were anymore much acquainted with them like prompted her to wonder of Delmon would he name for her a food group please, and Delmon was set even to speak of the chicken and hamburger shortcake one when he came to be inclined instead to point out the doorscreen towards the yard and tell to his grandmomma, "Daddy."

Of course his daddy hadn't but lately gone off to work that Delmon's grandmomma reminded him from the settee about but Delmon told her another time just, "Daddy," again and continued to point as he resaturated his Lorna Doone, which temporarily prevented him from illuminating his grandmomma to the extent he illuminated her when presently he said, "Buddy," as well and pointed and indicated one time further with renewed enthusiasm.

She joined him at the doorway once she'd taken up her black leatherette pocketbook off the sofa cushion and situated it behind the lamp on the endtable where she did not believe it could get plundered through in her absence, and her and her grandbaby Delmon watched Buddy Isom's dilapidated red half-ton fairly race towards them along the road beside the streambed with the dust and the grit churning and boiling behind it and gravel pinging off the undercarriage and knocking against the fenderwells. Buddy Isom slid and skidded on into the track and accelerated towards the house, failed even to slow partway up the hillside where the culvert had come uncovered, and so bounced head foremost off the cab roof and ejected from the truckbed the blackening piece of haybale he'd been carrying to no purpose since the previous July. He'd come to pick up Delmon's daddy not two hours past like he came to pick up Delmon's daddy every morning but for Mondays sometimes when Delmon's daddy laid out, and he did not generally return in the middle of the morning alone, did not generally return in the evening at such an extravagant velocity, and so excited the interest of most especially Delmon with his Lorna Doone who stood back of the doorscreen and wondered could Buddy Isom possibly stop his red half-ton before he ran up onto the front slab which Buddy Isom only barely managed to do by veering off into Delmon's momma's zinnias instead where he came at last to a halt with sufficient lurch and jolt to it to levitate two Pabst cans and an empty bar oil jug that all three together raised up off the bed and beat against the back windowglass.

Buddy Isom flung open the door, leapt from the cab, and fairly charged towards the house near about even gaining the front slab before he came to be prevented from it by Delmon's dog Sheba who'd been roused by the general clamor. She lay most of the day in a hole in the crawlspace but emerged every now and again to menace and bark, especially when she found herself presented with most any variety of human as Sheba did not possess much recall for faces and so departed from her crawlspace hole with fresh and evermore untempered zeal. She was as well a sizable and exotic dog, appearing to be the product of an intimacy between a bluetick hound and a goat, so she managed to thoroughly interrupt Buddy Isom on his way to the front slab by situating her prodigious wirehaired self between him and the door and barking and snapping ever so earnestly.

"Sheba!" Delmon's grandmomma hollered at her through the doorscreen and so caused herself to get barked and snapped at as well along with Delmon her grandbaby who, obscured and distorted through the screenwire, did not look to Sheba like anybody she was much acquainted with. "Sheba!" Delmon's grandmomma hollered another time and made as if to throw open the door and kick at Sheba's tender freckled underbelly which seemed to refresh Sheba's powers of recollection and she did in fact shortly recall how her hole in the crawlspace was where precisely she'd prefer to be.

Buddy Isom was wet. Buddy Isom was fairly sopping from his shirtpocket down and he seeped water out the creases of his brogans as he crossed the slab to the front door and drew up before the doorscreen where he undertook to concoct and maintain a dire expression as he'd carried with him an utterly dire piece of news. There is, however, a thing about dire news that oftentimes confounds dire expressions and renders them pretty wholly unsuitable, rendered anyway Buddy Isom's own personal dire expression unsuitable altogether as Buddy Isom could not somehow manage to be dire without appearing a little giddy as well. It was simply the pure and thoroughgoing strain of outright direness that did him in, and while he guessed he could be grim and could be sober as successfully as anybody might, he could not maintain the undiluted gravity to look dire truly and so stood before the doorscreen with his brow a trifle plagued and furrowed but his lips laid wide in a manner of wholly unsuitable smirk.

So he stood only semiforlornly upon Marie Huff's decorative doormat and dripped on both of the mallards together while he heard from Delmon's grandmomma how he should not even so much as hope to be admitted into the house proper to discharge upon the pile carpet as she simply would not endure it. She was pretty utterly confounded at why in the first place a man would find himself possessed to call in such a state, which put her in mind of a thing her Carl used to say about the demise of decent breeding among people, a thing she was threatening to invoke when Buddy Isom prevented her from it by telling through the doorscreen, "It's Donnie. He's dead."

And Delmon's grandmomma said to Buddy Isom, back "Donald?" and Delmon said to Buddy Isom, "Daddy?" himself and they heard together from Buddy Isom, "Donnie," another time like stirred Delmon's grandmomma to call into the kitchen to her girl Marie who told to her momma back how she'd already extracted from Delmon assurances adequate to suit her and did not believe anybody had been done in yet by a Lorna Doone in the middle of the morning.

"Drowned," Buddy Isom said, "in the Big Reed."

And Delmon and his grandmomma told to him, "Daddy?" and told to him, "Donald?" one time further, which seemed to Buddy Isom to so advance the general direness of the circumstances that his nervous smirk eroded intractably into a variety of toothy grin that he could not somehow help but stand atop the mallards and display. Delmon grew suddenly himself impressed with the unmitigated direness of the proceedings and so exchanged toothy grins with Buddy Isom through the doorscreen while his grandmomma, who he'd anticipated might wail and moan as his grandmomma was usually given to wailing and to moaning at the outset of most any species of distress, got lost instead in a reverie about her son-in-law, or about anyway her son-in-law's blue suit with the ever so faint and elegant stripe to it which she figured in death would render him distinguished most especially now that he could not dispute neckties with her and so would wear the satiny speckled one she'd bought him two birthdays past, the satiny speckled on he'd not ever previously removed altogether from the box.

Of course Delmon, being a child, was not much accustomed to dire circumstances and had grown sufficiently taxed and done in by his own present set of them to feel obliged to call for his momma to come from the kitchen and soothe him like seemed to his grandmomma a timely sort of a notion and induced her to holler once more for her girl Marie who was sitting at the dinette smoking a Kent and reading in a *Redbook* an altogether riveting piece of news about the resurrection of decoupage as a craft and a hobby. She had laying about the house countless tins and cast-off boxes that she undertook there at the dinette, with her Kent hanging out the corner of her mouth and her *Redbook* open before her, to fashion decoupaged which struck her as an appreciable advancement over cast-off alone, and she wondered at the likelihood of a woman maybe going into the decoupaging business and turning a profit by it, a woman possessed already of innumerable items to paste and varnish and thereby render quaint which struck Marie as the key to the entire endeavor since the appeal of quaintness appeared to her pretty much eternal as far as appeals went. So she sat at the dinette evaluating her prospects and got shortly interrupted at it by her boy Delmon and her momma Opal who called to her from the front room and heard directly back, "What is it?," which has not itself a sweet and charming sort of an inquiry.

And probably they would have insisted from out by the doorscreen how it was an acutely dire sort of a thing that prompted them to disturb her at all, or would anyhow have wailed and hollered further still but for a second half-ton pickup that raced towards them along the road by the streambed and slid and skidded onto the track, a blue half-ton that lurched over the culvert and nosed on into what of the zinnias remained to be crushed and run over. It was Frank MacAfee's brother Freeman who hopped out of the cab and stomped those few flowers that had suffered somehow no abuse otherwise, and while Delmon's grandmomma was vaguely acquainted with Frank MacAfee she'd not ever previously had occasion to meet his brother Freeman and did not take him straightoff for a MacAfee at all due to how he lacked the ancestral MacAfee prodigious belly and had managed instead to fairly waste away from drink and dissolute living. Delmon's grandmomma insisted that a man wore his indiscretions like a cloak, though Freeman MacAfee advertised his own personal inclinations well enough with his noxious breath alone which was a potent mix of corn liquor vapors and stale cigarette stink that, once he'd dodged the onslaught of Delmon's sizable wirehaired dog, he shared a blast of with Delmon and Delmon's grandmomma by means of a "Hey," which failed somehow to melt and fuse the screenwire though Delmon's grandmomma in particular could not imagine how precisely.

The mere sight of Frank MacAfee's brother Freeman on the slab beside him proved a palpable irritant to Buddy Isom who guessed he could transport and communicate dire news well enough by himself and did not hardly need the likes of Frank

MacAfee's brother Freeman come to find out could he. "Gaither send you?" Buddy Isom wanted to know and so heard from Freeman MacAfee how little Gaither had in fact dispatched him. "Well wasn't no call for it. I told them already Donnie's dead. They don't hardly need to hear it from you," and Buddy Isom undertook to wonder of Delmon's grandmomma with a glance if the ways of some people didn't surpass understanding altogether which Delmon's grandmomma managed herself a glance about back.

"I ain't come to tell them he's dead," Frank MacAfee's brother Freeman said and then reached inside his coveralls to his shirtpocket from where presently he managed to withdraw a solitary Chesterfield that he held by the filter between his thumb and foremost fingernails, a relatively flat and disreputable-looking Chesterfield that Freeman MacAfee took some pains to fluff and tamp prior to laying the thing upon his lip. "He ain't dead no more."

Freeman MacAfee could not find his matches straightoff, could not find his matches even shortly and wondered aloud what in the world he'd done anyway with his matches that nobody offered to speculate about as they could not truly work up among them the spit to speculate and stood the three of them with their chins a little loose and lowslung and merely evaporated saliva while Freeman MacAfee hunted up his errant matchpack and lit at last his cigarette which he drew on with a pure and wastrel fury. "Was dead," he said and fairly covered his face with his flat open hand so as to snatch away his Chesterfield deep in his fingergap, "but he come around. Ain't dead no more."

"I seen him," Buddy Isom insisted partly at Frank MacAfee's brother Freeman but mostly in fact at Delmon and his grandmomma opposite the screenwire. "I hadn't never come across nobody more passed on than he was. Don't tell me he wasn't dead."

"Was dead," Freeman MacAfee informed him once he'd taken occasion to step across the slab and dislodge his scant ash into a clump of marigolds. "Ain't dead no more." And Freeman MacAfee explained how they'd all of them taken him for deceased and had figured together since he'd manage to get done in he would probably evermore remain it and would likely in fact have persevered at being quite thoroughly dead if little Gaither had not come to be touched off by the general circumstances of Donnie's demise, if little Gaither had not ascended to a level of irritation sufficient to incite him to snatch up Donnie Huff by his shirtfront and inquire of him how in the hell he'd managed to ride the skidder into the creek in the first place, the skidder that had only just lately been completely torn down and rebuilt at fairly prodigious expense to little Gaither, which little Gaither shared the news of with Donnie Huff prior to speaking to him as well of the myriad abuses he would likely have felt cause to visit upon Donnie Huff's person had Donnie Huff not finagled his way into the everlasting like was for little Gaither an additional source of peevishness and he vented himself as best as he was able by pounding and shaking and jerking the deceased and slapping the deceased one time across the face with his open fleshly hand and dropping the deceased back flat upon the ground prior to gripping him at his shirtfront and lifting him one time further so as to provide the deceased the opportunity to douse little Gaither's inflamed features with about a lung and a quarter's worth of creekwater.

"He come around," Frank MacAfee's brother Freeman told through the screenwire to Delmon chiefly and Delmon's grandmomma. "Ain't dead no more."

Delmon's grandmomma straightaway identified in the miraculous turn of events the very hand of the Almighty as it appeared to her Him alone the could snatch back a man from what, in the case of her own particular son-in-law, was surely the jaws of perdition. "It's a miracle," she said somewhat through the screenwire but chiefly to her grandbaby Delmon whose knobby shoulders she gripped and squeezed, her grandbaby Delmon who'd allowed his Lorna Doone to go unsaturated throughout the entire spell of excitement and dismay and so made some use of the general relief to rehumidify and rewilt his cookie that he shortly extracted and studied with his habitual wonderment.

"He's lifted the veil and seen past it," Delmon's grandmomma said, "been to the beyond and come back from it, gazed likely upon the face of the Savior."

"Well," Frank MacAfee's brother Freeman said and raised his leg so as to dip his ash upon his thigh and rub it into his coveralls, "little Gaither's right pissed off at him. If I was him I might have just stayed at the beyond."

Buddy Isom, who was still a little stunned by the course of events, aired for no one in particular his own personal recollection that Donnie Huff had turned a rather striking shade of bluegreen, and he polled the little Huff and the grandmomma and the MacAfee too so as to ascertain if a man could be blamed for figuring a fellow wouldn't likely recover from being dead and bluegreen both which they all three agreed a man couldn't, most especially Delmon's grandmomma who failed entirely to see how a Godless heathen like Buddy Isom could hope to anticipate an instance of divine intervention.

Freeman himself, having gotten in the first place dispatched to impart a thing other than just Donnie Huff's general revival, stirred himself to impart it, told through the screenwire to Delmon and his grandmomma, "They carrying him out to Galax to the hospital. Figured he might have strained an organ or something what with being deceased and getting bluegreen. Told me to tell you they carrying him out there."

"We'll fly to him," Delmon's grandmomma declared and called out towards the kitchen for her girl Marie to come quick if she would, her girl Marie who was endeavoring with a boning knife to cut out from her *Redbook* an elegant photograph of a lustrous black Lincoln Town Car on a wet shimmery street like had struck her as just the sort of thing that would look altogether smashing decoupaged on a box. Of course slicing around the contours of a sedan with a knife edge proved far too delicate an undertaking to allow Marie Huff to reply straightoff to her momma and so her momma called her a second time after she'd heard her call her the first time already, which she lifted her knife and spoke to her momma about, informed her anyway how she was at the moment engaged and made to solicit her momma's patience, told to her, "Wait a goddam minute," like would have probably by itself punctuated her momma quite completely if her momma had not already grown inclined to silence on account of a yellow two-door Ventura, a yellow two-door Ventura fairly streaking towards them alongside the creekbed flinging gravel and churning dust and, presently, slipping and skidding on into the track and making for the exposed culvert at a truly regrettable velocity.

As the zinnias had been ravaged and destroyed already, the yellow Ventura nosed on into the hydrangea bush instead and so crushed some reedy shoots and mangled a few gaudy blue blossoms while managing as well to dispatch a veritable cloud of aggravated bumblebees that thumped against the windshield in a peevish sort of a way and so flushed out from the Ventura Vernon Nevins's boy Alvis who retreated back so far as the culvert and swatted and dodged and jumped and swore and expressed with some vitality his own personal doubts as to the general usefulness of bees anyway, which Delmon's dog Sheba, who'd stirred already from her hole in the crawlspace, heard him in at the sideyard and so quickened on around the house and induced Alvis Nevins to return ever so directly to his Ventura from where he informed Frank MacAfee's brother Freeman and Buddy Isom and Delmon and Delmon's grandmomma of his own personal doubts as to the general usefulness of sizable wirehaired goatlike dogs as well which was not truly what he'd come all this way to run into the hydrangea bush for.

He'd been dispatched to tell how Donnie Huff would not after all be visiting the hospital in Galax as he'd taken upon recovery an accounting of his various parts and organs and had not found them to be much strained. Alvis Nevins did not believe Donnie Huff would be arriving home shortly either but had been led, most especially by little Gaither, to understand that Donnie Huff would be joining the efforts of Buddy Isom and Freeman MacAfee and Alvis Nevins himself to winch little Gaither's John Deere skidder up off the bottom of the Big Reed, which Alvis Nevins had been led as well to understand Buddy Isom and Freeman MacAfee could not loiter upon a front slab and be much effective at.

"Come on," he told to them from out the sidewindow of his Ventura. "That damned Gaither's iller than shit," which gave rise to a variety of riposte from Frank MacAfee's brother Freeman on the slab, a variety of riposte that Alvis Nevins could not begin to make out from his Ventura due to how Sheba the sizable wirehaired dog took the occasion of Freeman MacAfee's riposte to raise up her head and bark pretty much flush against Alvis Nevins's left eardrum, prompting Alvis Nevins to declare, "I'm gone shoot this dog," which he told towards the doorscreen to Delmon and his grandmomma and which he confirmed to the dog itself and so suffered his eardrum to be barked against one time further,

Alvis started his Ventura and backed it off the hydrangea bush while Buddy Isom, for his part, told chiefly to Frank MacAfee's brother Freeman, "Well," and so prompted from Freeman an altogether similar sort of a Well back, and the two for them excused themselves off the slab and made for their vehicles which they rolled by turns out from the mangled zinnias. They waved. The both of them flung their arms out their sidewindows in a salute to Delmon and to Delmon's grandmomma back of the doorscreen, and then they left the track for the road where they proceeded along the branch and on off around a thicket and out of sight, leaving nothing but the devastated flora and the rising dust to indicate they'd even come in the first place at all. Delmon watched the piece of road where they'd both just lately been while his grandmomma peered through the screenwire in the direction of the heavens, or up anyway into the reaches of the sugar maple out alongside the track which seemed to inspire her to a devotional sort of a discharge, a scrap of talk about the Lord taking folks up when nobody else might seem much inclined to, which she identified for Delmon as one of the holy Psalms and spoke beyond it briefly of the general wonders of the Almighty who was most certainly in, she told it, His heaven, and she inquired of Delmon if didn't it seem to him that all was in fact right with the world, but Delmon had his droopy cookie to contemplate and so managed merely to grunt at her back.

Delmon's momma Marie emerged at last from the kitchen with her boning knife in one hand and her Lincoln Town Car in the other and she spied her momma Opal and her boy Del-

mon over upon the threshold before the doorscreen and she
inquired of them, "What in the hell is it?" and so heard from
her momma how it was in fact a miracle but did not hear from
her momma what variety precisely of miracle it was due to how
Opal had opted instead to clasp her hands to her bosom in a
most theatrical and semiarticulate fashion that Marie made no
attempt much to decipher and fathom but joined instead her
Delmon at the doorscreen and looked out through it into the
yard. Of course the road dust had pretty much left off boiling
and churning and the flora, while still devastated, did not strike
Marie as ever so freshly crushed and mangled, which left her
still to wonder of her momma chiefly, "What is it?" that her
momma was actually set to speak of and reveal when she took
some notice of the black lustrous Lincoln Town Car in her girl
Marie's hand and so found herself compelled to tell to her
daughter instead, "Nothing but a glorified Ford. Your daddy
Carl wouldn't never have had one even if somebody'd come up
and give it to him," and she discharged through the screenwire
her customary wistful breath and intoned towards the leafy
maple treetop, "Ah," and intoned towards it, "Carl."

ii

It wasn't even his to cut which was part of the trouble in the
first place since he didn't want to get caught cutting it if it wasn't
his to cut and could not be made to understand that the stump
itself would suggest and imply that he had in fact cut it whether
he got caught at it or not. But little Gaither figured as long as
nobody slinked up on him while his saw was revving and the
chips were flying and the tree was hinging over then he could
contend well enough with just a stump alone, could wonder
along with everybody else how in the world it had come to be
one. So he went ahead and cut it in a rush, slipped across the
line that had been hacked out of the scrub and underbrush and
blazed with so very much orange stripping as to proclaim itself
the irrefutable end of one place and beginning of some place
else, and he paused briefly to sight up the trunk, which was
stout and straight and streaky walnut throughout, and calculate

the boardfeet like left him a little breathless and agitated. He wanted the thing drawn off whole and cut up someplace otherwise but came to be persuaded to reconsider by Donnie Huff in particular who could not begin to see how little Gaither's lately rebuilt but still dilapidated John Deere log skidder could be coaxed into hauling that entire walnut tree. Alvis Nevins who fashioned himself a fellow of uncommon discernment and penetration suggested that perhaps since little Gaither was prepared already to puzzle and wonder over the origins of a solitary stump he could embrace in his bafflement a heap of limbs as well which Alvis Nevins was enlisting by turns Buddy Isom and Freeman MacAfee to throw in with when little Gaither yielded to him and induced thereby Alvin Nevins and Buddy Isom and Freeman MacAfee to start up their own saws and sheer the trunk clean.

They got prevented by little Gaither from cutting the walnut at their usual fifteen feet as little Gaither was of a mind to slice the thing merely in half instead. He had visions of fully dressed twenty-five-foot walnut planks and so indicated what struck him as a middling point up the trunk and wondered, once nobody much had shown an inclination for it, might Buddy Isom or Freeman MacAfee or Alvis Nevins generate the gumption to step on up and cut the thing in half, which prompted Buddy Isom and Freeman MacAfee to nominate Alvis Nevins for the endeavor since they'd both of them just lately filed their chains and guessed they'd as soon saw through a Pontiac as a length of walnut trunk which Alvis Nevins, once he'd been nominated, threw in with them about like fairly ignited little Gaither's ire and he rained a dose of it on Alvis Nevins in particular, Alvis Nevins who came to be persuaded that he could always find the opportunity to sit and file his chain one time further most especially if he did not loiter so long in his obstinance as to allow little Gaither the occasion to impale Alvis Nevins on the pointy piece of limb he'd selected for that purpose, skewer him through asshole foremost, which little Gaither did not suppose would prevent Alvis Nevins from filing his chain in the future but would surely leave him reluctant to sit while he did it.

So Alvis Nevins discerned and penetrated to the very nug-

get of his predicament and offered quite directly to step on up
to the walnut trunk and saw it through in half-lengths. Little
Gaither let on to be delighted at the prospect and waved and
brandished his pointy piece of limb in what Alvis Nevins could
not take altogether for jubilation and so slipped sideways to
shield his posterior as he stepped up to the walnut treetrunk
and worked and wrestled his saw through the girth of it and
down slightly into the ground beneath it where he scored a slab
of shale that Buddy Isom and Freeman MacAfee informed him
it looked to them he had and so touched off some hooting and
some saw waving on the part of Alvis Nevins which could not be
taken altogether for jubilation either. Donnie Huff backed the
skidder up through the underbrush and Buddy Isom and Freeman MacAfee wrapped the chain around the upper half of the
walnut trunk and dispatched Donnie Huff down through the
woods and well across the property line to a flat place they'd cut
in the hillside just shy of the bluff above the Big Reed where
Donnie Huff meant to turn and angle off towards the mill in
the bottom and did even presently turn and angle off both but
not before the sizable piece of trunk had accelerated down the
slope, passed him across the level ground, and fetched up
against a puny hemlock that bent and shivered but failed to
pitch somehow entirely over.

Donnie Huff lingered on the flat place long enough to lean
out from the wire cage over the skidder seat and dispatch to
little Gaither up the slope a snatch of invective, speak briefly to
him of what variety of dumb lowly son-of-a-bitch would make a
man haul a thirty-foot hunk of walnut in the first place down
such a pitch and back of such a contraption which little Gaither
could not make out sufficiently to take acute offense at and so
took only moderate offense instead, offense enough to feel compelled to share with Donnie Huff a vile bilious variety of item
back that he adorned and complemented with an unseemly and
ever so expressive species of gesture.

As Alvis Nevins was himself anxious to discover who precisely might be obligated to go into the lockup were they ap-
prehended for poaching hardwood, Buddy Isom and Freeman
MacAfee consulted with little Gaither on the matter and they all

three agreed among them that undoubtedly Alvis Nevins would be the one to get incarcerated which Alvis Nevins begged, if he might, to be contrary about and lurched wildly around in the underbrush flailing his arms and exhibiting his thoroughgoing chagrin which culminated in a proclamation, culminated in fact in a pair of proclamations together. "I'll be goddammed," Alvis Nevins said. "I ain't never cut down that tree," and he stomped and flailed and just generally exhibited further still as he heard from Buddy Isom and from Freeman MacAfee both how he had not inquired who'd cut down the tree but had sought instead to find out who it was that would get incarcerated for it which they'd gone to the trouble to enter into a consultation about and had determined it would in fact be him. "I'll be goddammed," Alvis Nevins told them, and as his agitation increased, his stomping and his flailing accelerated, and his voice grew evermore shrill and squeaky the way they'd hoped and anticipated it might. "I ain't going to no lockup. I ain't never cut that tree," he said and careened through the milkweed and the viny scrub swatting and beating at the air and venting a manner of complaint that Buddy Isom guessed at Freeman MacAfee they'd near about have to be a pair of collies to hear.

Donnie Huff chugged and sputtered up from the bottom on the John Deere skidder and gained the plateau notched in the hillside from where he turned to climb up through the woods towards the remaining length of walnut that Alvis Nevins was patrolling roundabout as he flailed and declaimed. Once he'd wheeled the skidder around backend foremost, Donnie Huff rolled it full up against the limbend of the length of trunk as he did not suspect he had chain enough to hook around the rootend even one time which Buddy Isom, who sized up the girth, and Freeman MacAfee, who sized up the chain, consulted briefly together about and issued presently a joint finding of what Donnie Huff had gone on ahead and suspected already. So they slipped it around the limbend and waved Donnie Huff down the slope so far as to draw taut the chain and snug up the loop which gripped and held after a satisfying fashion as best as Buddy Isom and Freeman MacAfee could tell. Consequently, then, they dispatched Donnie Huff altogether with one variety

of wave further, and them and little Gaither watched him advance down the slope with the length of walnut behind him
until it had manufactured some additional momentum of its
own when it caught up with Donnie Huff and advanced for a
time pretty much alongside him instead. Even Alvis Nevins
managed to leave off flailing and stomping and screeching long
enough as to stand kneedeep in the viny underbrush and watch
Donnie Huff and his length of hardwood compete down the
hillside where they were engaged in what appeared to Alvis
Nevins a dead heat until they gained the notch when Donnie
Huff made to turn down the roadcut and head towards the mill
like seemed to run purely contrary to the intentions of his
ponderous piece of tree. It was apparently of a disposition to
keep on going where it had set out in the first place to go and
so failed to swing around back of the skidder, or failed anyhow
to leave off swinging around once the little end had been persuaded by the loop of chain to pivot. The rootend came briefly
into alignment along the roadcut but straightaway proceeded
on beyond alignment entirely, fanned about like an outsized
bathead, and squarely clubbed the puny hemlock that shivered
and shook and pitched shortly straight over backwards with its
shallow roots torn from the ground and uplifted like allowed
the length of walnut to fan about further still until the sizable
unchained end of it was dangling off the bluff out over the Big
Reed which was just the sort of circumstance to give rise in
Donnie Huff to some measurable consternation.

Of course, from up on the hillside high above the notch,
little Gaither and Buddy Isom and Freeman MacAfee and Alvis
Nevins could not determine the precise nature of Donnie Huff's
predicament and concluded between them that the assorted
imprecations he was screeching were just in the way of your
usual variety of profane banter and so served to prompt and
bait the bunch of them who imprecated back, spoke to Donnie
Huff of his various personal failings and entered briefly together into a consultation which resulted in an intensely unsavory sort of sentiment that little Gaither was appointed to
proclaim down the hillside and so proclaimed it. For his part,
Donnie Huff had by then wholly surpassed imprecating and

was embarking upon a bout of highly animated howling much to the amusement of the boys up on the slope who watched the log skidder swing around and nose back towards where it had just lately left which seemed to them a peculiar but diverting manner of stunt.

Little Gaither's mild myopia prevented him from detecting straightaway that his rebuilt dilapidated John Deere log skidder had canted back, though he came shortly to be convinced that he was viewing inordinately more of the yellow steel underbelly of the thing than he had any right to see which Buddy Isom and Freeman MacAfee confirmed for him by means of a fairly harmonious exclamation which seemed to little Gaither quite utterly ripe with wonderment. As spectacles went, this one impressed the four of them as particularly unforeseen and exotic, and they stood together high up the slope and exchanged perplexed expressions and breathy discharges while they watched the frontend of the skidder hang for a time in the air, hang without rising further and without dropping perceptibly either, hang for a time that appeared to them of some length and consequence and struck most especially Donnie Huff as an undeniable eternity. He sat on the seat under the wire mesh cage with his one hand on the wheel and his other on the throttle and his feet simultaneously on the brake and the clutch both while the general contents of his stomach, which were primarily a sausage patty and a half a hotdog bun toasted and buttered and the bulk of a runny egg along with one cup of Nescafe and two Blue Ribbons, crept up towards his esophagus in a most unpleasant and intractable sort of way.

Everything seemed slow to him, painfully and deliberately slow but irresistible as well, and while he had time to jump and considered leaping clear of the skidder altogether, he failed to let loose of the wheel and unhand the throttle on account of how he'd come to be enthralled, had cultivated a manner of magnetic fascination with his own advancing peril and so could not jump, could not even move truly but just sat gripping the wheel and gripping the throttle and mashing the brake and mashing the clutch and forestalling, as best he was able, his breakfast which showed an inclination to save itself. Though he appeared from up on the slope hung and balanced and fairly through pitching for a time, he was not truly hung and was not truly balanced either one but was enduring instead an ever so stately and gradual transition in the nature of his very circumstances, was ceasing that is to haul the log and was beginning to get hauled by it, not tugged and yanked and snatched away but drawn gently back, an alteration far more detectable in the depths of Donnie Huff's stomach sac than from high up on the slope along the property line where Buddy Isom and Freeman MacAfee and Alvis Nevins and little Gaither had become sufficiently accustomed to the sight of the exposed yellow steel underbelly to leave off plain marveling at it so as to enter into one earnest consultation further during the course of which they exchanged theories and debated prospects and were right there on the verge of resolving unanimously to go to the aid of Donnie Huff or to advance anyway down the hillside and thereby gain a fresh perspective on his predicament, when Freeman MacAfee wondered might he let it be known that he was seeing just presently appreciably more of the yellow steel underbelly than had occasioned their consultation in the first place.

They were intending to yell to Donnie Huff to jump, saw him peer out briefly from around the mesh cage, and were meaning to advise him to fling himself clear of the skidder altogether, but they came shortly to be wholly as captivated with the nature and magnitude of Donnie Huff's impending disaster as Donnie Huff himself was and so merely watched the still dilapidated though lately rebuilt John Deere skidder gain the perpendicular and begin to lever over backwards, a sight to charm and silence the bunch of them. Even Donnie Huff, who meant at least to shriek if he could not manage to leap clear instead, was a little too entranced to work up the wind for it and merely gripped the wheel and gripped the throttle and mashed simultaneously the clutch and the brake while he endeavored to marshal and retain his breakfast and suffered the bulk of his circulatory liquids to race towards his topnotch all at the same time. His horror was truly abject but, due chiefly to the sheer novelty of his circumstances, it was mingled with a peculiar strain of delight. So while he suspected what might become of him, he was acutely curious to discover would it and consequently stayed where he'd gotten to be and watched a piece of sky slip by above him as his length of walnut sought the creekbed.

From high up on the hillside little Gaither and Buddy Isom and Freeman MacAfee and Alvis Nevins remarked by turns on Donnie Huff's prospects which appeared to them diminishing most especially once the skidder had laid entirely over topside down and commenced to travel backwards towards the bluff with its rear wheels spinning fairly madly roundabout and its engine racing and sputtering and its cowling kicking up little plumes of dust as the entire contraption slipped and slid across the notch. It teetered momentarily on the knobby bluff but soon enough pitched over and sank altogether from sight. They waited up on the slope for the splash but did not hear a splash exactly, heard in place of it sort of a damp clank followed by a squeally distressed metal species of noise occasioned by the bending of some particular item that would have rather gone wholly unbent. Otherwise there was not any sort of a clamor to hear but just instead the immediate and utter absence of clamor which was in fact its own manner of uproar. They heard a jay back up the slope from them in a treetop and a heifer in the pasture off across the Big Reed and somewhat of the stream itself faintly trilling and gurgling and babbling that way streams will, but the fall, or more likely the instantaneous termination of it, had extinguished the diesel engine and silenced the clattering valves and, since the skidder was gone from sight and its racket was gone from hearing, little Gaither and Alvis Nevins and Buddy Isom and Freeman MacAfee found themselves of a sudden bereft and calamityless standing like they were in an empty wood staring down across a vacant notch at nothing in particular.

They were, as an assortment, numb and stultified and loitered aimlessly for a bit, as is the habit with numb and stultified people, though they grew shortly inclined to ramble down the hillside and arrived near about simultaneously at the notch from where they peered down into the Big Reed and spied the skidder upended in the water that splashed against the tires and washed in a shallow stream over the yellow steel underbelly while the offending length of walnut, still tethered by the length of chain, spun and bobbed in a eddy along the bank. They couldn't make out Donnie Huff, couldn't make out any sign of him, and among them endeavored to gauge the drop from the notch to the creekbottom which did not truly look to be an awfully severe sort of a height, not anyhow for a man just calculating could he leap into the creek and come away uncrippled and whole. The complication, however, of a backwards roll in a log skidder altered the matter pretty appreciably and Buddy Isom and Alvis Nevins and Freeman MacAfee and little Gaither concluded that were they any one of them Donnie Huff they supposed they'd be dead or, at the very least, busted all to pieces and writhing in torment. But they could not discover much trace of writhing under the surface of the water and scanned without success down the stream to find out had maybe Donnie Huff caught up on a rock to expire and thereby terminate his anguishment.

As it was after all his dilapidated skidder and his annihilated employee, little Gaither gained the creekbank first and waded on into the water up to his knees prior to lurching briefly downstream and sitting inadvertently in a hole which served to soak him pretty much up to his shirtpocket and tempted him briefly to wheeze and hyperventilate. Naturally little Gaither swore at the hole in the streambed and at the chute of water that had pushed him into it though he reserved his most colorful and animated snatch of talk for Buddy Isom and Freeman MacAfee and Alvis Nevins over on the bank where, it appeared to him, they were hardly exercising their full usefulness which he chastised them about, wished anyhow they could manage to be together worth even one solitary happy Goddam which Buddy Isom and Freeman MacAfee and Alvis Nevins found stirring and inspirational as far as snatches of talk went and so they sought in fact to be useful to little Gaither by any means possible short of actually wading into the water, which failed to win them much detectable gratitude from Little Gaither himself who'd gained the skidder and was standing alongside it with his arms laid out upon the steel underbelly in a most forlorn and desolate sort of an attitude as if he could not quite figure how in the world he might ever pick the thing up and right it.

Buddy Isom, who hated to trouble little Gaither, inquired nonetheless from the pebbly bank if little Gaither had perhaps spied some sign of Donnie Huff out in the water which did not straightoff prompt little Gaither to a response as he had not entirely satisfied his need to be forlorn and desolate and languish ever so hopelessly against the yellow steel plating. However, he indicated shortly that he'd taken after all some notice of Buddy Isom's inquiry, reached that is with his left arm down into the creek, and drew up by a clump of hair Donnie Huff himself from the watery depths. Little Gaither held him for a time out of the current clean down to his eyebrows which served itself to prompt from Buddy Isom an additional observation since Buddy Isom could not somehow be persuaded to believe that elevating a man's topnotch and forehead out from the water was truly much of an improvement over total submersion as far as any life-sustaining variety of respiration went. Of course that was just the sort of talk to produce from little Gaither a sidelong look and a species of exhalation meant to communicate his annoyance at the ways of some people he knew. He wondered above the din of the water if he was expected himself to do every little thing alone prior to attempting to raise Donnie Huff further still and succeeding in part, lifting him anyway to the bridge of his nose like served to expose his eyes, one of which was open and one of which was shut, that itself was enough of a sight to spook Alvis Nevins into suggesting to little Gaither that he lay Donnie Huff on back where he'd fetched him up in the first place from.

For his part Buddy Isom, who carried Donnie Huff to work but for Mondays sometimes when Donnie Huff laid out, grew sufficiently stirred by his bond to resolve to wade into the creek and draw Donnie Huff to the shore. He announced to Freeman MacAfee and to Alvis Nevins that he'd grown by his bond stirred and he waited to see might they show an inclination to grow stirred with him, but they only between them wished him success and watched Buddy Isom step off the bank into the chill

water. He slogged and lurched and sat presently in the very
hole little Gaither had himself only lately reclined in, bringing
from Buddy Isom an animated complaint which he came to
repeat once he'd staggered downstream out of the one hole and
dropped upon his backside into another.

Naturally Donnie Huff was not in the meantime recovering
awfully well from his mishap as best as Freeman MacAfee and
Alvis Nevins could judge from his follicles and scalp alone
which, due to some thoroughgoing arm-weariness on the part
of little Gaither, was all of Donnie Huff left exposed to them.
He appeared a bit bluegreen there at the hairline that they
sought from the streambank to inform Buddy Isom he did,
Buddy Isom who gained at last the upturned skidder and so
spied for himself Donnie Huff's peculiar fungal hue which gave
him cause to suggest to little Gaither that Donnie Huff had not
likely ever learned to breathe through his cowlick with much
success to speak of.

Together little Gaither and Buddy Isom raised Donnie Huff
pretty completely out from the water and laid him upon the
yellow steel skidder underbelly where he clashed most extravagantly but failed to show an inclination for any endeavor otherwise, did not anyway snort or breathe or groan but just lay
between the wheels where they'd put him and suffered himself
to be shaken and poked by Buddy Isom in particular who instructed Donnie Huff most sternly not to be dead. Buddy Isom
wondered was little Gaither acquainted personally with any life-
saving techniques, techniques that is beyond hairtuft pulling
and the like, but little Gaither was acquainted himself with no
maneuvers except the one that dislodged chicken bones and
Alvis Nevins and Freeman MacAfee confessed themselves sty-
mied by Donnie Huff's circumstances as well and suggested that
perhaps Buddy Isom should carry him to the bank where they
could all three together shake and poke him and produce
maybe an effect. So Buddy Isom took up Donnie Huff at the
armpits and wondered might little Gaither take him up at the
feet which little Gaither grumbled about but obliged him at
nonetheless, and they set off back across the stream, pausing
only so as to sit one time more in the hole they'd all but Donnie
Huff sat in one time already. They laid him out alongside the

water on a gritty siltspit and concluded together that he was a pretty grave and sobering shade of bluegreen, likely even a deathly shade of bluegreen, and by a show of hands they nominated Alvis Nevins to reach down and shut Donnie Huff's left eye as they were all uneasy about standing over and studying a seriously afflicted if not outright deceased individual who sprawled upon the siltspit and studied them back.

Of course Alvis Nevins was not altogether anxious to lay his fingers to a very possibly clammy and most certainly bluegreen eyelid but could not manage to get unnominated and so shut Donnie Huff's left eye with a piece of stick once he'd inadvertently pricked and jabbed Donnie Huff about the eyesocket prior to it which served to convince the pack of them that Donnie Huff was certifiably dead since otherwise he would undoubtedly have gotten to his feet and beat the unmitigated shit out of Alvis Nevins. They guessed they ought to tell his people. Buddy Isom anyhow figured one of them ought to ride out to see Marie which straightaway he got nominated and elected to do and so began there at the streambed to endeavor to grow suitably grim which, but for the smirk, he managed and improved upon even as he walked up out of the bottom towards his pickup beyond the mill. And he wasn't, in fact, even gone good from sight before little Gaither pitched his initial fit which, for little Gaither, was an altogether mild display. He stomped up and down the siltspit and gesticulated after the fashion of a warring baboon and spoke as well of his woes and afflictions which he let on to be quite utterly innumerable though he guessed he would engage in an attempt to innumerate them. He had a stump and a heap of limbs to account for on a tract of land he'd not paid to cut. He had an ever so lately rebuilt John Deere skidder upside down in four feet of creekwater. He had a dead and bluegreen employee who'd not been so extraordinarily dependable in life but had managed nonetheless to diminish quite completely his usefulness. And he supposed he had as well an obligation to call the law as they were evermore eager to discover how people had come to get deceased, which would lead them undoubtedly to where precisely the length of walnut had been dragged in the first place from.

And little Gaither said initially just to Alvis Nevins and Freeman MacAfee alongside him a vile and contemptible thing with more than his usual dose of passion and disgust. Then he stomped some further and persisted at gesticulating until he'd traveled to the pointy end of the siltspit and arrived back from it to loiter briefly over the outstretched bluegreen form of Donnie Huff in thoroughgoing repose without, it seemed to little Gaither, the assortment of woes and troubles little Gaither himself was afflicted with, woes and troubles brought about in part by Donnie Huff himself if not in fact brought about even primarily by him as best as little Gaither could tell like was just precisely the variety of revelation to heighten little Gaither's agitated state.

And he made into the air one additional unsavory proclamation with evolving passion and disgust and contemplated briefly Donnie Huff's bluegreen face prior, much to the shock and utter bewilderment of Freeman MacAfee and Alvis Nevins both, to falling upon Donnie Huff in a rage, falling upon him not in that way people are said sometimes to fall upon each other and tangle, but depositing in fact his entire tonnage quite directly upon Donnie Huff's exposed frontside.

"Christ, Gaither." Alvis Nevins told him but only once he'd managed to work up the means to speak which was well after little Gaither had jerked and shook and slapped even one time Donnie Huff flush across the face. "The man's dead," Alvis Nevins said though he failed by it to persuade little Gaither that a man couldn't be dead and a troublesome blameworthy son-of-a-bitch both at the same time together, which little Gaither had drawn himself conclusions about and so raised up Donnie Huff by his shirtfront in order to share with him an intimate snatch of vulgar talk on the topic of Donnie Huff's myriad shortcomings. As the occasion appeared supremely suitable to him, little Gaither damned Donnie Huff to hell prior to flinging him back down upon the spit, which proved shortly premature on account of how little Gaither recollected a colorful expression of loathing which he wished as well to impart to Donnie Huff and so lifted him one time further by his shirtfront and was pretty well set to impart it when Donnie Huff himself, who'd been sufficiently jostled and beat about, revived after a fashion, regurgitated anyhow a surprising quantity of creekwater which he expelled pretty directly upon little Gaither's inflamed features.

Being, of course, a wholly unanticipated and startling sort of a display from a dead man, the general dampening of little Gaither stilled him altogether and prompted from Freeman MacAfee an expression of undiluted wonderment while Alvis Nevins fairly squealed one time prior to leaping clear of the siltspit and charging up the creekbank into a rhododendron thicket where his headway came soon enough to be insignificant and turned even shortly into retreat that brought him once more in sight of Donnie Huff who'd commenced to wheeze and gurgle and so drove Alvis Nevins another time into the bushes. Little Gaither, not renowned for his solicitude and selfless concern, flung Donnie Huff back where he'd raised him up from which itself prompted one discharge further, and Donnie Huff spat water and coughed and drew off a sizable breath of air like served straightaway to improve his hue.

It was Freeman MacAfee who showed firstoff the temerity to venture forth an opinion, telling to little Gaither in the siltspit and to Alvis Nevins in the undergrowth and somewhat to Donnie Huff as well, "He ain't dead," which was becoming increasingly apparent as Donnie Huff lay upon the siltspit and quite plainly respirated, apparent anyhow to Freeman MacAfee and to little Gaither although Alvis Nevins, who lingered up along side the thicket, could not himself decide if Donnie Huff was after all alive or was in fact merely undead instead, and he suggested to little Gaither and to Freeman MacAfee that there was undoubtedly a pretty severe difference between the two. Alvis Nevins had rented lately from Shirley's #2 in Cana a movie about the undead which he began to speak of from up at the thicket, meaning to focus almost exclusively on the assorted ghouls in the picture and their various powers and propensities but finding himself irresistibly sidetracked by his recollection of the nubile starlet who'd demonstrated a thoroughgoing reluctance to keep her blouse buttoned and was evermore shedding the thing and dropping it to the floor.

"You ain't never seen such jugs on a woman," Alvis Nevins

said and could not help but wonder where in the world those
movie people came across creatures with such extravagant antigravitational powers, and he looked for illumination to Freeman MacAfee and to little Gaither and found himself looking
to Donnie Huff as well, Donnie Huff whose eyelids fluttered
and then opened altogether, which once more filled Alvis Nevins with foreboding and stirred him to announce how if Donnie
Huff was in fact undead he'd shortly feel compelled to busy
himself ripping out their entrails.

For a time, what seemed most especially to Alvis Nevins an
inordinately long time, Donnie Huff just lay on his back upon
the siltspit gazing directly above himself at the wispy clouds and
the treetops. He blinked every now and again, rubbed his irritated left eye, and twice wet his lips with the tipend of his
tongue but chiefly just lay still and breathed deeply in and
deeply out as well prior to raising up onto his elbows with, what
appeared to Alvis Nevins, disembowelment on his mind. Consequently, Alvis Nevins set himself to plunge on in among the
tangle of limbs and leathery leaves and was just about to instruct Freeman MacAfee and little Gaither to run for their very
lives when Donnie Huff, who'd sat now full upright, said,
"Christ," and said, "Jesus," and told to little Gaither directly
opposite from him, "Hey."

From up just shy of the rhododendrons Alvis Nevins determined straightaway that Donnie Huff did not sound so awfully
undead to him which altered his own disposition pretty appreciably, and he took entirely upon himself the responsibility to
step forward off the rise and tell to Donnie Huff where precisely he was and how precisely he'd gotten there since Alvis
Nevins had rented and viewed enough movies from Shirley's
#2 in Cana to know that people knocked senseless from a blow
most usually came around to inquire what they'd done and
where they'd ended up and who perhaps they might be as well.

"You had a fall," Alvis Nevins said and pointed out midcreek
to the upended log skidder, "and fairly drowned from it, likely
did even for a time. You're Donnie Huff of the Barren Springs
Huffs," and as a service Alvis Nevins was just beginning to slowly
spell out "Donnie" when Donnie Huff himself swung around
on the siltspit and requested of Alvis Nevins, "Shut up."

Freeman MacAfee figured they should one of them undertake to prevent Buddy Isom from spreading among Donnie Huff's kin news of his death which Freeman MacAfee volunteered himself to do and wondered what variety of news they might together spread among Donnie Huff's kin instead whereupon Alvis Nevins advised Freeman MacAfee and little Gaither as well that they'd best carry Donnie Huff to the hospital at Galax on account of how Alvis Nevins had heard somewhere that violent death and the subsequent recovery from it advanced dramatically the likelihood of organ strain in a fellow.

"Organ strain?" little Gaither said to him from his squat on the spit.

And Alvis Nevins assured little Gaither, "Can't never know. Best to be safe once a man's been bluegreen and expired," and he turned and inquired of Freeman MacAfee, "Isn't it?" that Freeman MacAfee, once he'd flicked his dwindling butt into the creek, assured most especially little Gaither it was.

While Freeman MacAfee set out himself in pursuit of Buddy Isom leaving Donnie Huff under the watchful care of Alvis Nevins and little Gaither, Donnie Huff rolled his head around so as to stretch his neck, which appeared to Alvis Nevins such a symptomatic variety of endeavor that he vented a throaty contemplative sort of a noise prior to stepping up behind Donnie Huff and poking a kidney with his extended finger as a kidney was one of the few organs he could readily locate. Donnie Huff, once he'd contorted and left off howling altogether, climbed to his feet and turned full around so as to offer to detach Alvis Nevin's poking finger at the joint, which struck Alvis Nevins as a telling response and he bobbed his head on account of it in a grave and doctorly fashion prior to sharing somewhat with Donnie Huff but primarily with little Gaither news of the condition of the kidney he'd poked, a kidney which struck him as relatively hardy and unafflicted. He was anxious to jab at organs otherwise and as he brandished his poking finger, Donnie Huff informed Alvis Nevins how he was fairly well set to jab a little himself and he displayed the knuckly item he was meaning to jab with, was meaning to lay most especially against that particular organ in the middle of Alvis Nevins's face where Alvis Nevins's poking finger most usually resided.

"Seems perky to me," Alvis Nevins told to little Gaither as he retreated across the siltspit towards the rhododendron thicket. "Might not have got strained."

And little Gaither, who looked from Donnie Huff out to the middle of the streambed to the underbelly and upraised tires of his dilapidated but lately rebuilt John Deere log skidder, told presently to Alvis Nevins, "Perky," back.

iii

She didn't usually greet him, didn't most evenings hail his arrival upon the porchslab but for every now and again when she instructed him from the settee to leave his shoes on the nappy mat and slip out if he would from his coveralls as she'd just lately Boraxed the rug. She was only ever so rarely up and about at the doorscreen itself when he climbed out from Buddy Isom's truck like she was lingering at it this evening along with her grandbaby Delmon who joined his grandmomma in a species of rousing salute that quite thoroughly startled Donnie Huff who was right there in the middle of crushing his Pabst can in advance of flinging it into Buddy Isom's truckbed which was not remotely the sort of endeavor he usually got saluted about.

Delmon Huff, for his part, extracted from his mouth the partial sheet of raspberry fruit skin he was laboring to sculpt and shape with his spit and his tongue in combination and called through the screenwire, "Hey Daddy," to Donnie Huff who'd recovered sufficiently from his surprise to be right there on the verge of telling to Delmon, "Hey boy," back when he got prevented from it by his wife's momma who issued a manner of proclamation herself, told to Donnie Huff, "Countenance like lightning. Raiment white as snow," and then gazed steadfastly upon a portion of treetop as best as Donnie Huff could tell, Donnie Huff who turned about and gazed a little himself but could discover on his own nothing but limbs and nothing but leaves.

Of course Sheba intercepted Donnie Huff before he gained the slab and she barked and snarled and displayed her acute reservations about him until Donnie Huff refreshed her with his brogan and looked to her of a sudden the very fellow who'd come home to kick her the night previous, and she said to him as best as dogs are able, "Oh," and rolled her eyes and hunkered onto her belly and crawled pretty much on her elbows back around the house.

"Look," Delmon Huff told to his daddy and pushed open the doorscreen so as to show him his licked and sculpted and partially masticated piece of fruit skin which Donnie Huff examined but failed altogether to identify as anything worth licking and sculpting and masticating and so enlisted the assistance of his momma-in-law of whom he inquired, "Isn't that something?," in the hope that she would illuminate for him what variety precisely of something it was, but Opal Criner merely told to him instead, "Risen indeed," and gazed ever so intently upon him as he passed into the front room and called out to his wife Marie, "Hey doll," called out above the racket of the local TV news where a man from Browns Summit who'd built a shed almost entirely out of bottlebottoms was enduring from a woman in a blazer inquiries as to why and appeared almost as curious to hear what he'd say as she did.

In the kitchen Donnie Huff's wife Marie was endeavoring to pour off and save a goodly portion of the drainage from her turkey loaf so as to thicken it with flour and render it into gravy for the whipped potato flakes. Consequently, she did not come flying into the front room to catch up Donnie Huff in a joyous embrace but instead called to him back, "Hey," with, as best as Opal Criner could tell, a subtle but palpable sense of blessed thanksgiving which came soon enough to be ever so resolutely confirmed for her once her girl Marie had found in fact occasion to depart briefly from the kitchen so as to carry into the front room a fresh Blue Ribbon for Donnie Huff who took up in both his hands the majority of his wife Marie's scant posterior and thereby persuaded her to bump her frontside against his own one which Opal Criner proclaimed to be a tender ritual of reunion and relief, proclaimed it primarily at her grandbaby Delmon who'd been steadily dissolving and shaping and even ever so hardly at all ingesting his raspberry fruit skin which he extracted and displayed for his grandmomma as a manner of response.

Donnie Huff was clammy, had not yet dried out entirely most especially along about his own posterior, where his wife Marie slipped her free hand into his coveralls pocket and then straightaway withdrew it as she did not care at all for a clammy man and apprised Donnie Huff of as much. "Been wet," Donnie Huff told to her.

"Hear you had a mishap," Marie Criner informed him back.

And Donnie Huff drew in a sizable breath, discharged it, and told to his wife Marie, "Yeah," in that casual, weary sort of a way men sometimes say "Yeah" so as to let on how they are in fact after all men. "Had a mishap," Donnie Huff added with ever so thinly veiled indifference and he made to be enchanted with a particular walljoint across the room, a walljoint he studied and admired as he moved about inside his mouth a dollop of spit that squeaked and gurgled.

His wife Marie was hopeful Donnie Huff would see fit not to dampen the seatcushion of his upholstered chair and she provided him with a section of the *Times and World News* from Roanoke to perch upon, spread it even atop the cushion for him, and watched as Donnie Huff opened his Blue Ribbon and knocked back a goodly portion of it in a gulp prior to fairly tossing himself into the upholstered chair where the jolt induced from him a burp near about as clammy as his backside, a burp for which he anticipated a stern and impassioned rebuke from Opal Criner but entertained from her instead a snatch of scripture on the topic of his own personal crown of righteousness that had been laid up already for him in the kingdom of heaven, which was news to Donnie Huff who glanced at Opal Criner what she took for inquiringly and so heard straightoff an additional recitation about who it was precisely that would get exalted among the heathen.

The national news had come on the television and Donnie Huff watched with some attention a story about a man in Missouri who'd dispatched twelve of his neighbors with several loads of number 2 shot on account of how his neighbors had peeved and irritated him,—though nobody could discover just how precisely unless of course they'd irritated him,—with their housecats that had come to be dispatched as well, cause for special consternation on the part of the correspondent who quite apparently had a soft spot for cats. Opal Criner, troubled herself by further news of the vile things people do to each other, looked from the settee towards her son-in-law with the intention of pulling at him a face meant to indicate where precisely her own soft spot lay, but she could not manage to catch Donnie Huff's eye as Donnie Huff was staring off into the empty air after what appeared to Opal Criner a thoughtful fashion, a fashion in fact so uncharacteristically thoughtful that she grew moved to ask of Donnie Huff what it was precisely he might be pondering so very deeply about. Donnie Huff for his part drew on his Blue Ribbon, shifted atop the *Times and World News* and, following a pause fairly ripe and bloated with drama, announced to Opal Criner, "Bet there ain't no cat's much left," and he snorted and added, "Furry puddles," that his boy Delmon found particularly diverting and discharged in his high humor a dribble of red saliva that dripped off his chin onto his shirtfront, leaving what his grandmomma assured him was an indelible stain.

"Shame what some people will get peeved and do," Donnie Huff observed primarily into the empty air and Opal Criner, who'd licked a Kleenex so as to rub at Delmon's shirtfront and thereby demonstrate for him the exact nature of indelibility, gazed once more upon Donnie Huff who'd not shown previously much inclination to be philosophical or to loose anyhow the sort of generalized statement of belief that Opal Criner could herself endorse and affirm with fervor like she moved straightaway to endorse and affirm this particular one, telling to Donnie Huff, "Yes," telling to Donnie Huff, "It is a shame what some people will get peeved and do," which quite apparently induced a low compassionate noise from deep in Donnie Huff's neck that did not sound to Opal Criner much at all like gas.

She ventured to express to him how what with such meanness about people were fairly itching to get smited by the Almighty like would be worse even than number 2 shot as the Almighty had a gift for smiting.

"I will come upon thee as a thief," she said, "and thou shalt

not know what hour I will come upon thee," which, for scripture, did not appear to strike Donnie Huff as ever so exceedingly tiresome that way scripture usually did; he failed anyhow
to curl his upper lip and look nauseated like was his general
habit in the face of inspirational verse and instead he appeared
to ponder and mull the wages of meanness and the prospect of
getting shortly smited prior to sharing with his mother-in-law
news of how people didn't seem to him any longer much count
at all which stirred and quickened Opal Criner who was pleased
to inform Donnie Huff that she'd never herself had much use
for anybody. "Not ever," she told him and watched as Donnie
Huff laid his chin upon the web of skin between his thumb and
his forefinger and thereby struck a pose that impressed Opal
Criner as quite clearly meditational, the variety of pose precisely to render even his thin scruffy beard vaguely distinguished and apt.

Being a woman sensible of the various delicacies in life, Opal
Criner had been reluctant to speak yet directly to Donnie Huff
of his mishap—his death and his subsequent resuscitation—but
the sight of him atop his *Times and World News* earnestly reflec-
tive and fairly comely on account of it induced Opal Criner to
observe at last in a general sort of a way how it seemed to her
there was anymore a regular plague of people dying and recovering from it, and she wondered was perhaps Donnie Huff
acquainted with a tract she'd received just lately, an installment
of *The Sword of the Lord* that she knew was roundabout somewhere or another and she managed truly straightaway to discover it in her pocketbook right alongside her on the settee like
she attempted to let on to be an unspeakably happy coincidence.

"There's a thing in here about people that got dead," she
told to Donnie Huff, "people that got dead but didn't stay it,"
and she opened her tract to a creased page and read to Donnie
Huff an altogether inconsequential paragraph on the topic
chiefly of downtown Indianapolis, which was not in fact the
paragraph she'd intended to read, and so she skipped shortly
down to the part about the man from rural Gosport who'd
traveled north to Indianapolis on a piece of business and had

managed to get done in there. "Pole fell on him," she told Donnie Huff.

And Donnie Huff said back, "Pole?" and assumed a variety of sober inquiring look that enhanced his scruffy beard itself.

"Fell on him," she told him and scanned down the column to refresh herself as to what variety of pole exactly, leading her shortly to learn that it was a stout pole which she shared with Donnie Huff who said to her, "Oh," and drew distractedly at his Blue Ribbon while he wondered where precisely Indianapolis was anyhow in relation to places otherwise that he knew about.

"Didn't fall right flush on him," Opal Criner announced as she refreshed herself further still, "but dropped from a building and glanced off him."

And Donnie Huff gazed pensively into his lap prior to inquiring, "Indianapolis up alongside Toledo?" and Opal Criner told him straightaway, "No," which itself prompted Donnie Huff to press his lips flush together and jerk his head as if he had in fact been actually edified.

"If it'd hit him square it surely would have squashed him," Opal Criner said and Donnie Huff assured her how he was convinced himself a stout pole was capable of it, or made anyhow in his neck a noise that communicated as much to Opal Criner who read on from her tract about how precisely the stout pole came hurtling down through the air and clipped the man from Gosport on the arm prior to clattering upon the walk alongside him, and it was that shock of the clip and the wholly unanticipated uproar of the clattering in combination that served together to send that man from Gosport into full arrest. "His heart seized up," Opal Criner said and then read from her tract a florid snatch of prose which laid out the various sensations of full cardiac arrest that were given to be exceedingly unpleasant and evermore culminated in a kind of queasy faint very much like the faint itself that man from Gosport suffered there on the sidewalk in Indianapolis where he crumpled and fell and beat his head upon the walkway.

"He expired," Opal Criner said. "They all of them agree he did, most especially that man from Gosport who knew well enough he was dead." And Opal Criner struck out reading a paragraph on the topic chiefly of fatty foods and constricted bloodflow but skipped shortly down through it to a dense and indented passage of testimony from the victim who apparently could manage, in retrospect, to be fairly poetical about his own demise. He described how he lay there in Indianapolis on his backside breathing in a shallow diminishing sort of a way and thinking about his wife back home in Gosport and his boy down at Fort Benning and his Chevrolet Citation in a garage off Martindale Avenue where he did not figure anybody would ever find it as he'd inadvertently left the ticket on the seat. His functions slowed and dwindled and, presently, his breath stopped altogether and that man from Gosport told how at the very moment of his expiration, when he expected to be plunged into eternal and thoroughgoing night, he felt himself rising instead, came to float free from his carcass and hover above it where he watched briefly his supine, he called it, form in addition to the unsupine forms of those people gathered about him who peered and milled and loitered and asked of each other was he in fact dead. Like a bird, he recalled, he sailed and flew high up above the people and the sidewalk and his carcass and the stout pole and he ascended above greater Indianapolis into the sky towards the light of the sun which grew ever so extravagantly bright and pervasive until there wasn't anything hardly but light, glorious white light that buoyed him upwards still towards a portal, he called it, a sizeable portal that he guessed he would sail on through, was pleased and contented in fact at the prospect of sailing on through it but came shortly to be moderately disappointed when instead of rising further still he awoke to find himself peering pretty directly up into the nostrils of a paramedic who'd managed to jar and cajole him to life.

"Portal," Opal Criner said, "gateway to the everlasting bathed in heavenly light," which was itself the product of some interpolation on her part though she lent to it with her tone of voice a measure of irrefutability and consequently did not hear from Donnie Huff anything contrary and endured only briefly from her grandbaby Delmon an exhibition of his dwindling fruit skin that he'd sculpted and fashioned into the shape of a seized-up organ though he did not specify which organ precisely.

There was as well testimony in Opal Criner's *Sword of the Lord* from a woman in Florida who'd suffered a surgical trauma and had for a time expired herself, had for a time floated and soared clean through the sizable portal and into the presence of the actual Savior who'd been pleased to welcome her into the Kingdom of God, had been engaged in leading that woman to her place among the holy when she came to be revived and fetched away and awoke with palpable regret as did a gentleman from Washington state who got dead on the highway in his Toyota and so rose up portalwards until he came as well to be resuscitated. The accounts were fairly endless as best as Opal Criner could tell, and she held up her *Sword of the Lord* and flipped through the pages of it for the benefit of Donnie Huff who could see even from over in his upholstered chair how dense the thing was with testimony not even to mention the splendid full-color artist's rendition of Christ in the portal, a haloed Christ backlit ever so dramatically by a regular flood of white heavenly light.

"And not hardly all Christian people either," Opal Criner declared, and she revealed to Donnie Huff how they'd some of them lapsed in their churchgoing and one or two were even in fact unseemly reprobates, and Donnie Huff wondered might she please hold up one time further the splendid full-color artist's rendition of Christ in the portal which naturally Opal Criner was delighted to oblige him in and so exhibited the haloed Savior once more and watched as Donnie Huff perused Him for a spell in silence prior to wondering in a general sort of a way if wasn't it surprising how many people anymore seemed to die and come back from it like was hardly the case, Donnie Huff recalled, in his own youth when people that managed to get dead usually stayed it. He was convinced it was all on account of some noticeable advancements, and he had the medical sort in mind, but Opal Criner begged if she could to differ and suggested that while the advancements were likely medical somewhat they were undoubtedly spiritual chiefly, and she proved curious to hear from Donnie Huff if he had this day, in the course of his own mishap, benefited from some new and revolutionary medical technique which Donnie Huff confessed to her he hadn't.

And Opal Criner said somewhat to Donnie Huff but predominately to the lightglobe overhead, "Blessed hand of Jesus," and she wondered if, while Donnie Huff was dead, he didn't soar himself maybe just a little.

"Wished I could," Donnie Huff told her. "A couple of feet would have got me up out of the water. I was wanting badly to soar."

"Well, you must have rose up some," Opal Criner insisted. "Everybody else seems to."

And Donnie Huff assumed one time further his flattering contemplative pose which he briefly diluted and fairly undid by laying back his head to draw off the dregs of his Blue Ribbon prior to crushing the can in his fingers, as was his custom, like freed him to become one time further grave and meditational. "I got kind of giddy," Donnie Huff said. "I do recall going weakheaded right there as I blacked out," and Opal Criner suggested to Donnie Huff how that sort of thing sounded very much to her like the onset of rapture.

She was anxious to discover had Donnie Huff dropped off in the course of his demise into pitchy darkness or could he recollect some manner of illumination, and while she did not expressly mention the Savior of the portal and the dramatic heavenly backlighting she did in fact fairly completely insinuate the both of them with a thoroughly beatific smile that Donnie Huff himself straightaway took the gist of and so endeavored to cast back and see if couldn't he remember even a dim sort of a glow, and he did in fact recall some little specks of light that floated before him there on the creekbottom, little green specks like a man might see if he gets up to quick or sits down to soon or stoops over once he's past the age for stooping. Opal Criner, however, was not in the mood to entertain much theorizing on the part of Donnie Huff since she guessed she knew well enough herself what little specks of light on a creekbottom meant most especially in the case of a drowning giddy semiconscious heathen in ever so dire need of a dose of blessed salvation, and she informed Donnie Huff, "You been lifted up."

"Have I?" Donnie Huff asked of her.

"Plain to me," Opal Criner said and she spoke again of the weakheadedness and the speckled heavenly illumination and suggested to Donnie Huff how he surely must have felt, there in his gravest moments right at the very crux of his personal crisis, like a man raised and buoyed.

"I was in a stream of water," Donnie Huff suggested as adequate cause for a man rising and buoying both.

And Opal Criner grew rather more severe as she reminded Donnie Huff, "We are speaking here of the miracle of redemption and everlasting life."

"Oh," Donnie Huff told to her and under the prodding of Opal Criner's steady and unflinching perusal he presently managed to stir himself to confess that maybe he had gotten lifted a trifle into the glories of the hereafter before little Gaither had seen fit to snatch him back like Opal Criner straightaway proclaimed was cause for rejoicing though Donnie Huff did not appear himself to share her enthusiasm. He guessed if he was going to pass away for a time he might as well have occasion to view a thing other than scant speckled light. "I ain't never even seen Indianapolis," Donnie Huff said which seemed itself to Opal Criner so quite altogether beside the point that she was briefly too chagrined to speak and thereby provided her grandbaby Delmon with the opportunity to pluck from his mouth his paltry scrap of fruit skin which he'd managed by the joint application of his saliva and his tonguetip to work a hole in the middle of.

And Delmon charged his daddy and charged his grandmomma with him to look please if they might at the portal he'd made which they were gazing in fact together upon when Marie wished from the kitchen that perhaps she'd live to see the day when somebody somehow would up and put the ice in the glasses without her having to ask them would they which Opal was intending straightoff to tell to her girl a thing about when Delmon's fruit skin portal, which was itself quite extravagantly lubricated, loosed upon the settee a sizable scarlet droplet and prompted thereby Opal Criner to advise once further her grandbaby on the properties of indelibility.

II

*T*he Reverend Mr. Worrell had
dreams and visions in which ways
of the Lord and the true path of
righteousness were revealed to him. Blessed with powers of
divination well beyond his ken, he could evermore distinguish
a genuine sign and a legitimate portent from just your regular
insignificant and unportentous variety of item, and he carried
forth with vigor and no little passion the lessons of the Savior
which the Reverend Mr. Worrell took as best he could to his
heart. But the reverend had come to be afflicted with weaknesses and beset by impure longings, had cultivated in particular an improper fondness for a checkout girl at the Food Lion,
the tall one with the yellowgold ringlets who managed by way of
her fully developed and thoroughly refined womanly curvature
to render her blue polyester Food Lion smock clingy and suggestive, surely an unmitigated triumph of womanly curvature if
ever there was one. She knew the reverend from his personalized checks with the seashells on them and so greeted him
usually by name when he unfreighted his buggy in her aisle
which he'd managed to make a habit of whenever he shopped
alone if her line was not congested with stray men otherwise
who appreciated curvature themselves. They generally exchanged polite and frivolous chat as Mr. Worrell's groceries

49

advanced between them on the rubber belt, and the reverend showed on occasion his teeth and vented, when he thought to, his preacherly laugh and had adopted as well the custom of envisioning that beringleted child quite wholly unsmocked altogether.

He had attempted to purify his impulses, though without too awful much success. The reverend had sought to be untainted by the baser passions, had endeavored as best he was able to evict his assorted urges, but had made no clear triumph of the undertaking until just the previous spring when the reverend had himself beheld a manner of miraculous occurrence, had seen with his own eyes a sculpted Jesus weep which he'd divined as a genuine annotation upon his personal failings, had witnessed anyhow in the company of Mr. Walter Ramseur an instance of peculiar seepiness on the part of a length of cedar that the reverend had figured pretty much for tears of holy woe notwithstanding Mr. Walter Ramseur's personal campaign to thwart the wonder and dispel the mystery and clot the entire episode with particulars.

Mr. Walter Ramseur had not at the time but taken up sculpting of late. He'd driven previously an oil truck as an occupation but had retired from oil truck driving which had plopped him pretty directly in the way of Mrs. Walter Ramseur who'd wished he'd find a thing to do and wished he'd find a place to do it and had undertaken in fact to wish the both of them so relentlessly that Mr. Walter Ramseur came shortly to feel driven to root out and light upon a hobby that would carry him out of the house and pretty much keep him there. He'd had for several years in his possession a little electric chain saw that had been given to him a couple of Christmases past by his wife's sister who'd seen the thing in the Western Auto at Hillsville and found it so darned cute and tiny that she could not somehow keep from buying it. As a tool and an implement, however, an electric chain saw is probably about as useful as a four-cylinder television, and a cute tiny electric chain saw suffers so completely from its cute tininess as to be even less useful altogether. Mr. Walter Ramseur figured he could probably cut through sticks with the thing and scant limbs and suspected he could find a way to saw through the cord as well but did not believe, aside from sudden and unanticipated electrocution, he could manage awful much with his cute tiny saw that he could not manage quite well enough already with his full-sized two-cycle Homelite. Consequently, the thing never got so terribly far from the box it had come in until that morning in March when Mr. Walter Ramseur found the occasion to sculpt.

He'd been busting logs in the sideyard, had fetched out a couple of loads of lapwood from a tract of land up along the New River and was breaking it to sticks with his eight-pound maul and laying it off to cure. He'd carried home oak chiefly, white oak and black oak along with a bit of hickory and a couple of sizable lengths of wild cherry that somebody else had cut and left, and he ran through the hickory straightoff on account of how clean it busted but felt compelled shortly to do penance by way of the wild cherry that had aired sufficiently to go stringy, was knotty and screw-grained with it, and proved for a time to be quite unbustable altogether. His maulhead bounced when it did not wedge instead, and Mr. Walter Ramseur battered and assaulted his initial length of log for near about all he was worth until it offered at last to break in two, cracked perceptibly anyhow, developed a fissure that Mr. Walter Ramseur flailed at for a time with some limited success like was hardly the variety of success he'd aimed for when he'd set out in the first place to flail. So he grew fairly intensely peeved and irritated and knocked that length of wild cherry over onto the ground where he beat and pounded at it and kicked it and stomped on it and paused only shortly to inform it how disagreeable in fact he found it to be before he played upon it a vigorous tattoo with his maulhead and persuaded the thing to lay open at last in halves.

He took up the leanest portion of it and set it onto his busting stump where he meant to split it to quarters and would probably have split it to quarters in fact had not his recent struggles and travails diminished his aim so appreciably as to cause Mr. Walter Ramseur to strike a fairly glancing blow at the thing and thereby hew out a mere sliver like served to heighten Mr. Walter Ramseur's general ill feeling towards his portion of wild cherry and he intended to club it with the flat buttend of his maulhead as a means of articulating his sentiments and had

actually raised and cocked his maul in preparation for the blow
when he came to be struck by a peculiar feature of that half a
log, a variety of knotty protuberance that looked awfully much
to Mr. Walter Ramseur like a nose. He lowered his maul and
laid it aside so as to free himself to squat and ponder the item
with attention and it remained, even upon inspection, quite
nasal altogether and suggested to Mr. Walter Ramseur a face
roundabout itself, a broad fleshly face sunk and hidden just
beneath the stringy screw-grained exterior and in need of some
rather insignificant aid and excavation on the part of Mr. Walter Ramseur who guessed he was just the man to aid and exca-
vate as insignificantly as anybody might.

He determined then that he would take a break from busting logs for a time so as to mine whatever variety of natural
portraiture was already quite plainly incipient in his length of
cherry, and he went off to the cellar after his spoon gouge and
returned to even gouge with it for a spell before he learned
shortly that his length of cherry would not yield up its natural
portraiture to a gouge alone, would not at all shave and shear
to suit Mr. Walter Ramseur who returned to the cellar to bring
forth his mortising chisel and his mallet and had even taken the
both of them up when he spied his electric chain saw box with
the cute tiny saw inside it. He could not imagine an item better
suited to shaving and shearing than a cute tiny electric saw and
he carried the thing out from the cellar and into the sideyard
where he laid it on his busting stump while he hunted his drop-
cord that he trailed across the yard and plugged into the por-
celain fixture on the backporch ceiling.

As Mr. Walter Ramseur had not ever previously made use of
a saw so delicate and diminutive, he felt obliged to rehearse his
sculpting technique on a piece of hickory and so sliced and
shaped and shaved until he grew to be at his ease when he
turned at last on his stringy screw-grained hunk of wild cherry
with the knotty protuberance and brought very quickly into
relief first one puffy cheek and then the other opposite from it.
He was hoping for a square manly chin and had set out even to
produce one before he miscalculated the full extent of square
manliness and consequently lopped the thing off at merely a
dainty sort of a length but did add a rather deep and thorough-

going cleft to it thereby insinuating more virility than a dainty chin might alone and unclefted suggest. With his chin episode to guide and instruct him, he produced with great care and deliberation a pair of full-sized if not truly outsized ears which he clefted after a fashion as well prior to shaping a hairline above them and a broad furrowed forehead that he managed with extravagant success since a furrow was not truly anything much but a cleft laid over.

He was not nearly so deft and surehanded in his lipwork but commenced with a kind of a clefted crescent and manufactured shortly around it a fairly genuine and toothsome grin prior to improving as best as he was able upon the knobby protuberance and creating with a light delicate touch a full head of minutely clefted hair. Mr. Walter Ramseur then stepped a few paces backwards, cute tiny electric saw in hand, and eyed his creation that could not yet quite eye him back on account of the blank stringy screw-grained place between its nose and its furrowed brow where Mr. Walter Ramseur sought shortly to saw out a pair of sockets and with his spoon gouge cut pupils in pretty much the middle of each of them. He rendered, by means of assorted and ever so delicate vertical clefts, a pair of highly prominent and irrefutably manly eyebrows of which he straightaway became so inordinately fond that he rendered an additional larger one under the knotty protuberance itself prior to leaving off with his cute tiny saw and proclaiming just out into the air, "It is done," or meaning anyhow to proclaim it while managing instead to say merely, "All right then," as he backed once more away from his stump with his length of natural portraiture upon it.

The results were plainly miraculous to Mr. Walter Ramseur, quite purely astounding in fact as he had not even begun to surmise that lurking back of the knotty protuberance and under the rough stringy screw-grained exterior was the very image of Mr. Tennessee Ernie Ford who Mr. Walter Ramseur had with his cute tiny electric saw brought to the fore, sculpted and clefted and excavated so awfully near to life itself as to leave Mr. Walter Ramseur momentarily flabbergasted. He examined Mr. Tennessee Ernie Ford's various features, most especially his prominent outsized ears and his delicately clefted moustache, in addition to the slightly skewed and misplaced pupils which themselves suggested to Mr. Walter Ramseur that he'd managed some way or another to capture Mr. Tennessee Ernie Ford in a moment of abject befuddlement, like appeared to Mr. Walter Ramseur to render his own particular item altogether singular and unique as far as wooden chain sawed statuary of Mr. Tennessee Ernie Ford went.

He was anxious, of course, to induce Mrs. Walter Ramseur to become shortly flabbergasted with him as Mrs. Walter Ramseur had herself cultivated a particular affection for Mr. Tennessee Ernie Ford's rich and soulful singing voice and had ordered even off the tv a two-volume set of inspirational recordings which featured Mr. George Beverly Shea, Mr. Jim Nabors, and Mr. Tennessee Ernie Ford together and had been produced and manufactured for the benefit of those people afflicted with troubles and doubts and burdened as well with a major credit card. Mrs. Walter Ramseur still played her album every now and again and showed a marked partiality for Mr. Tennessee Ernie Ford's rendition of "He Leadeth Me" which she stood at the sink with her hands in the dishwater and sang on occasion herself in her own high-pitched and relatively desiccated tones. Naturally, then, Mr. Walter Ramseur could not hardly help but figure it would be an altogether unmitigated delight for Mrs. Walter Ramseur to discover hewn from a length of cherrywood the uncanny likeness of Mr. Tennessee Ernie Ford himself, and Mr. Walter Ramseur settled upon a plan to smuggle his natural portraiture into the house along with an armful of ordinary unsculpted wood and so loaded his crooked arm accordingly, careful not to bust off the knotty protuberance, and slipped on into the mudroom and passed through the kitchen and the dining room into the den where Mr. Walter Ramseur's sheetsteel stove threw off a thoroughly dehumidified and stifling variety of heat that Mr. Walter Ramseur controlled with a lever by which he could manipulate the damper back of the ashdrawer and thereby choke down his fire to moderately searing or ventilate it clean up to incendiary.

Most usually Mr. Walter Ramseur stacked his wood behind the stove in the fireplace and, with the exception of his length of natural portraiture, he went on ahead and deposited his armload back deep in the firebox under the flue. As for his cherrywood likeness of Mr. Tennessee Ernie Ford, he situated it on the hearth alongside the stove to the left and then shifted it over alongside the stove to the right where he grew convinced the light was more suitable somehow and enhanced most especially the deftness and artistry of Mr. Walter Ramseur's assorted cleftwork, seemed very nearly to breathe palpable life into Tennessee Ernie Ford who appeared there at the right of the stove on the verge of breaking into deep soulful song or muttering at the very least a "Peapickin'" or two in moderately deep and soulful tones of their own. Mr. Walter Ramseur's length of cherrywood struck him, in short, as the most stunning example of natural though cuty-tiny-electric-chain-saw-aided portraiture he'd ever personally come across and he lingered and admired it for as long as he dared prior to slipping back out into the sideyard where he awaited the arrival of Mrs. Walter Ramseur who he just knew would charge presently across the lawn and stand before him for a time too winded and breathless to speak of the ever so marvelous item she'd discovered on the hearth.

Mrs. Walter Ramseur did not, however discover Mr. Walter Ramseur's ever so marvelous item with quite the dispatch Mr. Walter Ramseur had himself anticipated on account of how she'd come to be engaged in the bathroom in a fairly concentrated effort to remove from just back of the tubdrain the green unsightly stain that she'd not, of course, have been obliged to get down on her knees and remove if Mr. Walter Ramseur had replaced the washer in the cold watertap and thereby stoppered the drip like several weeks previous he'd assured Mrs. Walter Ramseur he would. Consequently, then, as Mrs. Walter Ramseur scoured and scrubbed she grew increasingly irritated and determined how she might best have a word with Mr. Walter Ramseur on the topic of his various domestic duties and responsibilities now that they were both of them home all the day and all the night and lived pretty much on top of each other like lizards. So she washed and wiped and seethed and muttered and vanquished presently her green stain and was meaning to carry directly to Mr. Walter Ramseur the news of how she'd had to like put her on a route up the hall and through the front room and around into the den where she grew peeved afresh at

the sight of Mr. Walter Ramseur's ever so marvelous item upended on the hearth alongside the stove which was quite plainly
no place for it since there was obviously a stack of similar ever
so marvelous items in the firebox under the stovepipe, not even
to mention the dwindling and inflamed ever so marvelous items
growing ashen on the grate which she opened the stove door to
look upon and poke at and determined how one more ever so
marvelous item could not possibly hurt, all of which served as
preamble to the grasping of the knotty protuberance and the
hefting of the length of cherry which Mrs. Walter Ramseur
held a moment in her arms without taking even the meagerest
notice of the deft and artful cleftwork but merely shifted her
grip a bit instead so as to enable her to pitch Mr. Tennessee
Ernie Ford on into the firebox and shut the stove door back
of him.

She arrived pretty shortly thereafter in the sideyard, had
thrown about her shoulders Mr. Walter Ramseur's old worn-
out tweedy coat from off the peg by the back door and had
stepped off the porch and around the house where she discovered Mr. Walter Ramseur busting a length of wood with uncharacteristic good humor, judging from his wide toothy grin
that he displayed for Mrs. Walter Ramseur once she'd said to
him, "Walter," and inquired behind it if he possibly knew what
it was just precisely she'd lately been up to.

"Can't say," Mr. Walter Ramseur told to her back, apparently quite amused that she would ask of him such a thing in the
first place and, in an effort to undo Mr. Walter Ramseur's
amusement altogether, Mrs. Walter Ramseur shared with him
her most recent escapade of the stain scouring, the accompanying seething and muttering, and the hefting and pitching of
the misplaced length of cherry, which served alone to wholly
puncture Mr. Walter Ramseur's gay mood which had been already in fact on the wane.

Of course Mrs. Walter Ramseur forged on ahead into her
partially prepared text and she spoke earnestly of domestic
duties and responsibilities and lizards and such but suffered
herself to be interrupted by Mr. Walter Ramseur who exclaimed, "Tennessee!," flung down his maul, and departed al-

together from the sideyard, charged on around the house towards the backsteps which Mrs. Walter Ramseur went ahead and amended her text on account of. However, no amount of chagrin, regardless of Mrs. Walter Ramseur's colorful phrasing, could rein in Mr. Walter Ramseur who climbed the steps at a trot and dashed on into the house, where Mrs. Walter Ramseur came presently upon him squatting by the hearth alongside his smoldering length of cherrywood that he'd fished out from the stove. The knotty protuberance had gotten near about burned clean off and the cleftwork was so thoroughly charred and ruined that the artful deftness of it was no more to Mr. Walter Ramseur than a wispy memory, a sooty wispy memory which Mrs. Walter Ramseur departed quite entirely from her prepared text to speak of, and she wondered was Mr. Walter Ramseur acquainted with what the smoke from a smoldering hunk of wood might do to her wall and ceiling paint, but Mr. Walter Ramseur did not trouble himself to confess that he was or to confess that he wasn't either one and merely told to her instead, "Hunk of wood?" prior to speaking directly to Mr. Tennessee Ernie Ford, prior to inquiring of him if wasn't this life fraught in fact with woes and hardships.

Notwithstanding the utterly unambiguous response to his maiden exhibit, Mr. Walter Ramseur's passion for cute-tiny-electric-chain-saw-aided portraiture only heightened and grew and he found himself sculpting presently near as much wood as he stacked and burned until the weather warmed in May when he sculpted the very wood he'd stacked to burn. His native flair for cleftwork became more dramatic in the ensuing days after his Tennessee Ernie Ford fiasco, and he honed and refined his technique, did not need a gouge even for pupils any longer but could bring out the slightest nuance with his bartip alone. Of course knotty noselike protuberances did not naturally occur near so frequently as Mr. Walter Ramseur would have preferred, so he developed a talent for nose relief that he was quick to make use of when a protuberance failed to present itself to him. He could raise and channel ears with surprising dispatch as well and was purely a genius with sideburns in particular though he was highly artistic with sundry varieties of hair otherwise which was why he was especially partial to bushy men and women with extravagant locks and tresses and noticeable hormonal imbalances.

Mr. Walter Ramseur worked tirelessly at his sculpting in the sideyard and every few days presented Mrs. Walter Ramseur with a selected fruit of his labor which she evermore endeavored to appear pleased about even though no house can stand too terribly much natural log portraiture since natural log portraiture clashes acutely with most anything that is not natural and log and portraiture itself which it clashes with only somewhat instead. Mrs. Walter Ramseur had Teddy Roosevelt on the bureau in the front bedroom, Teddy Roosevelt in a jolly mood with his big square front teeth exposed, and the general Mr. Robert E. Lee atop the toilet-tank lid in the full bath where he glared towards the lavatory looking grim and sober and constipated. Out of a scant length of soft mealy cucumber trunk Mr. Walter Ramseur had fashioned the likeness of Mrs. Walter Ramseur's mother's sister Ida from Willis who'd not in life been a comely woman and did not truly get much improved in cucumber. She made, however, a passable stop for the door at the head of the hall where an accumulated coating of filmy dust shortly softened and enhanced her assorted uncomely features. In the front room on the endtable back of the gilded lamp and the framed snapshot of Mr. and Mrs. Walter Ramseur's girl Leona was a rendering in poplar of a jowly bearded gentleman who Mr. Walter Ramseur had insisted at the outset was Moses but had confessed presently was in fact Mr. Hank Williams, Jr., instead.

Upon the request of his wife Mr. Walter Ramseur had carved from an unusually sizable hunk of hornbeam a bust of Imogene Coca who Mrs. Walter Ramseur was most especially fond of and, as an artistic innovation, he'd flattened off the top of her head and laid a piece of windowglass upon it thereby making of Imogene Coca a truly exotic sort of a table that Mrs. Walter Ramseur professed to be so thoroughly taken with that she felt inspired and obliged to situate the thing in the den between the recliner and the radiator where a fellow would near about have to climb in through the window to see it. Mr. Walter Ramseur managed to slip into the kitchen in the corner by the dinette an oaken version of Mr. Benjamin Franklin who was in fact the result of a sort of mutation on account of how Mr. Walter Ramseur had set out to sculpt Dale Evans instead but had carelessly bestowed upon her appreciably more forehead than any woman generally has cause to be afflicted with. So he innovated and he mutated and he clefted afresh and managed to draw out from his balding Dale Evans a fairly astonishing likeness of Mr. Franklin who Mrs. Walter Ramseur did allow him to stick in the corner in the kitchen though she straightaway thereafter terminated the flow of natural log portraiture into the house relenting only so much as to permit a Maybelle Carter and a Douglas MacArthur either side of the back door on the landing.

With no regular outlet, then, for his work Mr. Walter Ramseur began to mass and collect it in the sideyard where he laid his excess portraiture up against the wire fence on the one side of him and up against the drystack foundation on the other and set out a few pieces just here and there upright on level spots of ground in the nature of a moderately organic and freeform portraiture garden. Of course his assortment was varied and far-reaching by the shank of May when he received upon the third Sunday of the month a visit in the early afternoon from the Reverend Mr. Worrell, the Reverend Mr. Worrell who'd come to spread the Gospel and stood upon the front porch and spoke briefly with Mrs. Walter Ramseur, expressed his curiosity as to the state of her immortal soul, wondered was she troubled and was she plagued or had she taken in fact Christ for her Savior which Mrs. Walter Ramseur did not possess the leisure or the inclination to speak of as she was washing the dinner dishes and listening on the radio to devotional music from the Baptist station in Roanoke which seemed to her all the activity her immortal soul could just presently stand. She did, however, recommend to the reverend that he step on around the house and consult instead with Mr. Walter Ramseur whose own immortal soul was most certainly altogether unengaged, and so the reverend departed from the porch and gained shortly the sideyard where he came upon Mr. Walter Ramseur who, with his cute tiny electric saw, was roughing out a bust of Mr. Willie Nelson from a length of red and ever so aromatic cedar.

"Morning brother," the Reverend Mr. Worrell shouted and exclaimed over the considerable uproar that Mr. Walter Ramseur's tiny electric saw tended to raise as he cut and shaped with it, and Mr. Walter Ramseur turned just far enough to take in the shiny blue suit and the printed tracts and the calfskin-covered Bible in addition to the Reverend Mr. Worrell's broad and relentless proselytizing grin, evidence sufficient to clue in Mr. Walter Ramseur who said, "Hey here preacher," back.

He didn't leave off sculpting but merely invited the reverend to speak at him if he must over the fuss and flying chips or wait if he preferred until Mr. Walter Ramseur's burst of inspiration flagged, which seemed itself agreeable to the Reverend Mr. Worrell who smiled in return his affable accommodating grin which looked so very much like his relentless proselytizing grin as to be wholly indistinguishable from it. But the reverend revealed his inclination soon enough as he roamed about the sideyard admiring Mr. Walter Ramseur's range of work, or admiring initially anyway the whole of Mr. Walter Ramseur's output prior to becoming taken with and captivated by a particularly voluptuous piece of portraiture, a stick of ash with inordinately deep and extravagant cleavage to it.

"Who is this creature?" the Reverend Mr. Worrell inquired of Mr. Walter Ramseur once Mr. Walter Ramseur had left off with his saw and stepped back from the stump to size up his progress on the length of cedar. "Such delicate work," the Reverend Mr. Worrell added and gestured vaguely with his hand towards the voluptuous portraiture so as not to get construed to be acutely taken with the cleavage alone which he did not hardly get construed to be.

"Oh him," Walter Ramseur said once he'd looked down the fence past in fact the voluptuous portraiture altogether. "That's Porter Wagoner. I had a time with his hair. Look how it swoops and sweeps."

"He is blessed with a head of it, isn't he." the Reverend Mr. Worrell observed ever so gaily prior to adding back of it, "Well, who's this then?" and he gestured on this occasion incisively towards the cleavage itself and so heard from Mr. Walter Ramseur, "That's Dorothy Lamour. *Road to Bali.*"

And the reverend said to him, "Hmm," and stepped back as

if to admire the general artistry of the thing, assuming a contemplative posture that did not appear truly the least bit indecent.

For his part, Mr. Walter Ramseur returned to his red cedar sculpture where with his cute tiny saw he ever so lightly honed and shaped and got joined presently by the Reverend Worrell who'd come over to admire Mr. Walter Ramseur's striking piece of portraiture in progress which the Reverend Mr. Worrell identified straightaway as quite plainly a tormented Christ. Of course it was only Willie Nelson instead though Mr. Walter Ramseur had shaved him down to such an uncharacteristic angularity that Willie did in fact resemble the Savior except for his bandana which did not truly look much like a crown of thorns. Nonetheless, Mr. Willie Nelson appeared sufficiently drawn and underfed to suggest to the Reverend Mr. Worrell Jesus in His suffering on the cross, most especially once the reverend had spied on the ground off alongside the stump a rendering of what he took to be the Virgin Mary who appeared to him quite plainly intent upon adoring Jesus above her. It wasn't exactly the Virgin Mary, however, and was instead Aunt Pittypat with a rag on her head, Aunt Pittypat with her eyes a trifle uplifted like made her appear to be gazing upon Willie Nelson in fact.

He was meaning to say a thing, the reverend was, had been stirred and moved and rendered fairly prayerful by the cedar Jesus with the deepest anguished gaze, and he was hoping to speak of the glories of Christ now that the allure of deep and symmetrical cleavage had abandoned him for a time, but just as the reverend dropped his chin and told to Mr. Walter Ramseur, "You know, friend," he spied on the cheek of the cedar Jesus a glistening drop of what turned out to be in the final analysis sap though it hardly got taken by the reverend for sap at all.

He was extensively dumb struck and made a point of sharing with Mr. Walter Ramseur the news of it, professed and proclaimed how he was far too bewildered to speak but managed nonetheless to muster up the breath and the wherewithal to ask of Mr. Walter Ramseur if wasn't that truly a tear on his Jesus. Now Mr. Walter Ramseur, who understandably failed to follow the Reverend Mr. Worrell's line of inquiry, told to the reverend what he was prone to tell whenever he got put to him a question or entertained an observation he could not decipher and comprehend, told to him, "Yeah," and issued a jolly and companionable sort of a snort while the reverend himself, who was persevering at being dumbstruck and was growing in fact evermore garrulous about it, stepped up snug alongside the stump and bent to peer pretty exclusively at that tear alone. Mr. Walter Ramseur, who could manufacture a suitably twangy voice by singing chiefly through his sinuses, broke into a passably melodic version of "For All the Girls I've Loved Before," which he intended for accompaniment to the Reverend Mr. Worrell's close and particular inspection, but the Reverend Mr. Worrell found himself drawn up short by most especially the lyric which struck him as a piercing indictment of his own personal and thoroughgoing licentiousness and he dropped into a variety of prayerful squat, so as not to sully his shiny blue trouserlegs with any actual kneeling, and petitioned the hunk of cedar portraiture for divine forgiveness and grace.

Of course Mr. Walter Ramseur allowed his sinuses to straightaway fall silent and he could not help but wonder what in the world the reverend had ever possibly done to Willie Nelson to feel obliged to drop into a prayerful squat before him. He said even one time, "Preacher?" but did not get much rise on account of it and was set to say, "Hey" and was set to say, "Preacher?" again when he heard the Reverend Mr. Worrell call that piece of portraiture Lord and call that piece of portraiture Christ and watched him reach up with his foremost finger to touch at the sappy tear which had beaded and clung along about Willie Nelson's moustache and had seeped in the first place from his finely clefted nose and so was not a tear precisely but was just instead a manner of effluvia that appeared nonetheless miraculous to the Reverend Mr. Worrell who laid his finger upon it and drew off the entire item in one stringy dollop.

"Preacher," Mr. Walter Ramseur said to the Reverend Mr. Worrell once he'd risen full upright to consider his fingerend, "that ain't Jesus."

As much, however, as the Reverend Mr. Worrell hated to dispute with Mr. Walter Ramseur, he guessed he knew the Lord and Savior when he saw Him and so assured Mr. Walter Ramseur that he was plainly mistaken and had doubtless sculpted a Christ, his cute tiny saw guided by hands unseen.

"That ain't Jesus, preacher," Mr. Walter Ramseur insisted. "He's over there alongside the vent," and Mr. Walter Ramseur indicated a piece of portraiture up against the foundation, a length of sugar maple just beyond Little Jimmy Dickens and just shy of Veronica Lake who the Reverend Mr. Worrell could not somehow help but notice was remarkably voluptuous on her own as opposed most especially to Mr. Walter Ramseur's actual Jesus who was drawn and gaunt and unrelievedly unvoluptuous himself.

The reverend raised up his sappy forefinger and pointed down alongside the vent in what appeared to Mr. Walter Ramseur a pathetic though moderately inquiring sort of a fashion and thereby caused him to tell to the Reverend Mr. Worrell, "Jesus," afterwhich the reverend redirected his sappy finger towards the length of cedar on the stump and so heard from Mr. Walter Ramseur, "Willie Nelson," which got augmented with and complemented by the reemployment of Mr. Walter Ramseur's sinuses in a doleful rendition of "Blue Eyes Crying in the Rain," which Mr. Walter Ramseur did not truly know all the words to and so sang what of it he could and otherwise carried through with the melody by means of an adenoidal hum.

He identified Aunt Pittypat upon request and supposed, once he'd been pressed and solicited, that he could possibly have misconstrued the whole business himself had he not known already it was Pittypat on the ground looking at Willie Nelson on the stump which provided some measure of relief for the Reverend Mr. Worrell who hoped Mr. Walter Ramseur could see fit to put from his mind the entire silly episode, forget that the Reverend Mr. Worrell had shown up of an afternoon on a Sunday and had dropped down in a prayerful squat before what he took to be a tearful tormented Christ when he'd seen in truth only Willie Nelson's nose run instead. Of course since Mr. Walter Ramseur could not in the wake of his recent retirement and newfound aimlessness much tell anymore where one silly episode left off and another one took up, he assured the Reverend Mr. Worrell that the facts of the matter were growing for him rather murky already though, for the sake of clarity, he felt obliged to inquire if did the reverend mean for him to put from his mind entirely the prayerful squat and the stringy dollop of effluvia or just the Willie Nelson-Aunt Pittypat part of the thing like prompted the reverend to tell to him, "Just Willie. Just Pittypat," and he offered to Mr. Walter Ramseur a tract out from his coatpocket, a tract on the topic of hell and how to burn there which he hoped Mr. Walter Ramseur would find engaging.

Then he took his leave, grabbed up Mr. Walter Ramseur's hand in his own sappy one and shook it wanly prior to retiring from the sideyard and leaving Mr. Walter Ramseur to look from his tract to his stump and back to his tract again in momentary solitude before he screeched and hollered and hooted and thereby led Mrs. Walter Ramseur to fear he had sliced off a significant piece of his own personal anatomy with his cute tiny electric saw like served to dispatch her out the back door and down the steps and around the house at a kind of perilous velocity and she arrived ever so shortly in the sideyard where she discovered Mr. Walter Ramseur quite whole and utterly unsliced, Mr. Walter Ramseur who had for her an altogether pressing query, and he gestured alongside himself towards his stump with his length of cedar upon it and asked of Mrs. Walter Ramseur, "Who is that?"

So it wasn't Jesus exactly, though the Reverend Mr. Worrell had figured it for Jesus, and it hadn't been truly a tear but had looked nonetheless to the reverend like a tear precisely and he sculpted and shaped and honed a little himself and delivered the Sunday following to his congregation at Laural Fork a stirring bit of testimony in a choked and tremulous voice, a refined and partially fabricated account of his own personal silly episode in which a chain-sawed cedar Christ wept. The congregation received the news in fairly reverent silence until Mr. Porter Ogle's sister Arlene stepped into the sanctuary aisle and pitched presently over into a faint, a manner of endorsement that liberated and unhinged assorted people otherwise who grew themselves infused with holiness and twitched and chattered and babbled and shrieked and made just in general a fairly gaudy display of their infusement.

The Reverend Mr. Worrell's flock gathered at a comely little church at Laurel Fork situated in a swale alongside an ancient and extravagantly gnarled white oak that dropped its leaves in the churchyard and tended to loose, most especially of a Sunday, its acorns onto the tin roof in an apt and punctuational sort of a way. The rise to the southeast and the rise to the northwest were fenced for cows, and Mr. Bobby Kemp from out towards Stuart kept a herd of Charolais up on the one hill and a herd of polled Angus down on the other and assorted numbers from each contingent tended most mornings to collect at the opposite fencerows and exchange niceties across the churchyard. The building itself was frame and white clapboard on the outside and painted matchboard on the inside with a half-dozen sizable though unleaded windows along each side of the sanctuary and an unadorned wooden pulpit up front atop a carpeted riser that thumped like a drum whenever the Reverend Mr. Worrell strode across it. There was no accommodation back of the pulpit for a choir as there was no choir to accommodate and instead high upon the wall hung a portrait of Christ the Lord in prayer, Christ the Lord quite larger than life altogether with His relatively doleful eyes upcast and His clasped hands resting upon a rock. A brass incandescent lamp clipped to the top of the frame illuminated most especially the clouds above the Savior's head that looked to swirl, and gather and threaten a storm which did not appear, as an imminent prospect, much troubling at all to Christ the Lord Himself who simply kneeled before His rock in the midst of the vast waste that sprawled about Him clean to the horizon, a scrubby, sandy, boulder-strewn waste. an arid unpopulated piece of territory with apparently just the Lord upon it in addition to an item off in the middle distance over Jesus' near shoulder, an item that looked very much like a duck though nobody lately had climbed a ladder to find out was it truly a duck in fact.

The pews were varnished hardwood with rolled and sculpted backs and rolled and sculpted seats which had both somehow gotten rolled and sculpted in the wrong places precisely and so did not actually bulge into people's dips or dip under people's bulges, attesting either to the ever evolving state of posteriors or the general haplessness of the pewmaker who'd seen fit as well to provide the pewseats with a steep and fairly extravagant lip which itself allowed unmindful individuals the opportunity to pour off onto the church floor. Those among the congregation with wearying parts and failing vessels and byways had seen fit in the majority to carry with them pillows to the sanctuary that they left from week to week on their pews at their customary locations along with tissues and mints and lozenges and ballpoint pens and sufficient personal effects otherwise to render their seats cozy and familiar like apparently served to soften the rigors of their theology and help make the news of their lowly states and the talk of their harsh prospects appreciably more endurable.

They advertised themselves on a sign out front over the double doors as a FULL GOSPEL PRIMITIVE MISSIONARY HOLINESS CHURCH which, as a title and a claim, got augmented and illuminated by a floridly lettered scrap of verse painted on the casing just above the lintel, a rhyming couplet meant to suggest how a man might go to hell most any old way but could travel only one route to heaven which sounded, in a couplet, a moderately wry and jolly piece of news. For a congregation, most especially for a full gospel primitive missionary holiness congregation, the people in the swale south of Laurel Fork were not too terribly much given to lively infusement, though Porter Ogle's sister Arlene was prone to collapse every now and again from rapture and Mr. Denton Gravely's wife Louise spoke on occasion in the sort of tongue a Chinaman might use were he driven to a consuming peevishness. Otherwise they just sat and amened chiefly and lavished every now and again the Maker with spontaneous praise though never so often or so loudly as to offer a serious intrusion to the Reverend Mr. Worrell's sermonizing which itself occupied only the shank of the service with the bulk of each Sunday morning being given over instead to a spell of testifying for Christ on the part of most anybody whose woes and troubles had undergone in the course of the week an alteration or who'd heard talk of some burdens somewhere being lifted. There were prayers as well for the sick and afflicted and remembrances of the dead and most usually a textual exchange with the reverend citing one piece of scripture and the congregation sharing with him a complementary piece of scripture back before turning more often than not, to a general raising of voices in spirited song.

The Laurel Fork Full Gospel Primitive Missionary Holiness Church had housed at one time an upright piano and had numbered among its congregation three passably competent piano players, two of them being the sisters Harriet Ann and Ocala Pugh who'd themselves played alternate Sundays until they fell out with each other on account of a casserole, a casserole that they'd neither one of them made but that they'd both of them tasted at a manner of potluck soiree and had agreed was a dish of altogether meager appeal though they'd disputed hotly the causes why, with Ocala insisting she tasted too awful much cumin in the thing which had struck Harriet Ann as nothing but airs alone since she did not suspect her sister Ocala would know a dose of cumin if it came up and beat her about the head and shoulders. Of course that was hardly the sort of talk Ocala Pugh guessed she should have to endure from a woman who mixed on occasion ketchup and mushroom soup and called it a sauce, and she told as much straightoff to her sister Harriet Ann who had indulged previously in the notion that her ketchup and mushroom soup sauce was considered widely a triumph which her sister Ocala served to puncture and deflate and pretty utterly do in quite entirely.

So they disputed and contended and presently fell out with each other irredeemably and Ocala Pugh determined how she would not herself play an upright piano that her sister Harriet Ann had laid her fingers to before Harriet Ann arrived shortly on her own at a similar conclusion which freed Harriet Ann and Ocala Pugh to pass their Sundays seething at each other across the breadth of the sanctuary while Mr. Eason Dunleavy of Fancy Gap applied himself to the upright piano with immoderate zeal, only middling ability, and a thoroughly mitigated success that probably would have produced some congregational strife had not the general raising of voices in song so wholly stifled and concealed Mr. Eason Dunleavy's shortcomings as to render them altogether inconsequential. And had Mr. Eason Dunleavy not fallen into sloth and been dropped from the church rolls he would likely have been allowed to persevere in his variety of musical torment, but he cultivated a manner of acute bursitis that would not permit him to hinge most especially at his knee and shoulder joints like he had in the past been given to and so he chose to lay about in his front room, yielding quite entirely to his complaint and bringing upon him the disapproval of the congregation otherwise who left off endeavoring to heal Mr. Eason Dunleavy through prayer and resigned themselves to going pianoless like surely would have proven more of a disappointment and a calamity had not Mrs. Nelson H. Allen agreed to carry with her to the sanctuary her mouth organ with which she generally endeavored to establish a key and improvise a preamble before getting rendered by the uplifted voices extraneous.

The women had all come somehow to be persuaded that they were sopranos of an operatic variety and they engaged weekly in a lively competition that consisted primarily of trilling and wailing mingled with occasional brief instances of screeching outright on those hymns marked and notated with a screeching clef. The bulk of the men were convinced they were blessed with deep rich tonal qualities themselves and endeavored to create of a Sunday their own variety of trembling shock except of course for those few scrawny tenors who sang in their necks with sufficient vigor to go fairly purple from the temples down. The collective result was a species of reverential uproar that even the cows at the fencerows most usually picked up their heads and looked at each other about, a species of a reverential uproar that commenced with a brief harmonica prologue which evermore gave way to a near about detectably melodic explosion led in part by the Reverend Mr. Worrell's wife in the front pew who'd previously once been praised for her soothing lilt, but led in fact primarily by the widow Mrs. Opal Criner back of her who considered her own tones purely angelic as she'd heard countless times from her Carl that they were.

Opal Criner had not taken straightoff to the Reverend Mr. Worrell when he'd come to the pulpit at Laurel Fork, but she'd warmed to him presently once the Reverend Mr. Worrell had displayed an inordinate passion for his Jesus in conjunction with the notice he gave one Sunday shortly after his arrival to

Mrs. Opal Criner's own particular brand of trilling which he insinuated was afterall angelic in fact, suspected anyhow that angels on high could pretty much hear it where they were without likely even having to leave off plucking their harps to do it, suspected it so sweetly and in the company of so awfully many teeth that Mrs. Opal Criner could not seem to help but grow passably charmed and flattered.

Consequently, the Reverend Mr. Worrell enjoyed soon enough the warm regard of the widow Mrs. Opal Criner who sat of a Sunday immediately back of Mrs. Worrell and endeavored to signify how profoundly in her own depths she trembled, felt obliged to communicate to the Reverend Mr. Worrell that he did quite utterly plumb her very reaches though she did not wish to hoot and blather after the fashion of Mr. Denton Gravely's wife Louise and so issued from time to time only decorous subdued sorts of discharges by which she managed to suggest both moderate infusement and mild indigestion together. Wednesday evenings the Reverend Mr. Worrell, in conjunction with his wife, conducted Bible classes in the sanctuary which Mrs. Opal Criner attended without fail, driving herself to the church in her Carl's beige Coronet and sitting often in a folding chair up alongside the reverend just shy of the pulpit from where she was handy to get called upon to cite and intone and frequently volunteered as well to school her Bible classmates in the nuances of versifying and the vagaries of Hebrew inflection notwithstanding how her Bible classmates weren't themselves hardly ever looking to get schooled.

They were all of them chiefly hoping to discover illumination and solace in the Testaments and were meaning for the most part to issue fairly rapturous proclamations once the light had dawned upon them which, as a course of action, served to render the Reverend Mr. Worrell's Wednesday Bible classes lively and unpredictable since there was never truly any telling when in fact the light might dawn and upon whom. They had, then, scripture to discuss and passionate discharges to entertain in addition to the various unanticipated points of interest that assorted members of the Bible study group found themselves inclined to raise and touch upon from time to time which served together to prevent the bunch of them from making too terribly much headway through the Good Book, and after four and a half months of concentrated study they were only just beginning to leave off with Deuteronomy and dip into Joshua primarily on account of how they'd all of them gotten hung up in Exodus, most especially where Moses ascended to the mountaintop and received from God His commandments that nobody much kept anymore as best as the Reverend Mr. Worrell's Bible study class could tell. Of course they'd felt obliged between them to discuss just who precisely it was they knew that bore false witness and stole and plundered and swore and coveted and diddled most especially their neighbors' wives while failing sometimes even simultaneously to keep the sabbath like was widely taken to be a terrible disgrace, and Mr. Troy Haven from Snake Creek had seen fit to inquire if didn't people seem anymore noticeably and maybe even acutely sorrier than they used to be which had naturally touched off a spate of extensive anecdotal evidence to that effect.

Presently, however, they did pass on through Exodus entirely and made in fact pretty short work of Leviticus and Numbers both prior to running up in Deuteronomy on the Ten Commandments all over again which gave rise to further talk of stealing and plundering and swearing and coveting and diddling too on the part of those people that nobody much had thought to speak of previously but who, in the intervening weeks since Exodus, had come to mind, like would include Mr. Roy Berrier of Sylvatus who'd taken up in a carnal way with his second wife's third husband's least girl which troubled the Bible study class and would likely have even scandalized and appalled them had they proven successful at tracing and deciphering Mr. Roy Berrier's Kinship to his second wife's third husband's least girl in the first place. There was mention as well of Mrs. P. D. Averill's sister Brenda who'd moved to Roanoke where she shared a house with a man and his spaniel, a man she wasn't even so much as betrothed to but flaunted nonetheless and had carried home at Christmas to present roundabout, telling to people, "This is Gerald, my lover," in the sort of flat declarative voice with which a decent woman might see fit to introduce her dentist.

In the wake of such tales as these it was quite understandable that Mrs. Gloria Hawks and Miss Cindy Womble, who were
together delicate of disposition or claimed anyhow to suffer
both from a burdensome sensitivity to sin in most especially
other people, should find themselves put upon to wonder
rather harmoniously if there was in fact any shame left on this
earth, precisely the variety of inquiry to shunt the Reverend
Mr. Worrell's Bible class off the scriptures entirely. Consequently, they passed two Wednesdays regaling each other with
tales of abject and unmitigated shamelessness which appeared,
as a variety of narrative, purely inexhaustible since the world
seemed anymore ripe with blacksliders and heathens outright.
Extended talk of the weak and the fallen quite understandably
served to blacken the mood of the Bible classmates who feared
that their world was retreating from the light and slipping ever
so steadily into darkness like cast a pall over their endeavor,
looked to thwart and diminish their pursuit as best as the Reverend Mr. Worrell could tell and, in an effort to dispel the
gathering gloom and dilute the general woe, the reverend decided to invite to the Bible study class a fellow he knew, a man
from Mt. Airy he'd met at a conclave down at Roaring Gap, a
former missionary who'd carried the Gospel to Thailand and
Korea where most everybody was in fact an earnest pagan idol-
ator which struck the Reverend Mr. Worrell as an altogether
grimmer state of affairs than they were threatened with here at
home by their domestic strain of shiftlessness and casual depravity.

So they entertained at the Laurel Fork sanctuary the missionary from Mt. Airy who brought with him his carousel projector and his trays of slides and gave a show against the blank
back wall, narrated a tour of the East where the vegetation was
lush and green and the people were nut-colored when they
were not pale yellow instead. He told of conversions and bap-
tisms and chicken in a sesame cream sauce and, standing in the
wash of the projector bulb over the fan motor, he shared as well
news of the love of Christ for all peoples everywhere which
itself touched off a mild bout of dignified infusement among
the Bible classmates who spoke of the bountiful Lord and the

sway of His ceaseless affection which got augmented by a query from Mrs. Norma Baines who was anxious to discover the proportion of the cream to the sesame like induced Mr. Troy Haven's wife Olive to wonder was it the seeds or was it the oil or was it the both of them somehow in combination which opened the way to a lively cultural exchange that itself helped to relieve the funk of the Bible classmates who, with the anticipation of new and exotic dishes to pass through their necks, suspected that perhaps this life was ripe with prospects and possibilities after all and should not yet be given over entirely to woe and gloom.

In fact, the slide show and subsequent discussion proved to be so thoroughly enlivening as to beat back the oncoming despair pretty much altogether which allowed the Reverend Mr. Worrell to take up afresh the Book of Joshua and carry forward clean to Ruth which itself was such a slight bit of scripture that the reverend figured they would pass the bunch of them almost straightaway through it and direct into Samuel, but the tale of Ruth come from Moab to Judah where she took up almost straightaway with Boaz the Ephrathite struck a nerve with most especially Mrs. Gloria Hawks who could not herself much condone the mingling of Moabites with Ephrathites notwithstanding how she'd never personally cultivated an acquaintance with either stock of people. Mrs. Gloria Hawks simply did not believe that everybody was meant to mix and marry as some folks plainly could not be thrown together and made to mesh by which she meant most particularly Stroupes and Snavelys in this instance as Mrs. Gloria Hawks had lately attended a service meant to join together a Stroupe and a Snavely in everlasting holy matrimony.

"A Family Dollar Stroupe?" Miss Cindy Womble wanted to know.

"Them," Mrs. Gloria Hawks told to her. "Those Galax Stroupes from out along the fifteenth hole. Phillip and Rosemary who built that Tudor house with the timbers that pass clean through the walls, or their girl Nancy anyhow who took up some way or another with Billy Snavely's boy Billy."

"Billy Snavely that went to jail?" Mr. Troy Haven wanted to know.

"Billy Snavely that went to jail twice," Mrs. Gloria Hawks informed him.

And Mrs. Norma Baines's husband Larry, who was not acquainted with any Snavelys himself, sought to discover from Mrs. Gloria Hawks which Billy it was that had been to jail precisely.

"Big Billy," Mrs. Gloria Hawks told to him. "Beat a man with a scantling, a Turner from up at Poplar Camp. They were both of them drunk and fighting over the favors of some woman, and believe you me I do mean favors, pure charity work. I've seen hogs with daintier features than Billy Snavely's got.

"Big Billy?" Larry Baines wanted to know.

"Him chiefly, though his boy's surely cursed with a resemblance."

The Reverend Mr. Worrell felt obliged to volunteer how couldn't any of them truly blame a man for being unsightly that his wife Mrs. Worrell subscribed to straightaway and had near about, with a telling gaze, persuaded Mrs. Opal Criner and Mr. and Mrs. Ray Truitt to throw in themselves with her when Mrs. Gloria Hawks informed the Reverend Mr. Worrell how both Snavelys together had been born sightly enough but had managed, by dent chiefly of immoderate habits and violent inclinations, to erode their appeal. And Mrs. Gloria Hawks proclaimed, "I got a fuzzy rug in the half bath that hasn't been flogged near so often as both those Snavelys together."

Mrs. Gloria Hawks set out to describe the ceremony which had taken place in the Methodist church east of Galax and had drawn a sizable crowd of assorted Stroupes and in-laws of Stroupes and neighbors and acquaintances of Stroupes as well, in addition to a regular pack of Snavelys down from Pulaski and little Billy's buddies from the third shift at the carpet plant who would most usually have been at home asleep but, due to their extravagant affection for Billy Snavely, had managed this day to travel to the sanctuary to sleep instead. The bride wore a gown of white silk organza over taffeta with a sweetheart neckline, a basque bodice, and a deep wire-edged ruffled flounce that enhanced her hemline and gave way to a train so exceedingly far-reaching that she required for her walk up the aisle not just the elbow of her daddy Phillip Stroupe but the aid as well of her brother's boy Hinton Stroupe who served as his aunt Nancy's trainbearer though, being a slight fellow with the very so prodigious train to marshal and tote, he experienced some measure of difficulty along the aisle and on two occasions lost so considerably much momentum that he near about jerked his aunt Nancy over backwards and did noticeably muss her rolled-edged organza derby and her veil of bridal illusion.

The bridesmaids, who awaited the arrival of the bride up at the front of the sanctuary, wore flowing pale green chiffon gowns and carried bouquets of pinks and fern fronds while the ushers and the groom and the groom's daddy had opted themselves for skyblue morning coats with navy piping and matching skyblue trousers. Their cummerbunds were bloodred and their shirtfronts were exceedingly ruffled while their flies were, in the majority, partly open exposing their shirttails, apparently a congenital Snavely trait as it was only the lone Stroupe among the ushers who'd managed to secure his zipper shut. To the mind of Mrs. Gloria Hawks, the Snavelys looked more common somehow dolled up than they did in just their regular disreputable streetclothes as they plainly could not manage to get accoutermented and accessorized sufficiently to defeat and undo their accumulated unsightliness which appeared to become intensified and heightened by close proximity to even a skyblue navytrimmed morning coat.

Mrs. Norma Baines, who was by nature a reckless sort, ventured to inform Mrs. Gloria Hawks how she'd been personally acquainted with Stroupes that were no delight to look upon themselves, but Mrs. Gloria Hawks hastened to inform her back that she was speaking specifically of the fifteenth-hole Family Dollar Stroupes who were a handsome and comely assortment and deserved for relations a better stock than your garden variety Snavely by which she meant to full well suggest that such as Snavelys should stick to their own and not go mucking about with purer strains of folks which appeared to the Reverend Mr. Worrell, as a manner of sentiment, a trifle uncharitable and he suggested specifically to Mrs. Gloria Hawks, though somewhat to everybody otherwise as well, how it would do to remember that the Lord Christ loves us all without restraint and condition which left Mrs. Gloria Hawks to suppose back that the Lord

Christ had not likely ever seen a Snavely in a skyblue morning coat.

The reverend, in further pursuit of the matter, mustered up his deepest preacherly tones to inquire of Mrs. Gloria Hawks, "Would you cast Ruth, then, from Judah?" which itself compelled her to exchange briefly expressions with Miss Cindy Womble as preamble to inquiring of the Reverend Mr. Worrell, "Do what?"

They were quite apparently pretty completely mired up in the scriptures and the Reverend Mr. Worrell, fearing that they might not the bunch of them ever actually arrive at the Gospels to learn there of the mystical wonders of Christ, grew compelled to edit and condense the remaining books of the Old Testament and marshal the discussions as best he was able. Consequently, he finished up Ruth in short order and encapsulated for his Wednesday group the Book of Samuel and both Chronicles together while omitting entirely Ezra and Nehemiah and touching only scantly upon Esther the Persian queen, mention of whom incited Mr. Ray Truitt, who passed the majority of his Tuesday evenings at the reference table in the Hillsville library where he read indiscriminately in the *World Book,* to invoke the name of Mithridates the Great that he'd come across two Tuesdays previous and who he knew to be a Persian himself, a pretty conspicuous Persian as best as Mr. Ray Truitt could recall though he could not seem to conjure up conspicuous how precisely.

Upon arriving at the Book of Job, the Reverend Mr. Worrell felt obliged to pause and loiter for a time on account of the general appeal of tribulation, and he allowed the discussion to range wide and proceed fairly unrestrained, interrupting only infrequently so as to inquire why it might be goodly men and women were oftentimes obliged to suffer which nobody much of the gathered throng could truly make out the cause for though, being goodly themselves, they did not doubt they were highly qualified to attempt to. They'd all of them endured unwarranted afflictions as best as they could tell, had felt previously put upon and forsaken and wished by turns to speak of their trials on this earth which commenced with the mechanical difficulties of Mr. Larry Baines who'd blown a gasket on his blue Riviera and had spilled upon the old Roanoke road what of his motor oil that had not seeped instead into the cavities of his engine, news of which prompted from Mr. Troy Haven a disdainful snort, and he took the floor instead so as to inform most especially the Baineses together that he'd personally himself thrown a rod once down in South Carolina out between Columbia and Charleston where there wasn't a soul about to come to his aid. "Nothing but sandflies," Mr. Troy Haven said. "I had to take a bus home," which struck most especially Mrs. Gloria Hawks and Miss Cindy Womble together as a verifiable anguishment considering the element that anymore traveled by bus which Mrs. Gloria Hawks and Miss Cindy Womble exchanged fairly curdling expressions about.

As it seemed to him pertinent somehow, the Reverend Mr. Worrell took upon himself the obligation of reminding his Bible study group that there was all sorts of torments in this life and vehicular failure was just one of them. While he did not wish to belittle the travails of Mr. Larry Baines and Mr. Troy Haven and did not suspect he would much care himself to ride a bus home from South Carolina, the Reverend Mr. Worrell couldn't help but figure that they'd all of them endured disappointments and heartaches far graver than had yet been spoken of. "We've lost to the hand of death friends and relations," the Reverend Mr. Worrell said, "the young and the old, the fit and the infirm and we've wondered of our God in heaven why, have we not?" like was just the sort of preacherly observation to bring forth from the Bible classmates little sighs and confirming discharges and, in an effort to slip seamlessly off automoblies and make towards death and disablement instead, the Reverend Mr. Worrell's wife aided her husband by standing up out from her seat and speaking fairly dolefully of an aunt she'd had who'd been run over by a Plymouth and had come to be on account of it altogether debilitated for a time in advance of succumbing quite entirely. She'd been a kind woman, as fine an aunt as a girl could hope for, and had been walking on the left facing traffic, which served in combination to render the whole episode utterly senseless as best as Mrs. Worrell could tell, Mrs. Worrell who grew moderately teary and noticeably congested and confessed how she'd come to be peeved with her Jesus for taking from her her aunt who'd been a good and decent woman, an obedient Christian, and a conscientious pedestrian.

"It didn't seem right," Mrs. Worrell said. "Didn't look to me much reward at all," and she gazed sadly off towards the blank back sanctuary wall which of course provided the Reverend Mr. Worrell with the opportunity to interject briefly a word on the topic of the vague and wondrous workings of Christ that seemed to him to lurk oftentimes hidden and unrevealed in the midst of grief. " 'When I waited for light," the reverend cited, "darkness came,' " and he was allowing the phrase to ever so dramatically hang and resonate in the air when Mr. Ray Truitt volunteered how his own daddy had been struck down by a Gremlin, had been knocked over anyhow into the curbing where he'd suffered bumps and abrasions along with a ruptured femur which Mrs. Norma Baines regretted to inform Mr. Ray Truitt was a thoroughgoing impossibility since a femur was not the sort of an item that could even get ruptured.

"It's a bone somewhere," she told him which Mr. Ray Truitt allowed maybe Mrs. Norma Baines's femur was though he assured her his daddy's own one had been a variety of femur otherwise since it had in fact undoubtedly gotten ruptured itself that Mrs. Norma Baines was pretty well set to remonstrate about when the Reverend Mr. Worrell cited once further in his deep preacherly tones. " 'Happy," he said, "is the man that God reproves. He wounds, but He binds up.' "

He was meaning to speak specifically of Job, most especially of how afflictions came to meet him and his heart was in turmoil and never still, but Mrs. Gloria Hawks, who figured she'd stood so much reproving that she ought to be full well delirious, rose up from her chair and set out to share with her Bible classmates a tale of woe, spoke to them of her own people who'd passed from this life, her momma and her daddy both along with her baby brother Warren who had not yet passed completely himself but had fallen pretty thoroughly from Mrs. Gloria Hawks's favor as he'd lapsed in his faith and anymore just laid about and drank beer in front of the tv. "I raised him like my own," Mrs. Gloria Hawks said. "Momma was sickly and couldn't see to him and I wasn't but a little thing myself, but I washed him and fed him and hauled him about like he was a baby of mine. He had the cutest little blond curls," Mrs. Gloria Hawks told towards the kneeling Jesus on the front wall,"and the sweetest little face, and Momma and Daddy figured between them he'd surely turn out to favor in his looks and his ways Momma's own uncle John who'd been a prince of a man; everybody'd known him for one. But he didn't," Mrs. Gloria Hawks said, "he didn't at all," and she fell so significantly silent that she could not even bring herself to swivel her head so far as to exchange with Miss Cindy Womble expressions all freighted with remorse and disappointment. "I thought he'd be somebody," Mrs. Gloria Hawks said at last and thereby prompted the reverend to chime in with a manner of preacherly citation which itself benumbed Mrs. Gloria Hawks sufficiently to provide the reverend the opportunity to share with her and everybody otherwise news of how the Christian heart embraces most especially those souls lost to the ways of sloth and faithlessness.

"It's easy enough to love a man for his righteousness," the reverend fairly intoned. "The challenge is to love him in spite of his sin," which, as a sentiment, Mrs. Worrell found so utterly apt and well-spoken that she could not help somehow but infuse a little in the direction of the Reverend Mr. Worrell who preened in the glow of her infusement and consequently yielded the floor to Mrs. Gloria Hawks who gazed briefly Jesuswards in rapt contemplation prior to declaring into the air, "He wears those gauzy t-shirts with the straps to them and picks at his toes," and she shook her head and dropped it low as if to say how there were some things even a Christian couldn't love a man in spite of.

Of course Mrs. Gloria Hawks's baby brother Warren hadn't passed beyond recall and rejuvenation that Mr. Troy Haven reminded her about and spoke as well of his own unsavory brother who'd expired and thereby put himself beyond the embrace of Mr. Troy Haven's Christian heart that was a troubling state of affairs as best as Mr. Troy Haven could tell, and he was meaning to speak further of his anguishment, was seeking in fact suitable words to speak further of his anguishment with when Mrs. Opal Criner alongside him made the first in a string of her customary noises, loosed her initial slight semi-wistful breath in advance of commandeering the floor from Mr. Troy Haven and wondering why maybe they didn't tell of people they'd adored in life and lost to the Lord since while it seemed to her easier indeed to love a man for his righteousness, she guessed as well it was surely harder to give a righteousness man up.

"I had one myself," she said, "and I lost him," afterwhich she allowed somewhat of a rift in the proceedings that Mr. Troy Haven attempted to introduce himself into and thereby retake the floor, but before he could get fully under way the widow Mrs. Opal Criner interrupted him, indulged in an exhalation so resoundingly deep and so purely wistful as to forestall Mr. Troy Haven altogether while prompting as well from Miss Cindy Womble and Mrs. Gloria Hawks, in advance even of the "Ah" and of the "Carl," an exchange of unrelievedly bilious expressions.

ii

She'd meant it for her grandbaby Delmon, had bought it upon the occasion of his birth, and stored it away sealed in its box on her closet shelf until such time as Delmon could make capable use of it. In truth, she'd forgotten entirely about the thing and likely would not have come across it at all had not the strap on her leatherette pocketbook begun to stretch and yield which immediately struck Opal Criner as a legitimate menace to the security of her various documents and keepsakes not even to mention her folding money and silver that some hoodlum could likely relieve her of with little more than a moderate tug. She figured she'd might best change over before a grave misfortune befell her, and she considered fairly deeply upon the virtues of her various bags otherwise prior to concluding that most probably her blue beaded one would best suit her since she recalled having been attracted in the first place to its stout and significant hardware, its catches and rivets and grommets and buckles that had not looked in the least bit delicate to her.

As she could not straightaway remember where exactly she'd laid the thing, Opal Criner firstoff inquired, as was her

habit, of her girl Marie where maybe her blue beaded handbag
might be which her girl Marie ruminated briefly upon in advance of telling, as was her habit, to her mother back, "How in
the hell should I know," as preface to Opal Criner's actual pursuit of the item. She looked for it under her bed in among her
hatboxes and in the back of her bottom two chiffonier drawers,
but did not turn up any trace of the thing and guessed as long
as she was rifling bureaus she'd step on into her girl Marie's
room and pick through various of her and Donnie's possessions
so as to satisfy herself entirely that they'd not by mistake slipped
up and stowed her beaded handbag away which, once she'd
been discovered, she explained as her purpose to her girl Marie
who as much as took up her mother and pitched her into the
hallway before Opal Criner could learn from her the applications of Donnie Huff's Pyrex bong which had struck her as a
curious sort of an item for a man to keep in with his socks.

   She searched through the linen cabinet and probed deep
into the sideboard and well back into the reaches of the secretary where she came across an old postcard, a color-enhanced
view of downtown Belleville, New Jersey, with happy Bellevil-
lians lounging about amiably on the sidewalk exposing at each
other their altogether resplendent white smiles which, through
the magic of color enhancement, had largely gotten smeared
across their noses. The thing was addressed to her dead uncle
Benny from some woman named Ida or named Evie or named
even Ava maybe since her signature proved so exceedingly frivolous and baroque as to be quite completely indecipherable.
Judging from the text, she'd been suffering in Belleville from
the midsummer heat but had managed nonetheless to work up
the wherewithal to venture forth and purchase a pair of stunning pumps which she spoke of in appreciable detail in advance
of complaining about the humidity as well. Straightoff Opal
Criner did not much care for her and could not begin to imagine what possible attachment such a creature might have had
with her dead uncle Benny who'd been in life stern and sober
and hardly the sort of fellow most women would seek out to
speak of their pumps to. It was a genuine curiosity and she
sought to draw her girl Marie into it with her, called out for her
to come to the secretary if she would and see for herself the odd

item Opal Criner had discovered which she flapped and beat about in the air and thereby did in fact entice her girl Marie over to her, her girl Marie who discovered in the view of Belleville an ever so suitable candidate for decoupage and so straightaway took possession of the thing herself and admired how the colors seeped and laid without venturing to comment upon her great-uncle Benny's attachments since she could not recall a thing in the world about him except how one time he'd heedlessly dipped a cigar ash down her blouse.

Marie didn't even do the service of lingering about so as to entertain news of Opal Criner's disapproval of the manner of woman that would buy such homely shoes as apparently this woman had bought. She simply stepped back into the kitchen with her color-enhanced card that she laid straightaway to a convenient boxlid so as to gauge the effect while Opal Criner proceeded in her examination of the secretary by which she failed to come across her blue beaded bag but did presently discover a 1943 Lincoln penny partly mired up in a melted hunk of caramel nugget. Opal Criner scratched about in the endtable drawers either side of the sofa and found a shirtbutton and a plastic rain bonnet but scant trace of her beaded bag which she sought out in the coat closet in the hall where she happened onto her fox stole that she laid upon her shoulders and fastened about her neck with the foxjaw clasp prior to stepping across the front room so as to model the thing in the kitchen for her girl Marie who was not herself of a mood to admire a stole and so suggested to her mother, "Go on."

In her own bedroom back down the hallway, Opal Criner revisited her chiffonier drawers and dusted her dead Carl's color portrait that had grown fairly fuzzy from neglect. She reexamined her hatboxes under her bed and determined that she would at last peek once into her clothes closet although she was relatively certain her blue beaded bag was surely elsewhere since she kept in her closet just her dresses and her shoes primarily and her quilted housecoat that hung from a tenpenny nail in the back of the door. She'd laid up on the shelf a straw bonnet she'd been partial to back when her and Carl had cultivated a flower patch out alongside their basement steps, a bonnet she'd laid and situated atop of a homely striped afghan a woman friend had gone to the trouble to stitch together and present to her in her time of grieving, and while she'd savored and cherished the gesture she'd packed away the article itself as she'd never been much partial to puce and pink and brown and blue and orange laid and woven together in gay if not near about riotous proximity to each other. She stored as well on the closet shelf her electric vibrating foot basin packed up in the carton it had come in and, beside it, her silver service in a handsome feltlined hardwood case. There was not truly room much otherwise for a blue beaded bag, but Opal Criner reached up nonetheless and felt about on her shelf back of her bonnet and her foot basin and atop of her hardwood case where she did in fact discover an item, a white pasteboard box with some noticeable heft to it though hardly size enough to hold much more than a modest clutch purse.

Standing there in her closet doorway looking upon that box in her hand, she had no notion truly of what it might be or how she'd come by it, and even once she'd slipped off the lid and thereby revealed the front cover of a white simulated calfskin Holy Bible she could not hardly guess straightoff whose white simulated calfskin Holy Bible it was, though presently she did notice that the calfskin had been stamped and personalized down in the lower right corner, had been tooled in gaudy in-authentic gold with a *D* and an *R* and a *Huff* as well which normally would have suggested Delmon Ray and brought back to Opal Criner how she'd purchased that Bible in town against the day when her grandbaby might bask in the glories of the word of God and the miracles of Christ for himself. However, Opal Criner this day persuaded herself that she was surely caught up in a manner of mystery since the *D* that could be for Delmon and the *R* that could be for Ray might serve for Donald and might serve for Richard as well. Opal Criner could not help but believe it was ever so strange and providential that she'd find this afternoon, in pursuit of her blue beaded bag, a white simulated calfskin Bible that might be construed to have been in the first place tooled and inscribed for her boy-in-law Donnie who'd gotten just the day previous expired and hoisted towards the heavenly portal.

She upended the box, dumped out the Bible, and consequently caused to waft and spread a rich simulated calfskin aroma. From the spine Opal Criner learned that the text was revised and standard with the words of Christ in red, not a deep vibrant red but what turned out to be a pale faded muddy sort of a red instead, a light troublesome red of such meager contrast with the white of the page as perhaps to prompt a devoted and scrupulous reader to discover in the teachings of the Lord profound spiritual comfort and acute eyestrain both together. On the slick pages at the head of the text and the slick pages at the shank of it there were maps and charts and pictures of the Holy Land in addition to full-color artist's renderings of harps and trumpets and zithers and shofars, and leptons, and shekels as well. The editors had even seen fit to provide a handy instructional calendar so as to indicate how an individual of suitable gumption might read through both Testaments of his Bible simultaneously in the course of a year's time, setting out with the first couple of Books of Matthew and Genesis on New Year's Day and finishing up with the final installment of Revelation and the entire Book of Malachi on the thirty-first of the following December like struck Opal Criner as an extravagant return upon a fairly modest investment.

There was no picture of Jesus in the thing anywhere that she could discover which Opal Criner was disappointed to learn due to how she evermore found the picture of Jesus in her own particular edition a balm to her doubts and afflictions as the Jesus in her Bible, standing on a hummock in His robe and thongs addressing the multitudes, looked passably tough and cocky for a Lord and Savior like most usually served to impart a plucky resolve to Opal Criner in her times of trouble since she found she preferred a Jesus who was quite plainly tender and thoughtful but could very likely be pressed as well to kick some butt. The editors of the white simulated calfskin Bible, however, simply had not gone in for pictures of the Lord Christ, not Jesus teaching, not Jesus crucified, or Jesus ascending even into heaven though they had provided a full-color view of the Gulf of Elath looking across to Jordan and a prospect as well of the Vale of Jezreel.

Of course she forgot pretty entirely about the blue beaded bag altogether as she stood there at the closet doorway studying

the maps and the charts and the encapsulated easy-reference
Bible stories in addition to the muddy red words of Christ,
which she flipped to the Gospels and endeavored to make out
by turning on the closet light and inclining the text towards it
until she could pretty consistently distinguish her Ye's from her
Yea's without too awful much scrutiny and extended perusal.
She was quite plainly struck with how utterly suitable a gift a
white calfskin Bible would be for a fellow who just one day
previous had enjoyed a brush with rapture. She supposed even
her Donald, and she called him silently to herself her Donald
which somehow she'd never before been plagued with temptation about, might have worked up in the intervening hours
since his resuscitation an appetite for scripture; he had, after
all, just lately exhibited a disposition to rest his head on his web
of skin in a deeply meditational sort of a way. Accordingly,
then, she determined in her own mind that the gold-embossed
D was plainly for Donald and the gold-embossed *R* was plainly
for Richard, and she ran one last time her fingertips across the
slick simulated white calfskin cover prior to returning the Bible
to its box and settling the lid down upon it in advance of pausing to wonder if mightn't she ought to wrap the thing, do it up
with a ribbon as well and so make it out to seem a treat for her
Donnie just in case he arrived home fairly unmeditationally
disposed.

They had left over from Christmas a piece of a roll of paper
somewhere, a shiny gold foil paper printed up in a star of
Bethlehem/baby in a manger motif which ran riot across the
sheet in a festive fashion. Opal Criner recalled having stored
away the scrap herself and straightaway conjured up four different places she recalled having stored it but where it did not
happen some way or another to be. In an effort to determine
where, if she were a scrap of gold foil Christmas paper, she
might herself have ended up, Opal Criner paused at the front
doorscreen and sank into thought though hardly so deeply as to
fail to notice the current exploits of her grandbaby Delmon out
in front of the house where he was presently occupying a bald
patch with Sheba the wirehaired dog, not the big central wholly
barren bald patch there in the heart of the lawn but one of the
smaller satellite patches off towards the ditch that was, like the

bulk of the patches otherwise, framed and bordered and interrupted here and there by a hardy creeping sort of an item that
ever so remotely resembled actual grass except of course in the
late summer of the year when it sprouted forth in burrs and
assorted desolate blossoms the color of grate ash.

Delmon was plainly sucking on a rock, not a sizable rock but
a little round stone that he was rattling about in his mouth and
Opal Criner, who was well acquainted herself with her grandbaby Delmon's propensity for rock sucking, noticed straightaway what he was up to and admonished him for it, calling out
through the doorscreen, "Delmon son, you don't know where
that rock's been." On the contrary, however, Delmon had
turned the thing up himself with the jagged end of a stick and
so ventured to tell to his grandmomma, "Uh huh, " which was
hardly the sort of talk she ever saw fit to tolerate from a child
that she reminded her grandbaby Delmon about prior to sharing with him the news of how that rock had probably laid already in the mouths of countless creatures otherwise thereby
accumulating untold filth and contamination which Delmon
was presently taking into his gullet. "Spit that thing out," she
told to him, "and don't be sucking rocks," and she lingered at
the doorscreen until Delmon her grandbaby had ejected his
stone onto the ground where it accumulated straightaway noticeable filth and contamination further and captured the attention as well of Sheba the wirehaired dog who could not recall
herself having ever laid previously eyes on that particular stone
and so barked vigorously at it, bucking up off her front feet in
the throes of feverish alarm.

Opal Criner's girl Marie did not have that slightest notion of
where the remnants of the roll of gold foil star of Bethlehem/
baby in a manger wrapping paper might have ended up, or
screeched anyhow at her mother, "How in the hell should I
know!" once her mother had called out to inquire would she tell
to her please where that paper could possibly be. Opal Criner
searched through the sideboard and the secretary, peered into
the hutch, and visited briefly the kitchen where she intended to
plunder through the whatnot drawer but suffered herself to get
straightaway expelled back into the front room and so poked
about under the magazines on the bottom rack of the tv cart

instead. She paused at the doorscreen to inform her grandbaby Delmon that, as best as she knew, jagged sticks could grow as foul and unsavory as any rock she'd ever come across which Delmon did not air himself an opinion about but merely drew without comment his jagged stick from his mouth, his jagged stick that Sheba the wirehaired dog had not lately seen the slobbered end of and so greeted it straightaway with fairly boundless enthusiasm. Opal Criner, for her part, turned her attention to the closet in the hall where she paused to admire a topcoat she'd pretty much forgotten altogether she owned and took occasion to try on a hat she'd been partial to previously, a black brimless hat with a half veil and assorted speckled plumage. She parted here and there the hanging clothes so as to examine the closet floor and the corner joints though with no reward much but for a lone sizable hairball that twitched and traveled as the air stirred it and, shortly, she fetched a straight chair from the front room and stood on the seat slats to allow her to reach deep back onto the shelf where she landed at last upon the item she'd been seeking in the first place and called out in triumph, "I found it," called out in fact twice, "I found it" in triumph which would be once upon the chairseat and once on her route through the front room to the kitchen doorway.

She entered into the kitchen, turned full around one time on the balls of her feet, and encouraged her girl Marie to notice if she would how that blue beaded bag hung and laid snug up against her hip in a secure and altogether uninviting sort of a way which her girl Marie left off with her boning knife and picked up her head about so as to tell to her mother Opal, "Go on."

White gauzy box lining was the only sort of wrapping she could find and she dressed up that Bible box as best she could and then turned on the tv, settled onto the sofa, and situated Donnie's treat between her hip socket and the bolster which freed her up to manage the transfer of her assorted holdings from her black leatherette pocketbook with the feeble strap to her stout and heavily begrommeted blue beaded one which she found to have not two but three zippered pouches in the inside that struck Opal Criner as a veritable delight. It was the onset of the litigious hour on the tv and people were in court on most every channel either in the process of getting acrimoniously divorced, being tried for felonies, or whining and bickering over actual verifiable true to life petty slights and disappointments, and although it was this last variety of contention Opal Criner was most curious to see, she oftentimes found the actual verifiable true to life people so unpleasant to look at and endure that she usually switched over to the divorce proceedings where paid professional actors made out to loathe and despise each other and wore without exception altogether fine ensembles to do it in while the actual verifiable true to life people largely demonstrated a marked partiality for rayon blends and most usually appeared to have stopped off at the courthouse on their way to the bowling alley. This particular afternoon an unimpeachable true to life man from Barstow, California, was describing for the judge an especially unflattering haircut his showdog Princess Di had received at the hands of a so-called professional groomer who was herself present to refute the charges and illuminate for the judge the improvisational nature of showdog grooming. Princess Di, who was present as well at the end of the leather lead, had put forth sufficient new growth in the interim between her haircut and her litigation to cloud the matter, and photographs taken by her owner of the offending cut were, in the judge's estimation, too poorly lit to be of much use.

Presently the judge retired to contemplate the matter and Opal Criner would probably have lingered about for his considered opinion but for the dog groomer herself who'd seized upon the occasion of her television debut to advertise her business on a t-shirt notwithstanding how there was appreciably more of her person from the beltbuckle up than a t-shirt could suitably manage and contain. So Opal Criner changed over to take in testimony from an unrejuvenated slut in a silk blouse who freely admitted to having performed services and favors for a swanky sort of a fellow in an Italian suit who she indicated with her finger at the behest of the attorney for that man's estranged wife who was wearing herself just the smartest outfit Opal Criner had seen lately. She transferred her purse and her

documents and her compact and her rouge and both her lip-
sticks as well as her wholly invaluable accumulated scraps of
paper from her black leatherette bag to her blue beaded one as
she listened to the unwholesome accusations fly and sensed the
general welling up of the venom in addition to admiring the cut
of the stenographer's skirt which Opal Criner could not help
but figure not just any stenographer would have the legs for.

Opal Criner tested the grommets and the stout significant
hardware otherwise and, once she'd filled that beaded bag and
buckled it shut, wore the thing about the front room so as to see
did it lay full like it had laid just previously empty which, by and
large, she concluded it did and she was trying the strap to see
would it yield and sag if she pressed resolutely on the top of the
bag itself when the divorce proceedings on the tv gave way to
Andy of Mayberry, gave way in particular to the episode about
Otis's brother who comes with his family from out of town to
visit. As Delmon was himself most especially partial to Otis,
Opal Criner called out through the doorscreen to tell to him
that the show about Otis's brother had come on, and from his
small peripheral bald patch where he was presently sucking on
nothing in particular Delmon called to his grandmother back,
"Thinks Otis is a lawman?" which she informed him straightoff
to be the only episode about Otis's brother she was herself
acquainted with and she did believe that, were there additional
installments in which Otis's brother appeared, she would very
likely know of them.

"Thinks he got deputized," Delmon told her and stood up
from his bald patch so as to beat the dirt off the seat of his pants
and tell to his grandmomma one thing further which he went
ahead and did in fact tell though he failed to get heard at it on
account of Sheba the wirehaired dog who'd not seen Delmon
upright and afoot in such a considerable while that she could
not determine straightoff who precisely he might be and so
raised an immediate uproar which she persisted at across the
yard and clean up to the doorscreen where she grew by Opal
Criner persuaded to lay her ears flat and skulk on around back
of the house.

Partway through the show Opal Criner detected from the
kitchen the telltale sound of the opening of the freezer door

and the extraction from the freezer of supper which her girl Marie quite apparently flung onto the stovetop. As was the case every evening without fail, Opal Criner inquired sweetly from the sofa if could she possibly come into the kitchen and be of some help with the meal which her girl Marie told to her "No" about, a low undemonstrative sort of a No that, like usual, struck Opal Criner as an altogether unambiguous invitation to extend once further her offer, insist even that a summons to the kitchen would likely prove for her a thoroughgoing delight which evermore earned for Opal Criner one "No" further, a strenuous and emphatic sort of a "No" that was not hardly much encumbered with ambiguity itself. Upon the outset of the local news from the station up in Bluefield, Opal Criner, as was her custom, congratulated her girl Marie on the savory bouquet issuing forth through the kitchen doorway and she induced with a look her grandbaby Delmon to throw in with her, her grandbaby Delmon who vented an extravagantly appreciative variety of noise and learned shortly from his momma Marie how him and his grandmother were smelling like usual the oven heating up.

The news on the station from Bluefield was more distressing this night than even ordinarily it was due to how a man from Beckley had gone on a rampage through his neighborhood, had grown peeved and irritated on account of a letter he'd received from a Mrs. Alice Germond at the telephone company who'd found him to be in considerable arrears on his telephone bill and had flatly apprised him of how he'd straightaway lose his service if he did not make amends. Now of course the truth of the matter was that this gentleman from Beckley had not lately paid his telephone bill as he'd spent the money instead satisfying assorted unwholesome habits and he did not truly much care if he got disconnected but found he could not begin to abide the tone of Mrs. Alice Germond's letter which plainly insinuated her opinion that people such as himself were quite apparently trash and probably did not know anybody worth calling or hearing from anyway. Naturally this was just precisely the variety of sentiment to incense that gentleman from Beckley whose native propensity towards agitation had come to be lately chemically enhanced, simultaneously heightening his energy and diminishing his resolve, so while he intended to hunt down Mrs. Alice Germond and tear her into pulpy bits and pieces he determined presently that he might best beat his own wife instead as she was handy for it.

He went after her with a mophandle and inflicted numerous welts and contusions which the paramedic on the scene informed the news crew about prior to producing from the back of his truck the wife herself who exhibited her welts and displayed her contusions and endured from the correspondent a regular battery of impertinent inquiries. The responding officer speculated on camera that the alleged perpetrator would very likely have dispatched his wife altogether had he not seen out the window what he took for a phone company truck parked along the ditch a couple of doors up the road. Considering the original source of his agitation, that gentleman from Beckley was pleased to have before him the prospect of raising welts and inflicting contusions on an actual telephone employee, so he left off flogging his wife and ran out into the yard and across the street towards that truck which belonged in fact to the Lawn Doctor people instead that the perpetrator saw soon enough for himself it did but, feeling rather impetuous and devil-may-care, he neglected to curb his impulses and charged up into that yard following the unfurled hose from the truck to a man in green coveralls who was spraying a patch of fescue with weed killer and nitrogen-rich fertilizer mixed together in solution.

That fellow detected the company straightaway and was set to turn about and treat that man from Beckley to a big Hi Howdy! like was general Lawn Doctor policy in the field, when he came directly to be prevented and thwarted and rendered purely undisposed by the mophandle itself that caught him across the collarbone and on the knobby part of his wrist as well and dramatically altered the mood of that fellow who defended himself as best as he was able with the weed killer and nitrogen-rich fertilizer in solution which he directed in a potent stream into the face of that man from Beckley whose enthusiasm precipitously dwindled and diminished on account in part of the pressure of the spray but certainly due largely to how the Lawn Doctor special liquid lawn treatment smelled to have been discharged from a cow. That man from Beckley fell back in retreat and suffered himself to be chased and doused further until the hose gave out in the middle of the road where that fellow in the coveralls dropped it to the pavement and pursued that man from Beckley across his own ditch and up through his yard taking occasion to impart along the way where it was precisely he intended to shove that mophandle once he'd laid his hands upon it which was not truly the sort of observation to have much place in the general Lawn Doctor canon of sentiments that a neighbor, roused by the dispute, stood at her side door and came to be of the opinion of herself.

She had to figure the Lawn Doctor fellow had lost somehow his grip and so was an imminent danger to the bunch of them running like he was amuck through the neighborhood. Consequently, she called the law on him and painted for the dispatcher an altogether dire picture of events which got her straightaway two of Beckley's radio cars that came shortly screaming down the road with the responding officer issuing from the foremost vehicle and rushing across that man from Beckley's yard so as to subdue the local Lawn Doctor representative who was standing on the front stoop peering through the doorlight and speaking ever so passionately of his intentions which sounded to the officer very possibly unlawful and undoubtedly discomforting. So he drew out his stick and applied with it a glancing blow to the collarbone of the fellow in the coveralls since, aside from screaming down the roadways in their Chevys, there was nothing Beckley lawmen liked better than knocking people about the heads and shoulders with their nightsticks. Of course that man in the coveralls, who'd received a blow just previously on the identical collarbone in near about the identical spot, turned around to express and perhaps even act upon his displeasure which the Beckley policeman, being a professional law officer, had anticipated he likely would and so had danced deftly aside, thereby situating himself to apply chiefly to that fellow's windpipe a special professional law officer choke hold which the policeman demonstrated for the correspondent once she'd volunteered her trachea that he promised not to dent and crush.

Naturally they'd managed to straighten the whole business out once that man in the coveralls had regained consciousness, and both officers together had subdued the gentleman from Beckley by means of their implements and their techniques and their professional enthusiasm and had cuffed him and pitched him into the back of the squad car where he got filmed through the windowglass and looked to Opal Criner as evil a fellow as she'd seen lately with very possibly as dreadful a haircut as any dog groomer anywhere could improvise and inflict. "Trash sure enough," she told to Delmon her grandbaby. "World's full of it anymore," which Delmon had not hardly mustered up the breath to throw in with when a story came on about a man and his wife up at Pulaski who'd kept twenty-six dogs in their rumpus room in the basement for fourteen solid months and were only discovered at it once the wife threw open the door to the parcel postman to accept a package and fairly dispatched him with the ensuing aroma.

From around back of the house in her hole in the crawlspace Sheba the wirehaired dog detected the distinctive bump and rattle of Buddy Isom's red half-ton that contained, she suspected, people she'd not laid eyes on lately who she slipped off towards the front of the house to be openly wary of. She barked at Buddy Isom who she could see enough of above the doorpanel to touch her off and set in as well on Donnie Huff himself who tossed his Pabst can into the truckbed and, as was his habit, exhibited for Sheba his boottoe which Sheba, as was her habit, recalled straightoff the sundry uses of and so laid flat her ears and crawled on her elbows back across the yard. Donnie Huff had accumulated in the course of the day such a fairly thoroughgoing coating of dirt and shavings and sawdust and nonspecific grunge on his coveralls that he determined to unzip and step out of them on the porchslab before Opal Criner had cause even to ask him if he might which she took to be an awfully propitious sign of Donnie Huff's present disposition that appeared to her if not meditational then passably considerate at least notwithstanding how he failed to remove his brogans and so straightaway silted up the rug.

As he was not this evening damp anywhere much, Donnie Huff got allowed by his wife Marie to sit directly down upon the cushion of his upholstered chair from where Donnie Huff himself congratulated her on the savory aroma of issuing from the kitchen and so heard directly from Opal Criner what precisely he was smelling that her girl Marie corrected her about explaining that she'd just lately flung open the oven door and stuck supper in which Opal Criner insisted she could not personally have hoped to know, or was there anyhow in the midst of insisting it when Donnie Huff lifted his hand to stanch her so that he might hear on the tv the culmination of the sports report which consisted this evening of a think piece on the speedway at Martinsville. Taking occasion of the station break, Donnie Huff sought to learn from his boy Delmon what precisely he'd been up to in the course of the day that his boy Delmon volunteered a version of much to the amusement of Opal Criner who explained to Donnie Huff what particular items she'd herself seen that boy of his chew and suck on in the progress of the afternoon, and she went ahead and figured that only the Lord Himself knew where they'd been before they entered into Delmon's mouth where they'd posed, aside from the likelihood of contamination, the prospect of lodging in his throat and thereby strangling Delmon dead that Opal Criner assured her grandbaby he would not much enjoy. She invited him even to learn if he might from his daddy, who'd been after a fashion strangled dead himself, that there wasn't hardly a thing in the world to recommend it which Donnie Huff was just beginning to insist for the benefit of his boy to be the truth when Opal Criner fairly exclaimed, slapped herself soundly upon the forehead, and confessed to Donnie Huff that she'd picked up for him a little something which she'd forgotten altogether about until talk of getting strangled dead had served to remind her.

"Here," she told to him and produced from between her hip and the sofa bolster that package wrapped in box lining and festooned with a knotted length of yarn, the package that Donnie Huff merely watched her extend towards him and did not move straightoff to relieve her of due chiefly to how he was not himself accustomed to receiving from Opal Criner tokens and gifts on even legitimate occasions.

"What's this?" Donnie Huff sought to discover in advance of actually taking the thing into his hand.

But Opal Criner told to him merely, "Here," once further and persuaded her grandbaby Delmon to pass the box on over to his daddy who held it and admired, it appeared to Opal Criner, her artful use of yellow yarn which she told to him was nothing really before he could even see clear to suggest it might be anything much.

Donnie Huff shook the thing up alongside his ear but failed by it to gain noticeable illumination and so pressed Opal Criner once further, asking of her another time, "What's this?" which she guessed he might discover for himself were he only to open it that she saw on his own the sense of and so ripped free the artful yarn, tore off the paper, dispatched with the boxlid, and was shortly holding in his hand a white simulated calfskin Bible with his own name tooled in gold across the front of it which Opal Criner scooted down the length of the sofa to point out to him herself. He did not appear to her utterly dismayed at the sight of the Bible and struck even a marginally thoughtful pose as he heard from Opal Criner news of the red words of Christ and talk as well of how his personalized white simulated calfskin edition was both revised and standard and included among the scriptures the most stirring photograph of the Gulf of Elath Opal Criner had ever herself come across. She even briefly relieved Donnie Huff of his personalized Bible so as to indicate for him the assorted nonscriptural highlights, commencing with the zither and the map of the Hittite kingdom in the back and advancing up past the snapshot of the Vale of Jezreel and the aforementioned splendor for the Gulf of Elath so as to arrive ultimately at the Bible reader's calendar which Opal Criner took pains to explain the uses of to Donnie Huff who failed to remark snidely upon her observations and inquiries which struck her as a very propitious lapse indeed.

Upon receiving his Bible back, Donnie Huff even turned through the first few pages of the thing on his own, scanned about there in the Old Testament prior to declaring to Opal Criner that somebody had apparently slipped up and made the words of Christ as inky black as everybody else's words which Opal Criner took straightoff as a jest and so pitched back her head and laughed gaily prior to directing Donnie Huff to the

Gospels where he discovered in fact the muddy red print he'd been seeking. As was his practice when perusing a book or a magazine, Donnie Huff turned shortly clean to the back of the white simulated calfskin Bible since he preferred to start at the shankend of such an item, cock back the pages, and loose them to lay forward one at a time with his left thumb which was undoubtedly for Donnie Huff his most accomplished page-loosing finger. So he cocked in fact a handful of Testament and end matter together and freed some of it to lay and get perused but had not made his way quite altogether through the glossary and concordance before he got stalled and hung up by an illustration of an adder that looked to Donnie Huff awfully much like a copperhead which he sought the opinion of his boy Delmon about, Delmon who was fond of visiting the branch down across the road so as to turn up copperheads under rocks and crush and maim them.

Delmon himself was of the opinion that the adder in the picture was striped along the snout after a fashion that copperheads never came to be which Donnie Huff straightaway disputed telling to his boy Delmon, "Naw," and speaking beyond it of a stripe-snouted specimen he'd come across once previously himself that Delmon his boy was loath to believe and so informed his daddy, "Nuh uh," back.

For her part, Opal Criner admired the two of them together collected at the upholstered chair with the Good Book laid open between them, precisely the sort of a sight to fill her heart with passably boundless joy due to how she was able to bring herself to discount if not altogether ignore the fact that they were contemplating the both of them a portion of the glossary and concordance just ever so barely shy of the text itself which they might, she figured, arrive at shortly once they'd left off debating reptiles. In an effort to accelerate the proceedings, Opal Criner even volunteered that were Donnie Huff to loose with his left thumb some scant additional pages he'd come snug up on the end of the world which she pitched forward and insinuated to be a grisly manner of tale and consequently flushed Donnie Huff out from the end matter altogether and cleanly into the actual Testaments where he discovered quite immedi-

ately an observation by the Lord Jesus that struck him as a wry
and revealing sort of a thing for a Savior to say and inspired
Donnie Huff to flip a ways further. He was learning in fact
precisely who was the root and the offspring of David when his
wife Marie wished from the kitchen that somebody would see fit
to put some ice in the glasses without her having to call out
every night to wish it.

So Donnie Huff clutched shut his white simulated calfskin
Bible and Opal Criner took up her blue beaded bag and they
herded before them Delmon Huff who was speaking still of a
particular snake he'd squashed with a sizable hunk of stone and
caused thereby to ooze and seep which he described more viv-
idly than his grandmomma found polite, that she drew him
aside to inform him about while Donnie Huff showed to his
wife Marie most especially the personalized part of his revised
standard Bible with the words of Christ in red and was set even
to gain from her an opinion on the reptile of contention when
Marie Criner Huff prevented him from it so as to inquire of her
mother, "Isn't that Delmon's?" which her mother reflexively
told to her "No" about but asked pretty directly back of it, "Isn't
what Delmon's?"

"This here," Marie Criner informed her and laid her fingerend upon the simulated calfskin itself. "I remember one
time you showed it to me."

But Opal Criner confided to her girl Marie, "Honey, Delmon can't read," and flattened her lips together in a meaningful
sort of a way which Delmon himself found bothersome straightoff and proclaimed to anybody that cared to know it, "Can too,"
after which he hoisted his bulk onto the countertop, opened the
corner cabinet door, and removed from the shelf a cookie box
that he held upright before himself and read proudly from,
telling most especially to his grandmomma, " 'Nilla," whereupon Opal Criner extended briefly her flat-lipped expression
before apprising Delmon of how little she approved of him
laying his foul trousers upon their Formica.

Donnie Huff wanted to cite if he might for his wife Marie
from scripture which his wife Marie did not let on to care one
way or another about and made so much racket dropping open

the oven door, extracting their main course in its foil pan as well as the accompanying baked yams, and then shutting the thing with her foot that Donnie Huff grew discouraged in his intentions. Opal Criner, however, was anxious for Donnie Huff to cite for his wife Marie from scripture if he would, was purely delighted at the prospect and so instructed Donnie Huff to go ahead please and read from his text which Donnie Huff guessed maybe he would, took up his white simulated calfskin Bible, flipped deftly with his left thumb past the end matter, and intoned for the benefit of his wife Marie, "Surely I come quickly," adding beyond it for the sake of uttermost clarity, "Jesus Christ."

And straightoff he heard from his wife Marie back, "Him too," which Donnie Huff clapped shut his white simulated calfskin Bible and fairly hooted on account of, pretty much dissolved in mirth that Opal Criner could not so much as begin herself to endure the sight of and consequently turned about and made to be deeply engaged alongside the refrigerator. She drew open the whatnot drawer and aimlessly picked through it in order to cloak her dismay but succeeded nonetheless in coming across an item that she could not somehow help but exclaim in triumph about, declaring into the air, "I found it," as she raised up in her fingers the folded scrap of gold foil star of Bethlehem/baby in a manger wrapping paper that Donnie Huff and Marie Criner Huff and Delmon Ray Huff as well gazed together upon.

iii

Her Carl had bought his beige Coronet in the summer of 1971 off a lot outside Mt. Airy. They'd been making room there for the '72s and so had offered to Carl his Coronet at a spectacular savings, at a discount so excessively deep and profound that only once a pair of salesmen had worked jointly through an elaborate equation in largely hypothetical dealership mathematics had they succeeded at detecting their own niggling profit in the offer which they'd together assured Carl was appreciably less profit than they'd normally take but they were making

room for the '72s and everything had to go. They'd accepted
from Carl his Biscayne in trade, had conceded even a handsome allowance on the thing that got lost somehow in the mathematics and thereby failed to cancel out their meager profit
altogether, managed even to increase it slightly which they concealed from Carl algebraically and so hardly disturbed the pleasure he took in driving his new Coronet off the lot and wheeling
it across the highway into a Texaco station where he filled his
tank and assessed the levels of his various fluids.

Carl had been by nature a man of moderate velocity and
had found himself most easeful and serene at forty miles per
hour when he could lay his right arm along the seatback and
steer with his left hand alone secure in the knowledge that he
wasn't generating so awfully many rpms as to tax his valves and
strain his gaskets and hoses and fatigue his parts otherwise
unduly. Of course his casual speed allowed him to view the
countryside as well not even to mention the lively and antic
faces of passersby who, upon discovering at last a flat empty
stretch of road, would oftentimes slip up alongside Carl's Coronet and look upon Carl with discernible passion, share with
him even on occasion their animated and uncharitable opinions
prior to accelerating rashly so as to gain what appeared to Carl
quite unprofitable speeds.

Opal Criner had not in Carl's lifetime been allowed her own
car since she'd not, as best as Carl could ever tell, manifested
much feel for vehicles. She had, however, been permitted on
occasion to drive Carl's Coronet in the presence of Carl himself
who was never somehow, in the passenger seat, the man she'd
loved and married and whose child she'd bore and raised. With
the glovebox before him instead of the wheel and column, Carl
suffered a manner of transformation, quite utterly lost his sense
of repose and clutched at the doorhandle and stomped on the
floormat and issued directives to Opal Criner in a tone that was
oftentimes other than loving. Consequently, she did not usually
choose herself to drive back from wherever it was Carl had
allowed her to drive to in the first place but permitted Carl to
reclaim his station at the pedals and under the wheel, check his
various lights and gauges, adjust his mirrors, and inquire at

length of Opal Criner, "We off?" so as to hear straightaway from her how she had herself to suppose they likely were.

Carl had left the thing to her chiefly on account of how he'd not been intending to stroke and so had made no alternate provisions for his Coronet which passed, upon Carl's expiration, into the possession of Opal Criner who could not settle atop the seat of the thing without growing irritated and forlorn both together. In life Carl had built a carport for his Coronet, had sunk the posts and tacked up the corrugated roof himself so as to protect his finish from sap and windless rainfall and the acorns off the white oak along their fencerow. He'd invested as well in a green canvas tarp that hooked under his bumper on the front and hooked under his bumper on the back and made of his Coronet such a snug and comely package that Carl had often been given to admiring the lines and sleek contours of his automobile without troubling himself to even so much as uncover it. For her part, Opal Criner, whose feeble feel for vehicles extended to the lines and the contours, maintained in honor of the memory of her Carl his green canvas tarp which every now and again she troubled herself to fix and fasten properly under the bumpers but primarily just flung and spread as best she was able on account of how she parked his Coronet anymore in the shed back of her girl Marie's house which had actual walls to it and a weathertight roof and a slab floor and had been built years back for a tractor that somebody had quite apparently thought pretty highly of.

Opal Criner drove Carl's car to church service on Sunday and to Bible study Wednesday nights and carried her girl Marie to the Food Lion every Friday morning but did not go regularly anywhere otherwise and made only occasional excursion to the clinic up in Floyd when her grandbaby Delmon demonstrated some manner of unsettling symptom. Chiefly the Coronet just sat in the shed under its partially unfurled tarp doing most especially Donnie Huff no palpable good whatsoever, Donnie Huff who himself owned a blue Skylark that resided presently in the high grass off beyond the clothesline on account of a grave and compound mechanical complaint, a cracked head in combination with a balky piston together that had idled his vehicle for what Donnie Huff had insisted was temporarily until the tires had rotted and flattened when he began to doubt he'd ever likely collect the money and work up the gumption to put his Buick to rights. He hadn't truly supposed that with a Coronet in the shed he had much cause to trouble himself about his Skylark anyhow, had guessed he'd just cat about in Carl's Dodge instead, but Opal Criner, as was her custom, had invested her dead Carl's Coronet with altogether undue significance and had to wonder of her son-in-law what he imagined Carl might think were Donnie Huff to wheel that car out into the street with as little regard for rpms as he quite plainly possessed. Of course Donnie Huff had evermore himself been of the opinion that part of the beauty of being dead was not having to think about anything much at all, but he could not persuade Opal Criner to share in his perspective on the matter due primarily to her own resolute opinion that while Carl was surely treading the streets of gold he undoubtedly still found occasion to concern himself from time to time with the upkeep of his various worldly investments.

So the Coronet largely sat on the slab in the shed with the green tarp spread atop it while Donnie Huff himself largely resided upon his upholstered chair except for those evenings when Buddy Isom and Alvis Nevins saw fit to swing by the house and carry him with them out west towards Hillsville to the lounge opposite the motor lodge where they shot pool and drank beer and spoke between themselves of the various females in attendance, explaining just how precisely they'd exercise their inclinations upon them with a decided emphasis on which particular fleshy items they'd take up in their fingers and grip and hold to even if presently they were prevented and forestalled from it by the unsuitability of their circumstances and the probable reluctance of the women themselves coupled with and in addition to their own sorry places in this world that had failed over time to improve like they'd all of them fairly much quit even hoping they might. Otherwise Donnie Huff just sat usually with his child and his wife's mother before the tv and drained off Blue Ribbons while he engaged as well in various deft contortions of his pertinent muscles in the spirit of prac-

tical research so as to illuminate for Donnie Huff how he best
might break stealthy and wholly inaudible wind.

Opal Criner had never previously seen fit to object with any
enthusiasm to Donnie Huff's assorted leisure habits and pursuits. Certainly she had felt obliged to voice her unqualified
disapproval of them, but she'd never truly protested with vigor
and resolve until Donnie Huff had managed, through his death
and subsequent resuscitation, to rise quite appreciably in her
regard. While familiar with the exploits of the children and
in-laws of her various acquaintances who'd entered into gainful
and prestigious employment and lived in fine houses with rolling grassy lawns and ornamental trees and drove for the most
part luxury sedans of a terribly recent vintage, Opal Criner
could not herself name a one of them who'd come yet to be
dead but failed to stay it which was plainly Donnie Huff's do-
main alone, his singular and distinct designation that set him
quite thoroughly apart from most everybody otherwise. There
did not, however, appear to Opal Criner much use at all of a
man having crossed to the other side and gotten fetched back,
of having soared and hovered and caught sight even of the
heavenly portal if news of it did not circulate about and fall
most especially upon the ears of those people who'd come somehow to be persuaded that the wives of their children and the
husbands of their children and their children themselves as well
were somehow the Lord's own gift to life on this earth.

Consequently, it would not any longer do for Donnie Huff
merely to squander his evenings drinking beer and breaking
moderately inaudible wind as best as Opal Criner could determine. He had anymore a duty and an obligation to venture out
amongst the peoples of the world and tell of his journey into
rapture which would undoubtedly bathe him straightaway in
renown, and Opal Criner could not help but figure some little
part of it might slosh on herself. That Donnie Huff did not
purely share her view was apparent to Opal Criner who passed
several nights on the sofa before the tv endeavoring to spark
him to most any degree of devotional reflection, hoping to
inspire even the briefest of meditational poses with the web of
skin uplifted and the scruffy chin settled upon it. Donnie Huff,

however, proved reluctant to think deeply, was undisposed to grapple just presently with thorny spiritual matters, and while Opal Criner managed most evenings to situate Donnie Huff's new personalized white simulated calfskin Bible on the end-table alongside him, she failed to persuade him to dip in and partake of the scriptures no matter how many times she asked to see again if she might the Gulf of Elath and the Vale of Jezreel. Donnie Huff, who'd himself wearied of the both of them, had adopted the habit of telling to her simply, "Here," and tossing his Bible the length of the couch which he was oftentimes pleased in fact to have the occasion for since Bible tossing proved a suitable distraction to vaporize undetected in the clamor of.

When specifically plagued and pressed by Opal Criner, Donnie Huff complained of the pale muddy words of Christ which he insisted he could but barely make out and confessed as well that the bulk of the prose otherwise struck him as exceedingly antique and relatively upside down, said anyhow, "It don't none of it mean a thing to me," which Opal Criner persuaded herself to take for a semantical sort of affliction. Accordingly she endeavored to translate for Donnie Huff various biblical episodes into layman's terms, sought to interject them into station breaks and commercials, and succeeded with one terse installment on Noah and brief mention of the origins of Moses but ran overlong in her explication of the treacherous deceit of Jacob which, like most deceits, was convoluted and troublesome and had not entirely played out when the deep-rich-dark-instant-granulated-coffee-that-nobody-could-tell-from-roasted-beans commercial gave way to the show about the detective from Uranus which Opal Criner prattled overtop of until Donnie Huff grew obliged to inquire of her sweetly, on behalf of himself and his boy Delmon as well, if couldn't she possibly manage to put a cork in it.

Marie Huff did not, of course, prove on her own to be awfully much assistance to Opal Criner since Marie Huff had not lately had much use for Jesus herself and had become a source of acute heartache and incalculable distress for her mother whose disappointment grew rawer still once her girl

Marie had seen fit to excise from the end matter of Donnie Huff's personalized white simulated calfskin Bible a pair of shekels, three tetradrachms, a denarius, and a lepton so as to paste the bunch of them onto the lid of a lozenge tin and varnish them over in pursuit of a dainty decoupaged change-box which Marie Criner Huff could not be persuaded to feel remorseful and conflicted about. She'd turned even a ravenous eye upon Donnie Huff's harp and shofar that she suspected, with the addition of Donnie Huff's sistrum, would make for a comely and harmonious grouping, most especially once she'd gone to the trouble to situate and paste them upon her brassy wallplate, her brassy wallplate she'd lately prepared for decoupage. It had come to her sometime back with burghers upon it, Germanic alpine sorts of burghers that had been raised in relief on the brassy metal. Marie had taken to her plate a block of wood and a hammer and had thereby laid flat the upraised parts and brought level the indentations leaving unmashed only the inoffensive and wholly burgherless platerim which had to it a tasteful design of cornucopias alternated with what appeared to Marie Huff honeydews. She could not help but believe that a harp and a shofar and a sistrum arranged handsomely at the heart of the dish and varnished thickly over with her specially tinted concoction would hold considerably more appeal in conjunction with the tasteful platerim than drunken burghers ever might.

Naturally, however, Opal Criner could not herself begin to endure further defacement of the scriptures for the advancement most especially of bric-a-brac and she raised a righteous fuss, ascended into a lofty and verifiable dudgeon, and turned a deaf ear to the view of her girl Marie who protested how she meant to cut pilfer only those items adjacent to the scriptures themselves though she could not truly disguise her affection for the Vale of Jezreel that was situated right there in the eighth chapter of Kings but likely would not, she insisted be missed once she'd managed with her razor to excise it. Of course Opal Criner refused to be appeased and for three evenings running retired with Donnie Huff's personalized white simulated calfskin Bible to her bedroom down the hall where she sought from

the assorted residue of her Carl solace and inspiration, took up
and held in her fingers his framed portrait on the chiffonier
that brought to her its usual balm. She guessed she was fairly
awash in woes and made out in her prayers and supplications
that hers was a house raging with sickness, afflicted with decoupage and sloth and undue stealthy vapors, a frame and
clapboard Sodom of a place that she consulted presently her
Savior about and soon enough came to be blessed with inspiration, grew illuminated as to the course she might follow, and
marveled yet again at how the wisdom of her Christ blended so
awfully well with her own personal deviousness, manufacturing
thereby an altogether potent compound of higher truth and
common deception.

It was all exceedingly simple really. She let on to have cultivated a wart, allowed herself to appear so twitchy and ill at
ease upon the settee as to bring forth even from Donnie Huff
a solicitous inquiry as to whether could she please somehow
manage not to bounce so about, an inquiry which had to it some
considerable fretfulness and concern, although of such a
cloaked and subdued variety that Opal Criner was obliged to
delve and muck about to discover it. She believed it was an
inflamed wart and indicated how pleased she would normally
be to display her inflammation but it seemed to her this particular growth had cropped up in a private sort of a place that
truly complicated her complaint since not only was she bound
by decorum not to throw up her dress and exhibit the thing but
she did not believe she could so much as scratch it without
appearing vulgar and lowly. Understandably, then, she was perplexed and communicated as much to Donnie Huff who, in a
tone ripe with his own particular brand of ever so nearly un-
detectable compassion, asked of Opal Criner, "Why're you telling me this? I can't scratch your wart either."

Like usual, Donnie Huff had pierced to the heart of the
matter and Opal Criner declared as much to him prior to wondering could he tell to her please was there possibly any wart
medicine in the house since plainly nobody could politely
scratch her wart leaving her exclusively to pursue treatment
otherwise. She thought she'd seen somewhere a bottle of Com-

pound W but could not be certain it hadn't maybe been that little vial of earwax solvent since they were both of them of an identical size. Of course Donnie Huff was in no position to know precisely what Opal Criner had seen and informed her of as much prior to luring his wife Marie out of the kitchen so as to learn from her if couldn't she possibly do a thing about her momma that Marie Criner Huff assured him she would, if she could, have already done.

"She's got a wart," Donnie Huff told to his wife Marie so as to diminish the general scope of the matter, and Opal Criner added for emphasis and effect, "I do," and after what struck her as a suitable interval she informed her girl Maire as well, "It itches," that Marie Criner took time to consider and ruminate upon in an advance of voicing her own personal species of solicitous inquiry, asking anyhow of her momma on the settee, "So?" that her momma on the settee paused to mine for compassion prior to asking of her girl Marie back where the wart removal ointment might be.

"Still at the store," her girl Marie told to her. "I ain't never bought none of it and there can't be none here unless you did."

But Opal Criner, who dropped on the settee into a study so as to consider the likelihood of ointment about, could not recall ever having purchased any herself and so guessed it had been in fact the little vial of earwax solvent she'd seen which she declared to Donnie Huff to be undoubtedly the case as preamble to fetching out from her blue beaded bag her dead Carl's key ring with her dead Carl's ignition key and her dead Carl's trunk and door key and her dead Carl's little pewter insurance company charm strung upon it, and she tossed the thing ever so blithely at Donnie Huff who moved instinctively to catch it but got beat by it upon the beltbuckle instead and so gazed down towards his inseam to spy for the first time ever in his own personal possession the keys and the charm together which he was gazing still upon and puzzling still about when Opal Criner instructed him to bring if he would the Coronet out from the shed and around the house as she could not help but suppose they'd have to set out to town for some wart salve of one stripe or another.

"Get the car?" Donnie Huff wanted to know since he'd only previously ever heard from Opal Criner a contrary of a sentiment.

"Bring it on around," she told him. "The Revco doesn't close for an hour yet."

Delmon, who was anxious to ride out from the shed and around the house in the Coronet himself, accompanied his daddy into the yard where they together instructed and edified their wirehaired dog Sheba on their way to the end of the lot. They took each a corner of the green tarp and drew it back off the Coronet which had become unaccountably smudged and sullied on the hood that Donnie Huff attended to with his shirtsleeve, wiping and buffing and squatting at length to admire the finish. Donnie Huff gassed the Coronet unduly which Opal Criner from the settee detected even over the television and grew inclined to calculate rpms as best as she was able, excessive and quite apparently inordinate rpms far beyond the limit of her gaskets and hoses which she actively from the settee feared for until Donnie Huff dropped the Coronet into reverse and lurched off the slab with a telltale complaint from the tire rubber that served to shift Opal Criner's concern. Delmon engaged himself from the passenger seat in the trip across the yard by endeavoring to discover the Big Q-mix on the radio dial, the Big Q-mix that played the contemporary hits by your favorite stars as well as the classics by the stars that you were likely previously partial to, but Delmon did not know just where on the dial the Big Q-mix might be as he could not conjure up from the tv advertisement the call numbers and so rolled the needle up the dial and rolled the needle back down it until he came at length across a particularly treacly ballad of the sort they were most especially partial to on the Big Q-mix, a treacly ballad with a man and a woman singing together a sorry confession of how little anymore they cared for each other at all though they insisted throughout the refrain, roundabout and overtop of the simulated string music, that they'd been in fact pretty fond of each other not so awfully long ago. Of course Delmon was eager to discover if extravagant volume might render the treacly ballad more poignant and heartwrenching than

it quite plainly already was, or was anxious anyway to crank the
thing up and so played it robustly through the speakers in the
back windowwell that, due to general desiccation and thoroughgoing inactivity, had surrendered the bulk of their fidelity and
rasped and hummed after a fashion that Donnie Huff suggested to his boy Delmon he did not personally find pleasing.

Once they'd gained the driveway and had near about even
come to an absolute stop, Donnie Huff beat out a carhorn salute
for the benefit of Opal Criner who caught up her blue beaded
bag, stepped over the kitchen doorway to tell to her girl Marie,
"We're going to the store," and then left the house for the stoop
where she was obliged to further the education of their wirehaired dog Sheba before she could advance unmolested towards her dead Carl's sedan.

Marie Criner Huff, who was moderately interested in finding out just who exactly was going to the store, attempted from
the kitchen to learn it but could not manage to prompt a response and so got up from the table and entered into the front
room with her varnish brush in hand and the majority of a Kent
between her lips. She continued clear across to the doorscreen
but endured along the way a transformation of her intentions
and did not upon her arrival wish so much any longer to know
just who exactly was going to the store as she hoped to discover
in place of it if maybe some one of them wasn't acquainted with
the little knob at the bottom of the tv that turned the set off. She
withdrew even her Kent in preparation for her query but found
herself prevented and forestalled by the sight of Donnie Huff
at the wheel of her dead daddy's Coronet, Donnie Huff lounging against the doorpanel with his arm dangling out the window as he entertained from Opal Criner standing alongside the
vehicle a piece of talk, an apparently earnest scrap of news that
Opal Criner had stopped there at the cardoor to share with
Donnie Huff, a scrap of news Marie Criner Huff could not from
the doorscreen make out but failed somehow to take to be a
revelation of the troublesome and inflamed wart variety, neglected to suspect that her momma was apprising Donnie Huff
of her fears and apprehensions that her wart was presently
such a discomfort to her as to keep her from driving her dead

Carl's Coronet on account of the risk of an infraction which seemed to Opal Criner quite sizable at the moment.

"You drive," she told to Donnie Huff and made her feeble way around the frontend of the vehicle to the passenger door where she stanched sufficiently her wart-induced anguish and irritation to instruct her grandbaby Delmon, "Scoot over," as she let herself onto the seat, drew shut the door, and turned off the radio in one highly coordinated and inordinately fluid motion.

From over back of the screen, Marie Criner Huff held in the fingers of her one hand her varnish brush and held in the fingers of her other her dwindling Kent as she watched Donnie Huff guide the beige Coronet down the drive, proceed slowly over the uncovered culvert, and swing on out into the road where he flung by way of immoderate acceleration sufficient crushed stone to produce upon the face of Opal Criner a highly expressive sort a look that her girl Marie, even from up back of the screen, could make out plain enough and she told aloud into the air, "Must be one hell of a wart," as she watched the Coronet that Donnie Huff had never even one time previously sat beneath the wheel of disappear up around a ledgy outcropping with the upchurned gravel ringing against the underbelly and rattling about in the fenderwells.

Quite plainly Donnie Huff had not ever cultivated much regard for rpms, just as Opal Criner had suspected, and she took upon herself the chore of revealing to him how the valves tended to get taxed and the belts and hoses suffered avoidable strain when a fellow such a Donnie Huff laid his foot so to the gas pedal. She invoked as well the memory of her dead Carl and hoped that Donnie Huff might see fit to honor it with a lower velocity. Donnie Huff, however, was engaged already in an undertaking otherwise, was performing for Opal Criner the service of cleaning out her carburetor which he could tell even from back of the dash was undoubtedly gunked up from too awful much fretting on behalf of the valves and the belts and the hoses as well. And Delmon Huff, who knew a thing about cleaning carburetors himself, suggested to Donnie Huff, "Stomp it, Daddy," which returned to the features of Opal Criner her highly expressive sort of a look.

He was not in truth near so wild and atrocious a driver as Opal Criner had feared, was not so heedless with her dead Carl's Coronet as she'd anticipated he might be, though it seemed to her that Donnie Huff on occasion ate .up too awful much of the center line in a curve and showed a disposition to antagonize slower traffic with not just his lights and his horn but by means as well of a highly animated and exceedingly articulate variety of one-handed miming that struck Opal Criner as vulgar and altogether unbecoming. Otherwise he parked well enough and had gladly stepped with her grandbaby Delmon into the pharmacy to fetch for Opal Criner her wart ointment, had even refrained on Opal Criner's behalf from drawing snug up behind Mrs. Benjamin J. Worthington's green LeMans on the way home and engaging there in one of his more objectionable dumbshows. Instead he'd laid back a carlength or two and had exhibited for Mrs. Benjamin J. Worthington an assortment of gestures that were each and all considerably less vile than Donnie Huff had demonstrated already a capability for. He'd shown even a willingness to drive slowly down the gravel road before the house so as not to kick up an edgy stone and thereby rupture the gastank that Opal Criner had read somewhere about an instance of and had adopted straightaway as a personal apprehension. So all in all, she was pleased, was whole and sound as she climbed out from the Coronet before the house and stepped clear to watch her Donald guide the thing through the sideyard and back towards the shed in the company of his boy Delmon who switched on the radio in time enough to hear the electric piano interlude between the verse and the chorus of a plaintive sort of a ditty sung by a woman who'd lost her man and was apparently suffering on account of it heartache and hyperventilation together, was in fact wheezing in palpable torment when Opal Criner turned about and spied just beyond the doorscreen her girl Marie who'd heard the Coronet on the drive and had arrived in time so that her and Opal Criner might look back and forth between themselves that way mothers and daughters will on occasion when the one of them suspects what the other one knows already.

Over the course of the succeeding few days, it began to

appear to Marie that her mother was cruelly afflicted with an array of topical infirmities from her earchannels down, short-lived but severe complaints that required in each instance a salve or a balm or a particular bottled remedy that nobody in the household had been yet induced to buy. Aside from a rubberized earcleaning contraption to work in conjunction with the earwax solvent, Opal Criner required on consecutive evenings special swabs for her nostrils, a tiny plastic utensil designed to stimulate and thereby arrest receding gums, a liver-spot cream for a particularly sudden and unsightly liverspot, assorted digestive supplements meant to lubricate Opal Criner when she wasn't and unlubricate her when she was while con-trolling as well her attendant gases as a matter of course, and an exotic variety of corn plaster with a lilac scent that Opal Criner applied as a preventive since she had not yet truly incurred corns but was sensible of the likelihood of them most especially for a woman at her stage in life. Of course her natural appre-hension grew heightened and intensified and, since she could not know when a new and unanticipated affliction might arise to debilitate her, Opal Criner enlisted the services of Donnie Huff who, at the first sign of fret and discomfort, would dash off with his boy Delmon to roll the Coronet out from the shed and swing about the house to snatch up Opal Criner who would simultaneously shut and lock her cardoor and turn off the radio in advance of identifying her present complaint and prescrib-ing for herself whatever corrective it seemed to her the Revco might stock.

Oftentimes on the return trip, in the throes of their general relief, they would stop the bunch of them at the dairy bar alongside the Hop-in and allow themselves a soft cone apiece until of course Delmon proved incapable of ingesting his soft cone with the proper dispatch to keep it from liquefying and running down his hand to drip off his knobby wrist onto Carl's tufted vinyl. Opal Criner and Donnie Huff were together in agreement that a tongue was not intended merely for a fellow to sculpt and shape his food with notwithstanding how Delmon had created previously a study in vanilla of a ruptured bunion that Opal Criner and Donnie Huff were both pressed to admit had been exceedingly lifelike, so they punished Delmon by putting him onto cups instead of cones and thereby effectively stanched the dripping and pretty much punctuated the licking and the sculpting as well since Delmon could not manage with a cup a suitable working angle.

Once the onslaught of infirmities had been ongoing pretty much without interruption for a solid week and a half, Opal Criner came down with a private sort of a trouble, reported to her Donald and his boy Delmon in the midst of the *PM Magazine* on her advancing discomfort. But before they could both of them leap and strike out for the shed, she confided most especially to her Donald how hers this evening was a woman's complaint and she suggested, partly through audible speech though by means as well of a general and wordless insinuation that was comprised chiefly of inclined eyebrows, how it did not seem to her suitable to seek a cure for her present ills in the company of a child by which she meant Delmon specifically who she signified with one eyebrow alone. Donnie Huff explained, "You stay here," and reminded Delmon that shortly on the *PM Magazine* they were traveling to Georgia to speak with a man who'd made a lap pet out of a groundhog. Donnie Huff could not help but believe that there might be some reward in seeing such a fool as that. So Delmon grew persuaded to remain parked on the settee while Donnie Huff brought the Coronet around the house, picked up Opal Criner at the front slab, and rolled down the drive, passing gingerly over the uncovered culvert and into the road that Marie Criner Huff in the kitchen, who'd become lately acquainted with the process, did not rise to witness herself until she heard her child Delmon wheezing and coughing and grunting after a fashion in the front room like was normally his habit when he sat upon the couch and played with his fingers.

Though she was varnishing a root basket and so had assorted drips to marshal and see after, Marie Criner Huff found nonetheless occasion to step into the front room and speak to her child Delmon, ask of him, "Where'd they go?"

"Store."

"Why didn't you go with them?"

With his shoulders that he elevated Delmon informed his mother that he could not just presently say.

"What's momma's trouble tonight?" Marie Criner Huff inquired but did not watch Delmon work his shoulders once further and instead stepped clear across to the doorscreen so as to peer out towards the road and then off beyond it to the far bank of the branch where a vein of chalky gray shale ran down the slope and into the water.

"Man's got a groundhog in the house," Delmon told to his momma who did not straightoff tell to him anything in return but eventually and in what was for her an awfully tiny sort of a voice asked of her boy Delmon, "Does he?"

"He does," Delmon informed her, though he admitted freely that he could not himself say why.

Anxious to save her Donald from humiliation and distress, Opal Criner volunteered to proceed alone into the pharmacy and purchase herself the ointment she required which Donnie Huff was altogether pleased to allow and so drew up into the fire lane in a vacant spot before the Pinch-an-Inch and sat idling in the Coronet while his mother-in-law made her relatively feeble way into the store, displaying up the sidewalk the manner of halting step her particular variety of infirmity most usually induced. She was back in a veritable trice with a puny sack to show for her trouble which proved for Donnie Huff a disappointment as he'd discovered in the window of the Pinch-an-Inch a seam in the louvers that permitted him to view two complete sizable leotarded women and a piece of a third one who were together hopping and dancing about in a startling and highly ungainly sort of a way, moving with sufficient jiggle and agility to produce upon Donnie Huff a passably hypnotic effect since he did not often find occasion to watch women of such heft comport themselves so. He made even, upon Opal Criner's return, a fairly inadvertent comment on the assorted wonders of this life and how they did not ever seem to him to cease, exclaimed anyhow, "Good Lord!" upon the execution of a particularly rash and foolhardy maneuver that appeared to Donnie Huff destined to result in a pile of sprained women on the nappy wall-to-wall.

Naturally Opal Criner wanted to know from him, "What?"

Donnie Huff, however, did not speak to her of the daring maneuver and confided instead that his had not been a particularized and specific sort of a "Good Lord!" but was merely his customary discharge in recognition of the splendor of the evening.

"Is a nice night, isn't it?" Opal Criner said to him and heard very shortly from Donnie Huff, "Good Lord!," heard very shortly from Donnie Huff, "Yes."

She could not have personally wished on him a more suitable disposition and wondered, once they'd gained the crossroads, if couldn't they possibly take 58 to the east instead of 221 to the north and so swing about the long way around that Donnie Huff appeared to find pleasing as a prospect and consequently passed without objection straight through the light and down by the high school and on up around the bend towards Laurel Fork. The sky had gone chiefly pink all over which struck Opal Criner as a thing well worth Good Lording on account of, and she asked of Donnie Huff to turn about briefly if he would and look at how the sun had come to lay in the treetops upon the ridge back of them, a sight they agreed together was as certifiable an advertisement of the hand of God on this earth as anything might be, or Opal Criner said anyhow it was and Donnie Huff failed himself to tell her it wasn't which she took directly for a pact and a concord. In an effort to maintain and even perhaps improve upon her good fortune, Opal Criner did not speak this evening to Donnie Huff of his tendency to eat up the center line, neglected as well to stomp her floormat, and curtailed even her little cries of alarm on her way to mustering the breath and saliva with which to congratulate Donnie Huff in his successful maneuver roundabout a tractor in a blind curve. She'd been herself so foolish as to fear he might kill the both of them, but plainly her agitation had been altogether misplaced since here they still were alive and whole.

Only in a spate of talking about matters diffuse and sundry did Opal Criner at last make mention of her appointment that she straightoff departed from and only presently revisited so as to tell of how, as appointments go, it was fairly impending. Donnie Huff, who was not by nature an intensely curious individual, did not take any notice of the appointment at all until Opal Criner had circled back to touch upon it a third time in advance of instructing Donnie Huff to turn if he might off the highway and down onto a blacktop where she indicated her appointment lay. Still, however, Donnie Huff expended the majority of his attention on his one-fingered steering technique and failed to work up detectable interest in Opal Criner's engagement until he'd come to get directed to pull off if he would into the churchlot and saw fit to inquire of Opal Criner, "Here?"

"Here," she told to him and suggested to Donnie Huff that he not park anywhere at all near that white oak in the churchyard since it would surely drip and deposit onto the Coronet.

There were a half-dozen vehicles scattered about and Donnie Huff slipped the Coronet between an El Camino and a holly-hock prior to switching off the ignition and slouching down against the seatback in an attitude of unmistakable leisure. But Opal Criner, who'd not of course found yet occasion to apply and spread her ointment, requested of Donnie Huff his assistance on account of how her symptomatic halting step had grown since the pharmacy acute and troublesome enough to enfeeble her quite altogether. "Might have to hoist me," she told to Donnie Huff who circled around the car, clutched up the fingers Opal Criner had extended to get hoisted by, and drew her upright, from where she caught on straightaway to Donnie Huff's elbow joint and clung strenuously to it.

He led her across the lot and up the two steps onto the landing, and under the growing scrutiny of a half-dozen Charolais off to the one side of the churchyard and an assortment of polled Angus off to the other, Donnie Huff pushed upon the heavy paneled door and squired his mother-in-law into the sanctuary proper where the last of this day's certifiable advertisement of the hand of God on this earth had adequately drained off and diminished to leave the pews and the altar and the assorted occupants in a light so scant and murky that Donnie Huff, upon arriving full into the sanctuary and drawing the door shut behind him, squired Opal Criner directly into the back of a pew that she protested mildly about but endured well enough to persevere on up the aisle once Donnie Huff had managed to come across it.

From up at the altar the Reverend Mr. Worrell issued on behalf of the Bible classmates a hearty welcome to Donnie Huff in particular in whose company they were all of them, the reverend insisted, pleased to be, which went as a sentiment wholly uncontradicted but for the wry expressions Mrs. Gloria Hawks and Miss Cindy Womble swiveled about towards each other and indulged in that nobody but themselves appeared to take any notice of. While always grateful for a hearty welcome, Donnie Huff nonetheless apprised the Reverend Mr. Worrell of how he was merely delivering his mother-in-law to her engagement that the Reverend Mr. Worrell inclined his head inquiringly on account of but came to be forestalled from pursuing the matter further by Opal Criner who, though relatively enfeebled and utterly unointmented, would not be dissuaded by her twinges and torments from speaking enthusiastically of the sinking sun that her and her Donald had seen together laying upon the treetops on a ridge.

"It was a pure sight," Opal Criner announced and thereby prompted Mr. Troy Haven and his wife Olive to share with the group a joint description of just where lately they'd themselves seen the sun lay.

By the time Mrs. Norma Baines found occasion to speak with the intermittent aid of her husband Larry about an orb they'd together watched drop into the sound off Pungo, Opal Criner had slipped past Mrs. Worrell into the front pew and had drawn by the elbow joint her Donald in with her, her Donald who she persuaded to sit by the application of mere finger pressure to a particular arm vessel. Consequently, he could not help but oblige her and demonstrated in his various features rising irritation though he found cause nearly straightaway to express to Opal Criner his gratitude once she'd kept him, by her vessel pressure alone, from spilling directly out of the pew and onto the sanctuary floor.

He wasn't truly mad yet. His nostrils hadn't broadened and expanded and he showed no particular inclination to chew his

cheek as was Donnie Huff's practice once he'd come to be put
out. He appeared to Opal Criner fairly content to gaze about
and take in the various features of the sanctuary which he could
see well enough now that his eyes had adjusted to the light, and
he laid back briefly to look above himself at the ceiling and the
dangling lightglobes, eyed rather intently what he took to be
the sizable hooters of Miss Cindy Womble across the aisle from
him in the opposite pew, and spent as well some considerable of
his attention on the picture of the prayerful Jesus upon the
front wall which was undoubtedly the biggest piece of portraiture he'd come across lately and had even its own lamp to light
it. He studied the details of the thing, considered with interest
the knobby hands of the Savior and the rough uncomely folds
of His robe which he was admiring the tufts of when the Reverend Mr. Worrell began himself to speak. He told of the pleasure they all of them took in entertaining for the evening Mr.
Donald Huff but told of it in such ponderous preacherly tones
that Donnie Huff himself went quite wholly deaf from the gravity of the sentiment and consequently persisted in exclusively
admiring the painted Savior without paying any notice to the
reverend who refreshed the collected Bible classmates as to how
they'd all of them heard probably through the years a ranging
assortment of testimony from folks who'd seen the light, been
touched and transformed by the glories of God and snatched
from perdition by the love of the Lord, but he did not suppose
they'd any of them been blessed previously with the occasion to
learn from a man who's been dead of the splendor that lies
before them. Consequently, it was a rare pleasure for the Reverend Mr. Worrell to introduce to the Bible classmates Mr.
Donnie Huff who he hoped would receive a warm Laurel Fork
welcome which the reverend undertook to ignite with his own
hands that he beat together, got shortly joined at, and so quite
effectively roused Donnie Huff who looked about to find himself watched and applauded, even persevered merely at gazing
about once he was getting mostly watched alone but did grow
after a fashion incited to speak, got prompted by the attention
of the reverend and the Bible classmates to satisfy his curiosity
as to a particular matter, and once the warm Laurel Fork wel-

come had piddled out entirely Donnie Huff asked of anybody that might care to tell him, "Is that a duck up there?" and some of them thought it likely was and the rest of them figured it surely wasn't except for Mr. Troy Haven who'd concluded to his own satisfaction that is was instead a sheep.

In the wake, however, of his inquiry Donnie Huff did not appear much inclined to speak further and sat briefly undisturbed as he endeavored to construe a sheep himself. But the reverend was anxious still to hear of the splendors ahead and apprised Donnie Huff of as much, invited him even up towards the riser where he might best address the bunch of them which was precisely when, as best as Opal Criner could tell, Donnie Huff grew legitimately angry and turned about to exhibit his dilated nostrils at her as he caught up a flap of cheekskin between his molars. Being a woman of no little experience on this earth, Opal Criner showed to Donnie Huff back as pathetic a face as she could muster, not apologetic and contrite but just pitiful chiefly so as perhaps to suggest to what degree precisely she was tossed and buffeted by the forces of this life that made her to do things she'd not hoped and intended to do which appeared, as an expression, to forestall Donnie Huff from taking up Opal Criner by the neck and pitching her into the churchyard. Instead he laid wide his lips in a sickly smile and reminded Opal Criner how she'd somehow neglected to inform him that her engagement was in fact his engagement too, likely even his engagement primarily that Opal Criner worked up an additional face on account of so as to suggest further that a woman like herself, tossed and buffeted and just generally flung about, could not be expected to remember every little thing.

The Reverend Mr. Worrell was anxious personally to entertain news of the hereafter and so encouraged Donnie Huff to depart if he might from his pew and come forward, but Donnie Huff maintained his thoroughgoing reluctance until the reverend had enlisted the Bible classmates to express to Donnie Huff how awfully anxious they were themselves to entertain news of hereafter like would probably not have noticeably enticed Donnie Huff but for Miss Cindy Womble across the aisle who turned upon him her sizable hooters a she expressed to him her anxiety as well which inspired in Donnie Huff a sense of evangelical duty coupled with a notion of just where he'd be pleased to press and lay his face. So he got up from his pew, stepped past Mrs. Worrell out into the aisle, and advanced on to the riser so as to provide himself with the opportunity to turn about and gaze upon the hooters outright. Of course Donnie Huff was not properly dressed to witness, had not worn this evening to the sanctuary the sort of a getup that the bulk of people might testify in, but Opal Criner was proud nonetheless to see her Donald standing alongside an actual reverend just shy of a verifiable altar and pretty much under a picture of Jesus with perhaps a duck or maybe a sheep off in the middle distance. She guessed she could overlook his muddy brogans and his greasy twill trousers and his checked shirt with the torn pocket and the threadbare collar not even to mention his scruffy beard with a fleck of something caught in it just beneath his lip, guessed most especially she could overlook them once her Donald had spoken, once he'd allowed the reverend to ask of him if hadn't he lately been dead and told to the reverend, "I was," in a deep resolute voice back.

The effect upon the hooters was instantaneous as best as Donnie Huff could tell. Due to the short sharp breath Miss Cindy Womble saw fit to inhale, she managed to produce a noticeable elevation that Donnie Huff sought to induce her to repeat by revealing deeply to the Bible classmates that he'd not been just dead but had managed to get green as well which plainly palpitated Miss Cindy Womble to her very marrow.

From back alongside Mrs. Worrell, Opal Criner encouraged Donnie Huff to speak if he might of how he'd hovered and floated and thereby prompted him to disclose largely at the hooters, "I hovered. I floated."

The Reverend Mr. Worrell wondered if Donnie Huff might trouble himself to take them through his experience stage by stage so that they could know what he felt and learn what he saw which did not, as a prospect, much appeal to Mrs. Gloria Hawks who aired in the direction of Miss Cindy Womble a sour expression that Miss Cindy Womble did not pucker up her features and return since she'd grown already exceedingly curious and partially elevated.

"I was snaking walnut," Donnie Huff said, "twitching a length of it down the hillside to the bluff. It was a big piece of tree and got rolling and sliding and wouldn't seem to fetch up against anything much."

"Snaking walnut," the reverend told to him and heard straightaway, "Yes sir," from Donnie Huff back. "A big piece of tree," Donnie Huff said. "Got to slipping and skidding down the slope."

"Snaking with a horse?" the reverend wanted to know.

"Skidder," Donnie Huff told to him, and he turned about and explained to the hooters chiefly, "Skidder," as well though produced by it no noticeable effect.

"Gaither had cut a flat place with the loader," Donnie Huff said and held before himself his right hand with the knuckles uplifted so as to indicate what precisely he meant by flat. "I was aiming to swing about on it, but that treetrunk just kept on coming. I'd told him I hadn't no business pulling that thing."

"Who?" the reverend inquired.

And Donnie Huff informed him, "Gaither. His tree. His skidder."

"So he'd made you haul this log?"

"Yes sir," Donnie Huff said.

"And you'd told him already you didn't want to?"

"Thing was too big," Donnie Huff said, "and that damn skidder's a piece of junk," which was apparently just the sort of talk to cause those hooters to sag and decline, which Donnie Huff took straightaway some notice of and so expressed at the left one and the right one together his sincere regret at having spoken impolitely there under Jesus in the house of God. But he was hot, he told it, had not yet managed to wholly rein in his fiery passions like he had to figure might be the case with most men who'd been killed and gotten green, sent to certain destruction for hardly enough board feet to build an outhouse. "I'd figured I was in trouble," Donnie Huff said. "I'd guessed I was purely stepping in it."

"So you'd seen already your fate," the reverend told him, "endured already a premonition."

"Snaked already the little end of the tree," Donnie Huff said and allowed how that had served for him as premonition enough.

Donnie Huff didn't suppose he could know how many among them had ever previously found themselves in true peril which prompted Mr. Troy Haven to speak briefly of his exploits in the Pacific during the big WW when they ate, he told it, peril for breakfast which itself forestalled Mr. Larry Baines from telling of the time he'd been sat on by a pony which did not strike him, in the face of daily ingestible peril, as much of an exploit. Mrs. Gloria Hawks had herself hemorrhaged once previously, mention of which served to remind Mrs. Olive Haven that she'd hemorrhaged once as well. Opal Criner recalled how her Carl had years back cut off a piece of his foot with his Lawn Boy, and she was meaning to explain which piece precisely when Mrs. Norma Baines volunteered that her Larry had one time been sat on by a pony which Mr. Troy Haven in particular found ever so diverting.

Donnie Huff didn't suppose he could know how many among them had ever precisely found themselves in immediate danger of getting maimed and crushed and mutilated, could not imagine they'd any of them faced yet annihilation like he'd been put upon to face it himself, and Donnie Huff expelled a manly breath and told to the rising hooters, "Yep."

The reverend was anxious for Donnie Huff to speak if he would of his particular predeath circumstances, share with them his thoughts and feelings that Donnie Huff let on he'd be pleased to undertake and so told of how the log dangled and the skidder inclined which he illustrated with his right hand that he held before himself with the knuckles uplifted though plainly in a fashion other than flat. "I felt the thing laying back," Donnie Huff said, "figured it couldn't but pitch on over."

"And you tried to jump clear?" the reverend asked of him.

"No," Donnie Huff told him back and felt straightaway put upon to think of the sort of cause for it that two hooters most especially might favor.

"Had time to jump?" the reverend wanted to know.

"I guess I did," Donnie Huff said but then wondered straightoff hootwards if hadn't they all of them felt sometime or another gripped and held to a place that they had no business being.

"Charmed," the Reverend Mr. Worrell suggested to Donnie Huff who told to him back, "I'm sure," and then entertained from the reverend his own opinion that people in dire circumstances were oftentimes like deer in headlights which struck Donnie Huff as a miraculous revelation since he'd been himself about to say the same thing.

"I had time to jump," Donnie Huff said. "I just couldn't manage to do it."

"Enchanted," the reverend told to him. "Fascinated. Fated," and Donnie Huff audibly sucked a portion of saliva through a toothgap and informed Miss Cindy Womble's blousefront "Yep," once further.

He hadn't ever previously stood up before anybody much and said anything, but not because he was fearful of speaking or anxious about crowds. Donnie Huff simply had never yet come across an item worth standing up before anybody and speaking of. The people he knew of a dispostion to hold forth were plagued themselves with convictions and troubled with resolve while Donnie Huff did not hold himself too awful many strong opinions and was hardly tempted to squander his leisure in the cultivation of them since, after working in timber the day long, it was a chore for him to muster sufficient energy to believe in anything much at all. The Reverend Mr. Worrell, however, and his Bible classmates plainly shared among them a potent feeling for their Jesus that Donnie Huff would himself have likely taken for foolishness but for the hooters that heaved and jiggled and shifted about under the blousefront and thereby translated fervor into a language Donnie Huff could well appreciate and comprehend. So while he had not yet stirred himself to believe on his own in anything at all, Donnie Huff was grateful most especially for the rousing faith of Miss Cindy Womble which appeared to him a shining, melonlike example of what churchgoing might be given the proper equipment enlivened by a suitable ardor. Naturally he was hoping to work her up further still and so explained most especially to Miss Cindy Womble the gravity of his circumstances, painted for her a grim picture of his predicament on the skidder atop the bluff with the contraption hinging back and his fate quite apparently sealed and ordained.

"I knew I was a dead man," Donnie Huff told to the third button down with noticeable and immediate effect. "I just knew it," he declared to most everybody otherwise and entertained a query from the Reverend Mr. Worrell who sought to discover for the benefit of the group how precisely Donnie Huff had felt there when it had seemed to him certain he'd soon be deceased.

"I felt sick," Donnie Huff said. "Just sick."

Of course the reverend was curious to know sick how exactly and suggested to Donnie Huff that perhaps he'd felt mostly sick at heart faced like he was with the prospect of ever so shortly departing from this earth leaving a child and a wife and a wife's mother to grieve for him and never to see again the beauties of the day and the splendors of the night which sounded to Donnie Huff more appealing than nauseated and so he guessed maybe he had been sick chiefly at heart. "Life's just so sweet sometimes," Donnie Huff declared, "that a man's pained to give it up," which the reverend and the Bible classmates together could not keep among them from raising a chorus of neck-noises about.

Donnie Huff shared with the group the sensation of riding a skidder off a bluff backwards into a creek that he did not suspect they had cause to be acquainted with, and they listened to talk of his predicament with considerably more attention than the bulk of people most usually paid to Donnie Huff, enough of a tribute to prompt Donnie Huff to linger over the details he could recall and to manufacture the details he couldn't which he lingered over as well. Though he admitted to no personal recollection of splashing into the creek and settling upon the bed of it, Donnie Huff nonetheless reconstructed his impact as he could not help but suspect it occurred and painted himself as a brave and manly although semiconscious participant. The transition, of course, from getting dead to being it called for some severely advanced powers of description that Donnie Huff doubted he possessed until he'd seen fit to consult the hooters which served to buck him up and adequately invigorate him to tempt him to embark upon extended talk of his demise.

"I was under the water," Donnie Huff said. "I was caught against the wheel and wasn't but about half awake, just come around enough to see I was in a fix," and Donnie Huff told how he'd managed there at the end assorted tender thoughts about his wife and his boy and his loving life's mother which incited Opal Criner to turn to Mr. and Mrs. Ray Truitt just down the pew and reveal to them how she was her.

"Then I guess I passed on," Donnie Huff said and heard straightaway from the Reverend Mr. Worrell, "Gave yourself over to those icy fingers of death," which Donnie Huff assured the reverend was pretty much what he'd meant.

Though she did not wish to intrude upon the general course of the narrative, Opal Criner reminded Donnie Huff how he'd best not forget the floating and the hovering and Donnie Huff told to his loving wife's mother he was coming to that straightaway and he clapped shut both his eyes together so as better to conjure up his ascent into the heavens without for the moment the sizable hooters to distract him. He figured straightoff he might speak of the little green spots since he'd seen after all the little green spots outright, but Donnie Huff had to suppose that likely little green spots were considerably more in the way of a cardiovascular than a mystical phenomenon so he did not make mention of them and proceeded in fact pretty directly to the floating and the hovering instead. Naturally Donnie Huff had expected to get plunged into eternal and thoroughgoing night, had always simply figured that he'd pass probably from life into something dark and everlasting or descend maybe into the fires of hell but certainly not float and not hover above his moderately supine form. Donnie Huff wished the Bible classmates might imagine then his surprise when he was not just of the sudden dead but was floating and was hovering both.

Mr. Larry Baines, who was inquisitive by disposition, wondered if mightn't he interrupt Donnie Huff so as to learn from him just what of himself it was that raised into the air which Donnie Huff considered briefly prior to revealing to Mr. Larry Baines how it was chiefly the unsupine part of himself that had taken flight, which did not truly satisfy Mr. Larry Baines who was hoping to learn if the part that floated and hovered resembled the part that lay back of the skidder wheel on the creekbed that Donnie Huff lifted his web of skin and fairly meditated upon.

Presently, after what appeared to Opal Criner a dramatic and seemly pause, Donnie Huff informed Mr. Larry Baines that the part of himself to float and hover had resembled pretty closely his supine remains except for how the airborne portion was filmy and slight which the Reverend Mr. Worrell identified for Donnie Huff and Mr. Larry Baines both. "Plainly spirit," he told to them and explained to the Bible class in general how Donnie Huff had undoubtedly gotten prompted by death to vent his essence into the air which Donnie Huff allowed to be the case and guessed he would have spoken of it himself but for fear of seeming boastful and proud since it was not just anybody that could vent his essence and then find occasion later to tell about it.

Donnie Huff could not say precisely how he'd floated but did not recall beating his arms and so guessed maybe he'd risen on a draft of air or supposed perhaps a vented essence was inclined to float and soar which he sought from the reverend a ruling about and so learned directly that while goodly essences did rise on their own into the heavens, tainted heathen essences sank unaided into the bowels of hell which cleared up the matter pretty completely.

"I floated," Donnie Huff said. "I hovered and drifted about over the skidder and above the bluff where Gaither and Freeman and Buddy and Alvis had come down already off the slope to see where I'd got to." Donnie Huff explained that he'd undertaken to call and cry out but had to guess he'd been too filmy and slight to get heard at it and, inspired by the hooters primarily, Donnie Huff expressed to the classmates the painful sense of longing he'd endured deep within his gauzy insubstantial self, the ache he'd felt to be once more amongst his friends and employer, to clutch them tight in an embrace, and then Donnie Huff paused briefly so as to undertake to recall just what it was he'd been in fact speaking about.

In an effort so as to aid her Donald who appeared to have dropped off momentarily into befuddlement, Opal Criner called out from her pew to inquire where precisely Donnie Huff had floated and hovered to and, by way of further assistance, she rolled her eyes ceilingwards which Donnie Huff detected her at and comprehended sufficiently to inform Opal Criner how he'd floated and hovered up chiefly, sailed like a bird into the sky.

"Higher and higher," Donnie Huff said, "into the clouds and on through them." "Up," he told to one side of the aisle. "Up," he told to the other and produced a windy sort of an exhalation, blew through his teeth so as to approximate the sounds of the ether for those people who'd not yet ascended into it like would be everybody but him since he alone had vented already his essence.

Mr. Troy Haven labored for a short time under the impression that he was curious to discover if it was cold up in the ether for an essence, but once he'd shared his inclination with his wife Olive she persuaded him by means of a look alone that the temperature of the ether was not a thing he truly needed to know. In an effort to be pertinent, Mr. Troy Haven tested and then actually aired outright instead a question otherwise, sought from Donnie Huff to learn if he'd passed beyond the clouds and through the ether and on into the inky depths of space with the stars and the orbs which Donnie Huff could not straightoff recall and so merely repeated to Mr. Troy Haven his inquiry which Mr. Troy Haven recognized and confirmed thereby allowing Donnie Huff the opportunity to look to his loving wife's mother who assured him with a sour expression that he had most certainly not passed into the inky depths of space which Donnie Huff relayed to Mr. Troy Haven who guessed then he was interested to hear where Donnie Huff had gone to instead that Olive Haven allowed he was.

"Up," Donnie Huff told him, "higher and higher," which Mr. Troy Haven learned from his wife Olive he was hardly satisfied with alone and so pressed Donnie Huff further, asking of him, "Up where?"

Opal Criner endeavored to look blinded, blinked her lids

and worked her eyes about but gained by it only the acute
concern of the Reverend Mr. Worrell who asked after her condition and hoped she was not suffering from an irritation in her
sockets, but he got assured by Donnie Huff that Opal Criner's
present irritation was in fact elsewhere altogether. She was
meaning to tell herself of how sensitive her eyes were anymore
to light, most especially bright, bright light, but before she could
manage to tell it Donnie Huff fairly exclaimed, "Oh!" and recalled beyond it how he'd sailed out of the ether and up towards
the sun that Opal Criner grew straightaway soothed and relieved by the news of.

   "Wasn't much I could see there at first," Donnie Huff said,
"and I just floated and hovered and rose on up to where there
wasn't hardly anything anymore but light itself." And Donnie
Huff inquired if couldn't they all of them remember some particular afternoon when they'd seen the sunlight break in shafts
and beams through the clouds and fall thick and misty upon the
ground that they all of them but for Mrs. Gloria Hawks insisted
they could as Mrs. Gloria Hawks had determined to be contrary
since she could not herself much tell a Huff from a Snavely and
guessed she'd watched this particular resuscitated specimen
gawk quite long enough already at her and Miss Cindy Womble's assorted enticements. So Mrs. Gloria Hawks insisted how
she could not even imagine shafts and beams of sunlight falling
thick and misty upon the ground and had not certainly ever
entertained herself the sight of them which she shot at Miss
Cindy Womble a glance in the wake of, Miss Cindy Womble
who was even then already wondering of Donnie Huff if might
she share with him a personal memory of shafts and beams that
was especially dear to her which Donnie Huff let on to be delighted at the prospect of and encouraged Miss Cindy Womble
to favor them please with talk of her recollection.

   She'd seen her shafts and beams in a time of trouble and
despair, nameless trouble and unidentified despair but purely
legitimate doses of both, affliction enough anyhow to have sent
Miss Cindy Womble into a funk. Casting back upon this bleak
passage in her life, Miss Cindy Womble apparently could not
help but become a little teary and agitated like caused her pos-

ture to erode noticeably, induced an appealing sort of a slouch that, as best as Donnie could tell, truly set off the hooters to altogether tremendous effects and so sparked Donnie Huff to inordinate heights of commiseration by means of fairly soggy exchanges with Miss Cindy Womble who heaved and whimpered and thereby enhanced her personal enticements further still.

She'd just been taking the air and wondered if didn't all of them sometimes feel inclined to simply step out and imbibe a dose of it which Donnie Huff, speaking for the Bible classmates, emphatically assured Miss Cindy Womble to be the case and paid beyond it handsome tribute to air as a heady elixir when most all else had failed which touched and stirred Miss Cindy Womble and incited her to palpable jigglement. She'd gone out back of her daddy's house to walk in the pasture there up above the crossroads where Burke's Fork bends around and pours into the Big Reed, and she'd just wandered about for a while looking to keep mostly from stepping on a snake or treading in a cowpie as she wallowed, she confessed, in her black mood and felt herself a pitiful soul on this earth. Of a sudden, however, sunlight broke before her on a patch of ryegrass and dandelions, a thick and misty beam of it that fell upon the pasture like a veritable ray of hope, Miss Cindy Womble declared, and she told how she'd picked up her head towards the sun itself and seen thereby the shafts and the beams otherwise that fell thick and misty and golden upon the hillsides and touched her to her own very essence which she'd not yet had occasion to vent herself.

"They healed my sick heart," Miss Cindy Womble said, meaning the beams and meaning the shafts and she heard directly from the Reverend Mr. Worrell in a lowly reverential tone, "Praise be," which itself set off a smattering of similar declarations from the Bible classmates who watched as Miss Cindy Womble rose from her slouch, straightened and stretched herself most thoroughly and therefore entertained from Donnie Huff emphatic mention of the holy Father as well which Opal Criner fairly crowed to Mr. and Mrs. Ray Truitt about.

With Cindy Womble's gracious permission, Donnie Huff returned to his own demise and invited the Bible classmates to imagine if they would the glorious sensation a man might enjoy were he to rise on the wings of salvation through buttery shafts and beams of thick misty light towards the porthole of heaven, or invited then anyhow to imagine something very much like it which they all of them endeavored to do but for Mr. Larry Baines, who'd served in the Pacific on what Mrs. Norma Baines called evermore to his consternation a boat, and hoped to Donnie Huff that they would not all of them have to pass into heaven through a porthole unless of course their own vented essences proved to be inordinately slight and wiry. Of course Opal Criner felt put upon to announce how her Donald was most assuredly speaking of a sizable sort of a gateway to the everlasting bathed in heavenly light, what the most of the rest of them might know as a portal, the most of the rest of them who'd not after all floated and hovered themselves and so could not speak with much authority on the matter. In order to avoid confusion, however, Donnie Huff demonstrated a willingness to call the thing a portal himself and assured the Bible classmates how it had in fact been a large and ornate gateway to the everlasting bathed in certifiable heavenly light.

Mr. Troy Haven set up a kind of a disturbance by suffering briefly under the impression that he was anxious to know if it had been after all a pearly sort of a gateway, but Mrs. Olive Haven managed presently to win him over to another impression altogether and thereby squelched his query quite completely. So Donnie Huff advanced on to the latter stages of his excursion, drawing for strength upon the hooters as discreetly as he was able and gaining by them even a species of actual infusement which he injected as best he could into his description of the heavenly portal. He recalled it to be an arched sort of a portal with etchings about the frame of it and massive filigreed gates flung open wide either side of a manner of portal stoop that exhibited itself noticeable pearly touches which Mr. Troy Haven in particular was most gratified to hear about. As arched portals went, Donnie Huff could not imagine a more comely and alluring item and spoke specifically to the hooters, but also for the benefit of most anybody that cared to hear it, of the sense of calm that overcame him as he stood there on that heavenly stoop admiring the filigree on the gates and the etchings about the frame and feeling ever so deep in his essence no trace much of the distress and apprehension a man might expect to haul up through the ether and arrive at the heavenly portal freighted with.

"I was at peace," Donnie Huff declared for anybody that cared to know it and he explained how it was not ordinarily his custom to be at peace since he was partial instead to agitation and nagging doubt which Opal Criner issued a confirming sort of a discharge about.

Naturally they were all of them anxious to hear talk of the portalkeeper, restless to learn who'd greeted Donnie Huff's own vented essence which Donnie Huff made at last mention of, spoke of a creature he'd detected passing towards him along a particularly buttery beam, a tall, handsome, bearded and berobed creature who'd stepped up to fairly fill the portal and had raised at Donnie Huff his fingers after a fashion that Donnie Huff was pleased himself to demonstrate and so lifted a hand of his own with the digits only moderately extended and shifted it about with no vigor much to speak of, less vigor anyhow than a trip up through the ether might appear to rate. Donnie Huff seemed to recall having said to this fellow, "Hey," and labored under the notion that he'd heard a Hey back which Opal Criner ever so shortly corrected him about and took occasion to refresh Donnie Huff as to the actual course of events that he'd shared previously with her which clearly had not included any chat whatsoever between Donnie Huff's own vented essence and the tall, handsome, bearded keeper of the heavenly portal who'd indeed lifted and wagged his fingers but otherwise had merely stood in the thick misty shaft of light that had created as it fell upon him a highly dramatic effect which Opal Criner attempted with a look to insinuate the nature of for the benefit of Donnie Huff who watched his loving wife's mother endeavor with her lively facial features alone to communicate "backlit" and impart "behaloed" though he deciphered her contortions to be largely an uncontrollable by-product of the Salisbury steak they'd taken together for dinner which was demonstrating in Donnie Huff's own stomach an inclination to travel and churn.

The Reverend Mr. Worrell, eager to cut to the very heart of the matter, sought to know from Donnie Huff if who he'd seen was in fact the Savior and Donnie Huff had to believe it was and revealed as much to the Reverend Mr. Worrell who managed, through skillful interrogation, to prompt from Donnie Huff a highly detailed description of the portalkeeper, an account of His various features and traits that accumulated and accrued in the mind of Mrs. Norma Baines into the very image of Jeffrey Hunter who, ever since *King of Kings,* had been the Lord she'd prayed to and invoked. Understandably, Mrs. Norma Baines grew tempted towards infusement at the thought of an actual dashing sort of a Christ and contributed to the proceedings by means of a little cry, a modest and semispontaneous exclamation pretty much of the sort Miss Cindy Womble had been meaning shortly to loose herself as a show of polite but thoroughgoing fervor. But with her own little cry anticipated and usurped, Miss Cindy Womble altered her plans and gave voice instead to a kind of a yelp that produced in Mrs. Gloria Hawks such noticeable consternation that she could not help but make herself a noise, which touched off Mr. Troy Haven back of her who, taking occasion of the general disturbance, ventured forth with a dreadfully inappropriate inquiry on the topic of heavenly raiments, an inquiry that Mrs. Olive Haven managed to foreshorten with a yelp of her own.

There was about, then, clear indication of genuine spiritual electricity and Donnie Huff, meaning to galvanize the classmates further still, told how he seemed to recall that the fingers of that Christ of the portal, the very ones He'd fairly completely raised and shifted about, had come to be lowered, had come to be extended, and had come at last to lay upon Donnie Huff's own forearm, "Just here," Donnie Huff told to the Reverend Mr. Worrell and indicated a downy patch of skin shy of his elbow, a downy patch he flexed and taunted and rendered as ripply as he might prior to indicating it once further for the benefit in particular of Miss Cindy Womble who took occasion to voice at last the little cry she'd been kept previously from voicing and did so with such tantalizing abandon as to set Donnie Huff casting about for a thing that Christ might have said, a stirring variety of observation designed to render in particular Miss Cindy Womble breathy and flushed. Opal Criner, however, appeared to sense his inclination and made for the benefit of Donnie Huff a wholly dyspeptic sort of a face that she showed earnestly to him, a grave and flatulent variety of expression meant to indicate to Donnie Huff just what sort of exchanges plainly constituted chat which Donnie Huff quite naturally failed to decipher and so learned shortly in so many words from his loving wife's mother how he'd come in fact around before Christ could tell to him anything much worth repeating.

"I come around?" Donnie Huff said and entertained from Opal Criner a stern and confirming nod that he could not well mistake. "I come around," he told to the Reverend Mr. Worrell, speaking briefly behind it of the fingers that had surely lain upon the downy patch and the lips that had parted as if for speech.

"But you awoke," the reverend said and Donnie Huff confessed forlornly hooterwards, "Yeah. I awoke."

Getting snatched back to life through the ether from the stoop of the heavenly portal quite naturally bore some speaking of, but talk of the creekwater Donnie Huff had spit up and the organs he'd likely strained in addition to the skidder he'd been made to winch and upend did not stir the classmates after any detectable fashion, elicited no cries and discharges, and inspired only a solitary inquiry from Mr. Troy Haven who'd mistakenly suspected that the size of the winchmotor was a topic of interest to him until Mrs. Olive Haven had convinced him that it wasn't. It was all of it, however, better even than chicken in a sesame cream sauce which the Bible classmates agreed unanimously about and so joined with enthusiasm the Reverend Mr. Worrell in applauding Donnie Huff back to his pew where Opal Criner appeared to have effected a full and complete recovery from her acute female complaint and so was able to greet her Donald with befitting enthusiasm and announced for anybody that cared to hear it how he'd married previously her own child Marie.

As was his inclination and calling, the Reverend Mr. Worrell paraphrased for the Bible classmates most everything they'd just left off hearing from Donnie Huff while enlarging himself upon the bulk of the tale so as to illuminate the significant passages for those of his Wednesday evening flock who were perhaps not by nature so extraordinarily probing and incisive as he'd been blessed himself with a knack for. Of course the reverend wondered as well rhetorically what lessons a fellow might take from Donnie Huff's own episode which Mr. Troy Haven suspected briefly he had himself a notion about until he got straightaway corrected by Mrs. Olive Haven and so listened along with everybody otherwise to the lessons precisely a fellow might take and the assorted snatches of scripture he might best explain to himself his lessons with, snatches of scripture which Mrs. Ray Truitt and Miss Cindy Womble and Mr. Larry Baines contributed to with telling and pertinent snatches of their own that they'd cultivated over time a fondness for. Understandably, the Reverend Mr. Worrell invited the assembled classmates to join with him if they would in a prayer of thanksgiving for the deliverance of Donnie Huff who'd seen for himself the heavenly portal and spied with his own eyes the countenance divine but was likely just as pleased to have revived and recovered to enjoy further his days on this earth which Donnie Huff was meaning to endorse and welcome with ardor and enthusiasm, but the Reverend Mr. Worrell, having entered already into his praying mode, launched straightaway into a deep and resonant petition to his Father in heaven to listen if He might to the prayer of thanksgiving which ensued pretty shortly and endured for longer than seemed to Donnie Huff polite.

With the keenly anticipated but ever so eventual amen, the formal portion of the Wednesday evening Bible class ended and the informal, wholly unexpected part of it struck up, unexpected anyhow for Donnie Huff who was not accustomed to serving personally as a source of admiration, had not ever previously enjoyed the opportunity to induce moderate infusement and get congratulated about it by an entire Bible class that pressed round him and exhibited a collective fascination with most especially his patch of downy forearm skin which they

were all of them inclined to lay their own fingers upon. Mr.
Troy Haven was himself fairly bristling with queries and had
managed even to ask outright of Donnie Huff if it was in fact
cold up in the ether for an essence before his wife Olive removed him from the vicinity by means of a clump of his own
downy hair that she took upon between her fingers and yanked
upon. Opal Criner stood alongside Donnie Huff and proclaimed his virtues for the benefit of anybody that might care to
hear of them. She gave him out to be a sterling manner of
fellow and narrated assorted instances of unimpeachable behavior which she could not believe would ever pass entirely
from her memory. Though she'd been inordinately fond of
him for a goodly while now, Opal Criner did confess outright
that Donnie Huff's death and resuscitation had undoubtedly
served to advance him in her affections, and she told how he'd
been lately rendered by death contemplative and persuaded
Donnie Huff to apply if he might his web of skin in a pensive
sort of a way which Donnie Huff resisted straightoff but endured such agonizing perusal on account of it that he shortly
did in fact lift his hand and situate his chin as meditationally as
he guessed he was able which all the ladies but for Mrs. Gloria
Hawks found to be a handsome pose.

Donnie Huff persevered with his web of skin and his
thoughtful gaze for as long as appeared seemly to him and was
there in the midst of giving it over to a posture otherwise when
Mrs. Ray Truitt pressed forward upon him so as to tell lowly to
Donnie Huff a thing he could not well make out and would
have asked to hear once further had not Mrs. Ray Truitt punctuated her comment with a folded dollar bill that she ever so
surreptitiously slipped into Donnie Huff's palm outright where
Donnie Huff felt the thing with his fingerends, opened his hand
to look baldly upon it, and thereby undid the stealth of the
proceeding quite altogether which Mrs. Ray Truitt herself saw
plainly to be the case and so repeated for the benefit of anybody
that cared to know it, "For your ministry."

"My ministry," Donnie Huff told to her back and was so
thoroughly absorbed in gazing from the legal tender over to
Mrs. Ray Truitt in advance of shifting back to the legal tender

once more that he did not notice the veritable din of pocketbook catches as the ladies otherwise sought out tribute of their
own beyond the sort of fawning and fingerlaying they'd shown
themselves previously inclined towards. He did not truly revive
until Miss Cindy Womble had bore in frontside foremost upon
him to present Donnie Huff with a piece of folding money of
her own even though by the very proximity of the hooters
themselves Donnie Huff had already come to feel enriched.

   They hoped he might spread the tale of his vented essence
among most especially the lost and the downtrodden, the assorted unfortunates of this earth who could stand likely to hear
of one man's brush with the Lord Jesus which they all of them
confessed had, as far as tales of vented essences went, caused
them to fairly tremble in their own depths, all of them that is
but for Mrs. Gloria Hawks who was not herself so easily
plumbed and agitated which she undertook to share with Donnie Huff by means of a face she displayed and a a quarter she
donated in among the dollars in Donnie Huff's upturned hand
as she told to him simply, "Here."

   Since the gentlemen had not yet opened their wallets to him,
Donnie Huff was disposed to linger about for purposes of sopping up additional currency, but Opal Criner was herself im-
patient to make with her Donald as grand and triumphant an
exit as they might together manage before the Bible classmates
had dispersed and departed. So she took up the elbow of his
upturned and unfreighted arm, bade a general farewell back
over her shoulder, and guided Donnie Huff down the sanctuary aisle and out through the double doors onto the slab where
Donnie Huff took occasion to close his fingers about his oper-
ating funds and deposit the whole of them into his trouser
pocket prior to yielding once more to his loving wife's mother
who ushered him into the lot and fairly squired him towards
the beige Coronet under the steady perusal of a half-dozen
polled Angus beyond the one fence and a significant clutch of
Charolais beyond the other that watched Donnie Huff stand
with his loving wife's mother alongside her cardoor to no detectable purpose until his present utility dawned at last upon
him and he reached down to fling that door open.

She expected a manner of scolding, anticipated a show of at least mild reproach from her Donald who'd been plainly the object of her guile and deceit, had gotten lured unwittingly to the sanctuary, and tricked into testifying which was hardly the sort of thing her Donald would most usually endure with much grace. And likely he would have gnawed for a time on his loving wife's mother but for how his irritation had come lately to be blunted by the ever so happy combination of the sizable hooters he'd admired and the cash he'd been paid to admire them which appeared to Donnie Huff, as he started and idled the Coronet, the variety of thing that perhaps only the Lord in heaven could personally arrange. Consequently, Donnie Huff did not speak harshly to Opal Criner, did not even show to her a severe sort of face, but merely instead backed the Coronet out from between the El Camino and the hollyhock and nosed on into the street to the south towards 58. Opal Criner shifted from time to time her gaze to fall upon Donnie Huff as they gained the highway and struck out west upon it, but she could not well read his disposition and he failed to reveal to her his mood with a piece of talk since he showed a solitary inclination to chew his finger and stare blankly through the windowglass.

So they rode for a time in utter silence which Opal Criner could not sniff out the precise nature of and took for harmless, benign silence only when she did not take it for the wordless preamble to Donnie Huff's potent wrath instead like was just the sort of pastime to promote intense uneasiness in Opal Criner who collected at length sufficient spunk to observe from over against the far door how her own personal opinion of the Reverend Mr. Worrell had risen to the point where she took him now for wise and kindly almost all of the time when she had not in fact thought there at the first too terribly much of him.

As for himself, Donnie Huff did not let on to have come away from the sanctuary with much impression of the reverend at all, persisted anyhow in chewing exclusively his fingerends, and failed still to make clear the tone of his mood and intentions, discharged not even one throaty companionable sort of a noise that Opal Criner could over by the far door detect. So she was guessing he was ill likely, was figuring from lack of evidence to the contrary that he was very probably aggravated and would exhibit shortly his spleen which she was working up already her most accomplished pitiful face about when Donnie Huff withdrew his fingerend, shifted around slightly on the seat, and said to Opal Criner, "Portal?"

And shortly he heard from her, "Portal," back.

"Portal," Donnie Huff said again and shifted once more towards the windshield, stared even in brief, contemplative silence out onto the highway before he grew moved and bestirred to announce in moderately rich, deep, and singular tones, "Portal," once further that he was plainly pleased at the sound of and, spurred by his giddy sense of achievement, he reached with his thumb and his previously chewed finger for the radio knob and switched on the Big Q-mix where a man was singing of the sundry agonies of loving presently a woman he'd not somehow loved back when she'd loved him which she'd left off lately at. And Donnie Huff wondered of Opal Criner, "Ain't this world a funny place?" that Opal Criner could not hardly deny to him it was.

III

"Like this here," Donnie Huff said and provided with his upraised hands an approximation that overshot the truth quite altogether and suggested most especially to Buddy Isom the variety of creature that did not often occur in nature just up and by itself.

"Couldn't have been," Buddy Isom insisted. "Ain't no woman got such tits as those."

"Like this," Donnie Huff told to him and rendered his approximation slightly more ample still. "Seen them myself. Stared at them for the best part of an hour."

But Buddy Isom merely shook his head and expressed his doubts as to Donnie Huff's own personal grasp of human physiology, told to him anyhow, "Shit."

Alvis Nevins had known previously a woman to be blessed so, his aunt's neighbor in Mouth of Wilson who was chesty beyond belief which Alvis Nevins provided with his own upraised hands indication of that straightaway Buddy Isom objected about and proposed to Alvis Nevins how his aunt's neighbor had been very likely afflicted with some variety of imbalance that Alvis Nevins did not himself doubt since he'd evermore been mystified that she could stand upright at all which prompted from Buddy Isom a wildly ornate and exceed-

ingly animated observation that did not sound to Alvis Nevins
to have a thing in this world to do with hooters.

Little Gaither was himself partway through ingesting a
Micky cake, a squat lumpy cream-filled Micky cake with pink
icing and a grated coconut garnish that he'd swallowed some of,
was chewing some of, and was holding as well some of in his
fingers when he thought of a thing he'd heard from a fellow, a
pertinent sort of an item that he meant straightaway to share
and so announced to anybody that cared to know it how there'd
been one time this girl which came out part in breath and part
in masticated Micky cake that shot across the intervening few
feet of empty air and struck Freeman MacAfee on the back of
the hand he'd laid across his face to extract his Chesterfield
with.

"She had her some jugs," little Gaither said, "and she wasn't
hardly no proper lady," little Gaither told largely in the direction of Alvis Nevins who wanted straightaway to know from
him, "Who?"

"This girl with the jugs," little Gaither said. "She wasn't
hardly no proper lady at all."

"She was in church at Bible meeting," Alvis Nevins reminded
him and so learned precipitously from little Gaither and Buddy
Isom both how he was just presently hearing of a different
woman altogether than the one they'd been speaking previously of, inspiring little Gaither and Buddy Isom to exchange
between themselves exasperated exhalations which did not, in
the aggregate, show much trace of Micky cake at all.

"So she runs up on this boy," little Gaither said, "and he ain't
no bright light," little Gaither added and told for the benefit of
Alvis Nevins, who'd looked inquisitively upon him, "This boy.
The one she runs up on."

Little Gaither pushed the remainder of the pink coconut-
garnished Micky cake into his mouth and Freeman MacAfee
told to him, "Don't you say nothing," before little Gaither had
offered even to speak.

Alvis Nevins, who was not so terribly squeamish himself,
encouraged little Gaither to speak to him please further of that
woman with the jugs and the boy she'd run up on and conse-

quently learned straightaway from little Gaither in nearly equal parts breath and Micky cake how that woman had wanted to know of that boy if he was maybe inclined to hear some sweet music.

"He guessed he'd just as soon hear sweet music as not," little Gaither declared and told how that girl with the jugs led that boy on back off the road into the high grass and slipped shortly clean out of her dress which persuaded that fellow he could likely as not listen to what music there was with his trousers down around his ankles, didn't anyhow require them raised and fastened to appreciate a melody. "Got fairly naked himself," little Gaither said. "Shed of his shirt and shed of his pants too."

And little Gaither, not one to squander dramatic momentum once he'd gone to the trouble to manufacture it, told right-off how that girl with the jugs had cupped her hands and taken ahold as best as she was able of her pair of extravagant hooters so as to bring them most specifically to the attention of that boy she'd run up on who'd been paying them already a species of thoroughgoing and unbidden regard that he'd likely have had to get beat with a board to undo. "She told to him 'Sugar,' " little Gaither said, "told to him 'come to Momma,' " and, according to little Gaither, invited that boy to pitch on over if he might and sprawl upon her.

"He laid down fairly much atop of her," little Gaither said and told how that boy let on to be anxious to hear whatever variety of melody might come his way like was sufficient to get him informed by that girl with the jugs how he might best press his nose to her breastbone, fairly wedge his head between her enticements which she assisted him at by laying both her hands together along about his cowlick and drawing his face down flush against herself where he could not breathe with much success and failed as well to hear even the first little scrap of sweet music. He raised up shortly and told her as much once she'd grown persuaded to turn loose of him, siphoned off a measure of air and, according to little Gaither, declared to that girl how he couldn't hear a goddam thing, which troubled and confounded her there for a time until she'd paused to examine

with care their present circumstances and thereby grew illuminated. "And she says to him," little Gaither told to Alvis Nevins
and to Buddy Isom and to Donnie Huff and to Freeman Mac-
Afee too, " 'Well, it's no wonder. You ain't plugged in,' " that
little Gaither himself grew straightaway transported by the general hilarity of and wheezed and spurted and dredged and
coughed and aired assorted Micky cake he'd already in fact
eaten and commenced to digest.

They guessed they all of them could stand to hear a little
ditty themselves and spoke by turns of enticements they'd previously had the pleasure of wedging their heads between which
led eventually to the topic of Curtis Tilly's sister Maylease who
they unanimously agreed had likely played on her own more
sweet music than Guy Lombardo and Lawrence Welk put together. As for himself, Alvis Nevins guessed he could talk of
hooters all the day and was anxious to hear further of Donnie
Huff's acquaintance of the evening previous, who Alvis Nevins
indicated and described with his own uplifted hands that Donnie Huff corrected him about since she'd not after all been a
milkcow.

"She had on this blouse with pleats in the front of it," Donnie Huff said and explained most especially to Alvis Nevins how
those pleats had unfolded with every breath she'd drawn and
recreased with every exhalation. "It got my notice," Donnie
Huff allowed, "right there from the getgo."

For the sake of clarity and his own peace of mind, Buddy
Isom interrupted to learn from Donnie Huff if he had in fact
been standing with a preacher before a Bible class watching a
woman's blousefront and entertaining most probably impure if
not highly contaminated thoughts and impulses that Donnie
Huff considered, contemplated plainly upon, prior to admitting to Buddy Isom, "I was."

"Well what kind of holy man are you?" Buddy Isom wanted
to know and so heard straightaway from Donnie Huff back how
he was himself surely all man but only part holy which fairly
much satisfied and appeased Buddy Isom who inquired after
the size of the pleats which Donnie Huff suggested to be
broader certainly than any pleats he'd ever seen a woman, without the benefit of her fingers, unfold.

"What church is this anyhow?" Freeman MacAfee asked of Donnie Huff who pointed sort of off and up at nowhere much and told to Freeman MacAfee, "Church out towards Laurel Fork somewhere. They got this picture of Jesus with a duck."

"A duck?" Freeman MacAfee said and heard from Donnie Huff how it very likely might have been a sheep instead. He couldn't anyhow say for certain it wasn't since he'd been there on the sanctuary floor while that creature was up wandering the barren waste back of the Lord and Savior.

Alvis Nevins suggested to Donnie Huff that it had perhaps been a swan off back of Jesus on the barren waste since he seemed to recall a tale in the Bible about the Lord and a swan, recalled anyhow that there was one though he could not conjure up the various elements and circumstances of it but for Jesus and but for the swan itself.

Little Gaither for his part felt obliged to express his surprise at Alvis Nevins's acquaintance with the scriptures since little Gaither had never previously seen Alvis Nevins take up and peruse any printed matter that had not been published by the World Wrestling Federation. Alvis Nevins, however, hastened to inform little Gaither that he'd been in his youth a manner of biblical scholar and was still well acquainted with the tales and episodes of the Testament and he spoke briefly, at the insistence of little Gaither, of the story of Esau's brother's shoes which he had to figure was still his favorite yarn from the Good Book even if he could not recall presently what had become of the shoes of Esau's brother who he was under the distinct impression had been named Grady which little Gaither ever so precipitously ridiculed Alvis Nevins about since he was well certain himself that the brother of Esau who owned the shoes had been named Monroe instead.

Buddy Isom, who did not enter often into theological debate, expressed himself as doubtful that there was talk in the Bible anywhere of Esau's brother's shoes since he guessed he would recall it himself having been reared summers in Bible school at his momma and daddy's church in Indian Gap where he'd become quite intimately acquainted with the Testaments. He recollected plain enough the episode of Caleb's trousers, Caleb being of course the least boy of Jephthah that naturally went, little Gaither and Alvis Nevins let on, without saying. Buddy Isom could as well conjure up without much effort the lengthsome and altogether thorny narrative of the travels of Abigail, an outcast who had at one time been married herself to Esau's father's brother, but he could not for the life of him resurrect much of Esau at all, like incited Alvis Nevins to contort his face in a show of undiluted concentration from which he reaped very shortly the benefits and was able to inform Buddy Isom and little Gaither both how he remembered now that Esau had been set upon in the night by what he'd taken for common ne'er-do-wells and had been robbed of his shoes only to discover his brother Grady stomping about the house in them the following morning, his brother Grady who'd plainly coveted Esau's footwear that he'd stolen for his own. The lesson of the thing seemed apparent enough to Alvis Nevins who did not trouble himself to formulate and express it but ventured only to speak once further of the palpable profit he had gained from his exposure to the tale of Esau's shoes back in the days of his callow youth when he was not hardly so penetrating as lately he'd become.

"A man can do worse than study the Bible," Alvis Nevins proclaimed and anticipated that he would likely on this occasion go quite utterly unchallenged and so was surprised to hear straightaway from Freeman MacAfee an opinion to the contrary.

"My brother Frank reads the Bible most every night," Freeman MacAfee informed particularly Alvis Nevins. "Ain't done a thing for him. I hadn't ever known a bigger asshole. He'll shit all over a fellow and turn around and cite a verse at him."

Of course Alvis Nevins allowed how there was evermore that sort that would patently abuse the scriptures, but he suggested to Freeman MacAfee that perhaps he should share with Frank his brother a pertinent passage that Alvis Nevins had been since his youth acutely fond of and which sounded, in Alvis Nevin's richly intoned rendition, to have a thing to do with the goodly hearts of some men that well nigh gleamed and glimmered like carbuncles scattered upon a sundrenched patch of ground.

"Yeah, I'll run home and tell him all about it," Freeman MacAfee assured Alvis Nevins in advance of extracting his Chesterfield and flicking it into a tirerut half full of murky iridescent rainwater.

Donnie Huff, who had sat by in silence savoring in part his poignant memories of the extravagant hooters and absorbing as well some measure of the local discussion, volunteered for the profit of anybody who might care to know it how there were crowns of righteousness laid up in the kingdom of heaven to be claimed upon the last day in that final hour by the worthy and the blessed, told it in the tone of voice he expected his own wife's mother might use though with a considerably deeper pitch than she could likely muster. He added beyond it brief mention of the root and the offspring of David and the water of life to be taken freely prior to citing as well the Lord's own wry and revealing admission from the Book, he proclaimed, of Revelation where the world came to a fiery end and those people who did not rise with their hearts like carbuncles into heaven descended into the unwholesome depths of hell instead so as to burn and rot for all eternity.

And little Gaither informed Donnie Huff, "I'm eating lunch here," and set about uncellophaning his glazed dunking sticks which he did not mean to take with talk of damnation and the putrid fires of hell but was hoping instead they could get on back to jugs pretty straightaway that it seemed to him a shame they'd departed in the first place from.

But Buddy Isom inquired of Donnie Huff, "So you told those folks about damnation?" that did not have truly a chesty thing to it which little Gaither insinuated with a grunt and then yielded directly to Freeman MacAfee who'd had an uncle to burn in hell. "Last thing he said in this life was 'cocksucker,'" Freeman MacAfee told most especially to Donnie Huff and suggested beyond it how a man probably couldn't hope to die with "cocksucker" on his lips and then fly off to the open arms of Jesus which Donnie Huff detected the sense of and announced in his own wife's mother's tone he did.

"Now who'd want to sit still to hear about hell from you?" Buddy Isom asked of Donnie Huff who confessed how he'd not truly loitered much upon the subject of damnation but had shared chiefly the tale of his own unfortunate accident which consisted in the majority of the plummet from the bluff, the ensuing respirational difficulties and accompanying little green spots, followed by the thoroughgoing recovery which Buddy Isom and Alvis Nevins and Freeman MacAfee agreed they were gratified to hear of but did not find much at all in the way of fascinating. "Well, there's people that do," Donnie Huff shared with them and he asked of the pack of them together if they'd ever between them one time seen sunlight fall in misty shafts and beams upon the earth after such a fashion as to touch them deeply to their very cores and essences that they could not recall among them even a solitary instance of. "Well," Donnie Huff insisted, "there's people that has."

"Shafts and beams," Alvis Nevins said to Buddy Isom who himself said to Donnie Huff, "Shafts and beams."

"Yes sir," Donnie Huff told to him and inquired beyond it who maybe they might see fit to consult were they planning a trip to Richmond and had never previously visited the place which sounded to Alvis Nevins ever so suspiciously hypothetical and so rendered him straightaway testy and ill and prompted him to inform Donnie Huff how he did not personally have any business in Richmond to speak of and could not anticipate the occasion for any business there in the future like would give him no need to enter into consultation with anybody at all which he'd only just culminated and left off at when little Gaither supposed, with a complementary smattering of ballistical dunking stick, that he'd talk to somebody who'd been there which Alvis Nevins objected about since little Gaither had not even in the first place been inquired at.

"And if you're bound to get dead sometime or another," Donnie Huff said, "who is it you might want to hear from?"

"Some fellow who's been to Richmond," Freeman MacAfee told to him in advance of exhibiting his teeth for anybody who might care to look upon them.

"So what is it you know about being dead?" Buddy Isom asked of Donnie Huff who informed him straightaway back, "Doesn't much matter as long as you've heard already I've been it and know for certain you haven't."

"All right then," Alvis Nevins said to Donnie Huff, "you been killed. You been green all over. Go on and tell to us what it's like to be dead. Go on."

And Donnie Huff, who drew off at his leisure a breath of air and at his leisure released it, lifted his palpably reverential gaze towards the treetops and presently announced for anybody who might care to know it, "Being dead is pretty much like being alive only your balls never itch," which inspired little Gaither, not by nature a man of faith, to proclaim in breath and confection together, "Take me, sweet Jesus!"

There naturally ensued the possibility that the conversation would veer off beyond retrieval into an intimate and highly anecdotal regional history of chafing but little Gaither, who chewed and ingested the remainder of his last dunking stick, interrupted his own account of a fairly hellish rash he'd contracted so as to wonder of Freeman MacAfee if he was meaning to eat the half a sandwich that had merely lain for a while now atop of his flattened lunchsack. "I can't say I much want it," Freeman MacAfee told to him, "but I'd rather choke it on down myself than have you spit it all over me," which greatly troubled little Gaither and he voiced his growing displeasure with Freeman MacAfee who reviled little Gaither back and various of the bloodkin of little Gaither as well like earned for Freeman MacAfee a spate of unrestrained abuse which culminated in an assault on the half a sandwich that Freeman MacAfee undertook to contest but came shortly to get by little Gaither vanquished quite entirely, little Gaither who raised the battered trophy to his lips and ate heartily of it.

Alvis Nevins was himself a little curious about being dead since he'd rented lately a movie from Shirley's #2 in Cana on the topic of a man who'd come back from the beyond so as to plague his widow and his widow's boyfriend. They'd not seemed to him, in the course of the film, sufficiently terrified the way he had to figure he'd probably be terrified himself had his new girlfriend's dead husband come calling to throw geegaws at him and upend the couch. Little Gaither, with only the merest contribution from his semimasticated sandwich, sought to discover from Alvis Nevins if that widow had herself been in possession of a pair of those sizable antigravitational Hollywood hooters and Alvis Nevins paused to cast back and reflect prior to apprising little Gaither that her hooters on the movie box had been sizable and antigravitational both, but once he'd seen her in life it was plain to him that the box artist had overapproximated.

"They'll do that," Freeman MacAfee told to Alvis Nevins and to little Gaither both and spoke further of a movie he'd been baited by a highly optimistic bit of artwork to rent and carry home, a movie about the queen of some Amazon women on an island somewhere, carnivorous Amazon women that dined primarily on the genitalia of unfortunate sailors lured shoreward by the beauty of the tribe and the radiant splendor of the queen herself who'd looked on the boxfront inordinately sinewy and svelte but had obviously packed away lately too awful many genitalia for her own good. She'd gotten fat and she'd gotten homely and Freeman MacAfee supposed, were that Amazon queen to come up the track towards his house, he'd loose his dogs on her. "Ain't any good movies about Amazons anymore," Freeman MacAfee announced for anybody that might care to know it and ever so wanly shook his head from side to side as he plucked a Chesterfield out from the pack in his shirtpocket, and squeezed it back into the round.

Donnie Huff volunteered how the world had come lately to seem to him a mean and a sorry place and declared how it appeared to him that wasn't anybody much acquainted anymore with what's tasteful and fine that Alvis Nevins straightaway threw in with and spoke directly of a boy he knew who was trash and a girl he kept company with who'd toured the country on her back. "Wouldn't no decent man touch her with a pole," Alvis Nevins said but heard directly from Buddy Isom and Freeman MacAfee together who'd both interrupted that girl in her travels and touched her after a fashion with poles themselves.

"Well then, you ain't no better than she is," Alvis Nevins told to them but Buddy Isom on behalf of himself and Freeman MacAfee demonstrated back that a young girl like that who'd embarked upon a career needed all the local patronage she could drum up and so had persuaded the both of them into acts of selfless generosity.

"Four," Freeman MacAfee boasted though Buddy Isom could not himself believe that there were sufficient hours in a day for Freeman MacAfee to be successfully selfless so many times as that.

"Four," Freeman MacAfee insisted and confessed in particular to Donnie Huff, "Talk about supine, there's one girl that surely knows how to be it."

"She's probably got everything but the pink eye," Alvis Nevins told to Freeman MacAfee and guessed, while even though he was pretty severely fond of the women himself and they were plainly fond of him back, he could not help but wish there was more to his life than ceaseless romance and innumerable instances of his own personal selfless discharges. He guessed he'd like just one time to get somehow transported by something other than the tits on a woman though couldn't Buddy Isom or Freeman MacAfee or little Gaither make out between them why.

"I met this cow once," Alvis Nevins said, "walking down the road. It'd got loose and was coming the one way and I was going the other. We met up on that cement bridge over the fork and that damn cow stopped and looked at me like I never hope to have a cow look at me again." And Alvis Nevins cut his eyes and slowly picked up his head in an attempt to indicate just how precisely he'd been gazed upon. "I got fairly uneasy," Alvis Nevins said. "God knows I've done many a shameful thing but hadn't yet done nothing a cow should know about. He drove me right off that cement bridge. I couldn't get away from that place fast enough."

"What in the hell are you talking about?" Freeman MacAfee, on behalf of Buddy Isom and little Gaither, inquired.

"I don't know," Alvis Nevins said. "I just come here and saw all the day and then go home and me and Daddy eat supper and me and Daddy watch tv and me and Daddy fall asleep and I get up and come back here. Doesn't hardly seem like enough alone. Got to be a thing back of it somewhere."

"A cow?" Buddy Isom wanted to know.

And Donnie Huff intervening for Alvis Nevins, told to Buddy Isom, "Uh uh," told to him, "No." He admitted for anybody that cared to hear it how he'd been made jittery by live-stock himself, had entertained from dumb beasts significant and telling glances which put him in mind of a time not too awful long past when he'd been troubled and low, had gotten somehow distressed and tribulated and had determined to provide his assorted afflictions with an airing, had carted them up the road and struck out with them across a pasture where he'd just wandered about for a spell wallowing in his dark mood and feeling surely a pitiful soul on this earth. Ahead of him he noticed spotted cows mingling together high up the slope and they all of them raised their heads and heaved about to study Donnie Huff like Donnie Huff had to figure he would certainly have grown a little uneasy himself on account of but for the shafts and beams of sunlight that broke before him through the clouds and fell upon the cattle and fell upon the ryegrass and the dandelions about them all thick and misty and golden.

"Touched me, boys," Donnie Huff said, "clear down to my essence. Healed my sick heart."

"Shafts and beams," Freeman MacAfee declared once he'd extracted his Chesterfield, and he heard straightaway from Buddy Isom, "Spotted cows," after which a bout of earnest contemplation ensued that itself provided little Gaither the opportunity to announce for anybody who cared to know it, "Hell, I might never eat beef again," and he considered briefly his remaining scrap of Vienna sausage sandwich prior to informing most especially Freeman MacAfee, "Surely ain't had none lately."

"I know what you mean," Alvis Nevins told to Donnie Huff. "I know just what you mean exactly," and he was intending to enlarge upon his own mystical encounter that he guessed had bore deep and struck essence itself but he came to be prevented from it by Donnie Huff who reached through the slit in his coveralls and withdrew from his trouser pocket six dollar bills and one piece of silver which he exhibited together upon his open hand in advance of airing in his deep and biblical tones, "Sweet Jesus, boys. How about a little something for the ministry."

"They give you that?" Buddy Isom wanted to know.

"They did," Donnie Huff told to him.

"Just because you was dead and they weren't?"

"Seems so," Donnie Huff admitted, though shortly he allowed how he'd probably stirred them with his presentation. "Whipped them up, don't you know."

"She give you one?" little Gaither inquired.

"Aw yeah," Donnie Huff told to him.

"What one?"

And Donnie Huff uncreased the bills and lifted them singly to his nose where he sniffed and sampled their aromas that had not come yet to be contaminated altogether by the trousers and the coveralls and the stink of sweat and engine oil. He settled shortly upon one bill in particular and savored the bouquet of it, waved the thing before his nostrils, and snorted its fragrant scent. "Sweet as the flowers in June," he told to little Gaither and gave over to him the bill itself that little Gaither appeared in some danger of introducing full into his nasal passages but was spared the trauma of it by Freeman MacAfee who snatched free the dollar and laid it against his own face, that little Gaither and Buddy Isom watched him at while, for his part, Alvis Nevins gazed with noticeably less delirium upon Donnie Huff alone who declared presently, "Like this here," and provided with his upraised hands an inordinate approximation.

ii

He hadn't looked much of a prize to her. She recalled how she'd hardly been taken with him straightoff and wouldn't probably have spoken even to him but for Charlene her girlfriend who'd been at the time smitten with the Goad on the hood alongside him and had persuaded Marie to step with her over to the vehicle so that she might tell to that Goad, "Hey Gary," and prompt maybe a "Hey Charlene" back. He was laying, she recalled, against the windshield with his bootbottoms uplifted, sprawled there upon the hood of that red Chevrolet and he eyed her, Marie remembered, pretty much all over while her girlfriend Charlene made chat with Gary Goad and appeared, besmitten like she was and noticeably giddy from infatuation,

inclined to linger in the lot. But Marie at last drew her away
from Gary Goad and fairly hauled her on off towards the roller
rink where they rented together their skates and found themselves a place to sit and lace them. Naturally Charlene was anxious to hear from Marie if wasn't in fact Gary Goad just the
dreamiest thing in pants, and Marie allowed how he was maybe
a little dreamy but she did not suppose she cared much at all for
his buddy who she conjured up there against the windshield
with his bootbottoms uplifted while she entertained briefly
upon her features only a passably disgusted expression that her
girlfriend Charlene might likely have taken some notice of but
for the quandary she'd dropped into over her socks as she
could not decide whether to wear them rolled down to her
skatetops or pulled up to her knees, could not somehow determine, were she Gary Goad, which she would prefer.

Though it had given lately way to an all-weather flea market, the roller rink at Woodlawn had been in its day a sizable
sort of an item with a concession stand at the frontend alongside the skate window and ample murky recesses at the farend
where couples with an urge and an inclination might cloak
themselves in the shadows. Marie recalled how the rink itself
had been oval and hardwood and received every spring four
new coats of gym finish which kept the wood itself so awfully far
from the skatewheels as to be entirely out of harm's way and
provided as well high adventure in a fall since a skater could
skid and slide on his backside truly extraordinary distances
across the varnish. A Mr. D. W. Montgomery, up from Sparta
on a Masonic outing, had undertaken once a pirouette for the
benefit of Mrs. D. W. Montgomery who had voiced loudly her
reservations as to her husband's talent for pirouetting. According to firsthand accounts, Mr. D. W. Montgomery of Sparta had
accelerated about the rink to an altogether reckless velocity and
then had leapt, after a fashion, into the air and had landed
pretty shortly upon the seat of his trousers which, in combination with the gym finish, allowed for the transformation of Mr.
D. W. Montgomery's momentum from lift back to thrust and he
advanced off from the rink altogether, slid between two
benches, bumped across the threshold, and gained the porch

where he slipped beneath the bottom rail and came straight-away to be deposited in a clump of bleeding heart that he could not manage to bestir himself to depart from and so merely laid there in the shrubbery looking up at the eave of the porch roof and listening to the advancing clump and clatter of Mrs. D. W. Montgomery's skatewheels as she gingerly stepped out through the doorway and across the porch floor so as to lean over the rail and wonder of Mr. D. W. Montgomery if hadn't she told to him he couldn't pirouette.

Of course the women took some pretty nasty spills them-selves, but they were most usually the sorts of spills to cause their skirt and dressends to get cast up over their heads, thereby freeing their uncloaked thighs to catch against the varnish and bring them to a precipitous and fairly immodest halt, though every now and again one of them would show the poor judg-ment to rock back on her spinal column and slip and slide about the rink with her legs in the air and her dresshem flapping up against her earlobes. It was this sort of indiscretion that a group of local gentlemen were themselves most intensely partial to, and they collected Friday nights and Saturday nights on a pair of benches against the west wall where they smoked and yam-mered and razzed and lied and boasted when they did not have occasion instead to debate the finer qualities of ladies' lingerie once an instance of it passed before them on the rink floor with the lady herself still in residence.

Naturally there were graceful sorts as well. Marie Criner had never personally been one of them and her girlfriend Charlene rolled about the rink with all the native polish and ease of a dinghy in a gale, but there were generally in atten-dance people quite well beyond falling and sliding, those that could skate with velocity frontwards and spin right around and skate with velocity backwards as well, those that could leap and sail through the air, those that could even pirouette without calamity. And then, of course, there were the Pardues, Wade and Lenora Pardue, who showed up regularly at the rink out-side Woodlawn and put on for their own distraction a most extravagant and enchanting sort of an exhibition.

They'd gotten from somewhere skating costumes. Wade's

was black chiefly. His stretch pants anyhow were black and his
short little jacket was black as well though his shirt beneath it
was the boldest variety of red as was his sash which he wore like
a belt roundabout his waist after a fashion that was not in fact
locally customary. Lenora's costume was black mostly too, appeared to be a full-length body stocking interrupted midway up
by a flouncy ruffle that laid somewhat like a skirt and stuck out
somewhat like a parasol and was striped round in bands of
vibrant yellow and green. Unfortunately, Lenora had lately
yielded up to time and Nabisco her bodysuit sort of a body and
Wade had himself accumulated the manner of gut that even a
short jacket and a red sash in combination could not well contain, so they did not look together maybe so dashing and elegant as perhaps once previously they had but they were a
curious enough sight nonetheless and most usually came to be
fairly widely remarked once they'd rolled onto the rink.

The odd thing was that they were not the sort of people that
anybody much expected to wear sashes and flouncy ruffles except maybe in the sanctity of their own home where folks
roundabout allowed that a man and a woman could do whatever it was they pleased for their own amusement as long as it
did not carry them out into the yard. Wade Pardue worked for
the agricultural extension agency, tested for alkalinity in soil
and recommended sprays for mites and aphids and identified
funguses and sought out the sources of blights. He was a regular sort of a fellow and drove a green Toyota truck that the
roadsalt had gnawed on pretty extensively, while Lenora herself was active in the ladies' circle at the Methodist church and
volunteered her time at the office at the middle school where
she'd demonstrated all along considerable competence but had
yet to exhibit the flair for drama that would put a woman in a
body stocking and a black striped flouncy skirt out where somebody other than blood kin might see her. So there was little
chance then that anybody much who did not frequent the roller
rink outside Woodlawn could have well imagined the sight of
Wade and Lenora Pardue striking together a pose on the varnished floor, standing stock still in a variety of stylized embrace,
Wade clutching Lenora just above her flounces and Lenora

herself laid divinely back with her neck extended and her chin uplifted and her fingers raised ever so artfully into the air in preparation for the commencement of their endeavor.

There was music at the roller rink from a jukebox, and Marie Criner recalled how Mac Davis had been an object of extravagant affection among the ladies who fed their quarters and punched his buttons routinely when they were not feeling of a disposition for some variety of intensely funky item instead and so would key up perhaps the BeeGees who were succeeding along about then at turning adenoids into gold. Mr. Sherman Moser, who lived nearby and often stopped off to watch what lingerie might skid past him, showed a partiality towards Mr. Eddy Arnold himself, who was well represented on the roller rink machine, in addition to Miss Patti Page and Mr. Hank Snow who seemed to him to provide quite suitable lingerie-watching melodies. There did not, however, emanate from the jukebox too awfully many graceful strains, too terribly much lilting music that a man with a sash and a woman with a flouncy ruffle might skate interpretively to with their hands sweeping gracefully through the air and that look of glorious anguishment upon their faces which people in sashes and flouncy ruffles are oftentimes prone to display. But then Mr. Wade and Mrs. Lenora Pardue did not themselves seem to hear the music that everybody else heard. They manufactured somehow their own beat to swirl and swoop by and could circle together backwards in the most elegant and seemly configurations no matter what sort of clamor somebody might have paid their two bits to hear.

The management regularly saw fit to break up the free skating with a quarter hour here and there of men only and a quarter hour of women only and a passage of counterclockwise skating for everybody together in advance of a full thirty minutes for couples alone when the pride of the roller rink, an inordinately sizable ball on the ceiling tiled over with scant pieces of mirror glass, would come to be illuminated and rotated and thereby cast a lowly and shattered sort of a light that fell upon the floor and traveled about the walls and suggested to some people warm and flickering romance while reminding

others of assorted inner ear complaints. There were not usually
too very many genuine couples among the crowd though there
was no shortage of tentative incipient attachments—girls that
wanted to be couples with boys that wanted to be couples back
but lacked somehow the resolve to inquire after the disposition
of any solitary young woman and instead frittered away their
considerable hormonal energy standing about in gaggles and
groups hooting and yelping in a highly fabricated sort of a way
at nothing in particular. So only the verifiable sweethearts
skated under the rotating glass ball and the husbands and the
wives of a mood for it in addition to the Pardues who could
evermore themselves make the very most of shattered and lowly
light.

Nobody could figure where they'd learned to skate, how
they'd cultivated such flair and show. There was talk about that
they they'd traveled in their youths with an extravaganza on ice,
but people who'd known them could not recall Lenora or Wade
either one running off to get attached to an extravaganza like
they had to guess would have undoubtedly stuck with them.
They would assume an embrace, a contortional sort of a pose
that they'd hold together for several counts in advance of striking out in a coordinated circuit of the rink for purposes of
gaining the manner of momentum Lenora especially required
for her layback when she would, with the graceful support of
her husband Wade, arch herself over backwards so far as to put
her flouncy ruffled skirt almost perpendicular to the floor. It
was the kind of feat the bulk of women her age would have
required a chiropractor to undo, but Lenora evermore got
snatched upright by Wade alone who would heft her up and
tote her about for a time on the crook of his arm prior to
steadying himself to fling her back onto the rink when Lenora
would manage a circuit or two upon the wheels of merely one
skate alone while Wade himself held to the other uplifted one
and steered her by it. Wade got to spin and dip a little himself
and showed a marked partiality for a vigorous variety of splayfooted leap in which he was somewhat constrained by his accumulated gut that tended to slip out from under his short jacket
and sag indecorously over his sash. Chiefly, though, Wade's task

was to set off Lenora to her best effect, which called for some considerable arm sweeping and occasional leg holding coupled with the instinctive judgment to know at just what moment precisely Lenora might best be retrieved upright and thereby snatched from the jaws of a crippling disaster.

Of course Lenora and Wade were by themselves an odd enough sort of a sight but once they got joined and augmented by couples otherwise who lurched and veered fairly wildly about the rink while the countless luminous shards of romantic light circulated in the opposite direction, they became by contrast even more curious still, and Marie recalled how by the time she had this night approached the rail so as to lend her full regard to the Pardues, they had assumed together their stylized embrace with Lenora laid elegantly back and Wade holding to her just above her flouncy ruffle. Wade himself had already this evening adopted his look of glorious anguishment that caught straightoff Marie's notice as she liked a man who could be openly anguished in the company of his woman, and she turned about to wonder of her girlfriend Charlene if wasn't she herself partial to men that could work up some anguishment, but Charlene was quite busy still gauging what reception her socks might receive were Gary Goad, the dreamiest thing in pants, to step in from the lot and see them. Consequently, Marie Criner alone watched the Pardues circle about the rink, a pocket of graceful calm in the riot of the free skate which went clockwise for a time and counterclockwise for a time and gave way presently to the low broken circulating light and couples exclusively who lurched and wallowed and veered and crashed but for Wade and but for Lenora who, with fingers extended and postures contortional, glided together around the rink after a fashion that suggested to Marie Criner the sheerest sort of loveliness all gauzy and tender that a man and that a woman might endeavor together to create.

She was growing even a little transported at the sight of them clutching stylishly to each other when they were not spinning or leaping or looking from a short distance with palpable longing into each other's faces instead. It was just the sort of showy pageant to stir Marie Criner's girlish affections, and she

was caught up baldly in the romance of the Pardues before her
when Gary Goad did in fact step in from the lot and discovered
Charlene pondering with unaccountable absorption her sockcuffs which allowed Gary Goad to slip undetected up alongside
her and gaze upon her sockcuffs as well.

His buddy, who'd stepped in from the lot himself, guessed
at Gary Goad he might go on ahead and skate which he guessed
once further at Charlene who told to him, "Hey," and told to
him, "Donnie," prior to indicating for his benefit her girlfriend
Marie Criner over by the rail where the circulating Pardues,
with the flecks of light playing upon their dramatic black out-
fits, held her fairly much in their thrall. Donnie Huff picked up
a pair of skates at the window, shiny black skates that he laced
tight and knotted double prior to rising from the bench to
determine how his dungaree cuffs laid upon his skatetops that
suited him well enough he supposed, did not prevent him anyhow from setting out himself towards the rail, striking out on a
course for the comely posterior that he meant to swoop in and
settle alongside of, but Donnie Huff had truly never been much
accomplished at swooping or, more to the point, he could in
fact swoop well enough but could not hardly leave off at it when
he chose to. So Donnie Huff worked up a little momentum and
approached Marie Criner obliquely from off to her right, meaning to ease in alongside her but failing somehow to manage to
swerve like carried Donnie Huff on past the posterior and beyond the rail to the far wall where he braked himself with his
entire frontside together and set about calculating a new route
to swoop along.

He passed her going the other way and gained the far
reaches of the rink where he collided with an Utt who he'd not,
he explained, been intending to swoop in upon which that Utt
seemed well enough disposed to believe and assisted Donnie
Huff with a shove that Donnie Huff very nearly made triumphant use of as he succeeded at strafing Marie Criner's comely
backside but could not discover a graceful way to swing about
and stop like left him to proceed into the wall he'd collided with
once already. For her part, Marie Criner was admiring most
particularly Lenora Pardue's elegant finger placement which

she endeavored now and again to mimic with fingers of her own that she was pretty thoroughly involved in an instance of, was making that is to pluck an imaginary plum-sized sort of an item from an imaginary limb after the fashion she'd just lately seen Lenora pluck herself, when Donnie Huff, who'd determined to give over swooping for a less graceful but very likely more effective sort of a tactic, arrived at the rail alongside her, beat that is directly against it and careened off of it but managed to catch ahold of the thing with his fingers and thereby snatch himself off his feet.

He'd worked up a thing to say, a variety of salutation that he'd meant to air upright but went ahead and loosed in a heap. He told to Marie Criner, "Hey doll," from the hardwood that straightaway appeared to render Marie Criner's assorted features quite harmoniously nauseated and she displayed them briefly at Donnie Huff so that he might calculate his effect upon her and then returned herself to the contemplation of Wade and Lenora who were performing at that moment a taxing species of maneuver which called for Lenora to fall blindly back into the clutches of her Wade who she trusted to catch her at the armpits and who did in fact catch her pretty much at the armpits alone in advance of guiding Lenora about the rink, steering and propelling her around the oval while Lenora lifted her fingers and plucked and tugged gracefully at scant bits of empty air.

Donnie Huff climbed presently to his feet and managed to stand without incident alongside Marie Criner who did not let on to be at all aware of him until he declared his "Hey doll" upright which was how he'd intended in the first place to air it and earned thereby one nauseated look further that Donnie Huff flattered himself to find considerably less nauseated than the one prior to it. He was meaning to utter the next suave and manly item that popped into his head and had swung somewhat about so as to allow Marie Criner the pleasure of gazing upon his rugged profile while a suave manly item came to him, but he caught sight straightoff of the Pardues who he was not himself acquainted with and so demonstrated quite naturally a curiosity about them, inquired of Marie Criner, "Who in the hell is that?"

in a tone that did not suggest to her a proper regard for the grace and for the elegance and for the stylish fingerwork.

Understandably she snubbed him straightoff, first took occasion to advise him what trash he was but snubbed him just back of it. She turned away from him and openly admired Wade and Lenora which Donnie Huff watched her at and figured how he'd best find a way to admire Wade and admire Lenora himself that he undertook shortly by admitting to Marie Criner how there'd never seemed to him hardly anything like a red sash for setting off a black outfit. Of course she cut her eyes at him in an effort to detect a smirk, but he'd made already his deeply sincere face that he was fond of and accomplished at and so earned from Marie Criner her own opinion as to the value of a touch of red. She suggested as well how the stripes on Lenora Pardue's flouncy ruffle flattered Lenora in most especially her broadest places which Donnie Huff raised his eyebrows and shifted to his acutely intrigued expression on account of so as to hear further from Marie of the intricacies of stripes and flouncy ruffles together and the illusions they create which she spoke about in sufficient detail to allow Donnie Huff the leisure to look down the length of Marie and look up the length of Marie and loiter even briefly upon his favorite localities which he disguised ever so ably as attentive rumination.

Of course Donnie Huff had previously skated semiprofessionally as a boy of fourteen which he was loath to confess to Marie Criner but confessed it to her nonetheless and guessed he'd worn any number of suits and sashes himself that he was hoping she would keep just between them as their little secret since he could not afford to let it get out what a sensitive and artistic manner a fellow he really was down underneath his bluff and dashing exterior. Naturally she had not taken him for a skater largely on the basis of his arrival at the rail that had not struck her as even semiprofessional, but once Donnie Huff had reminded her of his sundry nuances, including the talent he'd displayed for folding up and dropping unhurt to the floor like only a semiprofessional could, she grew persuaded and convinced and showed to Donnie Huff an expression of her own that could not possibly be taken for much beyond passably queasy if that even. They admired together Lenora's flair for fingerwork and Wade's impeccable posture, or truly Marie Criner admired them and Donnie Huff threw in with her once it seemed to him time to throw in, and Marie Criner wished aloud she possessed the easy grace of Lenora Pardue which Donnie Huff did not personally suspect she had much need for most especially if it came with the doughy thighs which Marie Criner mined straightaway the gist of and actually showed to Donnie Huff her teeth about.

It did not require too terribly much persuading on the part of Donnie Huff for him to gain from Marie Criner permission to squire her out onto the rink where the couple skate was in full swing with the Pardues and the pairs otherwise circling the one way and the low glamorous broken light circling the other, light so low and so glamorous and so broken as to conceal for a time the various lapses in Donnie Huff's semiprofessionalism, cloak his tendency to pitch and bob and jerk about and hide his wan expression of sickly anticipation as he waited to fall and hoped devoutly he wouldn't. There in her girlish years, Marie Criner recalled, she'd been probably too awfully fond of tragedy and passionate distress which had seemed to her part and parcel of the deep and profound emotions that men could feel for women and women could feel for men, attachments and affections that a man and a woman together had no call truly to speak of and declare but could confess instead with a look alone, preferably of a lingering and soulful variety. So she'd simply been hoping from Donnie Huff for a sign of his lingering, soulful, ineffable inclinations but had not yet detected much romance to speak of in the looks he'd exchanged with her during those brief and infrequent moments when he did not feel in immediate danger of folding and dropping unhurt. So disappointment pretty much reigned for a time as far as Marie Criner was concerned and she saw fit to expend the majority of her attention upon the Pardues exclusively who her and Donnie trailed around the rink like allowed Marie the opportunity to study the elegant lines Lenora manufactured with her upraised leg and her divinely arched back and her arms that she lifted and swept and her fingers that she worked with grace through the air.

Of course Donnie Huff, left undisturbed to concentrate upon his balance, became presently accustomed to the sensation of the skates beneath him, and his confidence steadily increased until he was feeling sure enough on his feet to venture assorted surreptitious ganders at various features of Marie Criner's person, the sorts of features a polite manner of fellow could not gander but surreptitiously at. He was fond of what he saw, admired the shape of Marie Criner's parts and pieces but allowed his imagination a trifle too much latitude in the contemplation of them, envisioned Marie Criner's most savory enticements uncovered and exposed which straightaway advanced Donnie Huff into a state of unseemly excitement which he attempted to undermine and punctuate by conjuring up, as was his custom, instances of grisly carnage, but the proximity of Marie Criner undid him and they rolled together about the rink trailing the Pardues with Donnie Huff venturing every now and again to lay nonchalantly his hand to his inseam while Marie Criner made meekly to work and sweep her own fingers after the fashion of Lenora Pardue who provided for her constant instruction in the deft and fluid trappings of grace. Donnie Huff, in an effort to gain some immediate relief and relocate his agitated member, undertook on his own Mr. Wade Pardue's highly favored splayfooted jump which he grew obliged to fold unhurt to the floor in the wake of without somehow managing as well to ease noticeably his condition. He did not figure the couple skate would ever end, supposed anyhow that he would not escape from the rink until Marie had found occasion to bump against him and grow disgusted which contributed to the general forlornness of Donnie Huff's predicament and rendered him more appealing still to Marie Criner who eyed his features and took notice of his deepened despair. While she hadn't found much to admire there on the hood of the Chevrolet, Marie Criner recalled how the Donnie Huff alongside her on the roller rink appeared to her an altogether renovated manner of creature what with his open capacity for heartache and tribulation, his willingness to display for her the various pangs he'd come to know which appeared to her quite altogether as sharp as any pangs Mr. Wade Pardue had troubled himself yet to exhibit.

He had a little mole between his left ear and his sideburn in the shape of a kidney bean and Marie Criner recollected how she'd found it a comely mole, a distinguished sort of a mark that contributed to the general advancement of Donnie Huff in her regard in addition to the veiny backs of his hands and his knobby fingers which she approved of as well since they looked to her manly and useful and quite utterly suitable for a strapping sort of a fellow. Donnie Huff had, in fact, risen so dramatically in her estimation, had proven himself capable of such genuine and abiding anguishment that Marie Criner was legitimately pleased if not altogether eager to depart with him upon his invitation out the side door before the couple skate was entirely over and accompany him into the relative darkness of the gravel lot where Donnie Huff gave over his nonchalance for the brand of stealthy and effective fingerwork that brought him some genuine relief.

They closed on the Chevrolet, proceeded across the gravel in their skates, and appeared the both of them in some real danger of folding and dropping perhaps unhurt to the ground, but they made together their way to the near fender and pitched against it backsides foremost, laid upon Donnie Huff's highly polished strip of ornamental chrome like Donnie Huff did not often encourage or allow and rarely made a practice of himself. She'd found his technique divine and spoke of how admirably he'd circulated about the rink to which Donnie Huff, in the nature of strapping sorts all over, made reply with a dollop of sputum that he discharged out the far side of his mouth by way of confirming the quality of his technique and the character of his circulation. Marie Criner had evermore wished she could dance and confessed to Donnie Huff in the ensuing silence beyond her compliment and his expectoration how she'd dreamed as a child of going to dancing school, and Donnie Huff told to her, "Yeah?" in lieu of any manner of discharge otherwise.

Marie Criner saw fit to speak of Donnie Huff's vehicle which she let on to be most acutely fond of and she wished he'd look at the way the thing dipped and bulged back along the door-panel, wondered how it was they'd decided where to dip it and how it was they'd decided where to bulge it out instead. Donnie

Huff himself couldn't say for certain though he allowed how his Chevrolet surely cut through the air like a knife. "Them fellows knew what they were up to," Donnie Huff informed Marie Criner. "Those boys at Chevrolet know how to make a car."

"My daddy drives a Chevrolet," Marie Criner said. "Couldn't anybody even give him a Ford." And Donnie Huff did not suppose he'd take as gift a Ford himself which Marie Criner straightaway construed as a remarkable coincidence.

Marie Criner inquired as to the origins of Donnie Huff, where he came from and who his people were and how it was she'd never come across him previously. She spoke as well ever so discreetly of her girlfriend Charlene's affection for Gary Goad which she bound Donnie Huff by an oath not to blurt out to Gary Goad himself though she guessed he might speak in a general and hypothetical sort of a way about her girlfriend Charlene so as to see what manner of face Gary Goad might feel inclined to pull.

"Charlene's on a diet," Marie Criner confessed in confidence to Donnie Huff. "She's not meaning to be chunky forever."

Donnie Huff laid his arms across his chest and ventured for the diversion of Marie Criner a recreational expectoration which she appeared to him to appreciate the various qualities of and then they laid together for a time in silence against the carfender, did not speak and did not spit but merely watched instead what of the rink they could see in through the open double doors, which was only a portion of it so scant and confined that the skaters passed by in singular unanimated poses, had come and were gone in one frozen instant, were framed and distilled there in the doorway for the merest of moments between what they were about to be up to and what they'd just lately left off at. Marie Criner recalled how somebody had punched Eddy Arnold on the jukebox, his rendition anyhow of "Make the World Go Away" that Donnie Huff allowed to her he was fond of as he was wanting every now and again to get the world off his own shoulders which he'd exhaled, Marie Criner recollected, most significantly about. She'd not herself had occasion by then to get weary of this life, had learned only from Opal her momma how best to mine undiluted joy from disappointment and snatch those jewels of delight from dark distress. She guessed there were likely people somewhere that got maybe worn down and done in and used up at last, but she was not personally acquainted with a one of them and suspected in her heart of hearts that they contributed by sloth and general sorriness to their own undoings. She'd learned from her momma Opal how men made their poor luck, manufactured their misfortunes by embracing temptation and turning from the good, and she ventured to make at Donnie Huff a sunny assurance as to the countless rewards of this life for those people who only but sought them out, petitioned him sweetly in her squeaky girlish voice to plug away here on this earth and resist if he could that deep and troublesome slough of despond where your pitiful leaden-hearted sorts of folks tended to muck about in the mire. She was hoping he might look around himself and take in the beauties of the world which, for beauties, were fairly endless and untold, and she suggested to him the native kinship between what a man reaps and what a man sows and had set out even to speak of dark clouds with their linings of silver when Donnie Huff interrupted her with an inquiry, swiveled about somewhat so as to say directly to her, "Let me ask you one thing. Who in the hell have you been talking to?"

And Marie Criner told him, "What?" leaving her mouth to lay open in the wake of it.

"Can't a fellow be tired?" Donnie Huff wanted to know. "Can't he have things go against him, have his luck ruined and spoiled? Can't a fellow just get a little sick and sorry every now and again?"

And Marie Criner who was hardly looking for a tiff, made at him a puny and altogether meager sort of a noise.

"I'll tell you, sister," Donnie Huff said, "there's more to this world than beauties," and Donnie Huff exhaled more significantly even than he'd exhaled previously.

Marie Criner had guessed she might best cultivate a rejoinder and was for a brief spell working one up, was selecting even a suitable tone in which to encourage Donnie Huff to lift his eyes to the far horizon where the sun would surely rise again on a new day, was casting about for the proper octave of earnest perkiness when Donnie Huff forestalled her by informing Marie Criner, "My daddy died," which Marie Criner was meaning to make her apologies about and was hoping as well to have occasion to suggest how the apparent ills of this life cloaked sometimes a deeper finer purpose, but Donnie Huff did not allow her to speak and carried forward with talk of how his daddy had come to be stricken with an internal complaint that slowly drained the life from him. "He was in timber," Donnie Huff said. "He didn't have a mill, just a truck and a saw and a pair of horses to snake with. Couldn't get anybody to work for him steady, not anybody sober and much count. He was always up and gone with light, out in the woods all day cutting and trimming trees and taking them off. Hauling to the mill. Hauling to the yard. Truck would break down, saw would bust, horse would go balky. Wasn't any money much in it. A man couldn't hardly hope to get ahead, and Daddy was just making it from one job to the next until he got sick. He didn't have anything laid by. He could have worked or he could have dropped dead, but he couldn't hardly afford to linger. We'll never get done paying for it."

And Marie Criner was meaning to share with Donnie Huff a comforting item of her own devising on the topic of the trials of this life that might lay low the weak but would find surely their match in the stout-hearted when Donnie Huff said to her, "My grandaddy, my daddy's daddy, he was the last of the farming Huffs. Hadn't any of them been in timber before him. They'd grown cabbage and peppers and feed corn and hay, kept cows and pigs and tended orchards, but my granddaddy lost his hay barn in a fire and the branch came up and muddied over his cabbages and took his corn away and the price of beef fell off and his pigs died of an infection and he just gave it all over I guess, took some work with a fellow cutting trees and when he kicked off my granddaddy just stayed at it, hired on his boys to work with him and Huffs been timbering since."

Marie Criner was intending to tell to Donnie Huff how it was undeniably pleasing to have a heritage of a sort, to be able to cast back and speak of your people's earnest labors on this earth, but Donnie Huff was not quite ready to leave off with the general woe of his circumstances and so forestalled Marie Criner, lifted his hand and showed her the wrinkly palm of it after a fashion suggestive of his wishes, and he drew a deep and deliberate breath and vented what was plainly a Make-the-World-Go-Away sort of an exhalation prior to explaining to Marie Criner in his most pitiful intonations how it seemed to him an undue burden for a fellow to have to come from people who hadn't ever done anything right, and as the time seemed to him quite ripe for an expectoration, Donnie Huff produced one and winced from the rigors of his condition in such a way as to suggest to Marie Criner the purest strain of glorious anguishment she'd ever yet had the pleasure to witness. He appeared to her fairly lacerated and did not begin even to ease off on his grimace until he'd noticed sidelong and surreptitiously an alteration in Marie Criner's own features, a melting of her countenance into the sort of soft and sympathetic expression that women had evermore seemed to him prone to when faced with an afflicted variety of creature—a kitten in a sack or a dog in a ditch or a fellow in a palpable funk.

"Don't be telling me about the beauties of this world," Donnie Huff said in the tiredest, most bedraggled tone he could manufacture. "I don't want to hear of them."

And while Marie Criner had set out to buck up Donnie Huff, speak to him once further of the far horizon where the sun would surely rise again on a new day, she did not somehow manage to tell it but produced instead, in the face of such torment and thoroughgoing distress, a slight and singular noise in her throat, a manner of wordless and breathy discharge that preceded by mere moments the laying of her fingers lightly upon the veiny back of Donnie's hand which was gesture and capitulation enough that even Donnie Huff, who did not truly know much at all about anything whatsoever, could tell even well enough himself. And she communicated to him with her own species of grimace a genuine sense of vicarious anguishment that Donnie Huff gauged and identified straightoff and accordingly laid some fingers of his own in advance of telling to Marie Criner, "Might be worse," in advance of suggesting to her, "There's people in harder spots than me," that Marie Criner in her neck alone disputed and shortly allowed herself to get gripped and held and fairly much embraced by Donnie Huff who she pressed her various parts snug against and thereby inspired in him a renewed sense of wonderment at how it was poor luck and forlorn extremity tended evermore to hold their sway with a woman.

So they pitched there, she recalled, against the fender of Donnie Huff's red Chevrolet bathed in the meager blue mercury light from the pole out by the roadway, and she did not speak further of the beauties of the world, did not feel in the least bit so inclined, but merely loitered in the clutches of Donnie Huff who she figured knew likely a thing or two about this life that she'd not yet heard from Opal her momma, items he might presently impart if she just laid and just loitered with him there in the night in the lot by the roller rink with music about them on the air and the skaters revealed through the open side door in scant and fleeting moments of enterprise. He showed her a planet low in the sky just above the treetops and a clump of stars that looked to him, taken together, like a turtle which he made plain to Marie Criner who could shortly see for herself the head and the shell and the little stubby feet. He guessed he'd be pleased to fly to the moon given the occasion for it as long as he did not himself personally have to steer the rocket, and he shared with Marie how his granddaddy's brother Warren had kept on his hearth in his front room a lump of iron that had dropped from the sky into Warren's dooryard, which put Donnie Huff in mind of a place he'd heard about down the other side of the world where it rained every now and again toadfrogs. He could not truly say why.

Donnie Huff expectorated and gazed up into the inky sky with the air of a man who's grateful for the strange and marvelous features of his life, and he guessed at Marie Criner how he maybe wouldn't himself mind seeing a frog shower, couldn't figure anyway the harm in traveling down the other side of the world just to learn what it was that went on there. "I surely don't mean to stick around his place forever," Donnie Huff told to her and struck subsequently, chiefly by means of his chin that he raised and uplifted, a bold and brawny sort of a pose meant to suggest to Marie Criner his steely resolve to wander.

"I ain't no farmer," Donnie Huff declared. "I ain't no timberman. Can't say what it is might become of me," which Donnie Huff had a look for as well and indulged in it for the benefit of Marie Criner who recalled how she'd never before met a boy so aggressively not one thing and resolutely not another like seemed to her curious and exotic and more than a little alluring. She suggested to Donnie Huff how it was in fact a big world that Donnie Huff did not contest with her about but only exhaled and dredged and snorted in advance of falling quite completely silent there in the lot where he conjured up assorted parts and pieces of Marie Criner all flushed and laid bare while she stood with her ear against his shirtfront and envisioned him and envisioned her down together somewhere beyond the southern ocean watching a cloudburst of toadfrogs rain thick from the heavens.

iii

Mrs. Lila B. Underwood had spoken in the forenoon to Mrs. Ailene Bunch's sister Dot who'd had occasion to hear earlier in the morning from a neighbor of Mrs. Troy Haven's who'd been out previously in her yard scattering toastcrusts for the finches when she'd run up on Mrs. Troy Haven herself engaged in the act of uprooting a milkweed from the fencerow. They'd exchanged remarks on the topic initially of weeds alone, for which they shared a common disapproval, prior to advancing into areas otherwise, discussing briefly a variety of wild green Mrs. Troy Haven had eaten as a child, which had set off in her neighbor the inclination to make mention of a mustard sauce she'd lately concocted for purposes of moistening her chicken dishes. They'd caught together sight of a common acquaintance up across the road and had spoken for a time uncharitably of her, featuring in their exchange various of her poorer qualities though they'd managed to speak kindly between them of her cat, not the white one with the spots and the tattered ear but the gray one with the goiter instead that seemed to them pitiful for a feline.

Mrs. Troy Haven's neighbor with the toastcrusts had asked after the condition of Mr. Troy Haven's prostate since she'd known it to have been lately inflamed, and while Mrs. Troy Haven had proven pleasen enough to share with her neighbor the news of her husband's dramatic glandular improvement, she was more anxious still to tell if she might of the meeting of her Bible class the night previous when she'd had occasion to hear from a man just ever so lately back from the dead, precisely the sort of thing to forestall her neighbor from holding forth the way she'd meant to on the topic of her own troublesome and infected tract that had given her lately no end of irritation and woe.

"Who got dead and come back?" she could not hardly help but inquire.

"That boy-in-law of Opal Criner's," Mrs. Troy Haven told to her. "Donald Huff."

She made him out to be a fairly glamorous sort of a fellow, allowed of course how he'd been wallowing in the mire of sinfulness and sloth but had suffered a fatal misfortune, had perished in an accident and soared consequently on up through the ether to the heavenly portal where he'd entertained upon his forearm the fingerends of Jesus which had served somehow to restore him to life, return his vented essence to his supine form, and he'd shortly awakened and revived much to the amazement of his associates who'd anticipated that Donald Huff would very likely stay dead. Understandably, his trip through the ether into the presence of the Lord had wrought upon him a miraculous change, rendered him presentable and appealing, and Mrs. Troy Haven endeavored to communicate across the fence to her neighbor the flair and aplomb with which Donald Huff had revealed to them his adventure. She confessed that she herself had been even stirred deeply and had laid in fact her own fingers to the forearm her Jesus had touched. "These here," she told to her neighbor across the fence and displayed for her the fingerends in question, lifted them, raised and extended them beyond the fencerow where her neighbor could not appear to help but meet and touch them with fingerends of her own.

Upon returning shortly to her kitchen, Mrs. Troy Haven's neighbor straightaway dialed up Mrs. Ailene Bunch's sister Dot

so as to apprise her of the tale she'd just lately heard and boast
of what fingerends she'd laid her own ones against, fingerends
that had themselves rested upon a forearm the very Lord and
Savior had deigned to touch which Ailene Bunch's sister Dot
entertained with hearty skepticism, failed that is to embrace as
firm and unmitigated fact on account of her first husband Wilton, a Methodist of some appreciable standing and regard, who
claimed to have been instructed by God to take up with a leggy
thing he'd come across at the Barbecue Barn and apply himself
rigorously to the salvation of her immortal soul. He'd employed
for his temple and sanctuary the far room at the motor lodge
out towards Stuart, the one with the yellow BarcaLounger and
the view of the Citgo where him and where her had customarily
engaged together in a variety of catechism, raising their voices
harmoniously on occasion in exultant praise and thanksgiving.
Straightoff, then, Mrs. Dot Bunch was not much interested in
hearing of the fingers of the Lord and where it was they'd laid
and loitered as she'd had already her fill of holiness. But in her
own personal version of the Donald Huff saga, his brush with
inky death and his flight through the ether, Mrs. Troy Haven's
neighbor embroidered the general facts of the matter with such
vivid concoctions of her own that Mrs. Dot Bunch grew presently swept up and enchanted in spite of herself. Donald Huff
sounded to her a manly and strapping sort of a fellow blessed
with an all too apparent passion for life on this earth, and the
grave perils of his trip through the ether all vented and unsupine, which Mrs. Troy Haven's neighbor gave out to be myriad
truly as far as grave perils went, conspicuously affected Mrs.
Dot Bunch who mined from them a trifle of genuine romance
and discovered in Donald Huff's encounter with his Jesus there
on the sill of the heavenly portal appreciably more drama and
allure than she'd expected to come across.

Consequently, then, even the taint of her Wilton and his
leggy infidelity for Christ could not altogether contaminate
Mrs. Ailene Bunch's sister Dot's enthusiasm for Mrs. Troy Haven's neighbor's highly varnished version of Donald Huff's
death and redemption at the fingerends of his Jesus, and once
she'd rendered what struck her as suitable improvements upon

the assorted details of the thing, Mrs. Ailene Bunch's sister Dot set out to broadcast on her own the news of Donald Huff's salvation, called her girlfriend Camille in Sylvatus and naturally her own sister Ailene who'd been the one to make mention of Mrs. Lila B. Underwood who Ailene suspected would be anxious to hear of the Lord. "You know how she is about Jesus," she'd told to Dot her sister who'd recalled pretty much in fact how Mrs. Lila B. Underwood was.

Mrs. Lila B. Underwood lived anymore south beyond Hillsville and partway to Fancy Gap where her momma's people owned land, had accumulated back years past an extensive tract of standing timber up the one face of a ridge and down the other and had bought up as well the adjoining bottom where Mrs. Lila B. Underwood's momma's relations grew feed corn and cabbage down on the flat and grazed Herefords on the slope to the treeline. They would have come maybe to be a prosperous pack of people if there had not been evermore so awfully many of them, brothers and sisters and uncles and aunts and nephews and nieces and cousins twice removed as well as countless assorted hangers-on by marriage who all seemed to leave for a time and strike out to make their way in this world as preamble to coming back shortly or coming back at last so as to lay claim to clearing enough for a house and a garden and an ornamental cedar that the guinea cocks and the guinea hens might scratch about in the shade of.

In their day, Mrs. Lila Underwood's momma and daddy and Mrs. Lila Underwood's aunt Fay Nell had appeared to be the exceptions, seemed to have stuck up in Poplar Camp where they'd bought a homestead along the east bank of the New River and had built a sizable frame house with floors of heartwood, walnut wainscoting, a round leadglass window over the doorway, and delicate fretwork high even in the eaves of the gable ends. There was a proper parlor and an airy dining room and a larder off the kitchen to the one end and a mud room off it to the other. Mrs. Lila Underwood's aunt Fay Nell occupied a downstairs bedroom with a sewing alcove attached while her sister and her brother-in-law enjoyed from their chamber upstairs a view of the river just where it bent and shoaled and washed in satiny flumes over a shelf of rock. Mrs. Lila Underwood had a room of her own with a slat bed her daddy had made for her and a dainty chest of drawers and a pine trunk and, off alongside her up the hall, her brother Elbert had a room as well, Elbert who nobody called Elbert and everybody called Jack instead.

He was a burly sort of a boy with big round shoulders for a child and ears that stuck straight out from his head and were evermore flushed and crimson. He had a scar on his lip from a dogbite, a scar inflicted by his daddy's hound Doc who Jack had seen fit to pitch into a thicket as a manner of prank which Doc, being a hound, had misinterpreted quite altogether and so had not truly responded in the spirit of good fun. Jack had one front tooth that was chipped and one front tooth that was cracked and twisted about and a lump on his noseridge from where he'd beaten it previously against a treelimb. He sported upon his forehead a deep and fairly sizable variety of dent where a Largent had succeeded in striking him with a rock from halfway across a hayfield after Jack had wagered with him he never would. He'd broken already as a child his left leg at the ankle and his right arm at the wrist, had twice caught his trousers on fire when he'd been intending instead to incinerate some item otherwise entirely, and had snagged as well the meaty part of his palm on a nailhead and laid it open nearly to the bone. So he'd been stitched and patched and salved and plastered over but had not ever seemed much mindful of his injuries and afflictions, just went on ahead and beat about this earth that way some boys are prone to.

He was not overfond of civil conversation but did show an inclination for whooping and yelping and hollering and carrying on in exceedingly loud and customarily congestive tones that his aunt Fay Nell found unmannerly and irritating and scolded him with regularity about but to no detectable effect as Jack was evermore ripe with exclamation and would not be curbed or corrected. He washed on occasion when pressed to but hardly ever came clean, and it was his habit at the dinner table to inadvertently dump over his milk most especially once his momma had shifted his tumbler to some relatively distant location that had struck her as secure and practically unassailable. He stomped across the floorboards, was not acquainted with any other means of transporting himself from one place in the house to another, and they all of them sat on occasion in the parlor, which would be Lila and her momma and her daddy and her aunt Fay Nell, and listed to Elbert upstairs roaming about like a draft horse. He could not ever seem to sleep the night through without rolling from his bed onto the floor which usually produced sufficient of a concussion to rattle all the windowlights in the house, and he was prone in his waking hours to engage on his own in earnest discourse, would sprawl in the sideyard atop the fescue or lay on a rock down by the river and share with himself the news of his disposition and the state of his opinions.

Mrs. Lila Underwood had not figured she cared much for him. She'd been at the time a young lady of seven who, under the steady tutelage of her aunt Fay Nell, had come to consider herself fragile and retiring after the fashion of proper ladies the world round who did not whoop and yelp and holler or approve of such behavior in gentlemen so inclined. A true and verifiable lady, Mrs. Lila Underwood had learned, should be known chiefly for her dignified bearing and unshakable composure and was wise to be habitually wary of men, skeptical of their designs and intentions since men were plainly devious and sly and should be regarded by proper women with inordinate caution except in the case of a certain Mr. Adderly of Wytheville who Mrs. Lila Underwood was instructed to loathe and despise due to how her aunt Fay Nell knew him already for a heel and a wastrel and so could caution against mere skepticism alone. As a child, then Mrs. Lila Underwood was not much encouraged to approve of such as her brother Elbert who was loud and coarse and antic and exhibited the seeds of deviousness, and she and her aunt Fay Nell together fretted over his prospects which seemed to the both of them meager and seemed to the both of them scant, and Fay Nell would tell into the air, "Oh that Jack," once she'd been by some ruckus made aware of him, and then she'd turn to her little niece and speak of the road her brother was traveling down.

Of course he was only eight and a half himself, but Mrs. Lila Underwood grew persuaded to disapprove of him nonetheless and frequently took occasion to share with Elbert her lowly opinion and offer to him as well instruction in the quality of his prospects to which Elbert paid only a fitful manner of regard as he was not personally capable of the undivided variety, was. evermore afflicted with impulses and inclinations and countless potent distractions which proved a thoroughgoing bane to his concentration. Consequently, he did not grow chastened and edified but did not become as well much affronted by the poor opinion of his sister, failed truly to absorb it at all, and patrolled about in his unrejuvenated state, whooped and yelped and hollered and stomped with wholly undiminished enthusiasm while his sister and while his aunt discounted his prospects further still and pulled at each other intensely disapproving faces, sat together on the porch or in the parlor or back deep in the sanctity of the sewing alcove, and displayed for each other fairly corrosive expressions as they told between themselves, "That Jack."

So he went about his business unaltered and unreformed, manufactured and maintained his customary uproar about the house and in the yard and down along the riverbank where he waded and swam partway through autumn when he amused himself instead by pitching most anything he came across out into the current to see where the water might take it. He did not allow winter to much thwart him but went about with his jacket undone and his knitted hat lost and forgotten and insinuated himself, even with the sashes shut and fastened, into the reaches of the house where his aunt and where his sister listened to him roaring about in the cold and the snow and grew together forlorn and despairing which they had between them faces for as well. Come the spring of his ninth year he had not gotten in the intervening months since eight and a half much transformed. He was burlier maybe and there was more it seemed of his crimson ears to stick out from his head, but he had not managed to grow significantly altered or noticeably improved and stormed around in the old way, welcomed the thaw with his usual unreserved enthusiasm, and went about like he'd hardly

yet seen a spring before, like this one was the first one he'd ever
had occasion to happen upon. Of course Mrs. Lila Underwood,
shut up through the cold with her aunt Fay Nell, emerged that
spring with an altogether richer and more highly refined sense
of skepticism and disdain than she'd been previously blessed
with, had advanced in her conviction that the deviousness of
men was the chief cause of heartache on this earth, and openly
shared her views with Elbert her brother who led her through
the woods to a stand of poplars where the ladyslippers and the
wild orchids had already poked through the forest floor, their
stems and shoots a wildly improbable green against the blackening leaves. He showed her a speckled trout in a pool of water
on the riverbank and a flattened place in the meadow across the
way where a deer had bedded and slept. He flushed for her
bluebirds out from the grass along the roadside and surprised
a grouse in a berry thicket, pursued her even with the first
snake of the season, a stubby black racer too chilled to coil and
strike. Naturally he hooted and he hollered as a matter of
course and received from his sister renewed instruction but was
not much inclined truly to think upon his prospects and fear
for the shabbiness of them what with the shank of May in the
offing when the days would lengthen and the water would
warm and he'd carry his pole to the riverside and fling his line
into the current.

But this was not to be much of a month for fishing, not this
May of Mrs. Lila Underwood's girlhood when the winds shifted
about and bore rain up out of the south, drove in the clouds
from off over the ridge where no clouds usually came, and
brought on the downpours and the long soaking showers that
would diminish on occasion and even sometimes cease outright
but would not wholly break and blow clear. The sky hung low
and the mist lingered late in the morning, rose early in the
night, while scant bits and pieces of cloud, detached and ragged,
passed along the treetops and presently went to tatters in the
wind. Often enough a trace of blue sky would reveal itself
through a tear in the overcast and thereby hint at the onset of
fair and cloudless weather, but the rift would heal over and the
rain would start up and the old mist would linger and the new

mist would rise and the runoff would sluice down from the ridge, washing the road into the bottom and the bottom into the river that grew muddy and headlong as it swelled in its banks.

They wandered together about the house, which would be Fay Nell and Lila and her momma and her daddy and her brother Elbert who himself would venture regularly onto the long covered porch across the housefront or the landing off the back door so as to peer up into the sky and gauge the progress of the clouds, so as to reach with his palm out from under the overhang and feel the rain upon it. Lila's daddy looked in on his cattle and fretted over his cabbage and otherwise amused and calmed himself by reading from a book about the queen of England, reading from it chiefly aloud to his wife and to his wife's sister Fay Nell who both went a ways further towards appreciating the charms of royalty than Lila's daddy could manage himself to do. Lila sat in the parlor and learned of the queen when she was not instead of a mood to retire to her room upstairs and groom her glassfaced doll in the long bespeckled shirtwaist gown with the sash and the bow who could not truly tolerate too awfully much grooming since her gown stayed evermore neat and comely and her hair was painted onto her head. But Lila exchanged talk nonetheless with her glassfaced doll, stood her against the slatted headboard in ladylike poses, and provided her a slight and dainty voice to speak of her engagements in.

Elbert her brother flailed about on occasion in his own room up the hallway but primarily roamed the house unearthing turmoil wherever he might, poking about places he had no business poking, and stomping and rough-housing and endangering the general furnishings to such a degree as to set off his momma and his daddy and his aunt Fay Nell too who would leave off respectively with their needlework and their regal disclosures so as to call to Elbert, "Jack!" so as to inquire of him, "What in this world are you up to?" and Elbert himself, following a long and deliberate silence, would inform them gravely, "Nothing." back.

Those times when the rain slacked off they would all of them leave the house and mill about the property, indicate to each other where the water had washed and run, identify what had been carried away already and what had been for the moment spared and uneroded. Jack took particular notice of the worms that had slipped up out of the ground and the bugs that had drowned in the torrents, and he made evermore a point of stepping down to the river in the company usually of his sister and in the company often of his aunt Fay Nell as well who would warn him off from the bank, draw him back to stand with them in safety and look out upon the thick silty water that had covered over the ledges and swelled high already well above the rocky shoal. The river was freighted with refuse from the surge, carried along in the current limbs and logs and entire trees torn up at the roots. There were fencerails and cowtroughs and chicken houses and hay carts and the greater portion of Mr. Howard Troxell's pig parlor in addition to the general refuse that had been pitched over the months down the gullies and into the streambeds. Numerous boats had been taken up and floated away only to be sunk and upended by the surging current and on occasion thrashed quite thoroughly to pieces. Fay Nell spied a highboy off along the west bank, a partially submerged highboy with a showy carved bonnet that she found most graceful and appealing, and Elbert took himself some notice of a dead cow that passed along the near shore entangled in a clump of wire. There was considerable lumber on the river washed off from the low-lying mills, and Elbert fished a perfectly good potato rake out of an eddy much to the forthright consternation of his aunt Fay Nell who could not find the sense in wagering life and limb for such an item as that.

Come evening the rain evermore set in again clattering gently at first upon the tin roof prior to raising presently a steady and ferocious din and the wind worked under the seams of the sheeting and backed the nails sufficiently to allow for ample water to pass into the attic and drip off the rafters onto the plaster which seeped and swelled. Of course the rugs and the draperies and the bedclothes got musty and dank and attracted the notice of Mrs. Lila Underwood's momma and Mrs. Lila Underwood's aunt Fay Nell who, being proper women, had cultivated already somewhere back in their olfactories a knack for sniffing mildew before it had come yet to be fuzzy and bluegreen. So they built a fire in the iron stove in the kitchen and kindled blazes downstairs on the coal grates and upstairs on the coal grates too and thereby dried out the furnishings and dehydrated the inhabitants who hoped with renewed purpose for the weather to break and their torments to cease.

And the clouds did at last begin to blow free and give way. Mrs. Lila Underwood recalled it was a Thursday in the forenoon when the rain left off for good, and for the first time in untold days a legitimate patch of sunlight fell on the sideyard where a clutch of chickens, slick and muddied clean up to the eyesockets, pecked at the wealth of grubs in the fescue. The river had not yet crested from the runoff but was higher nonetheless than even the Dunleavy up the road, who'd seen everything and been everywhere and heard already all there was to hear, had ever himself known about. The sizable sycamore partway up the far bank was standing in six feet of rushing water, and Mrs. Lila Underwood's own daddy's cabbage field off athwart the shoal had been lately transformed into a deep and expansive pond. Sticks and rocks and trash and wire lay about in tangled heaps where assorted sluices and rivulets had carried them to and left them, and much of the refuse of the river had fetched up and snagged along the banks, providing Mrs. Lila Underwood's brother Elbert the opportunity to pick about for treasures and curiosities notwithstanding his aunt Fay Nell's vigorous objections. She was fearful of moccasins and copperheads and could not personally say where that refuse had previously been though Elbert, in the spirit of enlightenment, did trouble himself to point back along the riverbed and inform her, "Been up there," which was precisely the sort of sass Fay Nell did not tolerate with terribly much grace.

They all of them guessed they should have likely foreseen the prospect of it. Fay Nell anyhow and Lila B. Underwood's momma and Lila B. Underwood's daddy too could not truly explain to each other or begin hardly to explain to themselves why they'd not feared for it and why they'd not protected against it knowing like they did how heedless their Elbert could be, their Elbert who spied presently from the bank a stick of

lumber that appealed to him, a lone length of plank that fairly
charmed him unlike all the planks otherwise that had caught up
in a splintery confusion along the shore. This one was whole
and broad, saturated and blackened, and afloat in the current
landward enough to seem worth venturing to snatch from the
flow, so Elbert climbed past a snag and stepped into the water
while his aunt Fay Nell was pondering at her feet a purplish
blossom on a flowering weed. Mrs. Lila B. Underwood had
recognized herself the foolhardiness of the undertaking and
guessed maybe she could have told to her brother a thing or
told at least to her aunt a thing on her brother, but she just
watched him instead as he stepped out onto the ledge and full
into the river he'd fished and waded and swam, seen the mist lie
upon in the morning and settle onto at dusk, been put at night
to sleep by the sound of, the river of his intimate acquaintance
that straightaway swept his feet from under him and dumped
him full into the current from where he failed to shriek and cry
out but merely looked instead upon his sister on the shore,
showed to her that face of his with the teeth chipped and twisted
and the noseridge scarred and the forehead dented and the
assorted features otherwise worked up together into an expression of unmitigated surprise, a look of pure and untempered
astonishment as Elbert had himself been trusting and foolish
and child enough to figure he'd somehow be spared.

Fay Nell could not manage to call out, gave over at length
her purplish flower for the calamity before her and could muster no wind to speak with while Mrs. Lila B. Underwood made
on her own the most trifling sort of a noise in her throat. Together they watched Elbert grab onto the plank that had enticed him so and proceed downstream in the company of it,
pass over the shoal and into the bend and float shortly from
sight, leaving Fay Nell and Lila her niece to gaze merely upon
the thick brown vacant silty water in advance of raising harmoniously a fairly incomprehensible alarm that Lila's momma
heard in the larder and stepped upon the landing to inquire
about like earned for her only a pair of elevated arms and
upraised fingers that pointed together past the shoal to the
place where the river twisted about and flowed from sight.

They managed shortly to contribute a piece of talk to the matter, succeeded at saying together, "Jack," with curious enough inflection to set off Lila's momma, induce her to step from the landing and strike out across the yard towards the riverbank where she learned in fits and starts of the plank and the foolhardy venture and she called down the river where her baby had gone prior to hollering back up the hillside towards the barnyard from where her husband grew inclined to inquire of a hen, "What was that?"

She lured him shortly, brought him down to the shore to hear from Fay Nell the woeful tale which she shaped and tailored so as to render blameless herself and her niece Lila who could not surely have curbed that Jack in his inclinations, thwarted him in his intentions sufficiently to keep him safe and dry, and she pointed to where he'd ventured onto the ledge and to where he'd gotten to be dumped and upended, and she indicated his course downstream out over the shoal and to the bend in the river, but Lila's daddy was gone already by then, had struck out afoot down along the bank prior to veering off across the road so as to meet the river where it straightened out of the bend. But Jack wasn't there either. Lila's daddy scanned the current down to where the glare undid him and discovered no trace of Elbert his boy. He looked along the shore where the clammy locust grew and the limbs and the refuse had fetched up and caught, but there wasn't any sign of his Elbert there as well like spurred Lila's daddy on further along the bank from where he shouted out when he thought to, "Jack!" that the deep steady roar of the water deadened and overwhelmed.

He collected assistance along the riverbank, called upon his neighbors downstream to help him please to find his boy who'd floated off, and they set out with Jack's daddy downstream, scanned with Mr. Wilbur Hunt's brother's spyglass the far shore where the banks had been undercut and washed away and the flecks of color turned out to be largely trash. They proceeded even near about to Allisonia though they did not any of them suspect and believe he could have been carried so far as that. They told his daddy he'd likely climbed out back up the river a ways, but they suggested between themselves with looks alone

how he'd not probably climbed out at all. There was low dis-
creet talk of all the things that might become of a fellow who'd
dropped into the New at flood, and salvation was hardly prominent among them. Some of them guessed he'd gotten crushed
against a rock or tangled in a snag while the prevailing view was
that he'd probably just been done in by the plunging water itself
that drove him deep towards the bed and held him there, and
they guessed he'd boil up presently, figured anyway he hadn't
probably boiled up yet though they looked for him still out of
courtesy to his daddy, examined the shore with the spyglass,
and called into the tumult, "Jack!"

Mrs. Lila B. Underwood's momma sat on the front porch
atop the wicker divan and pulled at her fingers as she gazed off
up the road and entertained from her sister Fay Nell assurances
about Elbert her boy who was strong and was hardy and would
likely haul himself from the water. Lila B. Underwood could
not recall precisely what she'd figured just then on her own but
recollected instead how she'd sat on the porch floor in her
dress, which would not normally have been at all tolerated, and
watched a bug on the banister, a black bug with a red dot on it
that wandered about on top of the rail until he came to be
weary of it when he proceeded down to the underside and
wandered about some more. She didn't much hear her aunt
who prattled pretty incessantly in an effort to buck up Lila's
momma who studied the roadway and tugged at her fingers
and failed even to volunteer polite and throaty noises for the
encouragement of her sister Fay Nell as she narrated, one upon
the other, curious cases of people who had not gotten dead and
done in when probably they should have. Come six in the
evening when her daddy had still not returned, Lila Underwood was escorted by her momma into the kitchen and fed a
meal on account of how she was a child and had to eat while her
aunt and while her momma both fretted exclusively and stood
by turns picket upon the porch until the light gave way leaving
little at all to linger upon the porch and see.

Mrs. Lila B. Underwood's daddy did not return home until
well after dark. He arrived in the company of an Allen from
down the road who swung his truck about in the sideyard and

declined to step into the house which left Lila Underwood's daddy to enter alone and render up unaided his pronouncement which consisted largely of a breath he exhaled and a slight forlorn movement of his head from side to side. Fay Nell, Mrs. Lila B. Underwood's aunt, was characteristically fond of clutching at items and wringing them to pieces which she performed as a service upon the news that their Jack had not yet been found dead even though he'd not yet been found alive either. She worked and twisted the thing and contrived thereby to milk some hope from it, but did not manage to persuade and influence her sister or her sister's child or her sister's husband either who grew moved himself to ask of Fay Nell her indulgence, raised up at her his hand that he held flat before her as he wondered if might they stand there in the foyer in peace.

Fay Nell herself put Lila to bed, which was not hardly her habit, and they prayed together for the deliverance of Elbert who Fay Nell insisted would turn up prior to drawing shut Lila B. Underwood's door and abandoning her to the darkness. She wriggled out from under her bedclothes and lay atop them on her back, listened to the rush of the water along the riverbed so low and unbroken as to not after a time sound much like noise at all, and she saw plain before her Elbert her brother bobbing there in the current with his arm flung across his plank and the wonderment of his circumstances plain upon his face. She saw him as well tiny in the bend and watched him from there in the dark atop the bedclothes get flushed from sight altogether. She hadn't much cared for him, reminded herself of his assorted failings, his meager prospects, his all too apparent seeds of deviousness, not even to mention the customary attendant uproar he'd raised and inflicted as a matter of course. She did not guess he'd been much use at all, and she recalled how he'd held her that time upside down by her feet over the wellhead which served to harden her further, left her to suppose he'd simply brought like usual his troubles upon himself that she had to figure was just the way of his ilk. And since she hadn't much cared for him, if maybe he didn't come back, if maybe he'd gotten already dead and drowned, it was not likely, she told to herself, the worst thing that might happen, which Mrs. Lila B.

Underwood clutched at and embraced and held to through the night as she lay upon the bedclothes awake and lay beneath the topsheet asleep and roused up at last in the thin light of morning when she could not straightaway remember what the matter was but got reminded shortly of it by the sound of her momma through the near wall, her momma who spoke in a high, plaintive, indecipherable voice and heard at intervals from her daddy back, "I know."

He rounded up a party for the hunt, enlisted most everybody he came across, told of his boy who'd been carried away in the flood, and they all of them helped him to look, beat about along the riverbank in the thickets and the tangled clumps of discharged limbs and studied the snags caught up and lodged in the current, sought to discover about them some trace of a child. But they failed still to find him even as the water fell and the flood slackened, and they told among themselves how the river would only yield him up presently and in time, would surely gnaw on him first for a spell which they kept from Elbert's daddy who called out still, "Jack!," hollered it down along the bank and waited even for a reply. Come dark, however, he arrived home again with just the exhalation and the slight forlorn movement of his head to show for his endeavor, and they sat the four of them in the parlor where Fay Nell made to lift their spirits with a piece of hopeful talk but got directly discouraged from it and so listened with the rest of them to the mantel clock that ticked and the timbers of the house that popped and creaked of their own accord, or listened likely beyond the ticking and through the popping and the creaking to the pure and profound stillness about them, stillness untroubled by such as a boy who'd had himself no use much for quiet, a boy gone and lost to them, out somewhere in the darkness, down somewhere under the water while they sat together safe in their house where the lamps burned and the hours chimed and the timbers shifted and groaned.

A Merrit found him, the eldest one of the four of them that lived together just across the river down beyond the bend. The third day when the water drew back further still, that Merrit discovered Mrs. Lila B. Underwood's brother Elbert in his beanfield, came across him sprawled upon his stomach in the mud clutching yet at his plank with his one arm while his other lay bent and wrenched oddly about upon his back. And that Merrit said to him, "Boy," said to him, "Hey boy," and poked at Elbert with his boottoe prior to returning to the house so as to fetch away the Merrits otherwise to come if they might and see the dead fellow laying in with the beans. They turned him over. That was all they did for him was turn him over and guessed they knew between them what boy it was even with the battering and the scuffing he'd endured, and they elected by consensus a Merrit to cross the river with the news, the least one who had still some manners about him, and he discovered Lila's daddy down the river along the bank poking about in a jumble of limbs and fencewire.

They washed him in the yard, laid him upon his plank between a pair of bucks, and rinsed the mud from him. He was scraped and torn up and his one arm was broken at the shoulder and at the elbow both, but he looked still pretty much like Elbert even dead and naked and wet and waxen and stretched out in the sunlight on his board. His daddy built him a box and his aunt Fay Nell made for it a lining of pale blue sateen that they laid him upon and then displayed him in the front room where his momma's people from Fancy Gap and his daddy's people from up past Radford came to view him and settle lightly their fingers upon his face, their palms upon his shirtfront while his little sister Lila sat in a straight chair by the hearth and watched him be dead and watched them be sorrowful and peered on occasion out the window where the treetops pitched in the wind. They carried him back to Fancy Gap to lay with his relations on a hilltop set aside for it. His daddy and his momma's middle brother dug the grave themselves so as it situate Elbert in repose at the feet of his granddaddy and allow him the shade come afternoon from a pair of cedars off at the edge of the plot. Elbert's uncle's child Larry who preached as a calling and an avocation performed the service at the graveside, read from the Psalms of how a man stands as a mere breath in this world, and led the family in a gloomy rendition of "Jesus, Savior Pilot Me" prior to taking up a knotted rope end and assisting on his own in the lowering of the casket that settled dully deep in the grave.

Elbert's daddy himself made the marker, made it from Elbert's plank that he cut and shaped and planed and found to be oak, hard sappy red oak which Elbert's daddy worked with his chisel and his mallet to inscribe. He etched a flower there at the top on a leafy stem and a kind of a lamb beneath it, a creature anyhow with plainly the head of a lamb but the body of a terrier, and underneath the flower and underneath the lamb Elbert's daddy inscribed the three names his boy had been given and the one name beyond it they'd called him instead prior to cutting below them the year of Elbert's birth and the year of Elbert's death which he was meaning to adorn and set off with a creeping vine that might frame Elbert's days on this earth, but the noticeable brevity of them remarked so upon itself as to leave no need for adornment at all. In place of a piece of scripture, Elbert's daddy concocted an epitaph on his own and cut it into the sappy oak, adorned it even with a length of vine itself prior to displaying the finished item for his wife and his wife's sister and his girl Lila who admired the flower and tolerated the lamb and praised the grace of the lettering and the stark sobriety of the dates prior to arriving at last upon the actual inscription which Lila's momma and Lila's aunt Fay Nell read together for the benefit of Lila herself, telling to her, "Carried off," that they found together to be apt and found together to be seemly.

They tried to stay on at Poplar Camp, made as if to take up and do what they'd done, be what they'd been, but there was just too awful much water about down across the yard and beyond the bank where the river poured evermore over the ledgy shoal, and Elbert's momma and Elbert's daddy and Elbert's aunt Fay Nell could discover among them no way much to escape the dull and ceaseless sound of it. So they picked up presently and departed together from their sizable house with the heartwood floors and the walnut wainscoting and the delicate fretwork and the round leadglass window, and they showed up again at the tract of land with the standing timber and the cultivated bottom and the Herefords grazing on the slopes, where they claimed a house a cousin had left from to strike out and make his way in this world, a small and modest sort of a bungalow with shrubbery along the front sill and spruce trees in the yard and mice in the parlor behind the matchboard, and they made it together cozy and rendered it together appealing and passed the four of them their evenings after supper on the front porch under the eaves where Fay Nell raised her customary chatter which required no response and encouraged no contributions and so allowed Mrs. Lila B. Underwood and her momma and daddy to sit merely there upon the bungalow porch and watch as the darkness came on.

And they assumed, like a trait of nature, from their Elbert a sense of spoiled luck and a feel for poor fortune, and Lila's momma and Lila's aunt Fay Nell developed in particular between them a talent and a gift for plumbing together to the poison at the heart of most any predicament and producing thereby some nugget of blight that they'd raise like a trophy for display. They instructed Lila their child and niece in the ways of disappointment and general hopelessness on this earth and advised her as how best to love her Lord Jesus who might heal and mend the afflicted and redeem with His grace the fallen while leaving a boy in his direst hour to his own meager devices. When she came to be of an age for it, Lila's momma and Lila's aunt Fay Nell warned her off of men and together they openly disparaged the Underwood Lila took up with and presently wed, the Underwood who accepted employment down off the mountain on a dirtfarm in Dobson, but he found frustration in the wages and discouragement in the labor itself and took work in a mill and took work in a grocery and took work in a garage prior to striking out for Louisiana, where he'd heard there were jobs on the Gulf. He promised to send for his Lila and wrote to her even a card from Alabama and a letter or two from Louisiana proper before that Underwood went on ahead and plain dissipated like smoke, vanished entirely but for some clothes in the dresser and some shoes on the closet floor that Mrs. Lila B. Underwood, following a suitable interval, burned with the trash.

So she came back to the bungalow the way her momma and

her aunt Fay Nell had figured all along she might, and she
determined evermore to go untempted by any man otherwise
and, consequently, stayed on at the bungalow, where she nursed
her relations in their illnesses and attended at their decrepitude
and gave them all over at last to their plots on the hillside until
they left Mrs. Lila B. Underwood alone in the house where she
occupied her time partly with her lilies and her peonies and her
gladiolas and her dahlias that she grew out back in the dooryard and partly as well in study of the scriptures as had become
a custom there in the bungalow where Mrs. Lila B. Underwood's momma and Mrs. Lila B. Underwood's daddy and Mrs.
Lila B. Underwood's aunt Fay Nell had been wont of an evening
to sit about in the front room reading each in silence from their
Bibles, silence that would come to be troubled and interrupted
by assorted significant necknoises whenever Lila's momma or
Lila's daddy or Lila's aunt might come across a postulation that
seemed to them dubious and farfetched.

   Mrs. Lila B. Underwood was given anymore to such humph-
ing herself most especially when she read in the Gospels of how
it was her Savior mended the sick and fed the hungry, brought
light unto the darkness, and cast away despair, precisely the
sorts of endeavors to give rise in Mrs. Lila B. Underwood to a
regular festival of necknoises, Mrs. Lila B. Underwood who,
like her momma and like her daddy and like her aunt Fay Nell,
had taken up and embraced her Lord as if on a dare and
prayed to Him evenings for the soul most specifically of her
dead brother Elbert who she still saw clearly and plain, not him
of the seeds of deviousness and the general uproar, but Elbert
instead in extremity and distress, Elbert awash in the surging
river with his arms flung across his plank and the disbelief
apparent upon his face. She could not hope to forget how he'd
craned about and looked at her prior to washing along in the
current down across the shoal to the far bend where his tiny
head and his tiny white face stood apart from the brown gritty
water until he was swept at last from sight. She guessed even
before her mother had come yet from the larder he was dying,
figured even before her father had arrived yet from the barnyard he was dead. So she prayed nights he laid easy now that

the astonishment had ended, and she read for her profit in the Gospels of her Lord who vowed to bring to the weary rest unto their souls which Mrs. Lila B. Underwood grew evermore throaty about.

So they knew, then, how she was when it came to her Jesus. Mrs. Ailene Bunch and Dot her sister along with all the rest of the Methodists from the rock church up the parkway were well acquainted with Mrs. Lila B. Underwood's disposition as they'd run the most of them up on the barbs of it and were consequently aware of how she held her Savior to a harsh and rigorous accounting. The Bunches, consequently, fairly delighted in the opportunity to pass along to Mrs. Lila B. Underwood news of a local fellow who'd come up lately on Christ Himself, soared through the ether to the portal of heaven, and entertained the holy fingerends upon his flesh. Ailene Bunch's sister Dot suggested even and insinuated to Mrs. Lila B. Underwood over the telephone how this fellow and her Jesus had chatted for a time there on the portal sill, had spoken perhaps of dead folks roundabout, though Ailene Bunch's sister Dot coyly demurred from guessing which dead folks precisely as she did not feel it her place to put words in the mouth of the Savior. Quite naturally Mrs. Lila B. Underwood, like Dot Bunch had figured she might, straightaway dialed up Opal Criner and learned from her further still of Donnie Huff's trip through the ether, heard about the vented essence and the bright and blinding glorious heavenly light and shortly invited herself on over for an interview.

They had tea together in the front room, tea with lemon which Mrs. Lila B. Underwood had requested of Opal Criner who'd fixed herself a cup as well although she was not truly much of a hot tea drinker which she innumerated for Mrs. Lila B. Underwood the assorted reasons for that Mrs. Lila B. Underwood failed herself to comment upon but merely blew into her cup and sipped at her beverage and looked about at the furnishings of the front room with what appeared quite plainly to Opal Criner disdain. She inquired after Mrs. Lila B. Underwood's people and discovered that the bulk of them were in fact

deceased while the most of the rest of them were only partly so
well as they might be. Mrs. Lila B. Underwood did not appear
herself much anxious to hear of Opal Criner's relations and did
not bother to inquire as to the health and pursuits of Opal
Criner's own people beyond wondering what perhaps that
racket was from the kitchen and Opal Criner explained how
her girl Marie was distressing presently a boxlid with a tack
hammer that appeared to produce in Mrs. Lila B. Underwood
a brief and flickering dose of interest.

Of course talk turned shortly to Mrs. Opal Criner's girl's
husband Donald who'd been lifted upon the wings of rapture
into the presence of the Lord, and as it did not seem likely that
Mrs. Lila B. Underwood was thoroughly acquainted with the
circumstances of the matter, Opal Criner shared with her the
tale of Donald's peril and deliverance, stepped even over to
the doorscreen so as to indicate just where precisely she'd received the news of his demise. In the retelling, Donnie Huff's
plummet into the Big Reed blossomed into a colorful and cap-
tivating episode replete with emphatic and sanitized outbursts
on the part of the principal and seemly dramatic exchanges
between the supporting players who were plainly wrought up
with fearfulness and despair. So as to heighten the tension of
the thing, Opal Criner alternated between the grave circumstances of Donnie Huff's earthly form and the ascent of his
vented essence through the ether towards the heavenly portal.
She spoke in detail of the balky attempts of his co-workers to
wade the creek and extract him from it and graduated presently to his pallid lifeless carcass upon the siltspit where Donnie
Huff lay obligingly while his wife's mother took up once more
with his essence that had passed clean through the ether and
into the bright and glorious heavenly glow.

Mrs. Lila B. Underwood's personal interest in the Lord and
Savior part of the thing was most especially keen and she plied
Opal Criner with necknoises in a fruitless attempt to accelerate
her, to alter the pace of the tale and forgo the drama, but Opal
Criner merely exhibited for Mrs. Lila B. Underwood her sour
and sickly smile and followed her personal inclinations on
through the heart of the narrative to the moment of crisis when

Donnie Huff's supine form lay expired upon the ground while his essence at the portal consorted with the Lord. She described the portalway itself and ventured to speak as well of the stunning portal gate elaborate like it was with filigree and assorted bits of sculpted adornment. Mrs. Lila B. Underwood, however, was not much interested in the various decorative qualities of the heavenly entranceway and suggested her disposition deep in her windpipe with no effect to speak of upon Opal Criner who persevered with the filigree and advanced only presently to the heavenly raiments themselves which she let on to be, for raiments, natty and fairly fetching though hardly the sort of ensemble that anybody but the son of God could hope to get away with.

Opal Criner had not been intending to represent to Mrs. Lila B. Underwood that her girl's husband Donald had exchanged with the Savior opinions, had passed with the Savior the time of day, but since Mrs. Lila B. Underwood had plainly been left by Ailene Bunch's sister Dot with the impression that Donald Huff and Jesus had stood there upon the portal sill and chatted, Opal Criner grew persuaded to render up a re-creation of their confab which had gotten itself under way, she gave out, with an exchange of salutations. Donnie Huff anyhow had told to his Jesus, "Hey," and his Jesus had answered with a Lordly nod back. Naturally, in the course of his departure from his supine form and his passage through the ether, Donnie Huff had grown curious as to his plight and wondered of the Savior where it was anyhow he'd ended up, providing Jesus the occasion to speak Himself to Donnie Huff's anxieties, to share with him a parable of a peach pit that had been cast aside with the leavings otherwise of the peach itself and had sprouted presently into a tree that bore upon its limbs peaches of its own with pits to get broadcast and spread and thereby take themselves root in the earth.

Opal Criner was under the impression that her Donald told then to his Jesus, "Oh," back and perhaps even gave out to be illuminated though he'd never in life demonstrated much grasp of the metaphorical which Opal Criner shared with Mrs. Lila B. Underwood the news of although she had to suppose there might be worse deficiencies in a fellow than a decidedly literal bent which Mrs. Lila B. Underwood seemed with a throaty discharge to concur about.

As best as Opal Criner had been yet able to glean from Donald her girl's husband, him and Jesus had not shown between them much inclination to speak further for a time but had stood merely together on the portal sill alongside the filigreed gate awash the both of them in the rich buttery heavenly light that Opal Criner paused to expand upon the qualities of for the benefit of Mrs. Lila B. Underwood who she suspected had not known previously anybody much who'd basked in the glow of the hereafter and returned through the ether to tell of it. Of course down on the siltspit Donnie Huff's supine form was attracting some attention of its own which Opal Criner shifted over to speak of in her ongoing effort to heighten the tension of the proceedings. She concocted for and ascribed to little Gaither various ministrations intended to revive Donnie Huff, told at length of his efforts to ventilate him and thereby snatch Donnie Huff back to life, harried frantic efforts that did not produce for the longest time any reaction at all in Donnie Huff himself who remained supine and bluegreen both and was beginning to appear altogether past revival when he did at last stir and rewarded little Gaither in his efforts with a measure of creekwater.

Along about that same time precisely up on the sill of the portal, Donnie Huff saw pretty much the last of his Savior. As Opal Criner herself had heard it from him, Donnie Huff was just before stepping clean across the sill and entering full into the kingdom of heaven proper when he felt a twinge there at the portal and so loitered and laid back, did not stride straightaway past his Lord into the hereafter which Jesus Himself took directly some notice of and as a consequence reached out and laid His fingerends to the forearm of Donnie Huff, rested them briefly upon a downy patch of skin. "Just here," Opal Criner told to Mrs. Lila B. Underwood and indicated on her own arm some skin in a similar location.

It was then that he got snatched back and revived, passed headlong once more through the ether, and reclaimed his su-

pine form as he rewarded little Gaither further still with co-
pious creekwater. Opal Criner did not believe her Donald
could recall upon waking much of what had transpired since
his plummet into the creek, but presently the vision of his Jesus returned to him, a vision he'd hurried home to speak
about and share and revel with his people in the wonder of.
It had been, Opal Criner insisted, the joyous shank of an ever
so remarkable day. And Mrs. Lila B. Underwood who'd absorbed the tale in relative silence, had not anyhow humphed
much lately, lifted her teacup to her lips, and drew off a
healthy draft in advance of settling the thing back upon her
saucer so as to free her fingers to lay upon some armskin of
her own. "Here?" she inquired of Opal Criner who directed
the fingers wristward a bit prior to confirming for Mrs. Lila B.
Underwood, "Yes ma'm."

Sheba the wirehaired dog would surely have heard the truck
flinging gravel along the roadway if she had not lately discovered in Delmon a troubling alteration, noticed how he'd given
over his pants seat for an uncharacteristic sort of a squat that
she was not herself acquainted with and consequently ventured
a query about, set up truly an investigation that so monopolized
her concentration and called for such undivided blandishments
as to prevent Sheba from taking any notice of Buddy Isom's red
half-ton until it had swung already into the drive and passed so
rashly over the exposed culvert as to launch and levitate Buddy
Isom's oil jug in addition to Buddy Isom's accumulation of
refuse that slapped and clattered against the back windowglass.
Quite naturally Sheba grew of a sudden alarmed and gave over
the uncharacteristic squat entirely so as to free herself to approach the half-ton and make of it assorted inquiries, sniff
anyhow the tirerims, and bark pretty relentlessly at the door-
panels. Donnie Huff, who most usually produced straightaway
a boottoe to display for Sheba the wirehaired dog, did not this
evening roll off of the truckseat with his usual dispatch as him
and Buddy Isom were enjoying together the dregs of their
beverages which Donnie Huff himself had treated them to.
With a portion of his ministry funds he'd purchased at the
Texaco a tall boy apiece for him and for Buddy Isom and they

were savoring still between them their additional four liquid ounces while Buddy Isom described for Donnie Huff a woman he'd seen once previously in the Food Lion by the dairy case. Explaining to Donnie Huff that he did not figure it would be seemly of him to piss on the peonies, Buddy Isom presently climbed out from the cab and urinated instead into the hydrangea bush, like attracted the immediate scrutiny of Sheba the wirehaired dog who could not fetch and could not sit and could not stay, refused uniformly to take any manner of instruction at all but managed evermore to answer the beckoning call of a trouser fly and would unfailing step in front of a fellow only once he'd cut loose and could not hope to choke off his flow. As a consequence, Donnie Huff heard shortly from Buddy Isom, "I'm pissing on your dog," and allowed himself how he'd pissed on his dog more times than he could say in advance of slipping out from the cab and flinging his can into the bed.

In the sideyard Delmon extracted from his mouth a rock he'd had the pleasure lately to suck on and rattle against his teeth and he told "Hey," to his daddy and "Hey" to Buddy Isom too and shared further with them news of an endeavor he'd undertaken lately with a piece of a limb, a complicated and seemingly ineffable endeavor that he could not well communicate the properties of most especially over the ruckus of Sheba the wirehaired dog who'd circled about the truck to discover Donnie Huff upright and afoot alongside the doorpanel before she got shortly thrown together with a boottoe that served itself to refresh and edify her. Donnie Huff, fairly giddy from his additional four ounces and agitated by his exertions of late, was considering pissing into the shrubbery himself, had reached even for his zipper tab so as to be prepared maybe to loose his organ and summon his dog both together, when he swung about and caught sight through the doorscreen of Opal Criner his loving wife's mother in the company of a lady he could not readily identify. She was shorter than Opal Criner and grayer than Opal Criner and had broadened and splayed considerably more than Opal Criner's own vanity would allow. She appeared to him as well sterner somehow than Opal Criner, had unaccountably mastered a sourer face than Opal Criner was even on her illest day capable of though Donnie Huff's loving wife's mother was gazing herself through the screenwire with visible distaste.

Together they were not the two of them much of an invitation, and though Donnie Huff unhanded his zipper tab he did not let on to take otherwise any notice of the ladies and appeared disposed to linger in the yard, but Opal Criner would not allow it, and she called through the screenwire a greeting to her Donald and informed him how he had a guest, wondered if wouldn't he look for himself and see there beside her Mrs. Lila B. Underwood come all the way from Fancy Gap on his account. Accordingly Mrs. Lila B. Underwood herself undertook for the benefit of Donnie Huff a variety of salute, inclined slightly her head and then disinclined it shortly thereafter, and Opal Criner allowed how they'd been speaking lately of him, wondered had his ears been afire as the air had been ripe with talk of his perils and exploits.

Although Donnie Huff's ears had not lately plagued him in fact, he was growing acutely sensible of the state of his bladder which was burning a little on its own and appealing after a fashion to get drained off and so persuaded Donnie Huff that maybe he'd might best enter the house, press with his own ones the fingers of Mrs. Lila B. Underwood, and then pass down the hallway to the toilet where he could put himself at unscrutinized ease. So he took his leave of Buddy Isom and advanced towards the slab and stepped through the doorway into the company of his loving wife's mother and Mrs. Lila B. Underwood both who interrupted him in his processional, would not allow him even in the wake of the finger squeezing to advance down the hallway but caused him instead to linger there before the door where his loving wife's mother sought to have him confirm for her as gospel most every little thing she'd told already to Mrs. Lila B. Underwood whose brother had drowned and whose people had succumbed and who gazed keenly upon Donnie Huff herself in hopes of detecting about him those qualities and traits that had purchased his salvation. Straightaway, however, he just appeared to her edgy chiefly and smelled to be rank and intoxicated which she worked up a caustic expression about, a look of such disapproval that Opal Criner grew fairly frantic to elevate Donnie Huff in her estimation and so escorted him over to the settee where she caused him to sit and settle and made of Donnie Huff an inquiry on the topic of his vented essence that had passed lately from his supine form and ascended into the ether.

Naturally Donnie Huff was not of a disposition to speak just presently of his excursion to the portal as he had on his mind a shorter sort of a trip altogether, but Opal Criner pressed and prodded him further, insisted that he tell to her please what she was meaning to hear, confirm how his vented essence had passed lately from his supine form and ascended into the ether, confirm it in fact twice over, once for Opal Criner who knew it already and once for Mrs. Lila B. Underwood who'd been the one to travel after all clean from Fancy Gap to hear it. Opal Criner was anxious to know if hadn't Donnie Huff gotten bathed in bright and glorious heavenly light as he soared and wafted towards the portal which Donnie Huff confessed to her he had and shortly shared with Mrs. Lila B. Underwood his recollections of those golden shafts and beams that were bright, he told to her, and that were glorious. As she could not help but figure Mrs. Lila B. Underwood was curious to hear of it, Opal Criner encouraged Donnie Huff to speak if he would of the portal itself before he proceeded on to the heavenly Savior, tell most especially of the filigreed gate that Donnie Huff obliged her in, and so conveyed to Mrs. Lila B. Underwood news of the gate that he let on to be sizable and let on to be filigreed both.

The additional and wholly uncustomary four fluid ounces that Donnie Huff had lately imbibed had brought him now to full saturation, had been filtered and processed and was ready to be expelled, was demanding pretty much to be discharged and straightaway that Donnie Huff could not help there on the settee but take some notice of, and he attempted to wriggle free of Opal Criner's grip on him, demonstrated an inclination to stand upright and slip off but got pinched and squeezed so as to thwart him in his desire. Consequently, he merely crossed his legs tightly one atop the other and embarked upon talk of the backlit and behaloed Christ who'd come forth to the sill to greet him, had stood there before Donnie Huff in His raiments all shiny and bright. Opal Criner was hoping that Donnie Huff might, for the benefit of Mrs. Lila B. Underwood, describe in some detail the aspect of his Jesus, tell to her how He looked and what He did and speak most especially of the parable of the peach pit that his Christ had shared with him, the tale about the one pit alone that had sprouted presently into a tree laid heavy with peaches itself.

"Oh," Donnie Huff told to her, "right."

And maybe it was the general strain of keeping his pent-up fluids pent up that brought to the voice of Donnie Huff a noticeable quiver or perhaps it was the acute discomfort of his loving wife's mother's grip upon his elbow joint that caused Donnie Huff to accelerate his speech and suggest in his manner a distinct sense of urgency if not fervor outright. Though likely instead it was the strain of his fluids and the discomfort of his joint flavored the both of them with Donnie Huff's general sense of irritation at having in the first place to sit there in the front room and speak of his Jesus at all that caused the timbre of Donnie Huff's voice to rise. He had wastewater to drain and flatulence to see after and he didn't much care if some woman he didn't know had driven over from some place she should have stayed at to hear him speak of how he'd passed through the ether and come across the Lord, and he guessed he'd just get up from that settee and declare as much to anybody who wished to know it, would loose himself from the elbow grip, and go off to make water and go off to break wind and pursue on his own just any little urge that struck him. He figured he would. He figured he ought to and he swung even slightly about but Opal Criner pinched him at a vessel like she'd evermore demonstrated a talent for and instructed Donnie Huff, "Go on," suggested to him, "Tell her."

So he was wanting to be elsewhere engaged otherwise, was encumbered with significant by-product that he had fair cause to vent, but Donnie Huff lingered there upon the settee balky and nerveless at heart while his loving wife's mother instructed and suggested and constricted as well and thereby promoted in her Donald the manner of agitation he was prone to once what he'd meant to do did not turn out to be at all what he did. But it looked like fervor and it looked like passion and it struck Mrs.

Lila B. Underwood as a palpable feeling for Jesus, a stirring variety of affection that Donnie Huff apparently could not well contain, and he told her of the ether he'd passed through and the portal he'd arrived at and the Lord and Savior he'd come into the presence of. He made even vague mention of peaches and nectarines both prior to speaking as well and in some detail of the pearly relief on the archway and the filigree on the gate, telling of them in such irritated nasally tones as to attract the attention of his wife Marie in the kitchen who'd left off for the moment inflicting distress and had to wonder what her Donnie had come home all lathered up about. She stepped across the linoleum and arrived at the doorcasing which she pitched against shoulder foremost so as to consider the sight before of her of her momma and her husband snug up together on the settee with Mrs. Lila B. Underwood in the upholstered chair alongside them, Mrs. Lila B. Underwood inclined attentively towards the settee herself. He was speaking by then of the raiments that had glistened and shone and the handsome wispy beard not terribly unlike his own one and the soothing voice and the long elegant fingers, and Donnie recrossed his legs and was meaning to tell of the tranquillity and fathomless peace that descended upon him there in the presence of his Savior but his boy Delmon interrupted him at it, had left the sideyard and arrived lately upon the front slab from where he attempted above the blandishments of Sheba the wirehaired dog to speak of how he'd managed just lately to chip off an incisor.

"Daddy," he said through the screenwire. "Daddy," he said again and so learned from Donnie and Opal both how he'd be best advised to hold for a time his tongue as they were just then in the middle of a delicate affair and could not presently tolerate a disturbance. They told to him anyhow together, "Hush!" with such a surplus of agitation as to impress even Delmon and Sheba who stood there on the slab gazing silently through the screenwire as Donnie Huff shared with Mrs. Lila B. Underwood the saga of the holy fingerends that got routed up from alongside the Savior where they'd laid and hung, advanced briefly through the air towards Donnie Huff there on the slab, and settled at last upon the downy patch of skin that Donnie Huff indicated for the benefit of Mrs. Lila B. Underwood though he grew persuaded shortly by his loving wife's mother to reindicate it in another place entirely.

"Just here," Donnie Huff said and removed his own hand from the way so that Lila B. Underwood might view unobstructed the place the Lord's fingers had touched. And she did for a time merely view it alone. There in the upholstered chair under the scrutiny of Donnie Huff and Donnie Huff's wife's mother and Donnie Huff's wife and Donnie Huff's boy and Donnie Huff's sizable wire-haired dog, Mrs. Lila B. Underwood contented herself exclusively with looking upon the downy patch of forearm that her Jesus had deigned to lay His fingers atop of, merciful Jesus, beneficent Jesus, Lord of the afflicted and Redeemer of the downtrodden, her Christ the son of God who'd apparently seen fit to bless this man before her, return to him his life that he'd lost and squandered through mischance and poor fortune, though she could not even guess why as Donnie Huff did not appear to her an especially worthy manner of fellow deserving more of grace and salvation than folks otherwise who'd kicked off themselves, but then that was just the quaint way of her Christ to turn up a wretch to pity and restore.

And he didn't figure she'd do it since she didn't appear prone and tempted, hadn't come to exhibit the rank wonderment he'd previously noticed on the faces of the women who'd laid their fingerends to him, but she did it nonetheless, canted forward and settled in fact some fingerends of her own upon the downy patch, pressed it, gripped it, smothered it over, and held to it as she glared about the room from Donnie Huff to Opal Criner to Marie against the casing and over to Delmon and Sheba beyond the doorscreen in advance of lifting her face and peering off towards the ceiling instead though hardly like a woman enraptured and infused as she looked chiefly to be contemplating the state of the drywall which she persevered at until she grew somehow persuaded that her obligation was spent and done when she discharged a noise from her neck and unhanded Donnie Huff at last like left him to reach with his own fingers for his downy patch that he rubbed and pinched and kneaded and endeavored to bring some blood back to.

IV

She'd neglected somehow to make mention of it, had returned come Sunday from the sanctuary in her blue speckled dress and her tufted hat with the stunning bird-feather bouquet, and had stood there in the front room drawing off her gloves by the fingerends when she'd seen fit to speak to Donnie Huff of pertinent matters otherwise, had described for him most especially the ensemble of Mrs. Ocala Pugh that had not struck her as deft and seemly on account chiefly of the cut of the skirt which had caused it to cling and to bind in the most unflattering sort of a way. But she'd failed unaccountably to disclose to him just what precisely had transpired there in the sanctuary between the doxology and the biweekly prayer for the shut-ins which left Donnie Huff quite unable to anticipate the visit he received come Tuesday evening from a Laurel Fork delegation, the call he entertained from Mrs. Troy Haven and Mrs. Norma Baines and the Reverend Mr. Worrell's wife Louise in addition to Miss Cindy Womble who'd seen fit herself to tote along with her her sizable hooters that Donnie Huff commenced straightaway to appreciate and know in his heart such gladness about that he left the ladies to stand for a time on the front slab while he simply gazed enchantedly through the screenwire until Opal Criner prevailed upon him to admit please the pack of them into the house.

Marie Criner did not prove herself quite so charmed by the
visit or nearly so enamored of the hooters as her husband Donnie Huff appeared to her to be. She did not in fact care much
at all for Miss Cindy Womble straightoff and the two of them
together bared at each other their teeth as a manner of salutation. Donnie Huff offered to the hooters a beverage and a
snack, made at them trifling talk on the topic of the weather,
which had been lately sublime, and inquired even after the
health and well-being of their attachments and relations in advance of yielding to Opal Criner, his loving wife's mother, who
wondered of the ladies what they might the bunch of them
want and require. Of course they wanted and required what
they'd all of them previously voted by acclamation upon there
in the sanctuary between the doxology and the prayer for the
shut-ins and, now that she'd been reminded and refreshed,
Opal Criner told to the ladies, "Oh," told to the ladies, "that,"
and gave way to the Reverend Mr. Worrell's wife Louise who
was not any longer herself in possession of the sort of enticements to engage Donnie Huff, or rather to disengage him entirely from certain attendant enticements otherwise. Consequently, Donnie Huff paid to Louise Worrell fairly scant regard
as she reported to him their intention to invite him please to
return to the sanctuary at Laurel Fork and speak on this occasion to the entire congregation who'd expressed this past Sunday, after the doxology and before the biweekly prayer, their
unfettered enthusiasm at the prospect of hearing from a fellow
who'd been lately dead. They did so all of them hope he would
bless them with his presence, and Louise Worrell, speaking on
behalf of the bunch of them together, pleaded with Donnie
Huff to come if he would the following Sunday to the sanctuary
and share his tale of doom and glory with the membership at
large which Donnie Huff did not appear truly much disposed
one way or another about until the Reverend Mr. Worrell's wife
Louise had left off speaking so as to allow Mrs. Troy Haven and
Mrs. Norma Baines and Miss Cindy Womble as well to petition
Donnie Huff themselves to favor them if he might come Sunday with his testimony which produced upon Donnie Huff an
agreeable effect due largely to Cindy Womble's own charming
and chesty way with a request.

He didn't truly realize what he'd guessed he'd do and where he'd guessed he'd do it until he'd squired the hooters back out onto the slab and watched through the screenwire as they receded into the twilight when his wife Marie joined him there at the doorway so as to exhibit at Donnie Huff her overbite which proved itself as utterly well-spoken as any hooters anywhere could possibly be. He raised at his wife Marie his shoulders in an effort to render up a declaration of his own but was spared further scrutiny on account of his loving wife's mother who fairly capered across the carpet and thereby earned from her girl Marie a supremely toothy grin herself that widened and expanded quite appreciably once Opal Criner had ventured to suggest to her child an outfit suitable for the sanctuary, a green corduroy shift she'd evermore been fond of that she figured Marie might wear belted on this occasion so as to keep her from looking too awful dumpy which was just the sort of talk to induce Marie Criner to retire into the kitchen where, apparently, she busied herself distressing the dinette.

Opal Criner suspected that with proper preparation Donnie Huff could truly convey to the congregation at large what being dead was all about, and she was eager to undertake to instruct him herself, was inclined even to set in straightaway at it. However, now with the hooters receded and gone from sight, Donnie Huff's enthusiasm wilted and waned and he flung himself into his upholstered chair where he sprawled with one leg over the chairarm and made as if to be inclined to watch the tv, but Opal Criner was not herself content to let him sprawl there before the set uninstructed when he'd agreed to give shortly a presentation before a collection of her brethren, her goodly churchmates who'd come to expect from their laypreachers a stirring sort of a spectacle, passionate if not inflamed testimony like was hardly the sort of thing a fellow could hope to work up on the spot. While Donnie Huff had succeeded well enough at Bible class, Opal Criner felt obliged to inform him that his ascent through the ether to the heavenly portal could stand nonetheless a little punching up on account of how the tale did not have too terribly much native zing to it. She figured he might improve as well on his plummet from the bluff, advance somehow the tempo of the thing, and add maybe a gaudy flame to trail behind the skidder on its way into the creek. She also guessed he could maybe be in retrospect dead for longer than he'd in reality been it, which would heighten undoubtedly the drama of the entire episode by contributing to it the chance of a hemorrhage if not general strangulation of the brain. She felt pressed as well to speak at some length to Donnie Huff of his pauses since he had not demonstrated previously much grasp of the considerable value of a pause, had not shown to her any feel for when to leave off and when to set in again and thereby profit from the lag between what he'd told and what he might tell next. And, most pertinently, Opal Criner was herself convinced that if Donnie Huff wore his blue suit with the ever so faint and elegant stripe to it and adorned and complemented the thing with the speckled satiny tie she'd made to him a gift of but had not yet had the pleasure to see him wear, then he'd surely hold most extravagant sway over anybody come to hear his tale of redemption in this life. Of course she could not help but believe that some general whisker removal was in order as well and employed her innate delicacy and grace in the insinuation of it but failed to produce much effect upon Donnie Huff who viewed on the set the decor of a starlet who lived quite plainly in glamorous digs.

Quite naturally Opal Criner perceived for herself a Christian duty to keep after Donnie Huff, and so she fetched out for him his white calfskin Bible and proceeded to offer up instruction and advice, cited for Donnie Huff useful bits of scripture, and suggested to him how he might, through controlled breathing and proper inflection, render himself inspirational. Donnie Huff, however, pretty much ignored her there for the balance of the evening and, come the following night, he did not straightoff demonstrate much inclination to alter his ways and take any noticeable heed of his loving wife's mother who read to him from the Book of John, explained to Donnie Huff the general appeal of life eternal, and reminded him how it was Wednesday already that he was obviously intending to squander before the tv like would leave him just three nights to come to be preacherly which Opal Criner did not appear to hold out much hope about. She had to guess the dismay would be rampant and general, would sweep like contagion through the sanctuary once Donnie Huff had revealed himself ill-suited and unprepared to testify on behalf of his Lord and Savior, precisely the manner of prospect to capture the attention of Donnie Huff who undertook to picture Miss Cindy Womble all infected with dismay, Miss Cindy Womble who would not surely heave and flush in the throes of deep and desolate disappointment as she'd demonstrated previously a talent for when suitably stirred and transported.

He came, then, to recognize the nature of his plight and fathomed as well the value of instruction once the benefits had been rendered for him real and melonlike. So he turned down the television and encouraged Opal Criner to share with him please the various qualities he might best conjure up to get taken come Sunday for preacherly. She was openly delighted to advise him and straightaway provided Donnie Huff with snippets of the Gospels to commit to memory, marked them for him with scraps of paper in his white calfskin Bible which she gave over to Donnie Huff so as to discover how he might be disposed to hold it. Of course, having gone his life uninstructed in the ways of the Lord, he did not grip his Bible to suit her, allowed it to lay upon his palm like most any tome otherwise until Opal Criner snatched it back from him so as to show Donnie Huff how a preacherly sort of a fellow might hold a Bible. She squeezed it there at the bottom corner opposite the spine with her thumb atop it and her fingers curled beneath it, and she raised it into the air and shook it until it flapped about which she did not even have to tell to Donnie Huff would serve him well in a moment of passion and rising fervor since he could appreciate well enough from his upholstered chair the immediate effects of Bible brandishing. She showed him how to let the scriptures sag and lay during those passages tinged with doubt and despair, and she ventured to demonstrate for Donnie Huff how, were he presented with an occasion tailored for it, he might flop open his Bible and wave it about though she confessed that this was an advanced form of brandishing which she could not help but discourage at this point in time.

Donnie Huff's posture was a worry to Opal Criner as he

tended to slouch and speak towards his shoetops in a voice that
faded and trailed away which no longer suited his calling now
that he'd come to be redeemed. He required, she figured, a
species of swagger and she drew Donnie Huff up out from his
upholstered chair so as to have him parade with her if he might
back and forth across the front room, providing her the opportunity to adjust his shoulders and alter his stride and elevate
his chin and just generally tinker with and transform his demeanor until they'd accomplished together the sort of comport-
ment that appeared to her a companionable blending of bluster
and humility and would likely communicate to a congregation
how here was a man who'd been places they hadn't been and
knew things they didn't know. Once she'd prevailed upon Donnie Huff to contribute to and complement the swaggering with
instances of judicious Bible brandishing, Opal Criner's satisfaction was for the moment complete, and she pretty ceaselessly
called for her girl Marie to step please from the kitchen and
grace them if she might with her opinion on Donnie Huff's
carriage across the front room until her girl Marie at last re-
lented and arrived in the doorway where she stood with a Kent
between her lips, crossed her arms before herself and watched
her Donnie march and brandish while her momma Opal
coached him at it which served, as a pageant and a display, to
inspire the revival of Marie Criner's wan, sickly, nauseated smile
which she had not much employed since her girlish days.

As Bible flapping was the kind of thing Donnie Huff could
sit in front of the tv and practice, he picked it up pretty directly
and, before the night was out, could fairly crack the scriptures
like a whip, but he failed to manufacture there on the chaircushion the manner of tonality and anguished inflection Opal
Criner had to figure he would likely require to produce upon
the congregation a full-blown and frenzied effect. Donnie Huff
simply could not project well enough from his upholstered
chair to cause his voice to quiver and catch, creak every now
and again like a floorboard underfoot, and he was far too weary
of swaggering and waving his Bible about to be tempted by
Opal Criner to rise and intone. So he remained there perched
upon his chaircushion with his white calfskin Bible that he

pressed and curled and snatched and just beat about in the air while he heard from his loving wife's mother a lengthy and semitheoretical presentation on the topic of diaphragmatic properties and respirational technique. She saw fit to conclude their evening together with a pertinent scrap of verse which she encouraged Donnie Huff to commit if he might to memory, a passage from the Book of Isaiah which commenced with a "Ho" that Donnie Huff found diverting since, while he'd been lately acquainted with a world with "Yea"s and "Wherefore"s, he'd not previously come across too awful many "Ho!"s. And he raised up his Bible to flog the air prior to telling to Opal Criner, " 'Ho, every one who thirsts, come to the waters,' " which she found to be largely delightful if a trifle topheavy with emphasis, and she read through the entire item for the benefit of her Donald who she instructed not to milk if he might his "Ho!" so.

" 'Ho,' " Donnie Huff told to her with lilt and restraint, " 'every one who thirsts, come to the waters. Seek the Lord while He may be found, call upon him while He is near.' "

Of course Opal Criner guessed she'd not ever in her days heard a finer scrap of Isaiah and she clasped her hands together and lay them against her breastbone prior to calling out in her agitated state to her girl Marie in the kitchen who, enjoying presently some agitation of her own, inquired of her momma, "What in the hell is it?" back.

Come Thursday in the forenoon Donnie Huff had already made himself pretty thoroughly tiresome there on the hillside above the Big Reed where he swaggered and where he intoned and where he waved, in lieu of his Bible, a slab of wood about and told "Ho!" most especially to little Gaither more times than little Gaither figured he had cause to endure it. Outside there on the slope Donnie Huff quite naturally felt free to hone his respirational technique and exercise his diaphragmatic properties, and so presently he moved beyond his "Ho!" alone and was announcing into the air instructions to those who thirsted and directions for those who sought the Lord in addition to declaring with regularity in his best preacherly tones, "Like this here," which allowed for the employment of Donnie Huff's free and slabless hand. The hijinks were truly infectious and set off

Buddy Isom and set off Freeman MacAfee who honed their techniques and exercised their properties as well until the territory roundabout was ringing with declarations that were scriptural every now and again but were primarily anatomical instead much to the uncloaked chagrin of Alvis Nevins who found on occasion some things sacred. He figured he was presently sentimental about the Lord who he wouldn't himself be inclined to make sport of which he shared with Buddy Isom and with Freeman MacAfee and with Donnie Huff as well who guessed he'd heard lately from the Lord a thing which Donnie Huff got invited to speak of and pass along and so shortly announced to Alvis Nevins in a startling and preacherly tone, "Ho!" that little Gaither across the slope objected about and swore on account of as he'd tolerated already "Ho!"s enough.

Marie Criner had lately decoupaged some crockery which had dried at last sufficiently to serve from and, come Thursday evening, she dumped their Salisbury steak out from its foil pan into her bowl with the grapes and the bananas on it which did not itself garner much notice from Donnie Huff and Opal Criner who entered the kitchen engaged in a discussion on the topic of the racking sob as a punctuational device and persevered at it as they set the table and took their seats, though Delmon did venture himself to wonder of his momma if wasn't one of her bananas upside down which earned for him a heated and detailed explanation of how there was no wrong side of a banana to be up or right side of a banana to be down. Donnie Huff, though it was not hardly his custom, volunteered to say grace and he shut his eyes and bowed his head and in a fairly deep and diaphragmatic voice beseeched the Lord to bless and keep their various holdings and relations which Donnie Huff named and identified for the benefit of the Savior, who might need to know which holdings and which relations precisely, and as a means as well of demonstrating his own coming mastery of the articulate pause that Opal Criner applied her shoetoe beneath the dinette to congratulate him about just barely in advance of a similar communication undertaken by Donnie's wife Marie who with her sneaker heel beat Donnie Huff emphatically upon a tendon and thereby created for herself a lull in which to tell to him, "Amen already."

Of course neither Donnie nor Opal could be troubled themselves to comment upon the crockery as best as Marie Criner could tell though Opal Criner did manage to complain about the Salisbury steak which she found to be gristly and unduly tough, that struck her somehow as products of the preparation which she managed quite successfully to imply and consequently got invited by her girl Marie to lay down if she would her utensils and shut if she might her mouth to prevent the inflow of food and the outflow of blather all at once and together. As for himself, Donnie Huff professed to prefer his Salisbury steak chewy and apprised his boy Delmon of the nutritional value of gristle which built, he told it, strong bones more ways than he could presently conjure up and identify, but Delmon guessed he'd keep his bones brittle and unimproved and so strung his gristle out roundabout his platerim and picked with his fork at his lean chewy leavings after such a fashion to appear to his mother to be little more than doodling with his food.

Naturally Marie Criner came to be obliged to speak herself of her crockery since nobody else possessed the decency to admire it uninduced, and Opal and Donnie showed between them a fondness for her serving bowl which Donnie in fact managed to seem weepy and choked up at the sight of much to the delight of Opal Criner who confessed to having been for a moment taken in by Donnie Huff's tortured expression. They aired the both of them their concern about the bananas which appeared to them upended, but otherwise they admitted to being charmed by the crockery quite altogether, admitted to it with such delicate and fabricated grace as to set off Marie Criner who guessed she wasn't yet fool enough to get seduced by an inflection and taken in by a lilt, though she supposed were she to find a way to love her Jesus she might soon enough become adequately stupid.

"Maybe the Lord would bless me with big tits like that woman that was here," she told across the table to Donnie Huff, who, in a demonstration of bold and potent thespianics, looked blankly upon his wife Marie and inquired of her, "What woman is that?"

"Go on," she told to him and told beyond it to her momma

Opal, "Go on, the both of you. Do whatever it is you been doing. Go on." And she turned her attention to Delmon her baby who was engaged in manipulating his strands of gristle into the shapes of assorted breadfruits that she alleviated for him the temptation of by collecting his plate together with the plates otherwise and dropping the pile of them into the sink.

"It's just a bowl, darling," her momma Opal told to her as she rose to crumb.

But Marie Criner, with her back to the table, declared to her mother's reflection in the windowlight over the sink, "It's hardly just a bowl."

Donnie Huff fairly much had his brandishing down cold and, demonstrating for his loving wife's mother his technique, he strode about the front room whipping and waving his white calfskin Bible in the air which served as a potent distraction for Delmon his boy who'd been hoping to view unobstructed the *PM Magazine* where a man was showing the leggy hostess how to make hoop cheeses which was just the sort of thing Delmon guessed he was curious to know. However, he could not well take in the cheesemaking process what with his daddy prancing back and forth across the front room being redeemed more passionately than there was truly much call for and his grand-momma Opal inciting him to be if he might redeemed more passionately still. It was almost more than a mere child could begin to endure, and Delmon was growing even a little peevish on his own when the *PM Magazine* gave way to the half hour of news from Hollywood which featured this evening, as it was prone to most nights, an array of bosomy starlets who threw in together to take up Donnie Huff by his ganglia and snatch him pretty much back through the ether to his upholstered chair.

Of course Opal Criner was not herself persuaded that Donnie Huff had advanced yet so far along in his general tonality as to be able just now to well afford the leisure of sprawling and laying about. But there was not truly a thing in this world his loving wife's mother could tell to him that would distract Donnie Huff from his pack of starlets who'd charmed and transfixed him already and held him there in their spell until the station break. Now Opal Criner, being herself a woman of no little insight and intuition, observed in Donnie Huff his affection for the bosomy starlets and proposed to him, once the news show from Hollywood had given way to the drama about the plumbing contractor who fought crime by night, that he could enrich perhaps his presentation by touching upon his foibles and shortcomings, the assorted lusts of his heart, so as to spice up the narrative and demonstrate simultaneously what an unlikely candidate for redemption he'd been.

"Tell to them how low you'd fallen before you rose on high," Opal Criner suggested to Donnie Huff and encouraged him to share with her if he might his urges and inclinations so as to provide her the opportunity to edit and revise them, but Donnie Huff was reluctant to speak to his loving wife's mother of what it was he'd been anxious just previously to lay his nose against and so he rendered up his highly thespianic expression and inquired of Opal Criner, "Tell you what now?"

She was quite prepared on her own to manufacture some foibles for him and so assigned straightoff to Donnie Huff a slothful disposition and an unreliable nature in addition to a wandering eye for the ladies and a luckless inclination to run evermore with the wrong sort of fellows. He'd been, she figured, by disposition profane and vile and had not demonstrated much willingness to alter his course on this earth right up to the moment he pitched off the bluff in his skidder trailing a tongue of flame. While Donnie Huff guessed it would be pretty much all stretch for him thespianically speaking, he determined that he would attempt to seem a wastrel and a reprobate if Opal Criner figured there were souls to be saved by it and spirits to be lifted, and he rendered up such a fairly exacting approximation of a wretched lout that Opal Criner approved enthusiastically and enlisted her grandbaby Delmon to tell to her please if wasn't his daddy as sorry a fellow as he'd had the misfortune to come across lately.

Here in the wake of his salvation, Donnie Huff had cause to be repentant of his evil ways and he called upon his loving wife's mother to coach him please in the nuances of remorse which she demonstrated and he mimicked and shaped for his uses and abilities until he could appear at an instant's notice altogether saddled with regret. When he saw fit to interrupt talk of his transgressions with a punctuational racking sob, Opal Criner herself grew noticeably radiant with delight and enlisted her grandbaby Delmon to join her please in an ovation which Donnie Huff acknowledged with a manner of grace that seemed very nearly native to him.

Friday he declaimed on the hillside up among the poplars a new verse entirely that his loving wife's mother had charged him to learn. It did not have a Ho to it much to the relief of little Gaither though it was afflicted instead with two "Yea"s and a "Wherefore" which Donnie Huff managed to intone with aggravating enthusiasm and so rendered presently little Gaither ill and irritated nonetheless, little Gaither who guessed he'd pray on his own to heaven that Donnie Huff might work in the future even half so well as he declaimed which did not strike Donnie Huff as likely though he was reluctant to discourage a man from prayer and so failed to share his views with little Gaither himself. Instead he furthered his acquaintance with his piece of scripture which was in fact a composite drawn by Opal Criner from several of the Testaments and amalgamated together after a fashion that seemed to her more suitable than the ancient scribes in their wisdom had managed. The thing set out briefly with a tribute to the King in His beauty, advanced on to make plain that hoary heads were crowns of glory themselves, prior to culminating with the news of how the Lord would descend presently from heaven with a cry of command, the archangel's call, and the sound of the trumpet of God. The "Yea"s and the "Wherefore" were interspersed indiscriminately throughout the item and shifted about in accordance with the whimsy of Donnie Huff who gave voice to the "Wherefore" whenever he was feeling transitional and gave voice to the "Yea"s whenever he was feeling emphatic.

Alvis Nevins, who counted himself a scriptural purist, objected stridently to the migration of most especially the "Yea"s from the head of the verse on down along to the shank of it, but Donnie Huff blessed and forgave him straightaway and thereby endeavored to defuse Alvis Nevins who'd not been looking to get blessed and forgiven by most especially the likes of Donnie Huff who plainly made up scripture as he went along which

Alvis Nevins could not apparently tolerate with much aplomb since fabricating verse did not strike him hardly as Christian and appeared to him just one instance further of Donnie Huff making sport of the Lord. Donnie Huff, however, managed to dissolve directly into what looked straightoff to Alvis Nevins a variety of respirational distress. He wheezed and he gurgled and he brought forth at length a racking sob in advance of reminding Alvis Nevins how those that thirsted should come to the waters and those that sought the Lord should call upon Him while He's near which Donnie Huff garnished with one racking sob further and thereby transformed the ire of Alvis Nevins quite altogether, rendered him meek and sorrowful while at the same time creating upon Freeman MacAfee a most favorable impression as he'd not himself witnessed such passionate thespianics since back a few weeks previous when he'd picked up on his dish a woman in the midst of an orgasmic reaction that had seemed to him genuine and real though Buddy Isom could not help but wonder how Freeman MacAfee might recognize a legitimate orgasmic reaction since he'd certainly not ever himself induced one.

Come evening in the front room Donnie Huff shaped his presentation with the aid and assistance of his loving wife's mother and his boy Delmon as well who was fondest himself of the fiery crash into the Big Reed but could tolerate the travels of the vented essence if Donnie Huff did not dwell too awful much on the properties of the ether or linger overlong upon the ornaments of the portal itself. Opal Criner spent some considerable of her energies on the exchange between Donnie Huff and the Savior by which she hoped to achieve an appropriate state of congeniality and render if she might the Lord Christ appealing without diminishing altogether His mystical qualities. Naturally they coordinated between them a suitable rendition of the parable of the peach pit which Donnie Huff endeavored at the outset to tell in the voice of the Savior Himself though Opal Criner could not believe it was tasteful to impersonate Christ. They agreed between them to terminate the general exchange once Jesus had laid His fingers upon the downy patch of skin and told to Donnie Huff, "Come."

"Come?" Donnie Huff wanted to know.

"Come," Opal Criner assured him and inquired if couldn't Donnie Huff recall having identified it previously as the sentiment of the Savior which Donnie Huff, upon consideration, seemed to recollect and told to Opal Criner, "Oh yeah," in advance of exhibiting his downy patch and sharing with Opal and sharing with Delmon as well, "Come," which he intoned deeply and lingered upon after a fashion that Opal Criner found ever so pleasing.

She guessed they'd be prudent to undertake a full dress rehearsal in the front room come Saturday afternoon, and she volunteered her services to Donnie Huff in the selection of his wardrobe, advised him anyhow to wear his blue suit with the faint and slender stripe to it and his black lace-up shoes and his navy socks as opposed to his skyblue ones in addition of course to his white shirt and his speckled satiny tie which he'd not yet found occasion to remove from the box but did not offer to dispute with his loving wife's mother about. So come Saturday just past lunch Donnie Huff endeavored to render himself swanky but found that his white shirt had a greasespot on the front of it that Opal Criner could not manage to cleanse away with spit and friction and so soaked the thing in the lavatory in a soapy solution and hunted up for Donnie Huff a white shirt her Carl had not himself cared much for the cut of, a white shirt she'd held to somehow as it had evermore seemed to her such a shame to throw away a man's clothes just because he was dead and buried.

Opal Criner had not herself imagined that the speckled satiny tie would set off Donnie Huff's eyes so or pick up with its speckles the stripes of the suit which proved such delightful surprises that Opal Criner attempted to entice her girl Marie into the front room to savor them for herself, but she could not find her girl Marie in the kitchen and could not discover her girl Marie in the back of the house and so was put upon to savor those delightful surprises in relative solitude though she did induce Delmon her grandbaby to concede how he hoped one day to have occasion to wear a speckled satiny tie himself.

As her Carl had been a sizable and strapping sort of a fellow, his white shirt provided Donnie Huff with an excess of shirttail which he attempted to situate and secure in his trousers, but it tended to creep on him with any exertion he made and fall in billowy folds out over his belt. Opal Criner, however, found that billowy folds were a good look for Donnie Huff since they made him appear to be wiry and likely even more ripply and svelte than Donnie Huff figured already he was. So she did not resituate his folds and billows but encouraged Donnie Huff to pace back and forth across the carpet with his jacket unbuttoned and his white calfskin Bible upraised in his hand from where he could whip and beat it about at will. Opal Criner instructed Donnie Huff to demonstrate if he would his thoroughgoing command of the dramatic pause which Donnie Huff obliged her in prior to rendering his tone creaky and tormented which he gave over shortly for an inspirational outburst that Opal Criner herself found fairly galvanizing.

Together they took the thing from the top and Opal Criner, in her role as the Reverend Mr. Worrell, introduced Donnie Huff to Delmon her grandbaby who she joined on the settee from where her and Delmon together watched Donnie Huff testify with considerably more polish and dash than Opal Criner had ever truly suspected he could muster. She grew in fact so completely transported by the performance that she fabricated for the benefit of Donnie Huff a racking sob to raise in harmony with his own one and encouraged her grandbaby Delmon to emit with her if he might stirring little evangelical noises when the moment seemed apt for it, though Delmon proved himself no judge much of aptness and squealed to praise his Maker in the most inopportune and unfortunate places. Donnie Huff, however, proved largely undistractable and pressed on through the ether and clean up to the portal proper that he lingered upon the features and adornments of in advance of sharing with his boy Delmon and his loving wife's mother Opal the parable of the peach pit that culminated in the fingers of the Lord Christ which laid upon the downy patch that Donnie Huff drew up his sleeve end to expose as he told to Opal and told to Delmon, "Come."

She guessed she was herself driven near about to tears, and Opal Criner confessed to Donnie Huff that he'd fairly well

melted her altogether with most especially his creaky quavering
episodes which Donnie Huff appeared gratified to hear of and
he accepted with grace Opal Criner's suggestion that he not be
tempted in the course of his presentation to reach with his free
hand as he's flapping his Bible with the other and undertake to
scratch himself at the inseam which had noticeably detracted
from the mood of the proceedings as best as Opal Criner could
tell. Otherwise she was terribly pleased with the presentation
and did so wish her girl Marie would join them there in the
front room to sit through a reprise of the narrative. Consequently, she dispatched her grandbaby Delmon to look please
for his momma and fetch her back with him to the front of the
house. Marie was not, however, anywhere down the hallway
and did not prove to be in the kitchen either although Delmon
managed to discover a piece of a pecan swirl instead right there
in the refrigerator back of the remains of a roasting hen that
had been picked over and feasted from and lay now wrapped in
foil on the shelf quite deflated and unenticing and serving no
other purpose than as an impediment for Delmon to delight. So
while he failed to fetch back his mother, Delmon carried into
the front room the scant scrap of pecan swirl he'd not eaten on
the way along with the cellophane packaging that he licked and
sucked on and the white cardboard sleeve that he scraped with
his teeth.

Straightaway his grandmomma wanted to know of him
where his momma might be though she could not help but
amend her query with the news of her own opinion of the sort
of young man that would suck on cellophane and scrape down
cardboard sleeves which was not, as an opinion, terribly gracious and favorable but failed itself to dissuade Delmon from
applying his toothedges to the sweet and gummy pecan residue
which he ingested every last morsel of prior to revealing to his
grandmomma Opal how his momma Marie was plainly not anywhere as best as he could tell.

She guessed then she would find her for herself, and so
Opal Criner rose up off the settee and sought her girl Marie in
the kitchen, looked for her out through the doorway on the
back slab, and passed along the length of the house and down

the hallway where she stuck her head into the bedrooms and peeked even into the linen closet. It seemed to her curious that her girl Marie would not be anywhere about, and she was aiming to step back into the front room to tell as much to Donnie and her grandbaby Delmon when she caught sight through the window of a flash of color out beside the carshed and discovered it to be the yellow shirt of her girl Marie who was sitting in the grass out towards the back of the lot between the trash pile and the furthermost clothesline post, settled upon a hummock with her back to the house and just sitting there quite wholly unengaged as best as Opal Criner could tell. She called over Delmon and Donnie both to look with her if they would at Marie in the grass and to tell to her if they might what it was she was up to. But a couple of minutes of fairly steady perusal managed only to persuade them that she was very likely not up to anything at all though she plucked every now and again a sprig of grass and cast it to the breeze which Opal Criner informed Donnie and Delmon both was not truly much of a gainful pursuit.

Being a mother sensitive to the subtle signs of her offspring, Opal Criner felt deep in the core of her being that perhaps her girl Marie had dropped off into a funk. She guessed in her years she'd learned to know a funk when she saw one and she did not suppose there was likely much remedy for it other than maybe a visit by her Donald out to the hummock where he could soothe Marie, listen to her plagues and worries, and supply her with whatever manner of assurances she appeared to him to require. Opal Criner suggested even a suitable tone of voice Donnie Huff might employ as he stroked and commiserated, a tone of voice Donnie Huff showed even a knack for and picked up straightaway and so stepped with confidence out through the back door and onto the slab. From the window Opal Criner and Delmon her grandbaby watched him cross the yard towards the hummock where his wife Marie did not appear to hear that he was coming or care that he'd arrived once he'd reached out to tap her with his fingerend and tell to her, apparently, "Hey."

Marie Criner did not offer to make room for Donnie Huff

upon her hummock but merely plucked further at the lawn and cast her pickings into the air, leaving Donnie Huff to shift for himself and squat after a fashion alongside her from where he reached out and laid his hand between the knobby points of Marie Criner's shoulder blades which Opal Criner soundly approved of and suggested to Delmon her grandbaby how tenderness between two people was surely sometimes a lovely thing. From the window they watched Donnie Huff speak gently to Marie his wife, make what appeared to Opal Criner an inquiry as to the particular plagues and worries that had driven Marie to her hummock in the first place. However, Marie seemed for her part reluctant to open up to Donnie her husband and share with him the nature of her present complaint. Shortly, though, with the kneading of his fingers upon her back and the sweet low inducement of his suitable tone in her ear, Donnie Huff plainly coaxed from Marie Criner a piece of talk that she swiveled about to share with him, a piece of talk that Opal Criner could not altogether make out but interpreted nonetheless as best as she was able and apprised Delmon her grandbaby how his momma had lately come to suffer nameless disappointments and unidentifiable frustrations. Opal Criner suspected herself it was very likely a temporary hormonal affliction which she informed Delmon his daddy would be pleased to explain to him once he'd returned to the house and had the leisure for it.

Now once she'd seen fit to loose a trickle of talk, Marie Criner grew inclined to fairly gush for a time and spoke at length to Donnie Huff from her hummock, Donnie Huff in his blue striped suit and billowy shirt and speckled satiny tie which rendered him particularly becoming in a squat, and Opal Criner identified for Delmon her grandbaby which parts of his daddy he might most especially admire. As for herself, Marie Criner could not appear to leave off spilling her torments and so remained swiveled about there on her hummock from where she spoke with animation and at length to Donnie Huff that Opal Criner, from back of the window in the niche, assured her grandbaby Delmon to be an auspicious course of events since it was oftentimes healthy for a woman in hormonal distress to air her emotions and speak, if she's able, with noticeable passion. Apparently Donnie Huff grew persuaded from the gist of his wife's sentiments to leave off kneading with his fingers and to rise as well out of his squat so that he might stand unengaged alongside the hummock and listen upright to his wife Marie who vented for a time further before allowing Donnie Huff occasion to vent briefly back which he made himself some animated use of and told to his wife Marie a thing she did not appear from her hummock to savor and care for. Consequently, she shared with her husband a vivid and fairly flagrant sort of a gesture which Opal Criner took pains to misconstrue for the benefit of Delmon her daughter's child who did not, she assured him, have much cause to lift and exhibit a finger of his own.

Donnie Huff returned across the yard to the back slab and entered into the kitchen where he paused to throw open the refrigerator door and survey, as was oftentimes his practice, the contents like provided the opportunity for his loving wife's mother and his boy Delmon to retire and gain the settee before Donnie Huff joined them in the front room and fielded straightaway from Opal Criner a query. She was hoping to learn from Donnie Huff if her girl Marie was feeling perhaps poorly and had settled upon her hummock to take the air which Donnie Huff allowed as a possibility but did not confirm as a fact since they had not between them spoken of her constitution, the sort of admission that Opal Criner seized upon in hopes of discovering what perhaps they'd spoken of instead. Donnie Huff, however, proved reluctant to tell to Opal Criner much of anything at all until she'd gone ahead and beseeched him outright when he revealed to her at last the nature of her girl Marie's distress, shared with his loving wife's mother how her girl Marie found her to be an asshole and found him to be an asshole with her and hoped the both of them together might discover some way between them to burn in hell.

"She wishes I hadn't gotten dead or had stayed it," Donnie Huff informed Opal Criner. "She doesn't much seem to care for a preacher in the house. Didn't like those women that come, got no use much for Jesus, isn't meaning this evening to cook us any supper."

And Opal Criner told to Donnie Huff, "My, my," and was intending to seek to know from him how it was her and her Carl could fail so in the rearing of a child as to drive her from the sweet embrace of the Lord, but before she could inquire, Donnie Huff, who'd only been pausing dramatically, cocked his thumb and pointed back over his shoulder in advance of declaring to Opal Criner, "Ain't a thing in there to eat."

Opal Criner could not see much cause for Donnie Huff to leave off rehearsing his testimony. Consequently, she encouraged him to pick the thing up if he might from the fingerends of the Lord and speak like they'd agreed upon of the passage of the essence back through the ether towards its rendezvous with his supine form expired upon the siltspit. But the acute disapproval of Donnie Huff's own wife had apparently dulled his enthusiasm where his vented essence was concerned. He was troubled by their encounter out at the hummock, besieged of a sudden by doubt as to whether or not he had much call to stand before a congregation and speak of the Savior since, while certainly he'd expired and perhaps even had seen with the tiny green spots some scant trace of Christ Himself, Donnie Huff was not at all convinced he'd passed in fact through the ether and lingered there at the heavenly portal in the presence of the Lord which he confessed to Opal Criner his loving wife's mother who guessed she'd been a Christian years enough now to allay on her own the reservations of a greenhorn. So she explained to Donnie Huff the elemental nature of faith itself, assured him how goodly God-fearing people only ever so rarely believed what they did because of what they knew of this world or suspected of the next. She guessed there wouldn't be sufficient challenge to that to keep from the ranks of the Christians just any old sort that grew disposed to show up and pray since it doesn't much test a man's mettle to take for a fact what he's seen to be true already. The trick of the thing, as best as Opal Criner could tell, was to believe unyieldingly in the Lord Jesus and the redemption of the spirit eternal as well as the basic goodliness of people at their core in spite of evidence to the contrary no matter how overwhelming.

Naturally Donnie Huff inquired of Opal Criner if she meant

to tell to him that he'd be best advised to suspect most everything he did know and believe most everything he didn't which Opal Criner would not herself endorse outright though she did suggest to Donnie Huff that the sorrier the world looked to him the more cause he had to rejoice.

And Donnie Huff told to Opal Criner, "Oh," and appeared to her so appreciably distracted and perplexed that she ventured to assure him and her grandbaby Delmon both that, in addition to bringing the pair of them to a better understanding of their Lord, she'd cook them for supper some eggs and some sausage and some fried potatoes as well.

Persuaded that a meal was forthcoming, Donnie Huff felt sufficiently optimistic in his prospects to carry on with his testimony and so provided his loving wife's mother and his boy Delmon with an ever so stirring version of his return through the ether to his supine form where he awoke on the siltspit, got roused by the ministrations of his associates who had not themselves looked sufficiently improved to him to shake his newfound faith which Donnie Huff contributed as an unscripted opinion that Opal Criner did not see fit to alter and excise. Donnie Huff "Ho!" ed with stirring vigor and cited flawlessly his verses in pertinent locations and drew from Opal Criner the advice that perhaps he should suggest to the congregation a selection from the hymnal as a means of bringing his presentation to a close. She was partial herself to "How Strong and Sweet My Father's Care" which Donnie Huff grew disposed to cultivate a partiality for on his own and encouraged Opal Criner to share with him please how he might best persuade the congregation to raise with him their voices in song which she was highly pleased to offer up instruction about.

Opal Criner was hoping Donnie Huff might feel inclined to dine in his blue suit since she figured it would be a delight for her to sit across the table and view him in his striped coat and his speckled tie and her Carl's white shirt, and Donnie Huff allowed how he would favor her in fact with his dressclothes at the dinette, leading Opal Criner to observe how simple it was for people to be pleasant with one another as she rose from the settee and stepped over to the window from where she was

intending to look meaningfully out across the yard at her girl
Marie who seemed lately unduly ill and spiteful, but the hummock was bare anymore and the yard was vacant.

Opal Criner didn't much like her eggs firm, so nobody got
firm eggs. She burned the potatoes as she was partial to burned
potatoes herself and fairly scorched the sausage and the coffee
both through undiluted neglect though she straightaway recalled how she was fondest of her sausage charred and her
coffee pretty much incinerated. Delmon did not himself care
for his food to be black and crusty and would not be persuaded
by his grandmomma Opal to a palpable appreciation of the
virtues of charcoal as a supplemental dietary element, and he
fairly liquefied his eggs with a sizable dollop of ketchup and
pulverized his sausage which he contributed to the concoction
that he stirred and whipped about with his fork until his
momma Marie advised him through the doorscreen to find
shortly another means of engagement as he was altogether done
piddling with his supper.

She'd discovered back in the reaches of the carshed three
magazines under a rag, two *Look*s and a *Collier's* that had together provoked her to a jollier disposition since there resided
between the covers of each possibilities for decoupage untold.
In her excited state she even displayed for Opal Criner and
Donnie Huff together a picture in her *Collier's* of a flower bouquet done up in quaint and faded shades of color as had been
prominent in days of yore which she apprised Opal Criner and
Donnie Huff about in a tone so even and kindly that a fellow
would surely have been hard-pressed to know she'd lately
wished the pair of them to burn in hell. Naturally they made
together as if to be transported by the bouquet themselves since
they were hoping between them to mend fully the mood of
Marie Criner on account of how her momma Opal meant to
carry her the following morning to the sanctuary and Donnie
her husband intended never again to sit down at the dinette to
a plateful of blackened and crusty supplemental dietary elements. Consequently, then, they admired the bouquet with an
excess of feeling, made to be more stirred than most people
would likely by a picture of a bouquet get. Marie Criner was

herself so enthralled with her discovery that she allowed her momma and her husband Donnie to enthuse as uncharacteristically as they pleased and only interrupted their assorted ejaculations to inform Donnie her husband how silly he looked to her at the dinette in his suit and to make of Opal her momma a solitary inquiry, point to her plate and ask of her, "You cook that in the fireplace?" that Opal Criner let on to be the cleverest inquiry she'd lately had the pleasure to field.

By morning Marie Criner had not still cleanly allowed that she would in fact travel with the rest of them to the church in Laurel Fork, so Opal Criner took motherly steps to persuade her, laid out upon the bedspread her girl Marie's green corduroy shift where her girl Marie would surely come across it. She selected as well a pair of shoes from the closet floor to display upon the rug and a belt that seemed to her suitable which she laid upon the shift so as to suggest to her girl Marie the aptness of it. Otherwise Opal Criner did not venture to persuade Marie to join them if she might at the sanctuary but she encouraged instead her Donald to speak please to his wife on her behalf and tempt her some way to load up with them in the Coronet. So Donnie Huff approached his wife in the kitchen where she was eating a toasted hotdog bun and clipping from one of her *Look*s a picture of a percolator that had struck her as most especially odd and antiquated. He stood for a time alongside the dinette until she saw fit to take some notice of him, and she allowed him even to tell to her, "Doll," before she assured him straightaway, "No," back.

He puled as best he was able, figured he would largely improve his chances by puling, but Marie Criner reapplied herself to her percolator and told to him distractedly, "No," once further prior to entertaining from Donnie Huff more puling still with a touch of fabricated anguishment to it, a catch in the throat manufactured with such exceeding mastery that Marie Criner, who was partial by nature to anguishment in a man, could not help but melt a little towards Donnie Huff who took occasion to confess to her how he was suffering just presently from a case of the jitters and feared that his nerves might incite him, once he'd stepped in through the double sanctuary doors,

to throw up in the narthex. It was hardly a prospect he took
much comfort in and he expected the accompaniment of his
wife Marie would produce upon him an effect so calming that
he could not well calculate it, calming enough anyhow to keep
his breakfast off the narthex floor. And maybe even still she
wouldn't have gone with them but for the second accomplished
necknoise that suggested to her deep and soulful distress which
was so very much itself like anguishment as to be indecipherable from it.

She discovered atop the bedclothes her green corduroy shift
with the belt upon it which she straightaway paused to resent
though, being a wife and a mother somewhat but still a daughter chiefly, she shortly donned her ensemble clean down to the
shoes of choice and applied a bit of liner to her lids and mascara
to her lashes once her mother had received her in the front
room and had believed aloud that, were she Marie, she'd see to
her lashes and lids together. Opal Criner, who'd not ever previously ridden in the backseat of her Carl's beige Coronet, opted
to attempt it this Sunday morning and slipped in past the up-
flung seatback so as to join her grandbaby Delmon and allow
her girl Marie to ride to the sanctuary alongside her husband
Donald as if they were the bunch of them just a regular wholesome family off like usual to worship their Lord. Donnie Huff
took the exposed culvert with more momentum than was ad-
visable and so lifted his child and his wife's mother off the
seatcushion entirely which only half of them drew open and
abundant pleasure from. Donnie Huff made as well, to Opal
Criner's mind, altogether too much headway up the gravel road
beside the creek and put himself in constant danger of skidding
and veering and producing with his heedlessness a grave calamity. Once he'd gained the blacktop Donnie Huff, as was his
custom, crowded unduly the center line which Opal Criner
drew herself up to the seatback to speak of but her Donald
looked to her so grim and dyspeptic that she determined not to
trouble him with her complaint and complimented instead his
scruffy scrap of beard which he'd groomed after a fashion, had
clipped here and there with his loving wife's mother's little gold
nosehair scissors, making him, Opal Criner confessed from the

backseat, considerably less boogery than he'd looked to her lately which she was meaning to elaborate upon, speak more specifically anyhow of Donnie Huff's former boogery qualities, when her girl Marie swung about to advise her to lay back if she might against her own seatcushion for the duration of their trip and speak, if she was so inclined, to Delmon her grandbaby alone, Delmon her grandbaby who'd unclipped his tie and was sucking on a tab of it.

As Donnie Huff could not recall precisely how best he might arrive at the sanctuary in Laurel Fork, Opal Criner was allowed by her daughter Marie to advise him provided she did not venture off onto topics otherwise, and so she told him where to turn and told him where to fail to and brought the bunch of them shortly to the churchlot which was packed this morning with vehicles and overseen up either slope by the Angus to the one side and the Charolais to the other. The men chiefly stood in clutches and gaggles in the churchyard smoking and spitting and plainly enjoying themselves more than Opal Criner found seemly considering where they were and what they'd come for. Consequently, once she'd climbed out from the Coronet she narrowed her eyes and leveled at the clutches and the gaggles both a stern and significant sort of a look by which she was meaning to alter perhaps the mood of the gentlemen at hand, but Donnie Huff himself was enough to shut the pack of them up, Donnie Huff in his blue striped suit and his own white shirt and his speckled tie and his black lace-up oxfords, Donnie Huff who alone among them had been previously deceased which Mr. Ray Truitt and Mr. Troy Haven and Mr. Larry Baines jousted for the honor of apprising the rest of the fellows about and thereby promoted the variety of devotional silence that Opal Criner had hoped with her narrow gaze to manage.

She guessed they should enter the church and situate themselves maybe midway back in the sanctuary so that Donnie Huff might, when summoned by the Reverend Mr. Worrell, stride dramatically up the aisle to the altar and create by it a manner of stir. Donnie Huff did not himself appear to feel strongly at all about where it was they sat in the sanctuary while Marie found her toes to be pinched up and laid together by the shoes

her momma had selected for her and consequently was anxious
to sit most anywhere they might come up straightaway on. They
got, however, forestalled by a gentleman in the lot, a fellow off
shy of the althea bush who interrupted their progress towards
the cement landing, called out two times over, "Excuse me," in
a loud and insistent tone that Donnie Huff and Marie and her
momma Opal and Delmon could hardly ignore.

He was pitched there against the fender of a babyblue sedan, was laying upon the wheelwell holding in his hands before
him a broadbrimmed black fedora. His suit of clothes was black
as well and his shirt was so awfully stiff and white as to look to
have been boiled in a pot. He wore about his neck a string tie
that was black itself and appeared most especially to Opal Criner to suit him awfully well, as he looked to her a string-tie sort
of a fellow, parted his hair high up on his head after a fashion
of yore, and wore under his nose a thin, comely, near about
theatrical moustache like Opal had in her youth known some
men to favor.

"You Huff?" he wanted to know and indicated pretty much
Donnie himself by twitching at him his broad black hatbrim.

"Yeah," Donnie told him, "I'm him," and he watched along
with the rest of them as that fellow in the string tie raised
himself off the wheelwell and paused to reach into his mouth
with his little finger so as to perform back in the vicinity of an
eyetooth some manner of excavation with his pinky nail. Once
he got under way, he strode himself with drama across the
intervening stretch of churchlot and created thereby his own
species of stir with most especially Opal Criner who recognized
in that gait the walk of a man of the cloth and so challenged that
fellow to tell to her please if wasn't he in fact a preacher.

"Why ma'm, you've found me out," he said and as he took
up her fingers and squeezed them with his own ones he announced to anybody that cared to know it, "Bob Jones University, class of fifty-four. How in this world did I give it away so?"

Opal Criner was meaning to confess to him that she was
blessed herself with a knack for knowing men of the cloth directly and straightaway but before she could manage to speak
her girl Marie confessed for her that her momma could smell a

preacher a mile off which served to shift about that fellow in the string tie with the northerly hairpart and the thin dainty moustache and, as he took up Marie Criner's own fingers, he told to her, "Dunbar, H. W. Dunbar. Pleased, I'm sure."

For her own part, Marie Criner told to him back, "Marie," and did not with her expression invite chat further which Mr. H. W. Dunbar quite apparently deciphered and so shifted about yet again and took up firmly the hand of Donnie Huff which he did not work and shake but merely gripped and held to instead as he looked squarely upon Donnie Huff who endeavored to look squarely upon H. W. Dunbar back and even in fact succeeded at it briefly.

"So you're Huff," H. W. Dunbar said to him.

"Yes sir. Donnie."

"Donnie," H. W. Dunbar intoned on his own and intoned shortly beyond it, "Marie," that he followed with a purposeful lull prior to telling for the benefit of the bunch of them together, "Like those Oswalds that sang. Them with the teeth."

"Yeah," Donnie Huff said to him, "them."

The Reverend Mr. H. W. Dunbar allowed how talk of Donnie Huff was widespread and general about the area and he'd heard mention himself of the drowning so far east as Stuart and so far west as Bridle Creek. Naturally, then, he'd figured he had to see on his own the fellow who'd ascended quite apparently to heaven as he'd not known anybody to rise into the presence of his Lord and recover from it since back when that Dalton from Piper's Gap had succumbed to an electrical charge but got revived by his wife's brother with whom he'd taken out lately a sizable loan, his wife's brother who'd found cause to resuscitate that Dalton but not before he'd drifted through the ether himself into the presence of his Lord and Savior who'd told to him, "Go on."

And Donnie Huff repeated, "Go on," which H. W. Dunbar confirmed for him to be the words in this instance of Christ Himself who'd dispatched that Dalton back through the ether and down amongst the quick as He did not apparently wish him to die in arrears.

"So he worked off his debt spreading the Gospel?" Donnie

Huff inquired of the Reverend H. W. Dunbar who seemed to recall how that Dalton borrowed in fact money from a cousin to pay his wife's brother and expired presently in debt still but to a blood relation. "The Lord took him in."

"I guess he did," Donnie Huff said and manufactured for the Reverend H. W. Dunbar a grave and telling expression which the Reverend Mr. Dunbar appeared quite plainly to appreciate the nuances of as he rubbed with his knuckles little Delmon's topnotch and told to him, "Hey son," that Delmon shortly lifted his head and informed Mr. H. W. Dunbar, "Ow," on account of.

"Ladies," the reverend said and showed to them briefly the bulk of his hairpart in taking his leave across the lot into the churchyard where he insinuated himself into a gaggle of men and straightoff wrested away the topic of talk so as to shape it to suit him.

"A preacher come to hear you," Opal Criner told to Donnie Huff and shared as well with her girl Marie, "A preacher come to hear our Donald," and Marie said to Opal her momma, "Yeah," and said to Donald her husband, "A preacher all right."

The Reverend Mr. Worrell had not himself known yet occasion to cultivate much taste for dramatic aisle striding and so would not be persuaded to allow Donnie Huff to sit midway back in the sanctuary or settle himself truly on a pew at all due to how the Reverend Mr. Worrell had gone already to the trouble of reserving the front pew for Donnie Huff's wife and Donnie Huff's wife mother and Donnie Huff's boy Delmon and had for the use of Donnie Huff himself placed a chair up on the riser under the Lord and His duck. However, as Donnie Huff had become already attached to the notion of striding dramatically somewhere, he endeavored to persuade the Reverend Mr. Worrell to shift at least that chair a little farther from the pulpit so as to allow Donnie Huff an interval in which to work up a suitable head of steam since he did not know if he could testify, lacking the opportunity to stride in advance of it, and Donnie Huff resurrected his grave and telling expression for the benefit of the Reverend Mr. Worrell who grew, in the face of superior thespianics, convinced that indeed Donnie Huff should stride if he was so inclined. So the reverend himself shifted that chair clean across the riser to the far wall that Donnie Huff confessed he was pleased ever so deeply about and even favored the reverend with a foreshortened taste of accomplished Bible brandishing.

As a means of fetching the congregation in from the churchyard, the reverend strode himself across the riser and threw a toggle switch that activated the carillon, or actually activated the tape machine that played the cassette Mr. Larry Baines had made with his portable recorder at the university in Blacksburg where he'd stood at the foot of the belltower during the noon hour and held his microphone skywards for the fifteen minutes the music played. It was certainly not all of it devotional music. The Christian portion of the program lay precariously between the zither theme from *The Third Man* and a medley of Bobby Goldsboro hits that commenced with "Honey" which had a devotional sort of a beat to it and so allowed the Reverend Mr. Worrell somewhat of a cushion. He could, that is, neglect to switch the thing off until well into the See-the-tree-how-big-it's-grown-but-friends-it-hasn't-been-too-long-it-wasn't-big part of the thing without startling his congregation unduly since Bobby Goldsboro on carillon sounded maybe Methodist at worst which was not so major a breach as to get remarked with any frequency. So the churchly music played from the speaker up high in the front gable and the malingerers grew persuaded to make their way towards the landing and pass through the double doors into the sanctuary proper where they settled into their customary places.

Miss Cindy Womble and Mrs. Gloria Hawks had suffered between them a falling-out on account initially of Donnie Huff whose salvation Mrs. Gloria Hawks had from the outset doubted which had promoted between herself and Miss Cindy Womble a mild and mendable schism that had grown lately ugly and insurmountable due to how Miss Cindy Womble had come to be apprised of an indelicate piece of talk attributed to Mrs. Gloria Hawks who'd made in confidence to her husband's brother's wife the observation that Miss Cindy Womble, in her striped high-waisted dress with the lowslung scalloped neckline, looked plainly a harlot to her, that Mrs. Gloria Hawk's husband's brother's wife, having learned it in confidence, did not pass along straightaway to anybody otherwise but revealed it only at length and presently to everybody that cared to know it. Consequently, Miss Cindy Womble and Mrs. Gloria Hawks reserved anymore their curdling expressions exclusively for each other, and when Miss Cindy Womble advanced in fact up the aisle in that very striped high-waisted lowslung dress the subsequent exchange of bilious toothy faces proved truly electrifying as far as sanctuarial moments usually go.

Miss Cindy Womble sat up front between Mrs. Louise Worrell and a Ludlow she was not acquainted with, a Ludlow up from Ararat who'd heard how a boy had passed through the ether and entered thereby into the presence of the Lord which that Ludlow had taken to be a thing, she confessed to Miss Cindy Womble, she guessed she could stand to hear further about which she enlisted her Willie alongside her to pitch forward and confirm that her Willie gladly obliged her in and admired, as long as he was pitched forward already, Miss Cindy Womble's assorted features and assets which seemed to him ample and bounteous and were plainly set off to fine effect by the high waist and scalloped neckline which Willie did not see fit to make across his wife mention of. Donnie Huff would himself have probably admired the features and assets as well had he not been prevented by an elaborate spray of daisies and gladiolas from seeing much of the congregation at all though he could spy well enough between the leafy stalks his loving wife's mother who was endeavoring still to instruct him through mime, was attempting to suggest that he adjust his tieknot and button his jacket and see please to his fly, touch on occasion his zipper tab to satisfy himself that it was elevated and secure which Donnie Huff made out some of but could not make out all of truly since it looked to him that maybe Opal Criner was advising him to bunt.

The attendant throng was in fact so eager to hear Donnie Huff's testimony that they'd settled themselves upon their pews well in advance of the opening carillon strains of the Bobby Goldsboro medley. There was considerably more of a crowd on this Sunday than the Reverend Mr. Worrell was accustomed to, and as he stepped up to the pulpit to welcome the faithful, he formulated an extemporaneous and hearty greeting that he shared with the congregation, advising the visitors to their sanctuary how best not to slide from their pews and spill out onto the floor which was largely a matter of simple footwork. The Reverend Mr. Worrell told a joke about a Presbyterian that drew a titter and he suggested that those who were so inclined might remember in prayer Mrs. Barbara Dunn who was planning in the coming week to check into the hospital in Roanoke and have a hip socket overhauled. He'd received as well a note from the immediate family of the late Mr. Johnny Caviness of Vesta who wished to express to the members of the Laurel Fork Full Gospel Primitive Missionary Holiness Church their appreciation for the kindness shown to them in their time of grief and were hoping also to discover who perhaps had left with them a ten-inch casserole lid which could be recovered, the reverend announced, at the home.

The Reverend Mr. Worrell took for the text of the day's proceedings a verse from the Book of Matthew which had to it a "Verily" and a "Whosoever," which the reverend intoned with such accomplished inflection and preacherly tenor that Donnie Huff could not help but sit in his chair against the far wall deep in the throes of admiration. Under his breath he practiced his "Ho!" and his "Yea" and his "Wherefore" and acknowledged with a nod the frantic dumbshow his loving wife's mother was performing from her pew, a dumbshow meant to indicate how something was terribly, tragically amiss with Donnie Huff's ensemble which Donnie Huff deciphered well enough to pluck at length the offending piece of thread from his lapel. He was not in fact quite finished straightening his tie and fingering his zipper tab when the Reverend Mr. Worrell saw fit to introduce him, spoke only ever so briefly of Donnie Huff's mishap before issuing to Donnie Huff an invitation to step on please over to the pulpit and testify. So Donnie Huff drew in a deep and steadying breath and exhaled it prior to standing upright and striding across the riser with appreciably less drama and considerably more velocity than Opal Criner could from her pew

endure serenely. Of course straightoff he forgot what he'd
come to the pulpit about and so stood there a moment in silence
to see if he could perhaps recall it. He looked out over the
heads of the congregation to the back wall and squinted what
seemed to Opal Criner becomingly. He gazed as well out a
sidewindow for a time so as to enhance, Opal Criner figured,
the tension of the moment. Donnie Huff persuaded himself to
look even upon the uplifted faces before him and had commenced a methodical survey of the faithful from the left side of
the sanctuary to the aisle when he came to be interrupted by the
striped, high-waisted, scallop-necked dress just below him that
cloaked plainly sizable enticements which he could not help but
exclaim to himself about, said with his breath alone, "Christ!"
who he'd come after all to speak of in fact which Miss Cindy
Womble by means of her anatomy kindly reminded him of like
prompted Donnie Huff to a brief moment further of silent and
heartfelt devotion.

He confessed directly to his heathen past, got under way
with talk rightoff of his sordid history on this earth, told of his
failings and his dubious pursuits, admitted to a slothful and
profane existence, a blindness to the ways of the Lord and the
ceaseless rewards of righteousness. He did not suspect he would
ever have found salvation on the road he was traveling, which
struck Donnie Huff as occasion for a creaky and mildly tormented tone that he managed with such exceeding success as to
incite assorted of the congregation, visitors chiefly following the
example of the Reverend Mr. H. W. Dunbar in the back, to
openly infuse, praise loudly their Maker with the sort of unfettered enthusiasm that the regular Laurel Fork membership
would not most usually condone since theirs was after all a
house of worship and not a wrestling venue. Donnie Huff, however, had learned so well the subtle applications of a quivering
tone that he stirred the congregation at large to apparently
involuntary evangelical outbursts which surged and swelled and
rose shortly to a thunderous crescendo once Donnie Huff had
seen fit to employ his racking sob as he unburdened himself of
the news that he'd been in fact previously a vile and unseemly
creature.

Miss Cindy Womble plainly could not contain herself and flushed and fidgeted and infused and heaved so enticingly that Donnie Huff got put off for the moment from his lowly state and attended to his zipper tab unduly which his loving wife's mother endeavored to wigwag up to the pulpit a comment about. He recovered soon enough to draw from Miss Cindy Womble's frontside a manageable dose of succor which he put to profitable use, grew quickened on account of, and came to be charged with a general and pervasive liveliness that complemented the narrative of his fiery mishap, rendered him sufficiently bold and able to depart from the pulpit and stalk the riser from one side to the other with his white simulated calfskin Bible in hand which he gestured and indicated with but did not yet brandish truly as he had determined already that he would conserve his brandishing for the vented essence through the ether part of the thing when he guessed he could create likely a stir with it. So he saw fit merely to thump his Bible instead as he relived for the benefit of the congregation his dreadful calamity, apprised them in his creaky tremulous voice of his circumstances that fateful morning, his predicament upon the skidder as it tumbled backwards off of the bluff and burst unaccountably into flames engulfing Donnie Huff in a regular inferno which, as a disclosure, prompted from the congregation a peppering of discharges that were largely righteous in their consternation but for a lone laggardly discharge from off back of the sanctuary that sounded to be in its consternation quite altogether secular and nondenominational.

"Hey!" somebody had said with no evangelical lilt to it, no mention of the Lord and Savior or suggestion of His native grace. Just "Hey!" somebody had said, and Donnie Huff interrupted his progress across the riser in order to gaze with concentration back into the reaches of the sanctuary where he discovered the Reverend H. W. Dunbar in his black suit and, alongside him, a woman in a brimless beveiled hat with grape cluster adornments upon it who was sitting herself next to a man in his shirtsleeves who had to his left a stout and hatless woman in a print dress who was glaring still on her own at Alvis Nevins alongside her, Alvis Nevins in the company of his daddy

Vernon who was himself gazing at the pewback before him while his boy peered steadily towards the altar with his eyes wide and his mouth fixed and his shoulders pitched defiantly forward.

Donnie Huff looked for a moment upon Alvis Nevins who studied him baldly back, shared with Alvis a brief and wordless exchange in advance of raising precipitously his simulated calf-skin Bible and whipping it in the air so as to manufacture prematurely what effect he might as he proclaimed how tongues of flame had escaped in profusion from roundabout the skidder bonnet and had boiled up about him like the very fires of hell which Donnie Huff paused to allow for discharges in the wake of and entertained truly a spate of them from murmurous prayerful intonations clean up to a reverent shriek, but he did not hear further from Alvis Nevins who watched Donnie Huff stand upon the riser with his Bible uplifted and watch him back.

Likely he wouldn't even have come but for his daddy. He'd told himself anyhow that likely he wouldn't have come if Vernon had not struck him as disposed for it, but he did not even believe it truly himself since it was him and it was Vernon that were in fact disposed together on account of how they'd lost lately their Hazel, Vernon's wife and Alvis's mother, who'd been among them one day and gone from them the next. In truth they'd done without her a while now, had laid her to rest the better part of a year back like constituted a decent, people called it, interval, but it seemed to Alvis and it seemed to Vernon just lately still which maybe they were hoping to remedy with their visit to the sanctuary, Alvis Nevins figured, hoping perhaps to render it other than lately somehow. It was anguish enough, as best as Alvis Nevins could tell, when folks had people to wither and pass away on them, but it was surely torment outright when they pitched over dead, were hale and healthy the one minute and plainly deceased the next like was itself the case with their Hazel who'd only intended to step into the kitchen after the Cheez-Its but had gotten snatched instead clean to the everlasting.

She'd suffered a vessel to burst, a crucial and significant

vessel that went fairly to pieces and allowed the life to spill out of her. It was a Sunday afternoon and Vernon in the front room and Alvis in the yard did not hear her collapse onto the linoleum and allowed her to lay there upon the floor in those last moments alone until Vernon figured his need for a Cheez-It had advanced already into a critical phase when he called out to their Hazel once with insistence and once with ire and once with troubled curiosity as well prior to struggling up out of his recliner and venturing over to the doorway from where he viewed briefly his Hazel heaped up upon the floor, viewed her exclusively without moving to take her up and lift her and without calling for his boy Alvis to come in if he might from the yard. The Cheez-Its had gotten spilled and cast about across the linoleum with their lively orange hue featured handsomely against the mottled green floortiles, and Hazel lay with her dressend indecently upraised and her legs splayed apart and her hairbun loosened and moderately unbound and an ever so scant trickle of blood easing out from her ear. Vernon himself had not ever previously had occasion to see an ear bleed and he lingered in the doorway to watch Hazel's trickle spill at last onto the floor and flow into a depression she'd made over time with her shoeheel before the sink.

He did call presently for Alvis his boy, remained in the doorway watching their Hazel as he hollered for Alvis to come from the yard and see a thing he'd discovered upon the lino-leum which was sufficient of a request to bring Alvis at length into the house where he joined his daddy in the doorway and looked with him upon their Hazel sprawled and splayed and laid out immodestly upon the floor with the garnish of Cheez-Its spilled festively about her like glitter. And they said to her, "Momma," said it together although they'd not between them schemed and determined to say it but merely stood there the both of them in the doorway and said harmoniously, "Momma," to her not just the one time alone but a second time beyond it before Alvis Nevins got encouraged by Vernon his daddy to demonstrate the temerity to step over to their Hazel and see what her affliction might be. He wouldn't surely have ap-proached her with more delicacy and deliberation if she'd been a cottonmouth coiled upon the floortiles, and he spoke to their Hazel as he advanced upon her, wondered if mightn't she tell him how it was she felt and why it was she'd seen fit to sprawl upon the floor, but Hazel did not share with Alvis her boy the mysteries of her condition and merely lay instead stiller than it appeared to Alvis Nevins customary for people to lay. The blood continued to drip off her earlobe into the depression where it had formed already into a pool and caught the light, and Alvis Nevins watched it shimmer and then gazed inadvertently upon his momma's exposed puffy thighs prior to studying a time her fingers against the green speckled linoleum where they looked to him excessively white and waxy and induced Alvis Nevins to attempt to discover with his own fingerend chiefly if his momma Hazel was in fact as thoroughly deceased as she appeared to him to be.

So he poked her and invited her to speak to him if she would, but she managed just one long breathy exhalation that she quite apparently did not endeavor to replenish, after which she lay merely like she'd been laying and dripped like she'd dripped whereupon Alvis Nevins turned about and told to Vernon his daddy, "She's gone," which Vernon his daddy straightaway disputed as he was plainly convinced that she could not be gone since he was not himself prepared for her to go. And he told to Alvis his boy, "No," told to Alvis his boy, "No sir," and retired from the doorway, returned to his recliner in the front room where he settled in before the television and concentrated his attention on the putting championship that was being contested alongside a highway in Ohio by a man in red trousers and a man in green trousers whose progress around the links was interrupted briefly by an advertisement for an instructional cassette for the benefit of meek, overweight, financially troubled people, an instructional cassette pitched and promoted by a gentleman blessed with near about as much muscle tone and fabulous wealth as hair.

Alvis Nevins came to stand for a time alongside his daddy, lingered there at the armchair as the station break expired and play resumed, and suggested at length how they might best call somebody on the telephone since he did not know himself what to do with their Hazel and did not believe his daddy Vernon was hardly in much shape to advise him. So Alvis Nevins proposed that they call their Hazel's sister Dorcas who lived just up the road to come down to consult with them, which Vernon Nevins did not object about and allowed without complaint or condition his boy Alvis to take up the receiver and dial the phone and speak with what delicacy he could muster of their present circumstances. Dorcas up the road, who was given to outbursts, wailed over the phone line and thereby jarred and discomforted not just Alvis Nevins, who was closest to the receiver, but stirred his daddy as well to rise from his recliner and give over briefly the putting championship so as to enter into the kitchen and gaze upon their Hazel who looked quite frankly dead to him, seemed in fact done in and gone and altogether incapable of returning to them ever again that Vernon Nevins stood upon the linoleum to weigh and consider as a state of affairs. He lingered there for a moment over his dead wife, looked upon her waxy fingers and her placid expression and her exposed underclothes as well as her scant puddle of blood that had grown lately clotted and crusty, and Vernon Nevins ventured even to poke his Hazel with a finger of his own in advance of retiring again from the kitchen and settling once more into his recliner where their Hazel's sister presently came upon him.

Dorcas had been entertaining up the road. Her and her friend Alice from Floyd had been enjoying each of them a plate of warm apple betty when the phone rang, and the news had so shocked and debilitated Dorcas herself that Alice, her friend from Floyd, had gotten enlisted to carry Dorcas down the road in her green Oldsmobile sedan. She'd been invited as well to assist Dorcas into the house and so had guided her by the elbow up over the sill and in through the doorway where Dorcas marshaled her faculties sufficiently to instruct Vernon her brother-in-law to get up out from that chair of his and shut off that goddam television that Vernon took under advisement but did not straightaway see fit to act upon. Dorcas pretty much loosed and unmarshaled her faculties altogether once she'd arrived there upon the linoleum in the presence of her dead sister. She shrieked and gurgled and panted and wailed and slumped down upon the floor so as to take up her Hazel's fingers and press them to her cheek which was more affection than they'd either one of them cared in a decade to exhibit.

Being anxious to learn from her sister's child Alvis what precisely had struck their Hazel down, Dorcas pressed him to narrate if he might the entire episode. Alvis Nevins revealed how, apparently, his momma had come in from the front room to fetch out the Cheez-Its, and he indicated assorted of the crackers featured like they were gaily against the floortiles in addition to the Cheez-It box that had come to rest over along-side the stove, and she'd pitched for some reason over dead with her dressend uplifted and her ear trickling blood.

Beyond that, Alvis Nevins could not say precisely what had happened to their Hazel, and he declared with gravity for the benefit of Dorcas his aunt and Alice, her friend from Floyd, how he was not himself a doctor and did not claim to be. For her part, Hazel's sister Dorcas from up the road, who was given to needless pronouncements, informed anybody who cared to know it that no soul on this earth could be certain of drawing breath from one minute to the next which Alice from Floyd confirmed to be ever so true indeed and contributed assorted of her own thoughts on the ever so fragile nature of this thing we call life which she concluded with the recommendation that they should likely all of them be prepared at any minute in the day to drop dead which Alvis Nevins's aunt Dorcas, from her seat on the linoleum, saw fit to concede to be the truest manner of thing she'd heard lately.

Though he obliged his aunt Dorcas and her friend Alice from Floyd in confessing to them what considerable comfort he'd drawn already from their exchange, Alvis Nevins was intent still upon transporting their dead Hazel off the kitchen floor and removing her some way or another to a more suitable location, which seemed to Dorcas and Alice together a wise concern. They determined between them how they'd likely ought to call the rescue squad notwithstanding Alvis Nevins's opinion that those rescue squad fellows were not probably at their best in treating the deceased. As sister of the late Hazel,

Dorcas felt obliged to make the call herself and, consequently, raised up her arms so as to get hoisted by them off of the linoleum prior to departing from the kitchen for the front room where she inquired of Vernon Nevins on her way to the telephone, "Didn't I tell you to turn off that goddam tv and get up off your butt?" that Vernon Nevins did not appear burdened with much recollection about.

Since Dorcas only allowed that her sister Hazel was presently in distress, the rescue squad van came screaming shortly down the blacktop and lurched to a halt in the drive back of Alice's green Oldsmobile. A paramedic leapt from the passenger side and brought out from the back of the van his tacklebox full of implements and bandages that he carried with him into the house, through the front room past Vernon Nevins in his recliner, and onto the linoleum where he immediately determined that Dorcas's sister Hazel was well past distress in fact.

"She's dead, ma'm," he told to Dorcas who confessed to having suspected she was dead already but, not being blessed herself with any measure of medical training, she'd been reluctant to act upon her suspicions, hadn't that is wanted to send to the undertaker a sister who was not expired entirely. Set at ease, however, by the assurances of the paramedic that her Hazel was well beyond recovery altogether, Dorcas enlisted those fellows from the rescue squad to carry please her sister out to Vaughan's in town with word that she herself would be shortly arriving with a burial ensemble. But the paramedic and the driver both were reluctant to take up Hazel and carry her off and were there in the midst of suggesting to Dorcas that she call out to Vaughan's on the telephone and have them come and fetch her sister themselves when Dorcas grew adequately weepy and distraught to persuade both those fellows together to haul Hazel on out from the house and pack her away in the truck prior to swinging back onto the blacktop and screaming, as was their custom, back down the road.

With the assistance of her friend Alice from Floyd, Dorcas retired to the back bedroom and selected from the clothes closet an outfit for her Hazel. Straightaway she passed over two flouncy print dresses in favor of a tan wool suit that Alice from

Floyd took under observation, and she declared at length how, while it was a fine enough sort of a getup, she didn't believe she'd want herself to wear it for all eternity. They both of them guessed they could live well enough with Hazel's pale green polyblend skirt and jacket most especially in conjunction with a beige blouse, and while they debated shoes and accouterments for a time they did at last reach an amicable settlement and carried their outfit of choice into the front room where Dorcas switched off the goddam tv herself and showed to Vernon and showed to Alvis their momma's manner of shroud which Vernon and Alvis neither one offered up to Dorcas a comment about that Dorcas plainly did not much savor as a turn of events since her and Alice from Floyd had gone plainly to some trouble to make their selection. She could only hope that Vernon and Alvis would dress for the viewing even half so well themselves which Alice from Floyd got encouraged to hope with her and so hoped it too.

Alvis accompanied his aunt Dorcas and her friend to Alice's Oldsmobile where he was hoping to discover how it was anymore that people got laid to rest since he'd not himself had cause to bury anybody lately. And Dorcas his aunt was kindly explaining to him the niceties of modern-day funeral decorum when Vernon hollered there that first time which naturally took Dorcas and Alvis both by surprise since Vernon was not usually given to hollering, especially hollering of a high-pitched throaty variety. Alvis could not help but guess he'd best go in and see to his daddy and was only halfway across the yard when Vernon hollered again, wailed outright like served to accelerate Alvis on up through the doorway and into the front room where Vernon had in fact lately gotten up off of his butt and removed himself to the kitchen. Alvis found him standing alongside the silver drawer gazing upon the little puddle of encrusted blood before the sink, and he said to him, "Daddy?" and moved even to lay a comforting hand upon Vernon who swung his head about to look on Alvis his boy, dropped open his mouth, and fairly shrieked once further as he could not somehow put into words and inquire what maybe he would ever do again in this life that would count for anything at all.

Two nights following, Tuesday in the early evening, Alvis and Vernon his daddy sat together on a sofa at Vaughan's in town and received the condolences of their friends and their relations who mentioned each of them their dead Hazel but did not see fit to dwell upon her, refused entirely to speak of her at length except of course to suggest that she looked to them blessed so in death with such sprightly vigor that they half expected her to leap out of the casket and jig about which Alvis's and Vernon's friends and relations appeared to construe as a soothing piece of news. Dorcas assumed her post at the coffinside and took active credit for her sister Hazel's ensemble while Alice, her friend from Floyd who'd been party to the discovery of the corpse and thereby felt a bond and an obligation, circulated among the mourners to pass word of the coffee urn in the hallway and the complimentary finger cakes. Dorcas had hired her preacher for the service as Vernon and Hazel had kept a slothful sabbath and did not any longer have a preacher of their own. The reverend was a Cox and he proved kind enough to drop in at the funeral home so as to size up the deceased and confer with assorted of the bereaved in an effort to discover what they'd best like to hear about her. While Dorcas was pleased to provide the Reverend Mr. Cox with the majority of his instruction, she allowed him to consult with Vernon and Alvis briefly in advance of retiring from the settee so as to make way for a Halpern from Sylvatus who'd apparently traveled over to Vaughan's so as to speak to Vernon and Alvis together fleetingly of their dead wife and mother and primarily of his tractor valves that he'd lately extracted and ground.

They buried their Hazel Wednesday afternoon in a rainstorm following a quarter-hour service in the Vaughan chapel where the Reverend Mr. Cox got most of their Hazel's names in a suitable order and was obliged to speak in general terms of the death of the body and the resurrection of the soul as he had not collected any personal and revealing anecdotes to suit him. Alvis and Vernon and Dorcas as well rode in a long blueblack limousine to the cemetery, the three of them abreast across the backseat and, due to the downpour, everybody crowded together under the canopy up alongside the casket and the wreaths and the rain hammered on the canvas as the Reverend Mr. Cox prayed once further over their Hazel and committed her to the earth after which he took up and shook the hand of Vernon Nevins and took up and shook the hand of Alvis Nevins too and grasped lightly Dorcas's own fingers that she'd lifted and proffered to him.

Their Hazel's sister Dorcas had arranged to receive the mourners at her house as it was spacious and orderly and had come lately to be adorned with a brand-new knotty pine buffet which Dorcas was anxious to put to legitimate use and entertain flattering talk about. She'd left her friend Alice from Floyd and her friend Gail Anne from Willis to see to the spread during the service, to sort through the dishes and concoctions that the neighbors had seen fit to drop off, heat the ones that called for heating and chill the ones that called for chilling, and set out upon the buffet those tepid dishes otherwise that could not harm the finish of the thing. Dorcas herself, who'd been fetched along with Vernon and Alvis early on in the day by the limousine, persuaded the driver to carry them home with some purpose and velocity and as little seemly blather as possible and so they arrived at Dorcas's house in advance of the full complement of mourners, allowing Vernon and Alvis to park themselves on the sofa as their Hazel's sister admired Alice's and Gail Anne's artful buffet presentation while she simultaneously rearranged it.

The new pine buffet proved an enchanting addition to Dorcas's general furnishings, and she greeted her mourners there before it so as to be handy to receive their sympathies and compliments both together while she handed to them their plates and identified for them various of the deep-dish items which tended to smell like nothing in particular and look like everything together and so did not hardly give themselves away. An apt and seemly eulogy in combination with an interment in a driving rainsquall quite apparently whetted and enhanced appetites, and most everybody ate with some noticeable relish but for Vernon and but for Alvis his boy who were given by Alice from Floyd plates fraught and mounded with food which they held for a time in their hands and settled for a time upon their knees and yielded at last to Gail Anne from Willis who carried them back to the kitchen in advance of bringing to Vernon and to Alvis a slice each of coconut cake which they held and settled and yielded presently as well.

For the benefit of the living who had to heal and mend, there was not too terribly much talk of Hazel, less talk anyway than there'd been already which had not turned out to be terribly much itself, so little in fact that Alvis and that Vernon had not yet had occasion to convince themselves that they were faced with anything much to heal and mend from. Their Hazel seemed merely more absent than dead and, once they'd chatted the afternoon away, Vernon and Alvis returned home together towards evening and half expected to find their Hazel in front of the television in her yellow print housedress and her black corrective shoes. But the front room, of course, was empty and still and while Hazel's reading glasses lay on the piecrust table in the corner and her gray cardigan hung on the knob of the coatcloset door, she was plainly herself not anywhere about, was gone for some reason from them which they sat down together in their funeral clothes to contemplate and absorb and perhaps even comment upon though they could not between them discover much fit to say.

It was all of it very unsatisfying as best as Alvis Nevins could tell. One day they'd had their Hazel and the next day they hadn't, and they'd buried her even before they could believe entirely that she was done in and gone. So they left her eyeglasses on the piecrust table and her cardigan on the knob, did not remove her dresses from the coatcloset or her creams and ointments from the vanity shelves, and they lingered together in peculiar circumstances since they could not at any given moment determine between them for certain if their Hazel was in fact deceased or just off somewhere and away. The thing ate at the both of them as it seemed to Alvis and it seemed to Vernon as well that when folks keeled over and died, got eulogized and buried and prayed about, some measure of peace that did not lie with them in the grave should settle instead among the living. Alvis and Vernon figured anyhow it should, and guessed if they were one of them the Lord Christ they'd make it their business to know if the grieving relations were finding as well some comfort for themselves since Alvis and since Vernon suspected that it was appreciably easier to be the one that up and got dead than the ones that didn't.

So they could not manage somehow to let loose of their Hazel and recollect fondly upon her, and instead they passed from one day to the next forgetting that she was dead and denying that she was gone and half expecting her to knock one evening upon the door and join them before the Motorola. But it was almost anymore a year now since she'd succumbed upon the linoleum, and Alvis had apprised Vernon his daddy how he did not believe they could hold to their Hazel forever, not that is the way they'd been holding to her. Consequently, he'd worked just lately to sell his daddy upon the mystical qualities of Donnie Huff who'd been himself deceased and so perhaps could tell to them a thing about the features of death that they had no way otherwise to come to be acquainted with short of expiring themselves which Vernon had not bothered to dispute and contest but had put on instead his white shirt that was chiefly yellow any longer and his brown wool jacket with the broad unstylish lapels and had accompanied his boy Alvis to Laurel Fork where Alvis had hollered already aloud, which even Vernon knew was no fit practice for church.

Alvis simply could not recall the tongues of flame though he did allow how he'd been still up the hillside when the skidder pitched and fell and so could not say for certain that the thing had not burned maybe a little, produced in its descent a modest inferno that the Big Reed had extinguished. Accordingly he was not truly tempted to voice a Hey! further and permitted Donnie Huff to proceed unchallenged into the realm of his vented essence where his oratorical skills purely sparkled and shone. Donnie Huff persevered in his Bible brandishing, though he whipped and flailed his Good Book about judiciously so as not to compromise the effect. Truly his passage through the ether did not call for much extraneous enhancement as it was freighted with intrinsic thrills enough to promote among factions of the congregation assorted rapturous outbursts since nobody much wanted to get left unenraptured while most everybody otherwise had plainly been taken up and transported. Consequently, every little smattering of infusement brought on shortly a broader display, and the general congregational uproar in turn charged and galvanized Donnie Huff who accumulated his succor from the sizable hooters and was able thereby to maintain a species of energetic arousal that drove him back and forth across the riser, promoted him to unprecedented rhetorical heights, and earned for him the flourishing ire of his wife Marie who watched her Donnie watch the hooters and heard her Donnie promote the Savior and showed her Donnie, when he deigned to look upon her, her thoroughly unenchanted expression.

As Donnie Huff had not ever himself had cause to stand before a regular throng of people and speak to them with conviction of a thing he guessed in his heart to be true, he had not anticipated it would turn out such a diverting sort of an enterprise even allowing how his conviction was largely theatrical and his heartfelt truth was doubtful at best. They looked as a throng upon him with frank devotion and called to him with fervor, most especially the ladies who'd plainly not married or consorted with men who'd themselves soared up through the ether, abandoned their supine forms for the portal of heaven where the buttery light might fall upon them and their Christ might take them in and then had returned to this life to speak with passion of it. Their men worked in the plants and the mills, stayed on the ground, avoided the ether, could not tell them much of this world or anything at all of the next unlike Donnie Huff himself who'd risen and soared and could speak with palpable flair of his triumph and salvation. So they looked upon him with feeling, the ladies did, admired his blue striped suit and his handsome speckled tie, remarked his stately carriage across the riser, and grew after a fashion smitten with his presence, enamored of his redemption, and taken even with his scruffy beard which Miss Cindy Womble in particular found dashing now that Donnie Huff had laid the nosehair scissors to it.

From back in the reaches of the sanctuary the Reverend Mr.

H. W. Dunbar promoted some neighboring enthusiasm with discharges of his own and studied attentively Donnie Huff's considerable technique that he appeared quite plainly to approve of and appreciate while, down the pew from him, Alvis and Vernon Nevins together endeavored to draw from Donnie Huff's ascent a useful measure of solace and instruction and attempted to gain from his heavenly encounter some scrap of Lordly wisdom to clutch at and embrace. They the pair of them even came to be a little stirred up on their own due to the contagious qualities of passionate infusement, and Alvis himself gave voice to a "Lord yes!" once a suitable sentiment had fallen upon his ears and had seemed to him to cry out for a discharge. The parable of the peach pit held most especially some charm for Alvis and his daddy Vernon who made to construe together that it spoke plainly to them and their purposes on this earth. Alvis anyhow made to construe it and took pains to promote his daddy Vernon to a similar sort of illumination, but Vernon did not prove much given to construement himself and returned to gazing upon the pewback before him in the blandly pathetic sort of way he'd come lately to favor.

Alvis, however, was not meaning to let his daddy spoil his own soulful delight at having drawn from the paraphrased words of Christ some discernible balm for his woes even if he could not persuade his daddy to get himself balmed as well. So Alvis turned his attention pretty exclusively towards Donnie Huff up on the riser and found himself touched and agitated most pleasingly by even the "Ho!" that Donnie Huff planted his feet and whipped his Bible and gave voice to in such bold and princely tones that Alvis Nevins could not at all imagine how that manner of exclamation had ever previously done a thing but thrill him. He thirsted, he guessed, for the waters and pined, he figured, for the Lord though he'd not previously been disposed to confess it. Not wishing, however, to waste a moment longer unredeemed, Alvis Nevins swung about to inform the stout hatless woman in the print dress alongside him how he, in fact, thirsted and pined together which she was clever enough to decipher and goodly enough to bless him about.

Donnie Huff had touched already upon the filigreed gate and had cited already, before his "Ho!," his additional composite verse with the "Yea"s and the "Wherefore" like left him to speak at last of the fingers of the Lord that he did not embark upon straightaway due to how his loving wife's mother managed to remind him by means of an extravagant dumbshow that a lull might be just presently apt. Since Donnie Huff could not see much harm in a lull himself, he manufactured one directly, paced silently from one end of the riser to the other expending the bulk of his attention in semisurreptitious glances upon the high-waisted, scallop-necked dress before him and the fleshy enticements that fairly animated it. He peered briefly as well upon those parts of Miss Cindy Womble above her collarbones and discovered that she was looking upon him steadfastly back and with hardly that expression of incipient nausea that Donnie Huff had become accustomed to from the sorts of women that had bothered previously to look upon him. In fact, it appeared to Donnie Huff during the course of his lull that nearly all the ladies and most of the men were perusing him after a kindly and attentive fashion as if they expected him to deliver shortly to them the sweetest sort of news they'd ever heard which he undertook at length to oblige them in, strode once more back and forth across the riser and struck in on the holy fingerends as he hoisted his jacketcuff and furled his sleeve and so prepared himself to tell at last to the congregation, "Come."

The rapture was general, the ecstasy widespread. Fervent exclamations issued forth from most every quarter of the sanctuary as the faithful savored the invitation of their Christ and blessed and praised the man who'd carried it to them, gave passionate thanksgiving to Donnie Huff up on the riser under the painted Jesus and His painted duck, Donnie Huff with his coatcuff uplifted and his sleeveend rolled and his downy patch of skin available and exposed. And maybe nobody would have clamored to grip it, though they all of them appeared a little inclined to clamor. Maybe nobody would have left their seat and advanced upon the exposed downy skin if the Reverend Mr. H. W. Dunbar back in the reaches of the sanctuary had not

failed himself to endure the temptation of that patch of forearm his Lord had touched, and slipped off from his pew to gain
the far aisle along the wall from where he struck out towards
the riser at fairly much a jog and, as he went, rained praise and
glory on Donnie Huff and the Lord and Savior together while
he closed upon the riser, advanced upon Donnie Huff who
merely stood and watched him come and merely stood and
watched him arrive and merely stood and watched him cover
with his fingers that portion of downy skin which plainly induced in that Dunbar a palpable shiver and a slight but discernible cry.

And they were pretty much on him even before he could
yield and give way, were stacked up back of that Dunbar with
their tremulous fingers and conviction enough to seek to lay
and apply them which that Dunbar moved to promote and
allow, had stepped even already aside quite entirely before Donnie Huff took notice, next to his oxford on the riser, of the
broadbrimmed black fedora laying upended upon its crown,
the broadbrimmed black fedora with already even the three
dollar bills inside it looking like they'd been flung and contributed and tithed though only the Dunbar had enjoyed yet occasion to donate, the Dunbar who lingered before the riser in
his black suit and his string tie and with his scant theatrical
moustache and northerly hairpart and greeted the faithful as
they proceeded up along the center aisle and advanced themselves upon the downy patch which they gripped by turns and
held to and thereby came to be quickened and came to be
enthralled. They proved, as a pack of people, exceedingly generous, took straightaway notice of the broadbrimmed fedora
and the three apparently flung and donated dollar bills and did
not wish themselves to seem stingy there in their brief splendid
moment of illumination and enlivenment. So they gave freely,
unpocketed their wallets and unhandbagged their purses and
contributed their silver and their folding money to that initial
stake, blanketed those three bills with such an utterly suffocat-
ing heap of currency that Donnie Huff on the riser could not
help but watch as it swelled at last up out of the hat altogether
and spilled onto the carpet like was enough in itself to provoke

Donnie Huff to cite once further with considerable passion and unbridled enthusiasm his "Ho!" and its ensuing verse that served to stir the congregation further still and impelled forward those members who'd guessed maybe they'd fingered already in one lifetime downy skin enough.

Alvis Nevins himself wasn't meaning truly to travel to the riser, had not intended to venture up to the front of the church for the pleasure of gripping there a forearm he could grip most any hour of the day he pleased without going truly much of anywhere to do it, and he informed a gentleman a pew up from him and the stout hatless lady alongside him how he was personally quite well acquainted with Donnie Huff, had known him way on back before he'd been dead and redeemed, and had discovered already occasion to take him up at the forearm more times even than Alvis Nevins could count which that gentleman and that lady appeared to appreciate as a disclosure and departed presently to take their turns at the riser where they each of them spoke of their intimate acquaintance with a buddy of Donnie Huff's who they jerked their heads and twitched their noses to indicate, a buddy of Donnie Huff's who'd led them to believe that perhaps, as friends of a friend of his, they might lay their fingers to the forearm and enjoy the sort of sensation that just any old body would not be privy to. They were hoping, if it was not too terribly much trouble, for an exceedingly mystical and uncharacteristically otherworldly manner of experience and, since they were after all chums of a buddy of his, Donnie Huff applied himself to the undertaking, concentrated ever so intensely his powers and faculties and plainly provided that gentleman and that stout hatless woman with gratifying jolts judging chiefly from their leavings upon the heap.

But Alvis Nevins himself wasn't meaning truly to travel to the riser and persevered in his conviction to stay there with his daddy upon the pew until a woman come clear from Speedwell reached with her fingers to the downy patch and was promoted by the encounter into a purely vaporish state. She wailed and shrieked and would undoubtedly have dissolved into a pile on the floor but for the Reverend Mr. H. W. Dunbar who'd learned

in his day to recognize the onset of a vaporish condition and
had consequently positioned himself so as to catch that woman
at the armpits and lay her in seemly repose upon the floor until
such time as her infusement slackened and she returned to her
regular senses. Now as Shirley's #2 in Cana did not stock for
rental the sorts of movies in which vaporish women might figure, aside of course from those women who wailed and shrieked
in advance of having their heads detached or their sternums
laid open, which Alvis could not take truly for vaporish behavior, he'd not previously been exposed to the variety of creature
who might just up and get felled by a dose of debilitating affection for Christ. Understandably he was curious to see one up
close and in the actual flesh and so excused himself from his
daddy Vernon and did in fact proceed up the aisle towards the
riser where Donnie Huff was entertaining for the second occasion this morning alone the delicate touch of Miss Cindy Womble who'd been rushed by the throng her first time around and
so had not enjoyed the leisure to lay previously her fingers to
suit her. Donnie Huff, for his part, was far too busy marshaling
his faculties and powers to take much notice of Alvis Nevins.
The full extent of his energies were required if he had any
hope at all of rendering Miss Cindy Womble flushed and enfeebled together, but Donnie Huff found he could not gaze
down upon the scallop-necked cleavage before him and work
up even sufficient spit to keep a field mouse lubricated much
less rein in his faculties and his powers to any effect. So he
merely instead allowed himself to revel in the proximity of the
hooters until Miss Cindy Womble saw fit to turn and cart them
off, leaving merely Alvis Nevins with fingers yet to lay.

  Alvis Nevins wasn't still convinced that Donnie Huff's arm
was much worth touching, but as he gazed there upon that
Speedwell woman who was gradually reviving and coming to
her regular unhysterical senses, he figured he might as well
grip for himself the downy patch since maybe he would enjoy
a potent flash of illumination, suffer to be revealed to him word
of their Hazel who'd ascended likely through the ether herself
and so probably did not need to be grieved for and longed after
by her boy and by her husband who could rest anymore easy

upon this earth. Maybe he would gain an instant peace that he could persuade Vernon to partake of as well. Alvis didn't anyhow know that he wouldn't as he'd never previously enlisted the services of the Lord and Savior and so guessed maybe he was due a revelation.

Donnie Huff, however, gave over the hooters for Alvis Nevins before Alvis Nevins could reach and could grip, and Donnie Huff shied deftly from the advancing hand, dodged and avoided it as he told lowly to Alvis Nevins, "No," and informed him beyond it, "Uh uh," and shifted and withdrew further still.

Naturally Alvis Nevins spoke straightaway back himself, said to Donnie Huff, "Hey!" as he pursued the retreating downy patch, stepped even up onto the riser and reached again with fingers he meant to lay, but Donnie Huff retreated once more and made at Alvis Nevins what he intended for an articulate variety of expression, widened his eyes and lowered his chin and endeavored to suggest his firm intention to go for the moment altogether untouched. It was purely an odd and ungainly time there in the Laurel Fork sanctuary before the largely infused throng and under the painted Lord and His duck and, from her place up just shy of the riser, Opal Criner attempted to signal to her Donald how he was venturing presently into palpable rudeness, but Donnie Huff could not be troubled at the moment to decipher her mime. He was far too busy being just presently disappointed in Alvis Nevins, Alvis Nevins who was plainly by nature silly and thick but had evermore seemed to Donnie Huff to possess himself sense enough to figure who maybe had the Lord in his heart and who maybe didn't and never would. Donnie didn't want those fingers on him, those fingers that would feel likely skin and armhair alone, would draw and conduct no solace but only absorb perhaps a little sweat at best. He was simply not aiming to get touched by them since it was one thing to entertain the fingerends of people who were largely themselves anonymous to him, folks beset by unspoken afflictions and secret disappointments, burdened with trouble and grief and assorted vague sorrows, blessed even on occasion with remarkable hooters as well, but it was quite another thing entirely to have a fellow he knew, a boy he swore at and swilled beer with and pissed on the ground in front of to come up and mean to touch him with reverence and hope because he'd arrived in his suit at a sanctuary and whipped and beat a Bible about that nobody would have bothered themselves to watch but for the ever so meager possibility that Donnie Huff had maybe seen with his eyes a thing they wished to see, been with his essence to a place they longed to go. And beyond the articulate face and in addition to the capable retreat, Donnie Huff told quite firmly to Alvis, "No."

There appeared to Opal Criner a legitimate danger that Donnie Huff's triumphant testimony would culminate with and dissolve into an unseemly chase about the riser which she was terribly anxious to prevent and so wigwagged most furiously but with no discernible effect upon Donnie or Alvis either one who retreated and advanced harmoniously together and would have perhaps completed shortly a circuit around the pulpit had the Reverend Mr. H. W. Dunbar not stepped up onto the riser to interrupt them. He established with his one hand a hold upon Alvis Nevins's wrist and gripped with his other the elbow of Donnie Huff who looked upon the Reverend Mr. H. W. Dunbar and heard shortly from him, "Believe me, son, there's easier things for a man to be than an instrument of the Lord," and he drew upon the wrist and manipulated the elbow and brought thereby the fingers to lay upon the downy patch of forearm, managed the thing with such grace and polish as to soothe and assuage even Opal Criner who left off with her dumbshow in order to view undistracted the apparent redemption of Alvis Nevins who felt obliged to start and twitch and muster a little moan prior to retiring from the riser and returning down the center aisle to the company of his daddy Vernon who did not trouble himself to inquire what Alvis his boy had started and twitched and moaned about but persevered merely in gazing at the pewback before him.

The Reverend Mr. H. W. Dunbar exhibited directly the presence of mind to suggest to the congregation a hymn, wonder if wouldn't they all of them care to stand and sing along with him and Donnie Huff "Softly and Tenderly Jesus Is Calling," and the congregation did in fact rise to follow the Reverend Mr. H. W. Dunbar into the melody while Donnie Huff, who was himself in no fit state to sing, was anyhow in no fit state to sing anything other than "How Strong and Sweet My Father's Care" which he'd cultivated a feel for, merely stood there on the riser in his blue striped suit and his speckled tie and his black oxfords and shut his eyes and lifted his head and clutched to his chest his simulated calfskin Bible which, taken together, suggested most especially to Opal Criner some noticeably deep and profound devotion and promoted in her such a glorious sense of unfettered joy that she lifted her voice with more vigor even than she tended most Sundays to lift it, raised her fairly piercing soprano to an unadvisable pitch and an unendurable volume and thereby praised the Savior and persecuted the congregation simultaneously.

Although Opal had persuaded her girl Marie to stand, she did not succeed with meaningful sidelong looks to persuade her to sing as well and so glanced throughout the course of the melody with disdain upon her child who gazed with what appeared to be indigestion back, while Delmon between them gave over his tietab for a plastic collar stay which he managed to extract from its sleeve and wedge becomingly between his front teeth. Fortunately, the Reverend Mr. H. W. Dunbar did not prove inclined to venture beyond the second verse of the hymn and drew the thing to a stirring close with an elevated and wholly unattainable note that most everybody fired wide of and nobody hit flush, which hardly prevented the Reverend Mr. Worrell from stepping himself to the pulpit and congratulating the faithful on the effort. He guessed they'd all agree it had been a stirring and fruitful service and, on behalf of his Laurel Fork congregation, he offered his heartfelt appreciation to Donnie Huff which Donnie Huff acknowledged with a modest nod of his head and a relatively papal elevation of his fingers that he was figuring to be the culmination of his performance until the Reverend Mr. Worrell wondered of Donnie Huff if wouldn't he favor them all please with a benediction which Donnie Huff let on to be delighted about and shut his eyes and dropped his chin to his shirtfront as he endeavored to calculate what precisely a benediction might be.

He knew it for a prayer of some stripe but could not say if it was perhaps of a regular or a freeform variety and so was reluctant to strike out blessing and praising haphazardly. The Reverend Mr. Dunbar, however, took upon himself the obligation of commencing the thing for Donnie Huff, made to be too altogether transported to resist it and thanked the merciful Lord Jesus for Donnie Huff His disciple on this earth who might show them all the ways of righteousness and devotion and guide them out from that thorny thicket of temptation into which they all of them wandered from time to time. He was anxious as well to praise, as a professional courtesy, the Reverend Mr. Worrell and his handsome flock who'd demonstrated such winning hospitality and palpable fervor which the Reverend Mr. H. W. Dunbar felt certain Donnie Huff was eager himself to touch upon and acknowledge like proved in fact an utterly uncanny piece of intuition as Donnie Huff did wish fairly exclusively to recognize the hospitality and give due to the fervor in advance of providing a blessing for the meals that the most of them would very likely partake of shortly that he punctuated with a "world without end" and a deep and resonant "Amen" which the Reverend Mr. Dunbar anticipated sufficiently to throw in with.

Notwithstanding how they'd been prayed over and dismissed, the congregation lingered and milled about and exchanged with each other talk of the jolts they'd entertained from the downy patch while, up on the riser, Opal Criner had joined her Donald so as to share with and filch from him to the extent that she might the glory of the moment that was moderately poisoned by Donnie's wife, Opal's only child, who would not be lured up to the pulpit and retired instead with her boy to the churchyard where Marie Criner, in her distraction, permitted Delmon to feed his necktie to a cow. As it was after all his broadbrimmed hat, the Reverend Mr. H. W. Dunbar moved quickly himself to take the thing up off of the carpet, and he collected as well the spillage from the rug and claimed discreetly the three dollar bills that he folded twice over and retired to his trouser pocket in advance of bundling up for Donnie Huff the bulk of the currency and setting aside for the Reverend Mr. Worrell a generous piece of money as well that the Reverend Mr. Worrell declined straightoff but was presently prevailed upon to take.

Donnie Huff recloaked his downy patch prior to stepping with his loving wife's mother off the riser and striking out down the aisle for the churchyard where they ran up together onto Alvis Nevins in the company of Vernon his daddy who held in his fingers a hat of his own, a felt, sweatstained, mousecolored fedora that he studied with apparent fascination as he twirled and circulated it about. Alvis Nevins could not hardly get over how he'd been induced to twitch and jerk and wished Donnie Huff would confirm please for Vernon the twitching and the jerking both, but Donnie Huff told to Alvis, "Aw," and told to Alvis, "Alvis," and allowed himself to be steered elsewhere by his loving wife's mother who did not approve of Nevinses, had not ever cared for them, and wondered had Donnie Huff noticed himself the stubble on that Vernon and the stink from him like maybe he'd just climbed up out of a gutter somewhere so as to come to a respectable churchyard with that wiry boy of his and be unsavory.

Marie Criner and Delmon were waiting already in the Coronet, and Donnie Huff had deposited his wife's mother in the backseat and was preparing to climb under the wheel himself and endure the displeasure of his Marie when the Reverend Mr. Dunbar called to him, "Huff," the Reverend Mr. Dunbar over by his babyblue sedan with his hairpart and his string tie and his dainty moustache and his black immaculate broadbrimmed hat that Donnie Huff watched him situate with care and deliberation upon his head. "Me and you'll be talking," the Reverend Mr. H. W. Dunbar said. "A man's got to make hay while the sun shines," which seemed plain enough to Donnie Huff who guessed at the reverend how a man best ought to that the Reverend Mr. Dunbar parted his lips and showed to Donnie Huff his teeth about before slipping with slick and sinewy ease into his vehicle and swinging it slowly out from the lot and onto the blacktop.

Opal Criner certainly was herself fond of that Reverend Mr. Dunbar and she wondered over the seatback of her girl Marie if perhaps he'd made upon her a favorable impression as well which Marie Criner showed no inclination to comment upon, leaving Opal Criner to confess how she was fondest herself of the wavy hair though she admitted to an affection for the scant theatrical moustache as well in advance of inquiring of her grandbaby Delmon if he'd share with her please what perhaps had become of his necktie.

Once Donnie Huff had settled at last under the wheel and drawn shut the door, him and Opal his loving wife's mother enthused at each other for a time, Opal Criner anyhow lavished upon Donnie Huff undiluted praise for his presentation, singling out for special recognition his opening bout of Bible brandishing and his timely invocation of scripture. She mentioned as well how she guessed it went without mentioning that she'd never in her days of churchgoing seen an anointed and palpated bodily part put to better use than Donnie Huff's own downy forearm, which Donnie Huff plainly took to be an awfully agreeable piece of news. He was simply pleased, he told it, to be of some service to his fellow creatures that earned him a gentle pat upon the shoulder from Opal Criner and some openly incredulous perusal from his wife Marie who Donnie Huff met straight on with a sweet and toothsome expression of his own that got augmented by and complemented with the wad of money he withdrew from his jacket pocket and exhibited, the sizable knot of greenbacks that Donnie Huff dangled and displayed between his thumb and his forefinger and thereby struck his wife Marie fairly dumb with fascination, his wife Marie who reached with some fingerends of her own which she laid and settled reverently.

As he was feeling festive and was able on this occasion to do a thing about it, Donnie Huff determined to carry his wife and his boy and his loving wife's mother down off the ridge to the fish house in Mt. Airy and so surprised them by striking out east along the highway and then south down the blacktop through the orchards and towards the quarry and, presently, into the fish-house lot. Their waitress's name was Wendy and she recommended the clam fritters, but heard for her trouble news of an illness Opal Criner had suffered previously as a young woman, a digestive complaint that her doctor had attributed to a clam, a fried clam very much after the fashion of a fritter itself, which had served to alter Opal Criner's views on shellfish altogether. She settled instead for the broiled perch while her girl Marie ordered the shrimp and her Donald ordered the combination plate and Delmon her grandbaby was persuaded to try the little landlubber's burger platter which Wendy his waitress assured him did not contain itself the variety of food that had come at all into contact with fishy secretions.

They watched a man at a table by the front window dump his water onto the floor and agreed together upon the slovenly hygiene of the busboy, and they troubled Wendy for more iced tea and troubled Wendy for more saltines and admired each other's entrees once they'd come to be placed before them. They passed upon request the condiments politely and circulated the hush puppies and the cocktail sauce, and Donnie Huff ate a shrimp off Marie's fork and Marie ate a scallop off Donnie's. Even Delmon made so bold as to sample the crabcake, and he extended to Wendy their waitress his compliments to the crabcake maker while his grandmomma Opal, whose perch had been dusted with too awful much paprika to suit her, failed to extend to the fish broiler compliments herself but ordered sweetly nonetheless her coffee and sweetly her pie. She was far too pleased this day to get put out by a dry, crusty, overseasoned piece of fillet, and she admired across the table her girl Marie in her green shift and her grandbaby Delmon in his little plaid jacket and between them her Donald in his blue suit with the faint stripe to it, her Donald who'd succumbed and ascended, who'd consorted at the portal with the holy Savior Himself, and who, in reaching for a hush puppy, dipped his sleeveend into his tartar sauce and told to nobody in particular, "Well, shit."

ii

He watched a slash of morning sunlight spread across the ceiling and operated with his fingernail upon a bump on the small of his back. Though he'd checked once already in the course of the night, Donnie grew anxious yet again as to the status of his proceedings in the nightstand drawer and consequently withdrew his wad of bills and counted them out onto the topsheet so as to determine that they still totaled eighty-seven entire dollars even after the fish house where he'd picked up the check and indulged Wendy with a sizable gratuity. Donnie Huff counted in fact his wad twice prior to taking up and stacking his bills with the presidents exposed and righted which proved a pleasing diversion for Donnie Huff who presently raised his currency to his nose and sniffed it in advance of announcing into the air, "For my ministry."

At length he joined his loving wife's mother in the front room, arrived in his shorts and undershirt and settled himself into his upholstered chair, casting a leg up over the arm of it in such a way as to inadvertently expose to Opal Criner more of his privates than she was inclined to see. So she coughed and wheezed and persuaded Donnie Huff to make himself decent on her behalf, to put on please some trousers over his undershorts like a proper gentleman might which Donnie Huff straightaway obliged her in and returned in time to catch on the tv with his boy Delmon and his loving wife's mother the lightning round played by a woman from Ohio with the assistance of a comely star of stage and screen who proved an impediment and a burden and fairly singlehandedly prevented that woman from Ohio from driving home in a brand-new Datsun sedan. Life, it seemed to Donnie Huff, was a gamble at best with stars of stage and screen strewn along its path to hinder and frustrate us. Donnie Huff suggested anyhow to his loving wife's mother that life was a gamble strewn with stars of stage and screen so as to see might he hold sway with her of a Monday in his undershirt like he'd held it already Sunday in his suit, and she told to him, "Yes," and she told to him, "Truly."

She'd had already a call from Harless McGee's wife Irene who'd not been herself in attendance at the sanctuary but had heard from a girl she knew of the downy patch, had been informed extensively of its mystical properties, and had dialed up to reveal to Opal Criner how her Harless had lately come to be afflicted with a growth that Irene could not help but believe a mystical piece of forearm might shrink and heal. Opal Criner, however, had been reluctant herself to commit Donnie Huff to tending after a growth since he was just, after all, starting out in the work of the Lord and the potency of his downy patch was still pretty vague and altogether uncalibrated. She hoped she'd done right by him to put off Irene and neglect her Harless, and Donnie Huff assured her she had, confirmed for his loving wife's mother how he presently was not disposed to do growths himself but was eager instead to promote merely a general variety of rejoicing.

"I'll tell you this," Donnie Huff said to Opal Criner and then allowed for a suitable lull. "There's some of us that weren't meant but for one thing alone."

And straightaway Opal insisted, "Yes," and insisted, "Truly," while Delmon her grandbaby on the settee alongside her exhibited for anybody who cared to see it the blue pen cap he'd attached by suction to the tipend of his tongue, from where it loosened shortly and dropped to the cushion thereby freeing Delmon to tell to his daddy and his grandmomma both together, "Ho!"

Marie Criner had come on account of the profits to be less ill, had retreated anyhow to her characteristic sour mood which seemed itself relatively merry and bright. She'd found a cookie tin to batter and abuse and was flailing away at it when Donnie Huff slipped up back of her in the kitchen and inspired Marie with his fingers to shriek and levitate which eroded her disposition pretty dramatically.

"If it ain't his holiness," she said to him once she'd settled and respirated, and Donnie Huff blessed her and reached for her downy patch foremost but she managed to dodge and evade him as she told to him, "Get away from me," in a tone he'd learned to take for earnest.

Donnie Huff opened the refrigerator and poked wanly about inside it and complained to his wife how he had not yet come across a thing worth eating, which prompted Marie to suggest to him that he might best manufacture some loaves and multiply some fishes which got her once more pursued by the forearm that she ever so deftly avoided. Donnie Huff settled

for potted meat on toast and joined his wife at the dinette
where he sought to learn from her the virtues of a battered
cookie tin as opposed to the regular unscathed variety and
Marie reminded him how he was after all trash himself who
didn't hardly know a thing in this world about what's tasteful
and fine. Consequently, she could not help but figure that talk
of a distressed cookie tin would be wasted upon him, so she
shunted him off from the topic altogether by inquiring if perhaps he was meaning to lay out this entire day from work which
Donnie Huff confirmed as his intention.

"I got no call to drive that skidder, haul them trees," Donnie
Huff told to her. "Got eighty-seven dollars back there at the
bedstead."

"Eighty-seven dollars," Marie Criner said. "You meaning to
retire on that?"

"Aw baby, that Jesus He works in mysterious ways, sees
pretty much after His own," Donnie Huff informed his wife
Marie and then bit off such a sizable piece of toast that potted
meat squirted out from either corner of his mouth.

"Well, let me tell you this, mister," Marie Criner said and
raised for effect her tack hammer to point and indicate with.
"We've got a child in there to feed and see after. Your Jesus
going to write you a check every Friday?"

And Donnie Huff elevated his prized downy patch so as to
display it for Marie his wife as he told to her, "It isn't always just
sweat that pays. You saw them. I've got something here."

"Hell, even those Christian fools will get worn out with you
soon enough. Somebody else will come along, somebody who's
been dead more lately than you and got pinched and fondled
himself by the Lord, some slick son-of-a-bitch that's heard the
angels sing."

"Well, he hasn't come yet," Donnie Huff informed her.

"He will. He always does." Marie Criner told to him and
played upon her cookie tin a vigorous tack hammer tattoo.

Donnie Huff guessed he'd go for a ride in dead Carl's Coronet, figured him and his boy Delmon would slip on into
town and see there what there was to see, and he stood presently alongside the settee with his hand upturned until Opal

Criner laid her keyring upon the palm of it, surrendered to
Donnie Huff her Carl's beige sedan that she was satisfied in
her heart he'd not abuse and cat about in, and she proclaimed
to him the nature of her satisfaction, insisted how thoroughly
convinced she was of Donnie Huff's fine intentions, and then
followed Donnie and Delmon to the door where she lingered
at the screen and watched Donnie Huff fairly fly over the culvert and whip the Coronet into the road. Delmon tuned the
radio, flitted about from station to station while Donnie Huff,
with his one arm laying out the sidewindow and his opposite
hand draped upon the wheel after such a fashion as to leave
him to steer with his wrist alone, discussed with Delmon his
boy the vagaries of spiritual well-being, argued why it was
precisely a forearm like his own one would maintain surely its
appeal over time since it was not just every day that somebody
up and floated through the ether and then got snatched
shortly back to life. Donnie wished Delmon would name for
him please anybody he knew who'd been resurrected, and
though Delmon was acquainted himself with a boy whose father had expired naked in the trailer of his wife's hairdresser
and so had likely already incinerated in hell, he did not know
of anybody whose essence had been vented temporarily the
other way, and so he told to his daddy just, "You," and
pointed with his radio tuning finger.

Donnie Huff found it curious that, considering his histori-
cally low opinion of Christian folk, it would be him that got
selected to fly to Jesus like he had to guess was just one more of
the mysterious ways in which the Lord worked, and he wondered if Delmon his boy had ever suspected he'd see his daddy
up back of a pulpit preaching to a congregation that Delmon
had apparently not bothered himself to suspect one way or
another about. "I had them right here," Donnie Huff told to
Delmon his boy and flipped over his arm so as to expose his
palm and guide for a time the Coronet with the bony topside of
his wrist. "You see them watching me, listening to your daddy?"
he wanted to know, and Delmon told to him, "Yeah."

"You see them flocking all around this thing here?" Donnie
Huff inquired and exposed at Delmon his downy patch which

Delmon reached out his stubby fingers and ruffled the hair of
as he told to his daddy, "Yeah," told to his daddy, "I seen them."

"There's something to be said for having people sit and
listen to a thing you tell them," Donnie Huff informed Delmon
his boy. "Not much at all wrong with it."

And Delmon himself, who could not see on his own the
harm in getting heard, shook his head to indicate as much.

They did not slip into town exactly but swung off north out
100 beyond Sylvatus and up through Barren Springs past Donnie Huff's homeplace and on towards Allisonia to the shankend
there of Claytor Lake where the New River spilled into it and
backed up. They drove up onto the headlands above the town,
left the Coronet on the roadside, and walked together out
across a pasture, through a stand of slash pines, and onto a bare
ledgy hump of ground that fell away towards the rooftops and
the water beyond them. Back before Donnie's Skylark had become enfeebled, him and his boy Delmon had gotten into the
habit of visiting together this rocky place up over Allisonia.
They could see from it back a goodly stretch along the river and
up a goodly stretch along the lake and were just themselves
level with the Methodist steepletop which was capped off with a
weathervane, a green copper weathervane with a sizable banty
rooster for a pivot, a banty rooster that Donnie Huff had struck
previously twelve times flush and nine times slight and glancing. Delmon's chore was to hunt him rocks, rocks with some
heft to them as opposed to the flat flaky variety that dipped and
sailed. Donnie liked a lumpy piece of stone that he could drape
his foremost fingers upon and hurl with some authority. So
Delmon rooted up what specimens he could find and deposited
them in a heap alongside Donnie his daddy who worked his
joints and tested the breeze and made a couple of preliminary
tosses with the poorer, slighter stones at hand.

Donnie reminded his boy Delmon how he'd previously
played ball back in school. He had been himself a fireballer of
some considerable repute with blinding speed and the accuracy
of a blunderbuss which he failed somehow to trouble himself to
remind Delmon of as well and instructed him instead, "Watch
this," in advance of squinting maliciously at the banty rooster

and sending his first rock into the limbs of a sycamore tree that was not even rooted in the churchyard. He landed a hunk of shale on the porch of the parsonage and fired a piece of milky quartz clean into the river. He would have hit surely the steeple at least with the handsome hunk of quarry gravel he'd taken up for that purpose if a puff of wind had not come up to disturb the flight of it which Donnie explained to his boy Delmon as a means of acquainting him further with the aerodynamics of quarry gravel. He made adjustments in his technique, tampered with his mechanics, and presently delivered himself of a stone that appeared in fact to threaten the banty rooster before it dipped and curled clear of the steeple and dropped down onto an Oldsmobile instead which prompted Delmon to vent in his daddy's honor a cry, lay back his head and holler into the air, "Ho!" which Donnie himself took up as a refrain, and they "Ho!"ed at the wide tosses and "Ho!"ed at the near tosses and threw in together on a bout of vigorous "Hallelujah"s once Donnie Huff had hit flush the copper steeple roof with what turned out to be a lump of clay that went precipitously to pieces and slid in scraps and nuggets down the shingles and pelted at length the gutterbottoms.

Delmon, who wasn't but six and a half, could barely fling a rock off of the ledgy hump himself. His arm was weak and his technique unsightly, but his daddy advised and instructed him, overhauled for Delmon his windup and altered his release point which rendered him presently capable of clearing the furthermost outcropping and raining stones into a garden patch down under the bluff where a fellow who was chopping weeds communicated with one shrill cry the news of for the benefit of Delmon who saw fit himself to "Ho!" back.

Donnie Huff didn't guess he cared if he never drove a skidder again or fed the mill or hauled planks off to be dressed, and he explained to Delmon his boy the liabilities of the hourly wage, stood there upon the ledgy hump tossing a stone in the air as he shared with his child the wisdom he'd accumulated over the course of his employment. It didn't seem to him that a man on the clock had much hope of getting ahead in this world. The bosses kept for themselves the bulk of the money and the government took most of the rest of it which didn't leave the working man much at all to show for his labor that Donnie Huff emphasized by sucking noisily a dab of spit through a convenient toothgap and thereby prompted Delmon to tell to him, "Yeah," which Delmon knew to be his part in the occasional parades of accumulated wisdom that his daddy was fond of inflicting upon him.

Donnie Huff hadn't ever himself been a boss previously. He hadn't ever had before a thing to be a boss about. "A man's got to have some goods," he informed Delmon his boy. "A man's got to have an asset," which Delmon appeared to weigh and consider prior to finding cause to tell to his daddy, "Yeah."

Donnie Huff confessed freely to never himself possessing previously an asset of much count, nothing anyhow of any detectable value beyond his ripply features and strapping physical attributes, and he apprised with gravity his boy Delmon, "Nobody was ever looking for me to do a thing in the world but sweat," afterwhich Donnie Huff fired for effect a rock that appeared momentarily a genuine endangerment to the banty rooster but suffered its contours to get blown upon and so dipped and veered into a carshed instead and cracked against the clapboards.

Donnie Huff couldn't figure himself that there was much premium truly on sweat and effort together since most everybody was capable of some of both that he allowed his boy Delmon to weigh and digest and say presently, "Yeah," about prior to advancing upon him the news that he, Donnie Huff, had not ever in his time been known truly for his sparkling intellect. "I hadn't never been sharp," Donnie Huff insisted, "and I won't try to tell you I am. Some of us just aren't meant for it."

"Yeah," Delmon assured him and pitched his own handsome hunk of quarry gravel out over the bluff and into the garden patch where it prompted a harsh bit of talk from that fellow with the weeds to chop who advised the sorry bastard that was flinging rocks upon him to prepare himself to get shortly throttled to a pulp.

But Donnie Huff didn't guess he needed truly to be sharp most especially now that he'd gotten blessed by the Savior, though that wasn't to say that he'd grown yet convinced entirely that the Lord had reached out in fact and touched him. He confessed in confidence to Delmon his boy that what he'd seen chiefly was spots, little green ones that floated and circulated about.

"Spots," Delmon told to him, "yeah."

But he had to figure Christ Himself had mingled there amongst them. Donnie Huff couldn't help but suppose, what with his downy forearm all potent and rapturous, that he had to have run up on Jesus somewhere and been gripped if only a little by Him. "I guess I was," he informed Delmon his boy. "I guess I had to be," and Donnie drew in a deep breath and expelled it as he determined how he might after all believe himself empowered, take as irrefutable proof the shivers and galvanic twitches of six gross of the faithful who'd been by him induced to vigorous displays. "I guess maybe I'm the Lord's boy on this earth," Donnie Huff suggested to Delmon his boy who assured his daddy without hesitation, "Yeah."

There was palpable peace for Donnie Huff in embracing his circumstances, which is not to say he'd previously endured torments and anguishment untold. But now that he guessed he'd go ahead and be a pawn of the Lord outright, he felt his anxieties drain from him and noticed an improvement in his aim, managed even to glance a rock off the louvered belfry before he confided to Delmon his boy, "I ain't never going to hit that chicken," and told to him, "Let's leave here," that Delmon obliged his daddy in, struck out ahead of him off the ledgy hump and through the slash pines and down along the edge of the pasture to the roadway where him and his daddy met a fellow, an ill and surly sort who unshouldered his hoe so as to quiz Donnie Huff as to his purposes and pursuits and consequently heard from him how he'd entered the woods in contemplation and found for his trouble balm and elixir which Donnie Huff breathed significantly in the wake of and thereby allowed his boy Delmon occasion for a "Ho!"

They stopped in at the Tastee Freeze for a double-dipped sugar cone apiece on their way home and concentrated between them entirely too much upon the chocolate sheathing without

sufficiently sculpting and marshaling their soft ice cream beneath it which melted and oozed onto their fingers, trickled
down their arms, and dripped from their elbows onto their
pantsfronts like was enough of a sensation and a circumstance
to heighten Donnie Huff's natural tendency to crowd the center
line and made thereby for a thrilling excursion. Donnie Huff
swung the Coronet into the driveway and passed rather heedlessly over the culvert in the judgment of his loving wife's
mother who'd heard him coming and had risen from the settee
to critique his approach. She held in her fingers a sheet of pink
paper torn from her notepad which was one of the dozen she'd
bought from that Unitarian child who'd come around raising
money for the youth fellowship. Her own name was spelled out
at the top of each page in clematis. "Opal" anyhow was im-
printed upon each sheet in leafy blossoming script, and Donnie
Huff's loving wife's mother was so terribly fond of her notepads
that she was reluctant to make any use much of them, fearing
like she did that she would run short of paper before the Unitarian youth fellowship ran again short of funds.

She'd been persuaded, however, that she'd come upon a suitable occasion and so had inked up a leaf and unstuck it from the
gummy binding, the very leaf she held now in her fingers as she
watched her Donald and her grandbaby Delmon lurch quite un-
necessarily to a stop and fling open and fling shut their cardoors
with nearly identical undue zeal. They each of them sucked on
their fingers and licked their knobby wrists while simultaneously
they entertained the blandishments of Sheba the wirehaired dog
who'd not lately come across Donnie balmed and elixired and
blessed plainly with such noticeable repose which she felt inclined to comment excessively upon. Opal Criner fairly yahooed
to them through the doorscreen, hoped they'd enjoyed together
a pleasurable outing here at the top of the week, and she loosed
the latch and admitted freely her grandbaby into the house while
interrupting his daddy at the threshold so as to inform him how
she'd come to be freighted with news to share, significant news
that would not hardly begin to keep.

Word of her Donald's testimony had plainly swept the
county. Opal had occupied her morning fielding calls from
chiefly the afflicted themselves as well as spouses and loved ones

of the downtrodden who'd entertained lately news of the mystical forearm and were hoping to find occasion to come somehow into intimate proximity to it and get thereby their turmoils becalmed and their doubts routed and swept away in addition of course to having as well their assorted growths reduced, their balky joints mended, and their stubborn internal debilities driven from them altogether. For the benefit of Donnie Huff, Opal Criner cited from memory specific plagues and afflictions she'd taken up the receiver and learned about, agonies of the spirit and discomforts of the flesh that she'd not, she made clear, committed Donnie to tend to though she could not help but believe that he might wish at his leisure to share his gift of salvation with the needy. She guessed anyway that had she personally been redeemed from the flames of hell she'd probably want to, and she pinched her lips together and confirmed for her Donald, "I would."

Beyond, however, petitions from the locally distressed, Opal Criner had received on behalf of Donnie Huff one call further which she told to him she had without revealing as well who precisely she'd received it in fact from. Instead she merely flapped in the air her pink sheet of notepaper and made at Donnie Huff a throaty sort of a noise that lacked altogether the Mrs. Lila B. Underwood variety of disdain. Coyly she kept her personalized leaf out from the reach of Donnie Huff as she flapped it further and waved it and shifted it about and only presently allowed him to snatch it from her, at length permitted him to pluck it away and flip it right side over and gumedge up, which exposed to him the "Opal" in clematis and beneath it, in his loving wife's mother's penciled scrawl, just "Dunbar" alone.

"Him with the hat?" Donnie Huff said.

And Opal Criner told to him, "Yes," meaning him with the hat precisely, him with the black suit and the string tie and the stiff white shirt and the scant theatrical moustache, him with most especially the full-fledged proposition. "That Dunbar," Opal Criner confirmed for her Donald. "Him."

iii

He'd purchased his tent from a Larrimore who'd trained for a living monkeys that wore trousers and jackets and homburg

hats and sat at little monkey-sized desks in monkey-sized places
of business while they pretended to be engaged in earnest com-
merce, screeched, that is, into monkey-sized telephones, and
berated with regularity their hairy beskirted secretaries. That
Larrimore, however, had tired presently of the glamour of the
enterprise and had unburdened himself of his monkeys, had
donated to charity their wardrobes for the use perhaps of scantling children born without nasal passages, and had sold to the
Dunbar his canvas tent which in foul weather smelled like a
cellar full of soggy alpaca. It made, however, for such a handsome and sizable structure and had proved for the Reverend
Mr. Dunbar such an exceedingly profitable venue that he did
not any longer mind the stink of it himself which was oftentimes a potent mixture of monkeys and mildew and promoted
in his clientele ever so suitably teary dispositions.

The Reverend Mr. H. W. Dunbar had never personally pre-
sided over a proper church or seen to the spiritual concerns of
a regular flock of the faithful due chiefly to the nature of his
ministry which was itself revivalist and evangelical at heart and
depended for its charm and allure primarily upon the fleshy
heel of the Reverend Mr. Dunbar's right palm with which he
thumped the penitent and the afflicted upon their foreheads
and thereby keeled them over into the arms of his brother-in-
law Eldon whose chore it was to settle them softly upon the
ground. The Reverend Mr. Dunbar's sister Sophia played for
her brother's services a plastic wood-grained electric organ that,
at the mere touch of a button, could manufacture its own rousing backbeat, and her and Eldon's child Frances, who the Reverend Mr. Dunbar evermore introduced as his lovely niece
Grace, sang lilting and doleful hymns of Christian yearning for
the benefit of the assembled. She was blessed truly with an
extravagant singing voice but was unfortunately a plain and
bony young woman and, in the flowing white dresses she favored, looked there up on the dais like Woodrow Wilson in a
ballgown.

Of course the Reverend Mr. H. W. Dunbar had not himself
enjoyed yet the pleasure of being deceased and reviving from it
and, while he was certain surely in time of the one, he was

sufficiently doubtful of the other to trouble himself to hold and
coddle any active hope for a rendezvous shortly with his Savior
with whom he'd had in fact no actual truck to speak of, no
visitations in his despairing hours, no portents in his times of
strife. His blessings instead were his silky manner, his deep and
seemly voice, and his dignified native carriage along with his
slight theatrical moustache that he groomed like a showdog. He
possessed chiefly presence that he managed somehow, at the
culmination of his sermons, to concentrate into his fleshy thumbjoint and render it there stirring and redemptive while he
drummed foreheads and reduced by turns the faithful to sundry heaps upon the tentfloor. But the reverend had been itching lately for a spark and an innovation that might serve to swell
his throngs and enrich his coffers, had wearied of thumping the
penitent, had tired of entertaining alone the parade of infirmities and the wan hopeful expressions on the faces of the downtrodden. He wished to provide them a distraction beyond his
fleshy joint and the lilting doleful stylings of his lovely niece
Grace.

Naturally, however, the Reverend Mr. Dunbar was mindful
still of his previous experience with a visionary. He'd hired a
Cotten to perk up his presentations, a Cotten who'd lapsed into
fits that allowed him to speak in tongues and consort with the
Almighty, visit anyway the hereafter and return with some recall of the excursion. He'd seemed evermore impressed with
how fabulously well the dead were making do on the streets of
gold which he'd been prone to share in regular English with the
assembled before becoming after his own fashion entranced,
rolling back his eyes and lifting his arms heavenward as preamble to a spate of curious discourse which that Cotten could
well have picked up from a chatty and irate infant. The Reverend Mr. Dunbar, who'd heard in his day tongues enough,
had never been much stirred and persuaded by that Cotten
himself although he'd proved fairly effective with the penitent,
most especially the ones in skirts and dresses who could not
seem to help but get by that Cotten a little wooed and inflamed.
He had a full head of wavy hair and big square teeth and a
cleft there at the point of his chin and, once the reverend had

bought for him a proper suit, he'd developed a manner that was passably suave and enticing and, with his trips through the ether to recount and his gibberish to vent, he proved for some of the ladies an absolute distraction from piety since they had to guess there was likely nothing finer on this earth than a handsome Christian fellow afflicted on occasion with holy entrancement.

So the Cotten had become a genuine attraction and had provided for a time a wholesome service alone, had lifted merely spirits in advance of finding occasion to lift for a change a dressend instead. It just turned out that his resolve to be goodly was weak and untested as he'd never previously been obliged to endure too terribly much temptation, had never before testified in a proper tent for the benefit in part of the sorts of young ladies who'd come to find Jesus but would just as soon settle for a Cotten who'd maybe run up once or twice on the Savior himself. So he wooed assorted of the congregation without meaning to woo them at all, inflamed most especially a flaxen-haired Sugg from Fort Chiswell who attended a week's worth of services there at the lot off the interstate outside Wytheville, and then showed up again the following week off the roadside at Woolwine where the Reverend Mr. Dunbar had contracted for the use of a fallow beanfield. She sat up front in increasingly immodest ensembles, arrived early and lingered late and lavished that Cotten with her praise and approval, found ample occasion to hold to his fingers for comfort, she called it, and grew at length so utterly overwhelmed by the hair and the teeth and the clefted chin in conjunction with the holy entrancement that she gave over herself altogether to the Cotten who'd not truly been looking to get given over to.

That last night in Woolwine the flaxen-haired Sugg followed that Cotten down the aisle after the offertory, trailed him into the beanfield, and caught up with him at last out along the tentwall, where she praised as a salutation their Jesus, took up for comfort that Cotten's strong fingers, and deposited them shortly upon her derriere which provided her apparently ample cause to inhale with dispatch between her clenched teeth and lift a scantily beskirted leg that she laid upon that Cotten along about his hip pocket. Straightaway the Cotten himself gave praise to the Maker and failed so resolutely to endeavor at all to mend the Sugg in her ways that he was visited precipitously with a judgment, unmasked directly as a duplicitous fornicator, suffered anyhow some untimely exposure to the congregation on account of how him and that Sugg had come to embrace at a place in the tentwall where the monkeys used to pass in from the outside and out from the inside, a flap of sorts that a breath of air raised and parted and thereby revealed to anybody who cared to see them the pair together who would not likely have attracted too awful much attention but for the unfortunate exclamation that the Cotten found cause to vent once he'd laid his free fingers upon the flaxen-haired Sugg's blousefront. He simply rejoiced with undue passion and so drew there directly the singular attention of a woman from Stuart who'd come to have a sinus complaint resolved and mended. She was on the verge of enjoying the ministrations of the Reverend Mr. Dunbar who'd cocked back his arm and was just about to deliver with his mystical fleshy joint a blow when that woman from Stuart loosed a little cry and then crumpled on her own into a heap before the reverend could thump her or his sister's husband Eldon could ease her to the floor. Naturally the Reverend Mr. Dunbar's attention was captivated straightoff by the sight of that woman piled up on the tentfloor, which prompted the reverend to gaze in turn briefly upon his altogether too potent fleshy thumbjoint that he was coming to appreciate anew when Eldon, his sister's husband, indicated with his nose primarily a portion of tentwall back over the reverend's shoulder, a portion of tentwall that the most of the rest of the congregation was watching already for themselves before the Reverend Mr. Dunbar had brought his own scrutiny to bear upon the windblown flaps that fluttered open to reveal that Cotten with the hair and the teeth and the clefted chin engaged plainly in something other than the Lord's own work though he applied himself to it with what was undeniably a missionary zeal.

There is not much otherwise that will more readily spoil the mood of an evangelical revival than a sudden dose of graphic and irrefutable evidence that a witness for the Lord has directly given over his entrancement on the dais for a passionate and immodest embrace alongside a tentflap. It's just the sort of thing to undo infusement quite altogether and did blacken in fact the disposition of that crowd from Woolwine who had to figure that Satan was likely among them himself if such a fine, handsome, beclefted man as that Cotten could be tempted by the wiles and seduced into the clutches of a wayward woman. They felt the group of them inclined to pray for the redemption of the Cotten but figured they'd best likely go on ahead and despise him first and so revealed to the Cotten and the Sugg together a veritable sea of unsavory expressions which they failed the both of them to notice for a time as they were quite supremely occupied otherwise. At length, however, the general scrutiny impressed itself upon them, grew fairly palpable on the air, and induced thereby the Sugg and the Cotten both to disengage each from the other and turn uneasily about towards the tentwall which was not, they remarked together, merely wall alone but was actually primarily flap instead. So they looked into the tent at the faithful who looked out from the tent at them, and that Cotten displayed his straight white teeth for whoever might care to gaze upon them and made as if to be performing on that Sugg a maneuver designed to promote salvation, thumped her one time upon the breastbone with his blouse-feeling hand, and shrilly exclaimed, "Demon be gone!" which the congregation at large did not appear to find a credible undertaking and looked still with loathing upon that Cotten and that Sugg together who became, as best as they were able, unentangled each from the other and slipped away from the monkey flap towards the darker reaches of the beanfield where the Cotten wished temporarily that he'd never himself come into possession of the manner or organ he'd be tempted to follow like a divining rod to strife and woe and very likely damnation but, with her ever so nimble fingers, that Sugg straightaway persuaded him to revise his views.

The Reverend Mr. Dunbar guessed he could still probably have employed that Cotten places other than Woolwine if that Cotten himself had not become irredeemably intoxicated with his Sugg's earthly enticements. So the reverend had grown inclined to alter his opinion and had been for a time already casting about for a replacement visionary when he'd heard tell of Donnie Huff who'd expired and recovered from it, Donnie Huff with his downy patch that had appeared to the reverend in Laurel Fork a livelier attraction even than the hair and the teeth and the clefted Cotten chin. He was set up north of Gladesboro back off the road in a grassy bottom that was swampier than that Dunbar had anticipated, was low and spongy and gave rise in the evening to wafting mists that saturated the tentwalls and served to release the primate aroma in dank and undiluted doses. The general humidity of the place had apparently served as well to short out the reverend's sister Sophia's plastic organ from which Sophia could not coax even one reedy note or the merest trace of syncopated backbeat. The reverend himself figured there was corrosion somewhere along the line from the organ to the generator and he wiggled what looked to him pertinent wires to no noticeable effect and wiggled as well those wires that had struck him previously as largely impertinent in advance of stepping outside of the tent and circling about to the generator itself which he kicked and battered as a species of persuasion but to no detectable electrical effect as the organ still refused to play and the wires remained, quite obviously, corroded.

Donnie Huff had carried with him his child and had carried with him his loving wife's mother who'd herself committed to memory alone the directions out to the bottom so as to better ensure her passage. Donnie drove her dead Carl's Coronet directly out onto the marshy ground which she vigorously advised him against as she feared getting mired up inextricably in the bottom, sinking into a swampy piece of turf clean up to the axles. But Donnie Huff struck out nonetheless down towards the tent itself and did slip and did wallow and did slide about on the soggy patches much to the consternation of Opal Criner though to the equal delight of his child Delmon who shouted with every yaw and shiver, "Ho!"

As she stepped from the car and was throwing the door shut back of her, Opal Criner was assuring still her Donald how they'd never again gain the blacktop unassisted which she was meaning plainly to elaborate upon, remind anyhow Donnie Huff just who precisely had questioned the wisdom of venturing off the road in the first place, when she found herself obliged instead to employ her breath and her assorted face muscles in the pursuit of another purpose altogether. She shaped and constricted her features, pinched and compressed them into an unmistakable I-can't-believe-what's-passing-up-my-noseholes sort of a face which she managed to sustain for an extraordinary length of time due chiefly to how the canvas tent itself was so appreciably more potent an item than both of Donnie Huff's feet together which Opal Criner most usually shaped and most usually constricted her features about. Even Donnie himself grew inspired to announce for anybody who cared to hear it, "Whew!" and he pinched and compressed some features of his own as he stepped into the tent proper and discovered there the Reverend Mr. Dunbar's sister Sophia fingering forlornly her plastic organ keys.

Opal Criner could not bring herself to approve of tent meetings or the sorts of people that conducted them for a livelihood since a revival was bound evermore to attract some trash like a regular sanctuarial service hardly ever did. She guessed if the day would ever dawn when trash could maybe be redeemed, she would alter her opinion, but for the moment she went on ahead and disapproved of the Reverend Mr. Dunbar's sister Sophia whose posture was poor and whose coif was unflattering and whose dress was outdated and whose hips were broad and whose organ was plainly broken. Sophia's child Frances, who slipped in through the monkey door to see who'd come there in the middle of the afternoon, did not fare much better herself in the estimation of Opal Criner who straightaway disapproved of her homely ungirlish qualities and had divined already on her own the relation between the mother at the organ and the daughter at the tentflap when Eldon arrived with an armful of folding chairs and a weak chin and a bony nose and a claim straightaway to paternity. Opal Criner didn't truly like the looks of any of them but then she had to wonder what decent handsome sorts of people would work in such a concentrated stench and, as Eldon was handy for it, she greeted him with the variety of toothy and seminauseated smile that her own girl had long since mastered and inquired if perhaps the Reverend Mr. Dunbar was somewhere about, the Reverend Mr. H. W. Dunbar who'd invited them most especially to pay him a call.

Eldon, the Reverend Mr. Dunbar's brother-in-law, bade Opal Criner and Donnie Huff and Donnie's boy Delmon to follow if they might the organ wire since, as best as Eldon knew, the Reverend Mr. Dunbar was loitering there at the end of it, and he told to them something on the order of, "Yar," and pointed up beyond the dais to where an electrical cable disappeared under the tentwall, and Opal Criner and Donnie Huff and Donnie's boy Delmon congregated at the spot and groped about fruitlessly together for a flap until Eldon directed them towards the monkey door which was not itself anywhere at all in the vicinity of the cable which Opal Criner instructed Eldon about.

The Reverend Mr. Dunbar had given over wiggling wires, which had impressed him at length as a dubious pursuit, and had taken up a sizable open-ended wrench with which he was bludgeoning by turns various portions of his generator and thereby attempting to induce the assorted parts and pieces to throw in if they might together and manufacture some detectable electricity. So far, however, he'd only succeeded in inhaling more exhaust than was healthful and he'd already grown quite noticeably wan by the time Opal and Donnie and Delmon had made their way back to where the organ wire went. While his scant theatrical moustache and his northerly hairpart improved even a pallor somewhat, they could not render the Reverend Mr. Dunbar altogether robust in appearance, and once Opal Criner had startled him with her fingerends and had caused him to lurch and hop about, she suggested over the clatter of the generator engine that he retire to a ventilated place and recover there his color while her Donald, who was ever so handy, mended his machine which her Donald had seen fit already to endeavor to do, had reached anyhow with fingerends of his own that he laid to a wingnut which he rotated and tightened down and heard consequently from inside the tent a

D and a middle C followed by a brief and glorious fanfare that
the reverend's sister Sophia was most especially fond of.

The Reverend Mr. Dunbar was himself plainly enchanted
with the turn of events and gave voice to a manner of Hosanna
in tribute to Donnie Huff who'd not ever been favored with a
Hosanna before and so had no cause to be acquainted with the
decorum of getting Hosannaed at, did not, that is, express mod-
estly to the reverend his heartfelt gratitude until his loving
wife's mother, by way of the skillful application of her elbow to
Donnie's tender underbelly, produced from him some gracious-
ness and relieved him as well of the most of his breath. After
just brief moments away from the generator motor, the Reverend Mr. Dunbar began to recover his native hues and started to
look there in his shirtsleeves and his string tie, and with the
added enhancement of his hairpart and his moustache together, more his dapper self. He had not suspected what danger he was likely in until Opal and until Donnie and until
Delmon as well, whose topnotch the reverend massaged with
his knuckles, showed up to warn and advise him which he
thanked them warmly for, took up anyhow the hand of Donnie
Huff and the fingers of Opal Criner while Delmon merely endured his cranium to get buffed once further.

The reverend was openly delighted that they'd troubled
themselves to drive out and see him, instructed both Donnie
and Opal together as to the quality of his mood and welcomed
them into the tent to sit please if they might for a time and
entertain his proposition that he was ever so pleased to have
occasion to speak of. As for herself, Opal Criner guessed she
preferred the open air of the marshy bottom to the monkey
and mildew miasma under the tentroof and, with a flourish of
her elbow, she persuaded her Donald to prefer it with her and
together they convinced the reverend to stroll with them
around towards the Coronet. Reluctantly and with marked hesitation, the Reverend Mr. Dunbar revealed to Donnie Huff and
to Opal Criner chiefly and somewhat to Delmon as well, who
squatted nearby in a puddle, how he'd suffered lately the loss of
his visionary, was making anymore do without his Cotten who'd
succumbed, the reverend suggested, to an organ complaint.

Consequently, the reverend had himself been lately casting about for a replacement visionary, had been hoping to come across some manner of fellow who'd gotten blessed one way or another by the holy Savior, had enjoyed perhaps a brush with rapture, had consorted maybe with Jesus before the filigreed gates. "I've been hoping for a time now to come across such a man as that," the reverend proclaimed to Donnie and proclaimed to Opal Criner, assuring the both of them, "and yesterday I did," which Donnie Huff took unprompted for a Hosannalike item and so ponied up unbidden an apt response.

The Reverend Mr. Dunbar wondered of Opal Criner and Donnie Huff if they were aware perhaps of the mere existence of the throngs and multitudes of wholesome God-fearing people who remained for one reason or another unaffiliated and nondenominational and required for their spiritual well-being independent preachers like himself who ventured out into the countryside and made convenient the lessons of the Lord. Some of these folks had lapsed, the reverend admitted, in the ways of churchgoing and had yielded to slovenly inclinations but they were goodly for the most part at heart and were looking merely to get drawn into the fold once more. Testimony from a former reprobate had simply evermore seemed to the reverend a boon in his endeavors, and he was hoping he might persuade Donnie Huff to join him in his charitable mission to go out among the lost and the lowly and chase away their darkness with heavenly light, and the reverend turned about so as to inform Delmon who was squatting still in his puddle, "Your daddy's a man that's risen and soared," which Delmon appeared to absorb and consider in advance of sharing with the Reverend Mr. Dunbar a distracted and halfhearted "Ho!"

Donnie Huff guessed maybe he could be persuaded to put up his forearm for hire providing of course that the reverend in his mission was not intending to be entirely charitable, was meaning, that is, to bestow upon Donnie Huff a regular and sufficient consideration, a consistent piece of money with which Donnie Huff might meet his expenses and maintain his downy patch that he suggested to the Reverend Mr. Dunbar was no small obligation and confided to him how he'd suffered already from strenuous forearm fatigue in the wake of his Laurel Fork testimony. "Got cramps," Donnie Huff said and he rolled up his sleeve to reveal as well a raw and tender place the parade of fingerends had inflicted. While Donnie Huff guessed he'd be pleased enough to give witness to the shining wonders of Christ and the welcome glories of the hereafter, he did not wish to risk for himself injury and endangerment to do it unless of course he was suitably seen after and his assorted traumas were taken into account.

"We're talking here a piece of the gross," Donnie Huff informed the Reverend Mr. Dunbar who unleashed upon Donnie and Opal together an accomplished bewildered expression and hoped devoutly that Donnie Huff did not figure the reverend's evangelical tent revival a highly profitable enterprise. "I'm just a poor servant," Mr. Dunbar told to them. "I take what by the grace of God I'm given and am happy to have it," which the reverend stooped humbly in the wake of.

Donnie Huff, however, had entered on his way to the marshy bottom into consultation with his loving wife's mother who had advised him sternly to insist upon a percentage off the top in addition to a modest but respectable retainer to be paid weekly in cash. It was after all Donnie Huff alone who'd abandoned his supine form to soar through the ether which made undoubtedly for a seller's market that Opal Criner had impressed upon her Donald who she'd instructed to stand pat in his demands until such time as she herself suggested an agreeable compromise. The wild card in the proceedings, however, was the Reverend Mr. Dunbar's own miraculous thumbjoint with which Opal and Donnie together were quite wholly unacquainted. Consequently, the reverend undertook to bring them to know it, spoke of its potent and inexplicable qualities and demonstrated for them how he most usually applied the thing, created on the spot a full-fledged simulation of his customary thumbjoint technique, summoned anyhow Delmon to him so as to bounce his fleshy joint off Delmon's forehead as he intoned a suitable incantation meant to chase away nonspecific illness and despair. And even though Delmon, who enjoyed just presently general well-being, failed to collapse into a heap, Opal Criner came most especially to be affected by the Reverend Mr.

Dunbar's display, his entire evangelical package which was intended at heart to provide general and miraculous relief to those troubled souls on this earth who might find solace in a fleshy joint, most especially one administered with the aid of such a sleek and theatrical moustache in conjunction with a genuinely princely manner.

Now while there was plenty to be said for Donnie Huff's laudable accomplishments in the areas particularly of Bible brandishing and creaky anguished discharges, the Reverend Mr. Dunbar invited Opal Criner and her Donald together to confess to him please that wasn't there as well appreciable room for improvement and polish which, once they'd consulted, Donnie and Opal jointly conceded as fact. Accordingly the Reverend Mr. Dunbar was prepared to apprentice Donnie Huff for a flat but generous wage and was willing to provide as well the prospect for advancement, the opportunity to work at length on commission once Donnie Huff had honed his technique and proved himself a legitimate draw for the downtrodden, an earnest and able revivalist, and had demonstrated as well an unshakable commitment to the work of the Lord, leading Opal Criner to wonder of the Reverend Mr. Dunbar if didn't it seem to him that a man who'd recovered from being dead and supine both would have cause enough to crusade for his Christ, and the reverend guessed it did in fact seem so.

The Reverend Mr. Dunbar properly introduced Donnie Huff and his loving wife's mother and Donnie's hale and sturdy child Delmon to Sophia at the plastic organ and Sophia's girl Frances and Sophia's husband Eldon who was particularly pleased to welcome into their endeavor a fellow lately back from the dead as he'd been himself awfully fond of that last boy they'd had who'd been deceased. "Got run over, didn't he?" Eldon inquired of Sophia his wife who seemed herself to recall that that boy had gotten squashed by a tractor, or would anyhow have gotten squashed if the ground hadn't been soft and muddy enough to prevent him from being crushed altogether.

"Just got the breath mashed out of him and had his rib cage to collapse," Sophia informed her Eldon and assured him how it hadn't been any serious sort of misadventure.

"Well, it killed him," Eldon reminded Sophia but Sophia did

not recall that he'd been so thoroughly dead and believed herself he'd advanced only maybe so far as death's door notwithstanding how Eldon her husband assured her he'd been utterly
expired albeit briefly.

Her Donald, Opal Criner announced, had been himself
good and deceased for a respectable stretch of time, had turned
in fact quite completely bluegreen, and had suffered the thoroughgoing interruption of his functions and the seizure of an
organ or two which Donnie Huff confirmed and he indicated
vaguely the location on his person of organs that had quite
thoroughly seized up. Opal Criner just could not herself believe
that getting ground into the mud by a tractor wheel was anything at all like drowning outright in the murky depths and
ascending into the presence of the Lord. So while the Reverend
Mr. Dunbar had employed maybe a dead boy previously, Opal
Criner could not believe they'd regularly enjoyed yet the testimony of a fellow who'd been as undeniably and fruitfully deceased as her Donald. "Tell them about the ether and the
heavenly portal," she suggested to Donnie Huff who was loath
to witness just at the moment but did manage to reveal to Sophia and to Eldon and to Frances their girl how the one had
been as inky as pitch and the other one hadn't, which they all of
them let on to savor as a piece of news.

The Reverend Mr. Dunbar had taken the liberty of cultivat-
ing an angle, had considered deeply the talents and circumstances of Donnie Huff, and had been blessed presently with a
notion of how they best might frame and employ them for the
diversion of the faithful who he had to figure had not likely
among them heard too awful much lumberjack testimony. The
reverend was of the opinion that Donnie Huff had no cause
truly to look preacherly as he was not in fact a preacherly sort
of a fellow but was instead a manner of roustabout who'd come
quite inadvertently upon the grace of the Savior. Consequently,
then, the Reverend Mr. Dunbar was not much partial to Donnie
Huff's blue suit with the faint stripe to it and favored himself
more of a timberman's getup, a fuzzy plaid shirt and stout
woolen trousers with braces in addition to brogans and whatever sort of cap it was timbermen were anymore fond of. The

reverend had toyed with the notion of having Donnie Huff tote about a camp ax upon his shoulder as he stirred and harangued the faithful, but he'd improved straightaway upon it and had decided instead to provide Donnie Huff with an appropriately battered copy of the Testaments,the reverend's own personal sizable leatherbound Bible that was creased and worn and crinkled and torn and looked itself the sort of tome that might have been hauled about in the big woods and consulted in those lulls and respites when the shavings weren't flying and the hardwoods weren't hinging over to the ground. Donnie would be, in short, as unrefined and homely as the crowd before him who'd sooner listen, the reverend figured, to a lumberjack in a lumberjack suit than a lumberjack in a blue one with a faint stripe to it.

The Reverend Mr. Dunbar wondered of Donnie Huff if he could possibly put together a lumberjack ensemble and show up at the marshy piece of ground the following evening prepared to share with the assembled the tale of his excursion which induced Donnie Huff to lift a hand into the air and rub the tip of his thumb against the tip of his two foremost fingers that fairly spirited as if by magic the reverend's wallet into view. Opal Criner witnessed the exchange of funds with no little satisfaction and took up her Donald straightway at the elbow so as to proceed in his company to the Coronet and in the company as well of her grandbaby Delmon who she snatched from a puddle and drew along by the wrist. Aside from being of the opinion, which she freely aired, that Donnie Huff had no business in lumberjack garb since he'd proven himself already wholly mesmerizing in his blue suit and his speckled tie, Opal Criner gave voice as well to her view that only a fool would have driven in the first place a full-fledged Dodge sedan down into such a low and swampy field where she expected they would succeed shortly at getting mired clean up to the wheelwells. But Donnie Huff merely spun up a little slop as he guided the Coronet up towards the break in the fencerow and out into the road and swung south through Gladesboro and west past Snake Creek towards the highway.

He didn't own any braces, hadn't ever previously had call

for a means to hold up his pants beyond his belt and the roll of flesh at the shank of his ripply torso which evermore between them had always done the job well enough, but Opal Criner's Carl had favored in fact braces himself, had been most especially partial to a handsome pair of green ones that Opal had laid up in a shoebox along with her Carl's wallet and her Carl's change purse and her Carl's silver cuff links and her Carl's pocket comb. Donnie Huff owned already fuzzy shirts enough to choose from and had come previously into a pair of broadcloth pants that had a woodsy look to them though they'd been manufactured for a sleeker sort of lumberjack than Donnie Huff had gotten to be and would not any longer button across his belly. His loving wife's mother, however, volunteered to let out Donnie Huff's trousers to fit him if he'd see clear on his own to buff up his brogans notwithstanding his view that no self-respecting lumberjack would shine his woodsman's shoes.

With assorted of her tins and boxes to engage her, Marie Criner did not enjoy presently the leisure to provide Donnie Huff with inordinate exposure to her sour, disapproving expression though she did find occasion to smirk openly at his lumberjack ensemble and demonstrated come evening under the topsheet a wholehearted unwillingness to extinguish for Donnie Huff the fires of his passion, advised him instead to discover if he could some way to get diddled by his Lord. She was not meaning herself to accompany Donnie Huff to the monkey tent and hardly intended for her child Delmon to see what his daddy had stooped to, and although Opal Criner laid out clothes the following afternoon for her girl and clothes for her grandbaby Delmon, Marie simply guessed she'd been daughter enough already and left her dress to lay on the spread while her and Delmon worked together at the dinette tinting varnish and clipping pictures and providing most especially for the tins and the boxes some additional distress.

Donnie Huff looked a fine and healthy specimen in his lumberjack ensemble, and Opal Criner was herself pretty well pleased with his getup and his general burly carriage. He looked to her wholesome and forthright and she admitted how, had she not already been saved and redeemed by her Lord Christ,

Donnie Huff would likely be just the fellow to tempt her to it. In advance of his departure, Donnie Huff stepped into the kitchen to get admired a little as well but failed to promote with his ensemble much enthusiasm on the part of his Marie who told only to Donnie Huff, "Go on from here."

On the way to the marshy field beyond Gladesboro, Opal Criner ventured to suggest to Donnie Huff that perhaps he might hook when he thought to his thumbs upon his belt-loops and strike thereby a manly sort of a posture which Donnie Huff let on to find agreeable and shrewd. He guessed he would resist as well the temptation to grow weepy and tormented, guessed anyhow he would attempt to resist it like any true woodsman might prior to yielding to his deep and soulful inflammation for Christ and dissolving into an appropriately agitated state like sounded to his loving wife's mother an altogether grand proposition and she congratulated heartily her Donald on his resourcefulness, causing him to fish with his thumb for a beltloop and attempt to look the rube as he informed his wife's mother, "Aw."

The low marshy field before the monkey tent was already fairly awash with vehicles by the time Donnie Huff had guided the Coronet beyond Gladesboro to the gap in the fencerow. He descended readily into the mire over Opal Criner's persistent forebodings which she shared with her Donald so that he might know plainly how she had every expectation of getting bogged down for sure in the slop the cars had churned up already if not the slop they'd churn up yet. But nevertheless Donnie wheeled the beige sedan pretty snug up alongside the monkey flap where the Reverend Mr. Dunbar's sister Sophia was applying with a dainty paddle blue glittering highlights to the eyelids of Frances her girl who'd caught up for safekeeping her white gauzy dressend in her fingers and stood with her knees clenched together and her elbows outflung and her slender bony face lifted and inclined as she endured the ministrations of her mother Sophia who endeavored with the dainty paddle to bring some allure to the eyelids at least.

Donnie Huff guessed it was a glorious evening to be outside a tent in a marshy field, climbed out anyhow from the Coronet, and suggested as much to Sophia and Frances together who failed to dispute him though they hardly appeared between them excessively charmed with the night. Opal Criner, who disapproved herself of glittering eyeshadow and assorted face-paints otherwise, treated the ladies to a wan smile as she passed with her Donald into the tent proper where the Reverend Mr. Dunbar's brother-in-law Eldon was distributing presently hymnals to those of the assembled who required them. The Reverend Mr. Dunbar himself, in his black suit and his string tie and with his broadbrimmed hat in his fingers, stood at the main flap greeting his flock as they slogged in through the mire and gained the sheltered tentroof. He praised back at them the Lord once they'd praised the Lord at him. He laid his knuckles to adolescent topnotches and exposed his incisors fairly ceaselessly while Sophia his sister gave over shortly the dainty paddle for her plastic electric organ upon which she played a light reedy processional that she punctuated at length in favor of a more rigorous item which, due to the limitations of her instrument, sounded a trifle light and reedy itself.

The Reverend Mr. Dunbar proved ever so terribly fond of Donnie Huff's ensemble and congratulated Donnie and Opal together upon the effect they'd rendered with the fuzzy shirt and the broadcloth trousers and the handsome stylish braces. As a result of considerable thought on the matter, it had come to be the reverend's intention to pluck Donnie Huff out from the congregation at large early on in the proceedings so that Donnie might share his experience with the assembled, make available his downy patch, and then yield to the reverend's bony niece Frances for a rousing selection that would itself preface a prayer of rejoicing from Eldon Sophia's husband who'd bring on the reverend at last like, taken together, would provide a suitable interval between the miraculous piece of forearm and the fleshy thumbjoint which fell themselves pretty much into the same category of religious implementa. The reverend was simply concerned that those people who'd lately been uplifted by the downy patch might neglect to get healed by the thumbjoint and he wished, by means of his organizational skills, to provide occasion between the forearm and the thumb for the fervor to dissipate and the ecstasy to subside, which Donnie Huff allowed to be a sensible pursuit.

He was, then, quite agreeable to his role in the proceedings and accompanied his loving wife's mother partway up the aisle towards the dais where they sidled along a row to a pair of vacant chairs and dropped anonymously into them which pleased most especially Opal Criner who delighted in how surprised their neighbors would surely be once they learned that they'd been sitting all along in the vicinity of a fellow who'd soared through the ether and in the vicinity as well of that fellow's wife's mother. However, Donnie Huff's neighbors did not appear to him disposed much towards amazement and wonder truly, hardly looked available for surprise or given to bouts of rapture. They struck him as just a little too worn and weary to get whipped to a froth, didn't seem in general awfully giddy about their Lord or prone, from exposure to the miracles He'd wrought, towards intoxication. For the most part, they sat glumly upon their chairseats watching the reverend's sister Sophia play her plastic organ which they'd leave off at every now and again for assorted exchanges of opinion accomplished in low and murmurous tones. Donnie Huff didn't suspect they could work up among them the vigor to care if he turned out to be the Holy Ghost Himself, took them somehow to be utterly beyond vigor and quite entirely past caring. Worse yet, he'd failed to spy so far an admirable pair of hooters in the pack.

Though it was hardly Opal Criner's habit to consort openly with the manner of people who'd congregated this night in the monkey tent, her overwhelming charitable impulses allowed her to sit serenely among them, and she discovered even on the feet of an unsavory woman a pair of pumps she fancied which Opal Criner took as a significant indication that there was plainly a measure of good lurking about in even the unlikeliest of places. She engaged briefly in conversation with the gentleman to her left, a sizable and fleshy sort of fellow who was cursed presently with an internal infection which he'd come to have throttled and expunged. His affliction had rendered him sore and tender about the kidneys and, once he'd persuaded Opal Criner to prod him with her fingerends, he winced with excruciating conviction. His wife alongside him was troubled by a bump in her ear and a history of sclerosis in her family. She was hoping for a jolt sufficient from the thumbjoint to remedy the both of them together. When pressed, Opal Criner revealed that she was blessed with good health herself and unburdened by complaints, but she indicated her Donald alongside her prior to disclosing how he'd lately expired and flown to heaven which served straightaway to inflict upon Donnie her girl's husband the prolonged scrutiny of that gentleman and his wife who examined Donnie Huff in his brogans and braces and broadcloth trousers as they heard from Opal Criner how her Donald had sailed clean through the ether and loitered before the filigreed gates.

"Did he now?" that fellow with the infection asked on behalf of his wife with the bump and the legacy, and Opal Criner assured them, "He did."

Upon the hour precisely, the Reverend Mr. Dunbar instructed Eldon his sister's husband to unfurl and shut the main tentflaps while the reverend himself proceeded to the dais to greet the faithful, to exhibit his handsome smile and his sleek and comely moustache as he bid the bunch of them welcome to his monkey tent and his evangelical service. The reverend opened customarily with a prayer for the plagued and the disenchanted, and Opal Criner, who'd not had the pleasure of hearing the Reverend Mr. Dunbar pray much previously, found herself thoroughly impressed with his tonal qualities and charmed by his grasp of the lingering pause. He petitioned the Lord for mercy, encouraged the faithful to devotion, and agonized plainly on behalf of those heathen souls who'd strayed from the path and wandered somehow into the darkness. He called as well upon the Lord Jesus to empower shortly his own storied thumbjoint that he was meaning to make available in time for the benefit of those with ills and troubles, and then he Amened deeply, much to the pleasure of Opal Criner who preferred on her own a preacher that could finish off a prayer with some resonance and vigor.

The Reverend Mr. Dunbar figured aloud he was plainly himself of a mood for a hymn of devotion, and he introduced to the congregation his niece the lovely Grace who entered through the monkey flaps and joined him by the pulpit where she endured briefly her uncle's loving perusal before his retirement from the dais which was left altogether to Frances and her bony joints and her gauzy flowing gown and her inordinately blue and glittering eyelids that she appeared to Opal Criner quite altogether too eager to bat and display and so spoiled largely by means of her vain pursuits the tone of her endeavor as best as Opal Criner could tell, Opal Criner who could not discover on her own the charm of "Sing with All the Sons of Glory" performed by a woman done up like a strumpet. She was hoping to communicate her freshly soured disposition to Donnie alongside her and so looked upon him with purpose and concentration, but Donnie Huff could not presently be distracted from pursuits of his own, was admiring intensely his downy patch and mussing the hairs of it with his extended finger, laying them over first the one way and then back shortly the other.

Once the Reverend Mr. Dunbar's lovely niece Grace had culminated her rendition, had lifted her head and shut her eyes to hit what seemed to Opal Criner an all too common and unexceptional note, she yielded the dais to the reverend himself who spoke ever so highly of his sister's child as he watched her retire through the monkey flaps and then turned his attention to the treat in store this evening for the assembled who were counting undoubtedly upon the thumbjoint but would enjoy as well one additional and unadvertised piece of anatomy that had passed itself clean through the ether and into the presence of the Lord. For purposes of contrast, the reverend painted a wholly unappetizing picture of the unredeemed Donnie Huff, he of the prepalpated downy patch who'd boozed and caroused and profanated, had hardly led a life of goodly devotion but had come to be favored nonetheless by the Savior Himself. And the woman with the bump in her ear turned to inform a lady alongside her just who it was that had loitered at the filigreed gates, afterwhich they both together engaged in some frank and shameless perusal of Donnie Huff down the row where he was buttoning shut his sleeve at the cuff in final preparation for bounding to the dais which he got shortly by the reverend invited to do.

Straightaway Donnie Huff took up the sizable battered Bible from off the pulpit, the Reverend Mr. Dunbar's own well-thumbed copy of the Good Book that had come through use to be worn and homely and so suited Donnie Huff in his present attire although it was a little too large and cumbersome a book to brandish with much effect and left Donnie to weigh for himself the prospect of creating a stir among the faithful against the likelihood of a scripturally induced muscle strain. He could barely heft the thing in one hand and hook upon his beltloop his free thumb simultaneously, could not anyhow sustain the posture and so laid pretty straightaway the Bible back onto the pulpit and engaged exclusively in the pursuit of appropriate rustic poses. There at the outset, he saw fit to provide the as-sembled with a colorful and highly fabricated description of the lumberjacking life, favored them with a brief and wholly man-ufactured history of timbering prior to proceeding to his own particular circumstances and his personal set of cohorts who he let on to be rough but seemly fellows with hearts pretty much of gold.

Donnie Huff confessed to having failed the bulk of his days to follow in the ways of the Lord. He looked out upon the faithful and admitted to a history of baser inclinations, gazed out onto the uplifted faces of the men and the women and the children who'd traveled to this low boggy place to sit in the monkey reek and hear of the miraculous Christ, who'd come out of hope and out of need and out of maybe desperation as well and endured from Donnie Huff his sorry tale of heathen pursuits. Taken together they looked to him an awful weary pack of people and rendered him up on the dais a little tired on his own as he was hardly so long from timbering that he could not recall their species of exhaustion, and he recognized the numb expressions and the deadened gazes as consequence of their labor not just of this day alone but of all the accumulated days previous and the anticipated and untold days to come. What with their prospects inordinately constricted and dimin-ished, they'd simply fallen into the custom of hoping doggedly for considerably more relief than they ever expected to get like was a burdensome and fruitless and a necessary endeavor. Donnie Huff confessed to them his assorted failings, his shiftless tendencies, his shameful episodes and native heedlessness that had carried him into Christian infringement and holy violation which he spoke of with palpable regret and sufficient of a quiver to stir most especially his loving wife's mother who'd been hoping he'd quiver all along.

Donnie Huff hadn't been prepared, he admitted, to fly through the ether and arrive in the presence of the Lord, though he claimed to the faithful to have enjoyed in his heathen days a mystical instant or two, and he described for them golden shafts and beams of sunlight he'd seen one time on a hillside off and away, assorted shafts and beams that had moved and touched him near about to the identical extent of the cow he'd come across lately, a speckled cow he'd met on the low water bridge over Burke's fork that had gotten itself loose somehow from the pasture and had struck out plainly with a destination in mind but had seen fit to pause there on the slab above the creek to inflict upon Donnie Huff some altogether significant and utterly unbovine regard.

"I was struck," Donnie Huff admitted to anybody that cared to know it, and he allowed how he was more than a little unnerved by the quality of the encounter that had seemed to him strange and mystifying and had touched him in his underlying parts which had usually themselves lain dormant and forgotten until the shafts and beams and the speckled cow had thrown in together to plumb them and suggest to Donnie Huff how there was maybe more to this life than he commonly saw which, as a prospect and a declaration, prompted assorted of the faithful to engage in ever so brief displays of meager and flickering infusement.

Donnie Huff hadn't figured on dying, couldn't guess much of anybody ever did, but he'd not at all even remotely suspected he'd expire in a fiery crash and fly to heaven. Even once the skidder had set to turtling over and slipping towards the bluff, Donnie Huff admitted how he'd supposed still he was sufficiently stout and ripply to come away from his impending ca-

lamity fairly whole and unkilled which he had to guess was just
the way with blustery Godless heathens like his former unredeemed self. He described for the assembled his plummet from
the bluff, spoke of the trailing tongues of flame, and produced
with his lingering pauses such unmitigated tension that Opal
Criner grew even a little overwrought herself and involuntarily
exclaimed after such a fashion as to garner the undiluted and
thoroughgoing perusal of that man alongside her with the tender kidneys and his wife beyond him with the prospects and the
bump.

Having established how he'd come to lay trapped and un-
conscious amongst the twisted metal on the creekbed, Donnie
Huff proceeded on to his vented essence where his oratory
truly glistened and glowed. It seemed to Opal Criner that he'd
never soared through the ether with such frank assurance, and
his rendition this night of the buttery light that shone down
upon him in the inky darkness was so stirring itself as to promote from Donnie Huff's loving wife's mother one plainly audible discharge further. Her neighbor with the kidneys reached
out his fingers and touched gently with them the back of Opal
Criner's near hand which he intended surely for a comfort but
Opal Criner, who was not truly acquainted with her neighbor
and could not say for certain what precisely he'd been with his
fingers up to, shifted and squirmed and rendered her near
hand and her far hand both quite completely inaccessible.

Donnie Huff saw fit somehow to take up his beltloops and
strike an unrelievedly rustic posture as he embarked upon his
description of the filigreed gates which did not seem to Opal
Criner an aspect of his enterprise that needed to get rusticated,
so she pulled assorted faces in an effort to elevate him to a more
dignified manner of narrative which Donnie took in fact as an
instructional endeavor and attempted accordingly to pull those
identical faces himself as he clung to his beltloops and persevered in his excruciatingly woodsy demeanor. Donnie Huff,
however, saw clear uninstructed to alter his tone once he'd
come upon his Lord and Savior who he described with a suitable reverence and gravity but for the re-creation of their salutations each to the other in which Christ's part was a spare

and apt "My son," while Donnie let on to have fairly hooted a "Hey Jesus." He related to the assembled a moderately intelligible rendition of the parable of the peach pit and the nectarines although he did manage to leave the thing sufficiently cloudy in its purposes and adequately obscure in its result to seem to be quite altogether infused with wisdom and ponderous significance. Donnie Huff figured he'd felt there on the heavenly stoop like a chicken in a rainsquall, and he allowed an interval for the congregation to decide among themselves how a chicken in a rainsquall might feel before proceeding at last to the pertinent nugget of the tale which was just precisely how the holy fingerends had been lifted and laid in compassion and grace upon the patch of downy forearm that Donnie Huff rolled up the sleeve of his fuzzy plaid shirt to display and which the bulk of the faithful gazed upon with noticeable and new-found liveliness. He guessed his patch still had some trace of the Lord upon it, felt every now and again a telling manner of tingle that he had reason to believe folks otherwise had gained with their fingerends evidence of. He'd seen them anyhow twitch and jolt upon contact with the downy patch, had watched assorted of them get reduced to senselessness which he was hoping to provide the faithful this evening the occasion for.

"Come forward with your troubles," Donnie Huff declared. "Come forward with your ills and woes and get ye restored," which he could not hardly leave to lie without contributing to it a rousing "Ho!"

Unlike the more reserved sorts at the sanctuary in Laurel Fork, the attendees in the monkey tent hardly required the Reverend Mr. Dunbar to lead and entice them to the downy patch. With troubles and ills and woes enough to stir them on their own, they rose from their chairseats and sidled into the aisle from where they closed upon the dais and congregated down by the organ where the steps led up past the pulpit. Eldon Sophia's husband had detected in the progress of the proceedings the imminent likelihood of insensibility and so had made himself available to field the vaporish, had taken up a strategic position at the lip of the riser from where he figured he could best thwart misfortune and head off litigation. Plainly these were largely the sorts of people who'd been healed before as they demonstrated a flair for twitching and a talent for wailing and an ever so casual willingness to collapse blindly into Eldon's waiting arms once they'd gained from the downy patch whatever measure of solace they'd been seeking. They were passionate and efficient and knew just precisely how best to flop about while they consorted with Donnie Huff's trace of the Lord, but there were among the faithful neophytes as well who'd not likely gotten healed before, had maybe not even been yet saved, redeemed, and born again in Christ, but had come to the tent in the low marshy field from extremity and possibly desperation as they simply could not figure what in the world else to do.

It was the girl that reached him first, a slight thing, a brunette with her hair piled up atop her head and hardly hooters enough for a fellow such as Donnie Huff to pay much mind to at all, but she was passably handsome nonetheless and prompted with her more savory qualities a toothy grin from Donnie Huff who proffered his downy patch, transported it into immediate proximity to the dainty fingers, and endured it to be clutched and gripped at by that scant young woman who was no bigger truly than a child but who'd been not so much as a year past a bride in fact, had wed her betrothed in the old stone chapel off the parkway, had exchanged with her Ricky vows and assurances before her assembled relations and in-laws to be and with her girlfriends for attendants and her brothers among the ushers and her tiny niece employed to scatter blossoms along the aisle. She'd cried at the altar when the reverend spoke of their love and her Ricky had squeezed her fingers and looked endearingly upon her there for everybody to see, taking her proudly for his bride with volume and resolve and having himself get taken by her sweetly for her husband. Her daddy had rented a piece of the inn at Groundhog Mountain, had leased a sizable room with a patio attached, a becanopied patio where a five-piece band clean from Winston-Salem was playing already a medley of lilting and treacly compositions by the time that scant girl and her Ricky had arrived from the chapel in their silver limousine which hauled chiefly the families of the deceased but got employed every now and again in carting about giddy couples lately joined together for all eternity by the bonds of holy matrimony.

Her momma had arranged for hot hors d'oeuvres, meatballs on toothpicks and chicken wings, and her daddy had sprung for sparkling wine by the caseload. The wedding party had all congregated before a rail fence and posed for pictures in advance of retiring to the patio themselves where that slight and fragile bride and her Ricky had circulated among the guests to thank them for seeing fit to share with the pair of them their happy day, and then they'd yielded presently to the wishes of the lead singer from Winston-Salem who'd badgered and cajoled them and persuaded them at last to take to the floor and favor their guests with their first dance as husband and wife. Ricky fed cake to his bride and his bride fed cake to Ricky and the mother of the groom danced a manner of jitterbug with the bride's eldest brother while the best man and the bride's father, who'd soaked up between them inordinate sparkling wine, connived together to wear their cummerbunds upon their heads like tribal crowns and dance as a couple a stately minuet. They could not any of them say when they'd had such a jolly time previously, and they'd lingered the bulk of them until the hot trays had been emptied and the wine had been drunk and the cake had gotten largely decimated when they'd collected there in the lot roundabout Ricky's red Toyota, which had been soaped and lathered and encumbered with cans, so as to be handy to pelt the bride and the groom together with what looked to be fistfuls of silage which they flung mercilessly onto the groom and onto the bride and into the Toyota and at each other as well once the bride and the groom had struck out across the lot en route to the coast of South Carolina where they'd planned to pass a week in fairly ceaseless consummation of their nuptials.

She'd simply guessed it would be different somehow, not the ceremony and the festivities and the subsequent intimate and uncloaked embraces upon an actual topsheet in an actual bed but the rest of it primarily which was in fact the gist and the bulk of the thing. Once her and her Ricky had returned to occupy the house they'd taken out towards Piper's Gap, she'd

figured the boundless riches of matrimony would straightaway
make themselves apparent to her, but there at the outset she
was far too distracted with assorted of her Ricky's uncomely
personal habits to have the wherewithal to savor the finer qualities of their union. It seemed to her that her Ricky had grown
indelicate and crude. He picked at and scratched himself with
unbecoming diligence and regularity. He left his hair to mat on
the tubdrain and urinated as often against the toilet seatlid as
he did into the bowl. He evermore pitched his dirty socks under
the bed and could not be persuaded to rinse his dishes and keep
thereby the foodscraps on his plates and the milk in his glass-
bottoms from growing crusty and troublesome. He never
wanted to watch a good story on the tv, wouldn't sit through the
show about the assorted young handsome professionals and
their conflicts and their dilemmas, or the one about the big
hairy boy who lived in the sewer and the regular relatively
unhairy woman who loved him, or even the one about the lady
detective and her husband the public defender where people
got gunned down every now and again and stabbed and assaulted. He was partial instead to the show about the kung fu
scientist who promoted the advancement of international understanding and goodwill chiefly with the bottoms of his feet
and the comedy about the habitually seminaked young woman
from the galaxy Hectar who was blessed chiefly with the talent
for displaying her bellybutton to handsome effect. He was inordinately fond of the Mafia drama where people routinely got
their arteries severed with piano wire and the show about the
private detective who fed beer to his Airedale, and Ricky would
sit of a weekend through most anything that came on, be it
bowling or a ball game or an imported movie about a lizard
from the deep or even that half-hour pageant of bald spots on
the heads of men who'd lately grown wispy almost wholly un-
detectable hair through the miracle of a mail-order ointment.

   He seemed to have misplaced his sense of tender romance,
and mere weeks after their marriage his appetite for the favors
of his new bride flagged and dwindled though every now and
again Ricky would load up on tall boys and let on to have some
ravishment in mind, apprise his dainty bride of what inordi-

nately angry item he meant to put where, but then drop off into a deep and unremitting slumber. He wouldn't after a time so much as speak to her of a baby, had announced already how they couldn't on what he made and she made together afford to have one, and he would not be persuaded that they might between them economize and sacrifice and make do. It appeared to his bride that her Ricky was ambitious merely to lay about on the sofa untroubled and unobligated, would park there after supper and all the weekend long while his new wife cleaned and his new wife washed and his new wife straightened and swept. She'd just thought it would all be different somehow and was ashamed at the fullness of her disappointment since there were people about who were ill and who were hungry and who were genuinely tormented while she was only frustrated and forlorn. But she hadn't ever hoped for terribly much, had dreamed merely modest dreams and harbored homely expectations, had wanted her Ricky to be sweet and true and to grace her with a baby who was whole and unafflicted which would, she'd figured, be enough to please her, enough to keep her. She'd always been a good child, obedient and kind, and had avoided mischief, had inflicted upon her people no extravagant distress and had never been one to press her Lord for personal considerations, had prayed instead for the lost and the fallen and the repose of the souls of the dead like she'd guessed would maybe gain for her some grace and ensure for her a measure of contentment in this life.

But she'd plainly been cheated and she'd plainly been duped and she'd seen already enough of her Ricky sprawled upon the sofa with his shoes under the coffee table and his socks back of the ruffled duster to conclude for herself what her prayers had been worth. So she'd come to where they spoke to Jesus, driven to the marshy field beyond Gladesboro to attend the services in the monkey tent that she'd learned from the flier on the Texaco doorlight would be conducted by a preacher with a mystical joint, a man who'd had some truck plainly with the Lord to whom she meant to make a show of her inordinate disappointment. But then she'd heard first from the lumberjack with the downy patch who'd soared himself through the ether and consorted with her Christ and seemed willing enough to get gripped and clutched and displayed meaningfully at. Donnie Huff had never personally seen such a look on the face of so slight and scant a young woman who tightened her dainty fingers about his forearm and glared directly at him while she failed to twitch and failed to flap about, demonstrated in fact no tendency whatsoever towards infusement and maintained exclusively her grim expression that she showed to Donnie Huff who attempted to gaze warmly upon her back and gazed even a little warmly in fact but without any noticeable effect upon that handsome though largely unbehootered slip of a woman who persevered in her expression, gripped doggedly that is to the forearm as she lavished upon Donnie Huff her utterly joyless contemplation.

He'd not in the sanctuary at Laurel Fork run up on much joylessness previously and so naturally had concluded that Christians were a fairly giddy and excitable lot with the good manners not to dwell upon their plagues and woes and muck about in their disappointments most especially when they had before them a fellow like himself bearing welcome news of the Lord and Savior and word of His comely portal and realm. It was Donnie after all that had to live with the little green spots while the rest of them might savor talk of the filigreed gates and take what comfort they could mine from the parable of the peach pit and the nectarines. If anybody should be driven to joylessness, Donnie Huff figured it was surely himself who had cause for it as he'd hardly been places he'd said he got to and hardly seen things he'd said he saw, but he guessed he had the grace about him to keep it to himself and he was hoping with a glance to reveal to that girl his opinions of the sorts that glared as they gripped and clutched the downy patch, and he trained even shortly a stern gaze upon her as he considered with attention the grim unanimated expression on the face of that girl who was no more than a child and who watched her fingers on the downy patch prior to shifting to the buttons on Donnie Huff's fuzzy shirtfront in advance of watching Donnie Huff watch her sternly back.

And it wasn't even in fact joylessness truly like he'd taken it already to be. It was plainly defeat instead on the face of that young woman who'd nursed over time an expectation that had lately dissolved before her, who'd believed with pure innocence in the merest of possibilities, had taken on faith that life for her and her Ricky together would surely be sweet and satisfying like was what she rated and what she deserved and what, from a just and kindly Lord, she'd guessed all along she'd get but she'd been undone. She'd been thwarted and throttled and rendered glum that Donnie Huff with his downy patch could not remedy and mend no matter how he focused his energies and concentrated his efforts in an attempt through his forearm to soothe that child if he could not jar and jolt her instead. And presently she let loose of him, opened at length her fingers and withdrew them from the downy patch as she prepared to leave the dais and retreat back down the aisle which Donnie Huff himself prevented her from, reached out with fingers of his own, and took her up briefly at the wrist so as to provide himself the occasion to share with that girl, "Bless you, darling," which she appeared as a sentiment to weigh and consider before telling to Donnie Huff, "Yeah," back.

He watched her go, watched her step with Eldon's assistance from the dais and proceed along the aisle, and the finer qualities of her sleek posterior barely impressed themselves upon him that way finer qualities most usually did on account of how her dark and disconsolate expression stayed with him and fairly much blinded him to the backside altogether, put from his mind his usual species of assessment, and provoked him to a sort of pained and compassionate expression of his own that did not have hardly any leer to it at all.

It turned out that they were the most of them hanging back, the ones with more than organs to mend and inflammations to clear up, the ones with burdens and disappointments, the ones with doubts about their Lord to whom they'd dedicated already their lives and their immortal souls like they'd guessed all along might entitle them to mercy and might entitle them to grace. The Wootens from down near Fancy Gap together approached Donnie Huff from across the dais once he'd dispatched his mystical and healing surges along the veins and byways of a fellow in the throes of some grave and painful bunion distress. They were familiar, the Wootens were, with the dynamics of a tent revival as they'd attended down in a Charlotte hotel a two-day seminar during which they'd come to have revealed to them the principles involved whenever a gang of people get together. But group dynamics was truly only a hobby with the Wootens, one of their sundry and assorted pursuits. Mrs. Wooten made hook rugs and knitted scarves and cozies and sculpted clay and danced on Tuesdays with Mr. Wooten who cut ducks out of shelving board with his bandsaw and hammered together picture frames from old wormy wood and tinkered with his Lawn Boy and shaped and molded his shrubbery and manufactured in the carport extravagant birdboxes. They were evermore between them searching for a means of distraction, seeking some manner of engagement that would forestall the both of them from dwelling inordinately upon their boy whose portrait hung in the dining room over the sideboard and whose baby pictures hung in the hallway and whose progress through childhood was documented in snapshots that the Wootens displayed in hinged silver frames upon their mantelpiece. He'd been Kendrick Monroe Wooten for Mrs. Wooten's momma's people and Mr. Wooten's dead least brother and he'd been sweet and polite and handsome and had loved, the Wootens had decided between them, life on this earth, had been so terribly fond of it that more was the shame of his loss to them, more was the pity of his fearful accident, his unspeakable mishap that had taken him from them on the twelfth of February of 1964 when their Kenny had somehow laid inadvertently the bore of his daddy's 20-gauge Bannerman up under his jaw and had by freak chance alone blown the top of his head clean off.

He'd been such a kind child, such a fine boy with countless friends and untold prospects but no luck much apparently which Mr. Wooten informed when he needed to Mrs. Wooten and Mrs. Wooten informed when she needed to Mr. Wooten back. So they knitted and sculpted and sawed and tinkered and danced and seminared but were drawn still to carry the news of their Kendrick's poor fortune to sanctuaries and tentmeetings where the fervent collected and the preachers had plainly received from the Lord His blessing and holy word. They'd not been anticipating a lumberjack with a downy patch but had been pleased at the sight of him up by the pulpit as he'd put them in mind of their own boy Kendrick who would himself have been forty-one come October. Upon crossing the dais with her husband, Mrs. Wooten straightaway informed Donnie Huff how he reminded her of her child who Donnie Huff guessed was likely a handsome and strapping and ripply sort of a fellow, which induced Mrs. Wooten to assure him directly back, "Oh yes," and she encouraged Mr. Wooten to speak if he might of what a fine specimen their Kenrick had been, which Mr. Wooten appeared meaning even to do before his wife prevented him from it by gripping Donnie Huff at his palpated and anointed spot and telling to him, "He was just a boy," in a voice that was low and that was soft but was unaccountably tormented as well. And they didn't speak of the mishap precisely, never anymore spoke badly of the mishap at all, but in the way that they revealed to Donnie Huff how their Kendrick was in fact gone from them forever, in the way that they looked each Wooten upon the other, Donnie Huff fairly calculated the mishap himself without having to get it explained or described or mentioned at all, and the Wootens by turns held to the downy patch and admired in the face of Donnie Huff what of their Kendrick they could find while Donnie Huff expressed to the Wootens together his heartfelt condolences here at their time of sadness and loss, which the Wootens failed to trouble themselves to reveal to Donnie Huff had commenced in February of 1964 since it seemed always truly their time of sadness and evermore their time of loss like rendered any show of sympathy and grief quite altogether unbelated and apt.

They seemed to draw scant comfort from the forearm, failed quite naturally to twitch and to jerk and to pitch about as their affliction was the sort that even a mystical patch of downy skin could not begin to mend and remedy, which was the way largely with those of the congregation who'd loitered and straggled and crossed the dais there at the end in what seemed to Donnie Huff a veritable pack. They hardly appeared to him prone to infusement, likely to come to be elevated and charmed on account chiefly of their own afflictions which they endeavored to speak of but failed for the most part to find a way to explain to the woodsman before them with the miraculous piece of forearm who could see that they were burdened and could tell that they were beset like they plainly could not take in through their fingerends much help for.

Donnie Huff had simply not previously found occasion to come across this particular strain of disenchantment since, aside from his wife Marie who'd been young and who'd been foolhardy, he'd never in his days had cause to run but with casual heathens chiefly and assorted varieties of layabouts and only your odd and sundry steadfast Christians who could not get sufficiently flogged and beaten back to falter in their passion for their Lord and Maker. Consequently, he had no experience much with the tormented and the defeated and the done-in to whom he offered his best comely smile for as long as he could manage it, but the weary looks and the hollow gazes took presently their toll upon him, and his toothy grin eroded and his resolve to be jolly gave way despite his loving wife's mother who engaged herself in a furious bout of wigwagging as a means of reminding her Donald how he was employed presently in the service of the Lord and so should look sharp or look at least passably enraptured. But Donnie Huff merely offered up his forearm with an evermore waning enthusiasm, and those of the laggards that felt disposed to touched with their fingers the downy patch while the most of the rest of them, who kept their own hands pocketed or otherwise engaged, gazed upon the skin in question to see if it didn't look to them in fact just a regular unmiraculous item like they'd suspected all along it would.

None of them twitched. None of them flapped about, and those with fingers and an inclination to lay them looked forlornly upon Donnie Huff as they held to his anointed place, peered at him with such deep and palpable sadness and remorse that Donnie Huff grew affected himself and fought off an urge to jerk free and shy away, thwarted a chill by blessing quite loudly each of those men and those women who'd come across the dais to share with him their keen distress, to pass along to Donnie Huff their considerable disappointment which a blessing from a lumberjack could hardly begin to relieve and undo.

Opal Criner was as furious with Donnie Huff as she dared anymore to get seeing as how he'd flown after all through the ether and come into the presence of the Lord and so was not probably any longer the sort she wished much to tangle with. But she was markedly peeved with him nonetheless as she'd hoped he'd gained from her in their lessons together not just the nuances of Bible brandishing and the subtleties of the dramatic pause, but the value as well of a steadfast Christian demeanor that did not melt and give way on account of no more than a handful of hollow gazes. And once Donnie Huff had left the dais, had entertained from his final laggard a purely forlorn expression in advance of returning to his seat, Opal Criner pinched her lips together and treated him to her own particular species of glance that was sidelong and significant itself and incited Donnie Huff to inquire straightaway of his loving wife's mother, "What?"

She simply could not believe that a fellow whose vented essence had passed into the presence of the Lord could afford to stand upon a dais and offer up the sign and token of his salvation so glumly as Donnie Huff had exhibited there at the last his downy patch. How, she asked of him, could he possibly hope to inspire the faithful to rejoicing if he did not make handy his forearm with joy and delight? How, she asked of him, could he possibly hope to perform with a blank expression the Lord's own work, which Donnie Huff did not trouble himself to make answer to straightaway but expended instead his attention upon Frances Sophia's child who'd entered through the monkey flaps to mount the dais herself where she stood alongside the pulpit in her white gown and her glistening blue eyeshadow and prepared, with the culmination of her momma's plastic organ preamble, to embark upon a hymn of praise and devotion which presently she in fact dropped her pointy chin and embarked at last upon singing in her sweet and glorious voice of her affection for her Savior which Donnie Huff abided and Donnie Huff endured until he grew inclined to shift about, pitched and leaned towards his loving wife's mother, and told into her ear, "Ain't nothing I can do for these people," which his loving wife's mother did not begin to weigh and consider but, as was her habit, straightaway disputed and apprised Donnie Huff of his sacred duties as a redeemed heathen, assured him how he could most certainly do for people more than he suspected, could buck up most especially the lowly who'd strayed and wandered like those laggards of his who'd plainly lost their way. "You just lead them to the Lord," Opal Criner suggested in a whisper to Donnie Huff and patted his hand after that fashion she was prone to which he generally did not much care for and, on this occasion, acutely disliked.

"They've been to the Lord," Donnie Huff informed her as he withdrew altogether from hand-patting range. "The Lord sent them back."

And his loving wife's mother shared with Donnie Huff a variety of Pshaw that was the verbal equivalent of a handpat in fact.

They were all of them waiting for the thumbjoint, had made what use they could of the downy patch but had been lured and tempted to attend by the thumbjoint itself, and they abided the intervening hymns and abided the prayers and abided the Reverend Mr. Dunbar's brief sermonette on the torments of hell and the sweet rewards of the herafter which immediately preceded his invitation to the afflicted and the gravely beset to join him please upon the dais where he might lay his mystical member against them. And naturally they all went forward again and shared by turns with the Reverend Mr. Dunbar the particulars of their infirmities, indicated to him where precisely they were pained, which the reverend evermore acknowledged with a doctorly nod in advance of bringing to bear his thumbjoint at last which he did not simply lift and simply lay but elevated with ceremony and deliberation and applied with fairly appalling velocity in the manner of a jab that the reverend saw fit to direct on occasion towards the balky organ in question, or the seat anyhow of inflammation and distress, though usually the reverend beat his joint against brows and foreheads as balky organs and seats of distress proved more often than not to be lodged and located in private, unseemly places where even a blow from a man of God might get taken for indelicate.

Eldon fielded the vaporish, caught them at the armpits and dragged them off back of the pulpit where he laid them upon a rug and committed them to the care of his girl Frances whose task it was to comfort and tend to the fallen until such time as it seemed to her their vapors should be dispelled and she could leave off with her ministrations and offer to the afflicted instruction instead, tell to them, "Get up," and thereby manufacture vacancies for those of the faithful who'd only just lately been rendered by the thumbjoint insensible. There was considerable wailing attendant upon the entire proceeding and the ecstatic discharges of the healed were followed hard upon by the discharges of their relations who were naturally anxious as to the talents and abilities of Sophia's husband Eldon who they feared might not field all his chances cleanly, who they hoped wouldn't boot their own particular loved one that they could not help of course but wail a little about.

So the proceeding itself was fairly lively up to a point, the air anyhow was ripe with assorted exclamations until the laggards began to filter their way into the mix and cast as best they were able a species of pall over the affair. They were headed up once again by that slight brunette with her hair piled atop her head, that young thing who was no bigger truly than a child, and she took her place before the Reverend Mr. Dunbar who stooped to lean towards her and make an inquiry as to her complaint. From alongside his loving wife's mother Donnie Huff watched with appreciable attention the Reverend Mr. Dunbar and watched with attention that girl before him and studied as well their exchange which consisted on the reverend's part of an economical query and on the part of that child of a lengthsome and fairly elaborate reply as she could not explain briefly to the reverend where it was she hurt precisely and why it was she hurt there and so undertook to speak of her expectations and undertook to speak of her circumstances and then endeavored with a look alone to characterize for the reverend the breach between the two which he made as if to comprehend and ap-

preciate, embarked anyhow upon a doctorly nod prior to elevating his thumbjoint and applying it to that young thing's
forehead, thrusting it upon her and bouncing it off of her lobe
like caused her to blink and caused her to lurch but hardly
induced her to fold to the floor, to collapse anyhow into the
sure and waiting arms of Sophia's Eldon who remained at the
ready until that slight young thing with the hair and the disappointment and the husband on the sofa at home took her leave
of the reverend under her own unecstatic head of steam. And
he didn't even seem to notice. Donnie Huff watched how the
Reverend Mr. Dunbar hardly appeared to pay any mind at all
to that girl who'd endured his thumbjoint upright, had taken
from his member a legitimate shot, and had simply retired with
the gap between the life she wanted and the life she had altogether unaffected. The reverend didn't even watch her go,
didn't expend upon her any additional regard at all but merely
kept the laggards moving through the line, received presently
the Wootens with the dead boy, and endured beyond them
sundry luckless people otherwise who he applied by turns his
thumbjoint to with no palpable effect on its part and no demonstrable concern on his, and he blessed and dispatched the
laggards and answered their meaningful sidelong glances with
a bland unchanging gaze of his own that did not falter and did
not erode as infusement grew evermore scarce and unlikely,
and he invited at last Sophia please to render upon her organ
a stirring instrumental as her beautiful daughter Grace and her
husband Eldon passed among the faithful to receive from them
their generous donations in pails that were handed along the
rows.

Though he confessed how he had no talent much for singing and did not usually inflict himself upon his congregations,
the Reverend Mr. Dunbar allowed how he felt this particular
evening sufficiently moved and transported to lift his voice in a
song of praise and rejoicing, which he let on to be a wholly
extemporaneous inclination as he jerked his head at Sophia and
prompted thereby from her a shift in key and a shift in tempo
and a brief plastic organ coda which allowed the reverend time
to work up sufficient spit and collect adequate breath in advance of striking out in his deep and pleasing baritone on a

stirring rendition of "Hark, the Voice of Jesus Calling," which Opal Criner demonstrated most especially a fondness for as a tune and a melody and she encouraged her Donald to savor with her if he might the elegant stylings of the Reverend Mr. Dunbar though her Donald did not look to her much disposed towards it.

The gentleman to Opal Criner's left and his wife alongside him were plainly pleased themselves to have been favored by the reverend with a song, and they expressed as much to Opal Criner once the reverend had culminated his rendition. They shared with her as well news of their improvements kidneywise and bumpwise too, news Opal Criner passed along to Donald her girl's husband whose own downy patch had aided surely in the shriveling of the bump and the soothing of the kidneys, but Donnie Huff could not seem to take much comfort in his successes and looked out over the congregation as the service concluded and broke up, watched most especially the laggards as they accepted from Eldon and Frances together the reverend's complimentary tracts and purchased, some few of them, from Sophia at the tentflap the reverend's inspirational cassettes before retreating into the evening with their goods and their afflictions both. Donnie and his loving wife's mother allowed the man with the kidneys and the woman with the bump to slip out by them down the row while they lingered in their chairs to await the attention of the Reverend Mr. Dunbar himself who saw off the last of his flock out in the marshy bottom prior to stepping back into the monkey tent proper and receiving from Eldon his sister's husband news of the haul they'd taken which had apparently been sizable judging from how Eldon rejoiced and Hosannaed.

The Reverend Mr. Dunbar had nothing for Donnie Huff but pure and uncritical commendation, and he identified for the benefit of Donnie and his loving wife's mother those particular passages in the lumberjacking testimony that had touched him most especially to his core which were countless truly, altogether too plentiful to speak of each in turn, so he just hit the high spots and rendered up to Donnie Huff a manner of bonus, pushed into Donnie Huff's hand a piece of money as a gratuity and a reward. Donnie Huff had a mind to take occasion to inquire of the reverend how it was he tolerated nightly those of the faithful that would not be stirred and infused, that would decline to admit into their troubled souls the holy and healing spirit of the Lord, got clubbed that is by the thumbjoint to no effect whatsoever or gripped maybe the downy patch the way they'd hold to any unanointed piece of skin, but he could not discover straightoff the words to inquire with.

The Reverend Mr. Dunbar, however, being by calling a sensitive sort of a fellow, could detect plainly in Donnie Huff a disposition to inquire and accordingly asked of him, "What is it, son?" and Donnie Huff even drew a breath to make in fact his inquiry with but found that he'd lost somehow the mood for it and relinquished the disposition and merely waved at the reverend his fingers to assure him that it was not in fact anything truly at all that he'd wanted to know, which was fine enough with the reverend who himself had been already this evening about as sensitive as he cared to be and so was pleased to dismiss Donnie Huff to go on home and rest if he might his downy patch in anticipation of the services to come.

The muck in the marshy bottom had gotten churned to a fare-thee-well and Opal Criner, who was herself wholly undisposed to wade to the Coronet, waited at the tentflap for her Donald to come and retrieve her, her Donald who slogged to the Coronet and then slipped and slid about in the field as he angled towards his loving wife's mother who deigned shortly to cross to the vehicle once Donnie had worked his way as near to the tentflaps as he could get. She'd not yet even settled full onto the seat when she shared with her Donald her acute apprehensions as to their immediate prospects, apprised him of how they'd never likely get up out of the bottom until maybe it froze and consolidated, which she'd not hardly left off being truly apprehensive about when Donnie Huff accelerated as recklessly as a fellow might and so skidded and slid prior to advancing precipitously up between the fenceposts and passing at last into the road for which Donnie Huff's loving wife's mother gave praise and blessed Donnie Huff for his skill and his daring and so earned for herself a look from her Donald and heard shortly from him a "Yeah."

On their way to the house Opal Criner found cause to unburden herself of appreciable chat and recounted for Donnie Huff her sundry impressions of his testimony with an eye towards where precisely he could stand in fact to punch up his presentation. She suggested to Donnie Huff that he/should consider perhaps engaging more readily in an exchange of toothy grins with the faithful as he was capable of such a comely toothy grin himself but seemed reluctant to make much use of it. She could not help but believe as well that he'd failed to catch and quiver as often as he might, and she did not know but that a white simulated calfskin Bible would after all suit a lumberjack with braces and broadcloth trousers, so she went ahead and advocated some brandishing but only of a vigorous and manly variety. And though Opal Criner encouraged Donnie Huff to throw in if he liked with her and speak of what renovations he saw maybe a need for, Donnie Huff did not so much as serve to encourage Opal Criner with low throaty conspiratorial noises and seemed to steer the Coronet quite heedless of his loving wife's mother alongside him, his loving wife's mother who was rendering still judgments and proposing alterations as they passed together over the culvert and eased up before the slab where Opal Criner came to be encouraged to step if she might from the vehicle, heard anyhow from Donnie Huff, "Get out."

So he proceeded alone to the carshed, swung the Coronet off around the end of the house and across the back lot, and guided it in through the doorway and up snug against the far frame wall. Donnie didn't straightaway shut off Carl's sedan and climb from it but allowed it instead to idle for a time as he sat there in the lowly green light of the dials and the gauges and held with his fingers to the wheel while he sought to conjure the manner of Lord and Savior who would squander any portion of His potent mercy and His divine love on an earbump or a bunion or an irritated organ when there were people about plainly lost to this world and all but given over from this life. But Donnie couldn't see such a Christ as that standing past the portal beyond the filigreed gates, and he tired shortly of trying even to see Him and switched on for distraction the big Q-mix where a woman was singing in a breathy voice of a fellow she'd found just presently cause to grow all tingly about.

V

*A*lvis hated to be contrary, had determined anyhow that a fellow like him who'd come to get blessed with infusement, had twitched after a fashion and tingled and flapped about, should undertake maybe to seem agreeable and pretty extravagantly well disposed towards especially your surly benighted sorts. But he made himself contrary nonetheless and doubted in fact that Donnie Huff was presently much encumbered with stones.

"Oh Lord yeah," Buddy Isom told to him and described with his crooked finger an item of such extraordinary girth that little Gaither, who'd enjoyed previously the privilege of passing some sizable spiny stones of his own, grew involuntarily induced to pucker his ducts and tauten his passageways and loose from his lips a low plaintive cry.

Freeman MacAfee had himself once floated away a stone on a sea of malt liquor and hoped aloud that Donnie Huff was blessed perhaps with wisdom enough to attempt to flush his own stones accordingly, but little Gaither, who guessed he'd suffered stones enough to know, assured Freeman MacAfee that there wasn't much other than Everclear that could bring a fellow relief, Everclear taken straight from a tumbler chased with a measure of Mountain Dew, precisely the sort of combi-

nation to prompt in Freeman MacAfee the puckering of a duct
and the tautening of selected passageways.

Buddy Isom could not himself speak with much certainty of
Donnie Huff's fluids of choice as he'd heard only from Delmon,
Donnie Huff's boy, who'd told to him through the doorscreen
of Donnie Huff's affliction, or had told him truly in fact, "Go
on," which Buddy Isom had performed the service of translat-
ing into a legitimate complaint as was his habit those days when
Donnie Huff saw fit to lay out. So he'd conjured up stones of
sizable spiny dimensions and had inspired thereby the puckering and tautening and the heated lubricational debate in addition as well to the objections of Alvis Nevins who hated to be
contrary but went ahead and was.

Alvis himself was of a mind that Freeman MacAfee and little
Gaither had no cause much to fret on account of Donnie Huff
and his spiny deposits due largely to Donnie Huff's ties of late
to the holy Savior, the actual son of God who'd gone lately to
the trouble, Alvis reminded Gaither and reminded Freeman
and reminded even Buddy Isom too, to snatch Donnie Huff
clean up through the ether, speak to him of assorted orchard
fruit, and then send him back down among the living to broadcast His word and make available, by means of the downy patch,
His soothing and healing touch. Christ himself, Alvis Nevins
proposed, would flush surely Donnie Huff's troublesome obstructions without the aid of malt liquor or grain alcohol.

Little Gaither and Freeman MacAfee and Buddy Isom contemplated Alvis Nevins in silence prior to shifting about to look
instead upon each other like preceded an inquiry on the part of
Freeman MacAfee who laid back against the planksaw carriage
and plucked from his shirtpocket a Chesterfield that he rolled
and rounded between his fingers as he asked of Alvis Nevins,
"What orchard fruit is that?"

Buddy Isom was anxious himself to learn from Alvis Nevins
if maybe this morning he'd endeavored to float away a few
stones of his own as he sounded to Buddy Isom fairly saturated
with some manner of fermented lubricant. "We're talking about
Donnie Huff here," Buddy Isom reminded him. "He hadn't
been anywhere but in the water and out of it."

And while Alvis Nevins was awfully loath still to be if he

could help it contrary, he went ahead and made himself one time further altogether disagreeable and assured Buddy Isom how Buddy could not plainly say for certain just where exactly Donnie Huff had been. Alvis on his own had cause enough to believe that their Donnie had soared in fact through the ether and loitered at the filigreed gates which he revealed to Buddy Isom and to Freeman MacAfee and to little Gaither too who did not themselves much care whether they were contrary or not and so threw in together to lavish Alvis Nevins with some considerable ridicule, which provided Alvis the occasion to smile blandly upon the group of them back like he'd noticed the Christian folk in the church at Laurel Fork were for the most part accustomed to smiling.

Alvis wished to speak if he might of the downy patch and deliver an account of his experiences in the sanctuary where he'd come to be soothed and put at his ease, and he ventured to tell how him and his daddy had traveled to the church in Laurel Fork, causing Freeman MacAfee and Buddy Isom and little Gaither as well to lift together their upturned hands in fairly identical gestures of extravagant chestiness.

"I didn't see her," Alvis shortly informed them back, though he did confess how he'd taken there in the churchyard notice of some bosomy ladies who'd been largely themselves moderately endowed and not even so much as passably alluring, but Alvis Nevins, charged like he'd come to be with goodly Christian impulses, was quick to discount the appeal of pendulous hooters and promote the innate charms of homely flat-chested women the world round, although Freeman MacAfee and Buddy Isom and little Gaither begged if they might to differ.

Alvis, however, would not be drawn into a debate of chestiness as a blessing and a gift and made mention instead of his own momma Hazel who'd busted a vessel and pitched onto the floortiles deceased, his dead momma Hazel who'd inspired him and inspired his daddy to travel to the sanctuary in Laurel Fork where they'd meant to take some solace and had hoped to mine the manner of balm that would provide relief for their torments and would serve to salve their woes. Alvis made mention of how him and his daddy Vernon had been able from their pew to gaze out over the entire congregation, the manner of claim to rekindle in most, especially Buddy Isom, optimism that talk of selected chesty women was in fact forthcoming after all, but Alvis spoke only instead of the wretched qualities chiefly that had brought the pack of them together, that had drawn them there to the sanctuary to find their ease in the living scriptures and the miraculous works of the Lord whose general majesty Alvis saw fit to linger upon and speak of at length and thereby set off little Gaither, who'd come himself to be primed to dwell upon creatures whose assets and attractions touched him nearer his inseam than at the core of his very being. Alvis, however, had been rendered by his jolt from the downy patch foolhardy and relentless and consequently ventured to bless little Gaither for the amusement he provided with his quaint opinions which preceded from Alvis Nevins considerable talk further on the topic of the general woe and wretchedness him and his daddy Vernon had seen there before them in the sanctuary, the disappointment and the fretfulness that, with the advancement of Donnie Huff across the riser to the pulpit, had fairly altogether dissipated.

Buddy Isom was inclined to believe that Donnie Huff had probably neglected to shut his fly and had consequently exposed to the congregation an item far too scrawny to much alarm the ladies or begin to rile the men and so had seemed a source of calm and relief, which struck most especially Freeman MacAfee as plausible and likely and he told to Buddy Isom, "Oh hell, yeah." But Alvis, who confessed to being amused and attempted even a semihearty manner of chortle, assured Buddy and Freeman together that Donnie's charms had plainly not resided in his trousers, or had not anyhow resided in his trousers alone. Alvis took occasion to remind Buddy Isom and to remind Freeman MacAfee and to remind little Gaither as well that their Donnie had lately been saved and redeemed by the fingerends of his Lord which had lain upon Donnie's downy patch, and Alvis Nevins explained for the benefit of Buddy Isom, who'd inquired which downy patch precisely, that it had not been in fact a nether downy patch at all. Through this piece of skin, Alvis told it, our Lord in heaven had communicated to Donnie Huff news of His mercy and grace, had reached out with His fingers to reveal thereby to a drowned heathen and a blasphemer a vision of the hereafter, a revelation of the heavenly portal and the filigreed gates with the Savior Himself loitering just beyond them in His blinding white raiments that looked to have been spun and woven from the very light of the sun, the Savior Himself who'd bestowed upon Donnie a gift, had empowered him to transmit jolts and surges to those of the afflicted and downtrodden who'd seen fit at the sanctuary in Laurel Fork to step forward and lay some fingers of their own.

And Buddy Isom asked of Alvis Nevins, "You mean to say there was people there to come up and take ahold of Donnie Huff, grab that boy at the arm like those ladies did?"

"I mean to say," Alvis Nevins told to him back, "there wasn't hardly anybody about that didn't."

And Buddy Isom wanted to know of Freeman MacAfee and wanted to know of little Gaither, "You hear that?" which they readily confessed to him they had and so threw in directly with Buddy Isom in a moment of marvelment over the curious ways of some people that they'd not truly left off pulling faces at each other about when Alvis fairly boasted to them, "Touched him myself," and he added beyond it in the silence he'd managed to prolong, "Took a jolt, as big a one as anybody might."

In an effort to establish firmly for his own benefit the facts of the matter at hand, Buddy Isom asked of Alvis Nevins if he meant to say that he'd traveled with his daddy clean out to Laurel Fork and visited a legitimate sanctuary for the purpose of resting his fingers upon the forearm of Donnie Huff and receiving thereby a jolt and a surge which Alvis could not claim to be the case in fact and explained to Buddy Isom how him and his daddy had traveled instead clean to Laurel Fork on account of their dead wife and momma who'd lingered plainly about and was causing them some sadness and torment.

"Hazel?" Buddy Isom inquired.

And Alvis Nevins told to him, "Yes sir," and explained for anybody who cared to know it how it was oftentimes a plague for the living to have a loved one to just pitch over dead. Little Gaither was himself of the opinion that it was likely pretty much of a plague for the loved one as well who'd probably not been hoping to pitch over, but then Alvis was guessing that the dead went undoubtedly to a better place than Gaither himself was figuring they went. Moreover, once he was pressed by Alvis Nevins and goaded, Gaither confessed how out of what loved ones he'd known to pass not a one of them had simply up and expired but they'd fallen all of them sick and had wasted after a fashion away like discounted, Alvis Nevins insisted, little Gaither's grasp of Alvis and his daddy's own predicament that Buddy Isom and that Freeman MacAfee could tell him themselves little about since they admitted the both of them to coming from the stout sort of stock that did not get usually felled by vessels and rarely succumbed to cataclysms without clinging for a time to life and allowing thereby the kin and relations to gather in the sick room and make to each other low murmurous mention of recipes they'd come across and vehicles they'd bought and people they did not among them much care for.

So Alvis alone was acquainted firsthand with the plagues and the torments of an ever so precipitously punctuated relation, and he assured little Gaither and assured Buddy Isom and assured Freeman MacAfee as well that they could not know the pangs he'd endured and the regrets he'd entertained when his momma Hazel had stepped into the kitchen for the Cheez-Its and had been stricken and felled and altogether extinguished before Alvis or Vernon his daddy could either one of them tell to her those things that people say to folks they're parting from likely for good. Alvis had himself shared with his momma a peevish comment over dinner, had voiced his disapproval of the yams and had ventured to speak poorly as well of the butterbeans in advance of excusing himself from the table and wandering out into the yard where he'd answered in an hour's time his daddy's shout and had found consequently how he could not tell to his Hazel anything further at all. She'd just gone from them, leaving him and leaving his daddy to endure their pangs and stew in their regrets that they'd proven too altogether able in, and Alvis had just figured they could stand maybe a service and tolerate some testimony from a fellow like Donnie who'd been dead and had passed plainly into the beyond and so could maybe inform them if he'd remembered still in heaven all the shabby things he'd been told by people in life.

"Well hell, Alvis," Freeman MacAfee said, "I can't remember half of what people tell to me now and the most of it is spiteful.

Your poor dead momma isn't going to lay about until that last trumpet thinking on things you said to her or things you didn't say. Nobody's momma would because mommas just plain don't. Sorriest scutter on the earth is some lady somewhere's sweet child. If it was me, I wouldn't much worry myself about Hazel."

"Isn't you," Alvis Nevins told to him. "It's me and it's daddy, and you can't know what it is we ought to fret about and what it is we ought to let slide. Your people don't ever drop dead. You hadn't had nobody to pitch over."

"So here you go off to Laurel Fork to take a hold of Donnie Huff," Buddy Isom said and heard directly from Alvis Nevins back how he'd not in fact planned to grip the downy patch himself but had been meaning only to plunder the testimony for what scraps and nuggets might seem to him pertinent.

And Alvis Nevins assured anybody who cared to know it, "I wasn't guessing Donnie Huff had anything about him much worth touching. I was just meaning to hear what he'd say."

"But you grabbed him anyhow," little Gaither reminded Alvis Nevins who admitted that Donnie had swayed and moved him with the tale of the travels of his vented essence and the news of his confab with the actual Lord Christ. But he guessed he wouldn't have gone up to the riser and laid to the downy patch his own fingers but for the people otherwise who'd seen fit to leave their pews and were plainly twitching and bouncing around up there at the pulpit, which Alvis confessed intrigued him as he'd not ever previously known good Christian folk to fling themselves about so. He'd simply never seen in life any-body get infused and found in the experience some legitimate allure even if it was only Donnie and his forearm serving to-gether as the instrument of infusement themselves.

"Well, what did he say to you when you come up?" Buddy Isom wanted to know and watched Alvis Nevins take occasion to cast back, watched Alvis Nevins recall what in fact had tran-spired between him and Donnie, and watched Alvis Nevins drop his head and tell to him, "Nothing. Just stuck out his arm and I latched on to it."

"And twitched?" Freeman MacAfee asked.

"Bounced around?" little Gaither inquired.

And they heard directly from Alvis Nevins how he'd felt on

his fingerends a prickly sensation that had traveled soon enough up his arm and arrived thereby at the rest of himself, inducing him to grow flushed, he recalled, and woozy which brought forth from little Gaither a snatch of his own brand of extemporaneous testimony since he'd gotten in his lifetime flushed and woozy on occasion as well and consequently concluded and proclaimed that he'd probably taken in the Lord through a bottleneck more times than he could tell and so had been all along blessed and redeemed without ever so much as suspecting it.

"Praise be," Buddy Isom told to him and Gaither lifted and flourished his fingers the way he guessed the Pope of Rome might.

As Alvis had come to be awash with salvation, he did not any longer see fit to grow irate and so failed to admonish Gaither and Buddy together and spoke instead of the evolution of his prickly sensation which had gotten transformed into an overwhelming warmth that had affected assorted of his parts and features though he would not admit to Buddy Isom, who put to him the inquiry, that his cockles had been in the least bit heated up.

"I felt like I'd laid in a tub of bathwater," Alvis Nevins said and confessed to having twitched a little and bounced somewhat about as a result, he guessed, of the alterations in his prickly sensation, and he admitted how he'd come straightaway to feel at his ease, had enjoyed an inclination to release his woes and his troubles and allow them to fall away from him. "I got soothed," Alvis Nevins told to Buddy Isom and to little Gaither and to Freeman MacAfee. "The Lord reached out and took my pain away, gave me instead some comfort and some peace."

Buddy Isom could not say himself when last he'd been so thoroughly touched and moved, and he mustered a couple of sniffles as he invited Freeman and invited Gaither to be if they might touched and moved with him, which they proved to be obliging about and grew moderately weepy themselves in a highly theatrical fashion whereupon Alvis Nevins informed Gaither and informed Freeman and informed Buddy as well how they could go ahead and cut up and have their fun but he was himself glad to have gone to Laurel Fork and discovered there some balm.

"So you went off to a church," Buddy Isom said, "and you grabbed on to Donnie's forearm and it's all right now that your momma dropped dead before you could tell her how you'd been after all fond of her yams. Is that about it?"

"Go on with you," Alvis told to Buddy Isom. "The bunch of you," he told to Freeman MacAfee and told to little Gaither too. "It don't hardly matter to me what you think. It was my fingers that got laid. It was me that got soothed."

"Well hell, Alvis," Gaither said to him, "didn't old Vernon get taken up and yanked about a little himself, let that Donnie build a fire under his cockles?"

And Alvis assured little Gaither, though only presently and only at last, "He did."

Of course he'd never figured himself for the sort of a fellow who'd get attached to a story on the tv, hadn't in his working years been prone to pass his evenings before the set and had resisted early on in his retirement the temptation to park himself in his upholstered chair. But Vernon had become in fact most especially fond of a story at last, a show about the lives and the loves of the people of Meadow View who were partial as a population to intrigues and extravagant displays of cleavage largely, needless to say, on the part of the Meadow View ladies, though Thorne the Swede, who worked down on the docks manhandling cargo, demonstrated a disposition for airing his own outsized pectorals whenever the opportunity arose. Nobody in Meadow View got on too awfully well with anybody else except for maybe the wife of the chief of police who eclipsed on occasion even Thorne the Swede in pectoral airing which proved a suitable social lubrication, and it didn't seem that anybody ever died in Meadow View either since people just moved off to Bay City and got replaced in town by folks up from Tippetsville, though Vernon could recall how on one occasion the loan officer from the Meadow View bank had apparently passed away and was absent from the proceedings for the better part of a month before it came to light that he'd not expired after all but had only, in a fit of amnesia, retired to the Meadow View woods where he foraged for nuts and berries while his agent and his producer negotiated the terms that healed him.

Hazel had been herself most especially fond of a story about the hospital at Park Ridge, which was the saga chiefly of the beautiful but conniving raven-haired administrator whose weakness for tender young flesh was legend and prompted her evermore to compromise her meager integrity for the sake of some wiry young intern before whom she'd fling herself upon a secluded gurney and invite examination. Her surgeons and doctors were for the most part lusty sorts themselves with weaknesses both for strong drink and lithe candystripers, while her nurses were regular temptresses with the exception of Mavis the radiologist who specialized in hard looks and icy indignation. The staff there at Park Ridge acted largely from motives and intentions which proved in most cases to be extraordinarily tangled and enormously unbecoming and conflicted with their employment as merciful healers since they were evermore having to interrupt their schemes and set aside their petty grievances in order to tend to some species of medical calamity, retrieve some poor mangled soul from the very brink of perdition. Of course the doctors and nurses at the hospital in Park Ridge were blessed with a truly fabulous variety of complaints and afflictions to see after and mend though they demonstrated an inclination to bandage most everybody about the head, perhaps in the way of a preventive. There plainly existed in the area a high likelihood of coma and a genuine threat of baffling symptoms that assorted of the doctors could gather together and disagree as to the causes of and just generally snipe at each other about. Disasters as well were commonplace. Houses caught fire, cars collided, airplanes fairly rained out of the sky and, on one occasion, dense soupy fog proved a contributing factor in a submarine wreck down off the beach head, which provided an ensign the opportunity to receive a gauzy head-wrap of his own and engage as well in a therapeutic dalliance with the raven-haired administrator one dark evening on the settee in the day room.

Vernon had straightaway come to be appalled by the thoroughgoing licentiousness of the Park Ridge staff and disgusted by their sundry unspeakable pursuits. Him and his wife Hazel had agreed between them that those doctors and nurses and bureaucrats at the hospital in Park Ridge were surely, excepting of course the general population of Meadow View, the sorriest bunch of people they'd ever heard tell of, and Vernon himself found he could not resist the opportunity to settle daily in his upholstered chair and grow appalled and become disgusted at just what precisely some people would do once they'd come to be whipped and come to be driven by their schemes and their urges and their fiery desires. He was most especially intrigued by how hale in particular the Meadow Viewites generally appeared to him to be. Obviously they thrived and flourished in their deviousness and so were rarely called upon to declaim their unwholesome intentions and give voice to their calculated deceits with tubing up their noseholes like evermore proved for Vernon a distraction there at the hospital at Park Ridge where folks were as likely as not to get struck down and debilitated before they could hatch altogether some manner of viciousness. So Vernon endured the tales of Park Ridge but savored the intrigues in Meadow View where undiluted spite apparently made the citizens lively and strong.

Time was, then, when Vernon and his Hazel would finish their lunch at the dinette and retire to the front room where they'd settle each of them into their upholstered chairs and switch on the Motorola in time for the afternoon's first scrap of medical malfeasance. They'd never bothered to speak much each to the other except for when one of them would rise to step into the kitchen and so would entertain suggestions as to what to fetch out, but they'd never been ones for bald and unadorned chat and Vernon, consequently, didn't find in the silence and the general stillness of his afternoons much worth grieving about since their days together had been largely silent and chiefly still and Hazel didn't talk so awfully less dead than she'd spoken quick and alive. That face, however, was gone from him, the one she used to work up and display with the onset of deviousness among the scoundrels at Park Ridge and those rascals in Meadow View, that face that had served to inform him how there were some things in this life that she could not possibly hope to digest, some ways she could not

fathom, some motives she could not understand which had
happened evermore in each and every case to be the things and
the ways and the motives that Vernon had no feel for as well.
She'd known what he knew and figured what he'd concluded.
She'd confirmed for him daily most everything he'd come already to believe, had seen on her own the same faults in this
life, known for herself the same dissatisfactions, and she'd reserved for him alone that face of hers that she'd worked up and
that she'd displayed when folks in their stories had plotted and
connived and acted, she'd figured, too terribly much like regular people might.

So there wasn't anybody about any longer to believe with
him what he believed and to trade with him significant expressions when an organ salvo sounded, nobody to look with kin-
dred disdain upon the deceitful orthopedist once he'd strolled
onto the ward, or snort on account of the police chief's wife
once she'd discovered occasion to uncloak her assets, nobody to
assure him across the endtable with a gaze how people were in
fact anymore mean and irredeemably sorry and the world was
lately a vulgar place to be. It was just him now and his boy Alvis
and they spoke only to each other that way fathers and sons
sometimes do, made idle talk chiefly to beat the quiet away once
they'd grown together uneasy in silence. Alvis was fond of admiring his supper as he ate it and spoke routinely of the suc-
culence of the meat and the delicate flavors of the vegetables,
and he made, at the culmination of each meal, his customary,
highly dramaturgical offer to wash if he might the dishes and
would even attempt feebly to intercede once his daddy had set
to clearing the table but would come to be persuaded by something less than main force to keep his seat and finish his tea and
wash the dishes some other time. Alvis carried home regularly
movies from Shirley's # 2 in Cana, gruesome sorts of items in
which starlets managed to frolic naked just prior to having their
appendages sundered and separated from the rest of themselves and their torsos laid open by some variety of maniac who
demonstrated usually extravagant artistry with a boning knife
or a hatchet or a reciprocating saw and so came forth nights to
slaughter coeds and eviscerate their dates and slept by day in a
hovel in the woods. Alvis was himself most especially intrigued

by the bloodletting, was anxious evermore to learn where the spurts had come from and how the gushes had flowed, and would run the pertinent episodes backwards and forwards until he'd grown satisfied as to how precisely those movie people had done what they did when he'd trouble himself to share with his daddy the news of their technique which Vernon was never somehow too terribly eager to know of.

But come that Sunday after the sanctuary when Alvis twitched and when Alvis tingled and when Alvis gained his measure of infusement, he appeared to Vernon to have misplaced plainly his passion for mutilation and did not, like usual, suggest to his daddy that they sit together before the Motorola and watch again the movie that they'd watched the night previous about that hotel where the guests were prone to come to be filleted. Alvis instead allowed his daddy to view for a time the show on the Charlotte station about the hand-hammered Chinese wok that could fry and could steam and could poach and could stew and would wipe clean with a rag, and he interrupted only at length to wonder of Vernon if perhaps he'd considered lately the splendors of the hereafter and the balm to be found at the breast of the Savior which Vernon confessed to Alvis his boy he'd not somehow lately considered. Alvis consequently felt obliged to sell if he might his daddy on the virtues of rapture and the ease and comfort a fellow might find once he'd come into the clutches of the Lord, and he wondered could Vernon recall how back in the morning hours his boy had been merely a lowly sort, beset by worries and sundry distresses, and he wished that his daddy would look on him now that he'd gone to the trouble to draw through his fingers infusement. And his daddy in fact looked briefly upon him, gave over the wok for Alvis his boy who made as if to seem soothed and made as if to feel eased and ventured to propose that Jesus perhaps was the answer for a fellow who'd suffered a loved one to pitch over dead.

"Momma's in a better place," Alvis declared to Vernon his daddy and figured aloud how it didn't likely suit to mourn any longer a woman who'd gone to her reward and resided anymore in the kingdom of gold. "Momma's on high," he told to his daddy who was not plainly on high himself and resided still in the house with the Motorola where a man in an apron was dribbling presently nut oil into his wok.

Alvis saw fit to pray over Sunday supper and blessed with passion the chicken that was left from dinner and the yellow squash and the hard biscuits and the coagulated gravy and he sought to engage his daddy in a lively theological discussion on the innate merits of salvation and the assorted rewards of redemption in this life, but Vernon was not much willing to be engaged and so tolerated his child in silence, endured the theology of his Alvis while he dined and while he cleared and crumbed the table and while he washed the very dishes that Alvis had asserted meekly he might be disposed to wash himself. They watched together on the tv a show with no gore much to it, a drama about a man who was battling bravely a grave illness and making of himself an inspiration to the fit and the infirm alike that Alvis found enriching and encouraged Vernon his daddy to be if he might a little enriched himself, and they set out as well to watch the escapades of the kung fu scientist who cracked this night countless skulls with his arches and dislodged numerous teeth and prompted thereby Alvis Nevins to turn off the set and wonder of his daddy if couldn't they please just sit for a time in devoted silence before they washed up and before they turned in.

Monday in the morning Alvis blessed the eggs and reconfirmed in prayer his ardor for the Lord before heading out in his Ventura for the creekbottom and leaving thereby Vernon his daddy alone at the house where he meant to clean and straighten and scour or round up at least the hairballs that skittered down the hallway and lurked back of the bathroom door but squandered somehow the morning hours in aimless unprofitable pursuits and found himself after lunch in his upholstered chair learning how, apparently, the raven-haired administrator had connived to have her way with and enjoy the favors of the ambassador's son Colin who'd fallen from a ledge out at the Park Ridge quarry and had been admitted to the hospital in a semilucid state. He did look, Vernon had to confess, rather dashing in his head bandage, and his lapses into and out of consciousness were managed with such undeniable charm that the allure of Colin for a creature so lusty as the raven-haired administrator seemed to Vernon quite altogether understandable though he was not clear entirely in his own mind as to the manipulations and possibly even medications that passionate administrator had employed in her efforts to render assorted of Colin's parts and pieces lucid enough to suit her. Plainly she'd driven him with her vigorous amours to the verge of some species of conniption. His doctor anyhow, in consultation with doctors otherwise, concluded that Colin the ambassador's son had deteriorated in the night from his dashing semiconscious state into a manner of musky love funk that remained for an ever so few minutes a medical mystery until the organ music swelled and rose and the gaggle of physicians together decided who alone there at Park Ridge General was capable of visiting upon a fellow such a wholly enfeebling affliction.

In Meadow View this day, Thorne the Swede fished from the harbor a beautiful lithesome woman in a sequined gown who'd apparently fallen off a boat, ventured that is with his pectorals a-bouncing down off the dock and into the surf from where he dragged that woman up onto the beach and resuscitated her by means of an age-old longshoreman's technique which looked equal parts breath and tongue together and served not only to bring that woman back to consciousness but persuaded her to attempt on her own to swallow Thorne the Swede clean down to his collarbone. So they grappled and groped and rolled about on the sand until that beautiful lithesome woman in the sequined gown regained sufficient of her strength to allow her to stand upright and grapple and grope afoot for a time as well so as to make apparent to Thorne her feverish gratitude in advance of explaining to him how she was herself the Duchess of Monsanto, which, to judge from her accent, was located off between Spain and France.

As fortune would have it, Thorne had traveled once on a frigate into the Bay of Lunt there where Monsanto's Leone Mountains tumble into the sea and he'd picked up a few native phrases which he aired for the Duchess who, though sopping wet and fairly exhausted and chafed as well about the mouth from Thorne's manly stubble, exhibited her delight and chattered in Monsantoian back, was instructing in fact Thorne in a

nuance of declension, when the Duke of Monsanto, who'd
fallen off the boat as well, got deposited on the beach himself by
the surging Meadow View tide and presented thereby Thorne
with a dilemma as he was growing quite personally fond of the
Duchess and did not just presently require the Duke to thwart
his advancing passion, enough of a complication to set off some
rising organ music and induce Thorne to show to the camera
his most accomplished blackguard's expression.

Vernon had settled on shortlegs for supper, roasted shortlegs in a cream of mushroom sauce which required in preparation the unwrapping of the chicken and the opening of the
can and the introduction of the elements together into the bak-
ing dish that Vernon undertook as he listened through the
doorway to the early news on the Charlotte station. He heated
as well a brick of frozen succotash and read at the table those
portions of the *Times and World News* he'd not bothered over
breakfast to read, and he rose presently to greet Alvis his boy
who bucked like usual against the front door so as to unstick it
and spill into the house. Alvis had been hoping to have occasion
to get if he wanted to reinfused but, what with Donnie Huff's
spiny stones that had laid him apparently low, Alvis had been
obliged to go this day downy patchless altogether and had suffered consequently his reverence to erode and his passion to
dwindle and wane. He loved undoubtedly still his Lord and
Savior who'd carried off his momma to a better place than his
momma had previously been, but he loved Him presently without the fervor that he'd loved Him with this morning and had
loved Him with last night, as he'd been obliged to pass the day
enduring from Buddy Isom and from Freeman MacAfee and
from little Gaither too some considerable ridicule and extravagant heathen abuse, surely the sort of treatment that could tell
on a fellow who'd only just got infused in the first place and
hadn't mustered previously awful much zeal for the Lord.

So Alvis was hardly, there at the supper table, terribly giddy
with praise and rejoicing that Vernon his daddy remarked as
he'd never seen his child forgo with such dispatch a newfound
enthusiasm. He wondered even himself might Alvis see fit to say
over their supper a prayer, which Alvis proved obliging about

though it was a truly pallid and utterly unspirited sort of a grace. Alvis had just figured that once a fellow had twitched and once a fellow had tingled, his disappointments and his distresses would be cast evermore in a different sort of a light like might allow him to see around them and beyond them and just past them altogether, like might encourage him plainly to mine from his woes the good that was bound to lurk there, and he simply had to guess, since his woes seemed merely woeful, that maybe he'd drawn just a scant and paltry dose of infusement, that probably he'd gripped too lightly the downy patch which spiny obstructions were presently keeping Alvis from gripping again. Consequently, he picked forlornly at his chicken and stirred about his succotash in the mushroom sauce but showed no inclination much to eat and surrendered presently his plate to Vernon his daddy who was not obliged this night to entertain from Alvis his boy a halfhearted offer to wash the dishes as Alvis had lost the will to be even passably insincere. He sat merely instead wondering where maybe his comfort had got to and wishing he knew where his balm had gone, and he allowed presently his daddy Vernon to usher him into the front room and deposit him on the couch from where Vernon hoped Alvis might enjoy with him please a movie on the tv as he'd learned from the paper that the Roanoke station was showing this night that film about the dentist that Alvis was ever so fond of, the dentist who'd plainly lost his way in this world and seduced unwitting patients to allow him please to bore out their abscesses with his Craftsman drill press that tended to render its victims quite altogether porous and well beyond the need for further dental care.

"Isn't he a rascal?" Vernon wished to hear from Alvis his boy once that dentist had commenced to dispose of a housewife with an occlusion, and though Alvis could not straightaway stir himself to reply, a lively freshet of blood that danced and squirted most extravagantly inspired shortly in him gumption enough to tell to his daddy, "Yeah," tell to his daddy, "Isn't he?"

ii

They were themselves most usually an inducement to romance, produced with regularity upon Donnie Huff an amo-

rous effect though he'd not ever been able to say exactly why
since they'd plainly not been manufactured with passion in
mind. Marie had bought them down at the theme park in Or-
lando and they had a speckled band about the waist and red
piping about the legholes in addition to the full-color renditions
of Daffy Duck on the frontside and Pluto on the backside which
hardly, taken together, would seem much likely to stir a man,
but somehow of an evening once Marie had seen fit to slip into
her special theme-park panties, she became invariably for Donnie Huff an object of incendiary desire. He could not even
begin to fathom the cause for it, preferred in fact not to think
much upon the matter at all as it was fraught plainly with the
species of unwholesome implications that might serve themselves to blunt the allure of Pluto and thwart the charms of
Daffy Duck.

Marie had come as well into possession of a t-shirt, a gray
t-shirt from the university up in Blacksburg, a shirt with GOB-
BLERS emblazoned in bold orange letters across the front of it,
and she'd taken her scissors to the thing and sheared off the tail
so that the entire item left off anymore along about where her
belly button began like produced as well upon Donnie Huff a
rousing effect, most especially in conjunction with the theme-
park panties, and he'd gotten so he could hardly bear up under
the sight of his Marie bumping shut with her backside the bedroom door and stepping towards the mattress with GOBBLERS
across her chest and Daffy Duck upon her inseam when she'd
generally see fit to inquire of him, "You awake?" and so would
hear most usually straightaway back, "Oh Lord yes."

But come Tuesday evening in the wake of Donnie Huff's
inaugural tent meeting, he failed somehow to discover in the
panties and the shirt and the intervening strip of flat stomach a
call to to his customary primal agitation. Plainly she'd dolled up
for him as she'd gotten lately into the habit of wearing to bed
one of her dead daddy Carl's white cotton dress shirts that
dangled pretty much down to her knees and smelled still of skin
bracer like routinely served together to dampen Donnie Huff
in his desires. But this night she'd fished out from her bureau
drawer her theme-park panties and her university t-shirt and
she'd lingered even in the bathroom rendering herself alluring

prior to stepping at last across the hallway and bumping the bedroom door shut when she'd seen fit to make of Donnie from there at the threshold her inquiry and had heard presently from him a wan and meager sort of reply with no zest at all much to it.

Opal her momma had told her of it, had entered into the house and made directly for the dinette so as to share precipitously with her girl Marie news of Donnie's triumph in the monkey tent where he'd produced results specifically upon an earbump and an inflamed organ but had improved plainly the circumstances and uplifted obviously the spirits of countless folks otherwise with complaints and afflictions unknown to Opal herself. He'd demonstrated, she'd insisted, a thoroughgoing mastery of the dramatic pause and had rendered up an altogether vivid account of his sordid heathen past before he'd come to be born once more in the ways of the merciful Christ. Opal Criner had embarked even upon talk of the parable of the peach pit and the nectarines which Donnie Huff had, to her mind, related this night with particular grace, but she'd found cause to leave off at it so as to wonder of her child what manner of foul thing she'd seen fit to plunk down right there on the eating table where they'd all of them been known to dine previously and would likely be obliged to take some meals yet.

It was a boltbox Marie had discovered out back of the shed where the rainwater from the roof had dripped down upon it and weathered the wood and rusted the nailheads and thereby rendered that item an altogether suitable candidate for decoupage which Marie had taken notice of straightoff and so had cleaned off that boltbox with a wire brush and carried it on into the house where she was making of it an accent there on the tabletop. She'd spread of course a section of the *Times and World News* underneath the thing, but Opal Criner had developed long since her own theories of just how it was filth came to be transported and communicated from one object to another, theories that had no basis whatsoever in demonstrable fact but had come nonetheless to serve for Opal Criner as steely convictions. So she expounded for the benefit of her girl Marie her views on filth in general, which were acutely uncharitable, and her notions specifically on the capabilities and devious talents of

debilitating germs which Marie allowed her to finish even ex-
pounding upon before she shaped her features into a highly
expressive manner of arrangement and suggested to her
mother, "Go on."

Donnie plainly seemed to Opal cursed this night with a need
to malinger and, once he'd entered at last into the house, Opal
wondered of him where he'd been and what he'd been up to
that Donnie did not appear disposed to speak presently of and
so jerked merely his head out towards a place through the
doorway prior to lighting briefly upon the seatcushion of his
upholstered chair so as to discover what it was Opal Criner had
tuned in on the tv which she could not herself think of the
name of but informed Donnie how it was in fact the show about
the blind attorney who waged himself a personal war against
injustice in this world with the able assistance of Darren his
driver and lackey and Queenie his sizable longhaired guide
dog. It seemed to Opal Criner this evening that the blind attorney was meddling somehow in the black-market baby racket
where he'd sniffed out a noticeable inequity though she'd only
herself just turned the set on and could not be certain what it
was that lawyer was up to.

"Oh," Donnie told to her and loitered upon his seatcushion,
staring blankly at the tv before he rose to his feet and stepped
into the kitchen where he told to his wife Marie, "Hey."

"Well," she said to him as she pasted onto her boltbox a
picture of a wood duck, a speckled greenheaded wood duck
she'd excised from the encyclopedia they'd purchased some
few volumes of at the Kroger in Galax before the management
had grown weary of the encyclopedia promotion and switched
over to scrolled flatware instead. "Moses himself," she told to
him and Donnie Huff squirted in reply a measure of air between his shut lips.

"See much rapture this evening?" Marie Criner wanted to
know and busied herself in centering her duck, which prevented her from spying on Donnie Huff's face the species of
expression which would surely have apprised her that he'd seen
this evening no rapture much in fact.

"What's that thing?" Donnie Huff asked presently of his wife

Marie as he nodded towards the dinette and she said pretty much through the doorway and out of the kitchen altogether, "Box of filth," that Donnie Huff failed to make straightaway or make even eventually an inquiry about and thereby gained at last the attention of his wife Marie who watched Donnie Huff look more or less at her boltbox, gaze anyhow in the general direction of it that he persevered at as he heard from Marie how her momma had figured that boltbox to be chocked full of disease and riddled with contagion.

"Did she?" Donnie Huff managed to ask at length and then selected up towards the ceiling a piece of air to gaze for a time off into.

And Marie Criner stoppered and set aside her glue and watched momentarily Donnie Huff as he watched in turn his piece of air before she troubled herself to ask of him, "What?"

He mustered up a feeble attempt to suggest to her that he could not himself imagine how she'd come in the first place to feel inclined to inquire "What?" of him, or made anyhow a quizzical face which he gave over shortly for a bout of gazing further and so heard once more from his wife Marie, "What?"

And he guessed even he might tell her if he could find somehow the words for it, speak of who he'd seen there in the monkey tent up on the riser, make mention of how they'd looked at him as they gripped with their fingers the downy patch and failed to twitch and failed to jerk and managed to elude infusement. But he could not discover a suitable thing to say, lacked the means to explain to his wife Marie why he'd stepped there into the kitchen to stand in her presence and gaze forlornly off at a piece of empty air, so he told to her an unsuitable thing instead, informed Marie his wife, "A woman came to see would Jesus heal a bump in her ear."

"I heard," Marie told to him and endured from Donnie Huff an odd and troublesome sort of a grin with no mirth much to it, which Donnie Huff sustained and prolonged as he gazed merely for a spell further at his piece of air in advance of shifting about and declaring towards the boltbox chiefly, "There's no end of unhappy people in this world," which his wife Marie did not herself offer to throw in with but instead

simply looked upon her Donnie who gave over the boltbox for
the backsplash off beyond the stove which he perused forlornly
for a time before confessing at length to Marie at the dinette,
"I'm tired," which Marie guessed for herself she could see well
enough he was and figured even maybe she'd be a little weary
as well if she'd had call to hang around Christian folk all the
evening. They just plain worked on her like a drug as best as
she could tell.

And Donnie Huff confided to Marie his wife, "I'm worn
out," which prompted her to suggest to him, "Well, go on to
bed," that Donnie appeared to weigh and consider as a possible
course of endeavor but lingered still to gaze further at his vacant piece of air until his wife Marie insisted, "Go on," when he
turned in fact and stepped into the front room where he endured from his loving wife's mother news of what a terrible
tragedy it seemed to her that there were folks still roaming the
earth who'd sell a baby for profit that Donnie Huff did not
express, as best as Opal Criner could tell, adequate consternation about, and she was hoping he might linger there in the
front room for a time and field from her lamentable disclosures
that he could practice looking aggrieved in the wake of, but
Donnie proceeded towards the hallway, paused momentarily to
look in upon his boy Delmon who slept with the bedclothes
kicked off and his arms flung up over his head, and then continued on back to the bathroom at the end of the hall where
Donnie switched on the fluorescent bulb and passed some few
minutes contemplating himself in the mirror over the sink.

In the kitchen at the dinette, Marie Criner failed to resume
her pasting and sat herself looking for a time into Donnie Huff's
piece of empty air as she heard in bits and snatches the blind
attorney's appeal in court to the decent and wholesome impulses of the jurors who he was hoping might see fit to convict
the depraved scoundrel in the docket before them, and Marie
couldn't help but wonder what manner of depravity that scoundrel had undertaken though she was hardly willing to make an
inquiry of her mother in order to find it out and so just figured
that scoundrel had engaged merely in some lurid and extravagant species of tv depravity like freed Marie to leave off think-

ing of him and allowed her to return to her Donnie who had seemed to her troubled and fretful and woebegone and maybe even done in a little with Opal her momma and the assorted wages of Christian living. She suspected maybe he'd come at last to see enough of goodliness and had partaken of and perhaps endured sufficient prayerful exchanges to hold him for a time, had satisfied maybe his urge to nose around among the churchgoing sort and discover for himself what it was precisely they evermore saw fit to lavish their devotion upon. She just figured maybe he'd gotten finally his fill between the sanctuary at Laurel Fork and the monkey tent at Gladesboro and the nearly ceaseless company of Opal herself who Marie had to believe could likely on her own drive the Pope to the Devil. So she calculated he was maybe ripe to be claimed and won back, and she lifted from the dinette her boltbox and set about tidying her mess prior to retiring from the kitchen herself and lingering long enough in the front room to learn from her momma what a shame it appeared to her to be that there were folks still roaming the earth who'd sell a baby for profit.

Marie drew up the bedclothes over Delmon her child and passed a moment in just looking upon him before she continued down the hallway and stepped into the bedroom, though shortly she withdrew with her nightclothes in hand so as to dress and primp before the lavatory mirror. From the settee in the front room, where she could see down the hallway to the bathroom door, Opal took notice of how her girl loitered unduly in amongst the fixtures, and naturally she was wondering if constipation perhaps were the culprit and the cause that she intended to make, when the time came, mention of and so waited for the knob to turn and the door to swing open when she set herself to air in fact news of the wonders of a fiber-rich diet but got by Marie's ensemble put off from it quite entirely. She could hardly bring herself to approve of the scanty t-shirt and the naked midriff and the ever so slight and revealing satiny panties with the duck upon them that, taken altogether, said plainly to Opal "sex kitten," and induced her to alter her demeanor, prompted her to give over the expression she'd cultivated for talk of digestive complaints and put on view instead

an arrangement of her features intended to suggest to her girl
Marie how awful much decadence there plainly was about like
earned for Opal from Marie Criner down at the end of the hall
with the GOBBLERS across her chest and the duck on her pelvis
a treacly sweet variety of adieu that Opal Criner merely endured. She hardly deigned shape a reply.

Donnie Huff had discovered in the darkened bedroom a
vacant piece of air worth expending some attention upon, and
he was sprawled there atop the spread in his undershorts all
caught up in the rigors of soulful perusal when Marie Criner
stepped in from the hallway and bumped shut the bedroom
door with her posterior in advance of inquiring of Donnie Huff
in low and moderately dulcet tones, "You asleep?" which
Donnie Huff confessed at length he'd failed yet to come to be
and allowed, in response to one query further, how he would
not in fact mind if Marie switched on for a moment the boudoir
lamp atop the bureau. It was a puny sort of a thing and cast but
a dingy, feeble light, which proved nonetheless illumination
enough to show off Marie's ensemble to handsome effect, and
Donnie Huff saw fit to give over for the moment his piece of air
and his extravagantly pitiful expression so as to indulge instead
in some undiluted scrutiny of his wife Marie who strolled over
to the window as if she had legitimate cause to fiddle with the
curtains and was not merely carrying her parts and features on
an airing. But even with the tailless shirt before him and the
exposed midriff and the cartoon duck and the cartoon dog on
the skimpy lingerie with the piping about the legholes and the
speckled waistband, Donnie Huff failed to achieve straightoff
his customary frothy state and neglected to make of Marie his
wife the manner of lewd proposal that he usually plied her
with. Instead he merely admired her in her travels over to the
window and back again to the bedstead where she came briefly
to settle at the footboard and asked of her Donnie, as a means
of advancing the festivities, if he had there about him an item
he was intending shortly to inflict upon her like usually
prompted Donnie to rummage about his person and come
across in time his own distinctive manner of pigsticker which
Marie would let on to be as steely a piece of equipment as she'd
lately had cause to see.

Donnie Huff, however, did not appear himself to be harboring any intentions to speak of, and he did not seem at all of a mood to grope playfully about his person and produce at last his prize and his token. Instead he admired a little sadly his wife Marie there at the footboard where she stood exhibiting for him her belly button as she hoped he might perk up and grow lively but watched him merely leave off at last from looking upon her and return to his piece of air that he lavished with attention. And Marie called to him by name in a way she hardly ever anymore was prone to, said to him, "Donnie," the two times it took to prompt him to tell to her, "Yeah?" back though he failed with it still to look upon her, given over like he was to the potent enticements of his particular piece of air.

"Donnie," she said to him yet again and stepped around the footboard so as to slip up onto the spread where she lay raised upon her elbow and looked merely for a time inquiringly at Donnie Huff who did not offer to reveal to her what charms he'd discovered up roundabout the ceiling but persevered in his thoroughgoing distraction until Marie asked of him, "What is it?" in the variety of tone and with the manner of inflection meant to suggest to Donnie Huff how her reserves of compassion were low and dwindling that he appeared himself to decipher and appeared himself to remark and so loosed straightaway a number of significant exhalations prefatory to informing Marie his wife how earlier in the evening he had discovered there in the monkey tent beyond Gladesboro, the occasion to have a word with a young woman, a little slip of thing that was no more than a child truly who'd come he guessed to be healed and seen after.

"Her with the bump?" Marie Criner wanted to know.

"No," Donnie Huff told to her. "No." He couldn't himself say what precisely her complaint had been but he'd hardly taken it even there from the outset for a bump or an abscess or a localized inflammation since he guessed maybe she would have indicated to him the seat of her ills if she'd been herself able to. He simply hadn't figured her for sick and hadn't figured her for ailing but had seen there even right from the first how that child was plainly saddled with troubles. "She wasn't but a little thing," Donnie Huff said and lifted in a gesture his hand so as to suggest to Marie his wife what a delicate creature she'd been, far too fragile for woes and afflictions and too close yet to her girlhood for the torments she was plainly enduring, though Donnie Huff, upon his wife Marie's inquiry, could not name those torments precisely and told instead how he'd stood there up on the dais in the monkey tent and looked into the face of that young woman where he'd seen plain enough that something was wrong, that maybe even everything was wrong, and had offered to her nonetheless his downy patch, which she'd taken up for a moment and gripped with her fingers in a stranglehold though clearly she knew and clearly he knew that no piece of skin could do her much good, not even one that maybe the Lord Christ Himself had laid for a moment His fingers upon.

"Wasn't any help for her," Donnie Huff told to his wife Marie. "Wasn't nothing plaguing her that might have got jolted and twitched away. It just didn't seem that things had played out to suit her. What's a fellow supposed to do about that?"

And Donnie Huff left off with his piece of air so as to look imploringly upon his wife Marie and thereby encourage her to tell to him if she would how it was a guy like him, who through sheer happenstance alone had soared off beyond the ether and loitered there at the portal with the holy Savior, might be expected of an evening to make the world with his forearm a finer place for such as that dainty slip of a girl who'd had things go plainly sour on her. He wished his wife might tell him what maybe please he could have said as well to that man and said to that woman who'd come up onto the dais to speak to him of their dead boy, that man and that woman who were looking clearly for balm and for comfort and didn't in the downy patch discover for themselves much trace of either. How is he supposed to mend these people, Donnie Huff wanted to know, the ones without the earbumps and the inflammations, the ones that might be otherwise afflicted and beset.

Of course Marie Criner, sprawled there atop the spread, saw fit to pass a moment or two in contemplation of Donnie Huff's inquiry so that it might appear in fact an item worth pondering deeply upon, and she shared with him presently in reply an inquiry of her own, asked of her Donnie, "Why is it up to you to make everything right for everybody?"

Straightaway Donnie Huff squirted between his lips one boisterous and moderately exasperated breath of air that he allowed to serve briefly as commentary and rejoinder prior to troubling himself to frame for his Marie the news of how it had after all been him that got killed, him that had passed into the everlasting and consorted and malingered with the Savior in advance of getting at last snatched back to life.

"You mean to say you can look me here in the eye and swear to me you floated up through the ether and chewed the fat with the Lord who told you maybe things you didn't know and showed you maybe things you hadn't seen and then sent you on back down amongst us to act a fool a time longer in the flesh?"

"Yeah," Donnie Huff told to her, "I can," and he looked Marie squarely in the face and made as if he might shortly insist at her where he'd been and who he'd seen there and he probably would have insisted it but for how she looked at him back, which was hardly like Opal looked upon him and hardly like his congregations had seen fit to study him yet since Marie was among them the lone creature who'd just as soon he'd not in fact soared and not in fact loitered and had hardly found cause to consort. So Donnie Huff after all did not declare where he'd been and did not confess who he'd seen there but returned instead briefly to his piece of air which he subjected to a dose of fairly penetrating perusal before making of his Marie one inquiry further, seeking to know in a theoretical sort of a way if a fellow could expire, if a fellow could manage to be deceased and lay dead for a time and then get at length spared and resuscitated without having come in the interval to be somehow uplifted and redeemed and rejuvenated in the ways perhaps of goodliness and grace. He wanted to know if a fellow could get maybe saved and revived and then just be again like he was and do again what he'd been doing notwithstanding all those folks about who wanted him altered and wanted him transformed, needed him delivered from his wickedness and sloth. Donnie simply wanted to learn from his wife Marie if wasn't it a waste for a man to go to the trouble to be dead without deriving from it some manner of profit and undergoing by it a species of renovation. He just couldn't understand how a fellow who'd found occasion to vent his essence could ever be again somehow the same fellow he once was.

Marie Criner, for her part, selected up about the ceiling her own piece of air to study and she gazed with attention upon it as she endeavored to formulate for her Donnie a suitable reply, hoped to discover a way to tell to him how that fellow who'd been killed, that fellow whose functions had ceased and whose breath had left him, that fellow who'd maybe even vented his essence and toured for a time the ether had no cause truly to return to this life quite utterly overhauled since merely reviving itself was surely testament enough to the better qualities and the decent inclinations that had made him worth saving in the first place. Marie Criner wanted to share with her Donnie what a fine sort she'd evermore known that fellow to be before he'd grown by her momma persuaded of his salvation and convinced of his duties to the faithful. She was meaning to remind him of his wholesome and kindly tendencies and his charitable native impulses, was designing even to recount assorted of his more noble undertakings in his pre–heavenly portal days before he'd come yet upon occasion to float and soar. She intended in short to make for her Donnie a case for his place on this earth regardless altogether of whose fingers had laid upon his downy patch and whose fingers hadn't and never would.

And she opened even her mouth as if to reveal there atop the spread some portion of the things she'd devised and formulated to reveal, but she could not manage to phrase and express even the first flattering sentiment as she'd never before had much call to enlarge for Donnie Huff upon her thoughts and explain to Donnie Huff her opinions. They were simply not the sorts who held together consultations and engaged in highly reasoned exchanges, had not ever between them seen truly the need to get by on talking since she was like him and he was like her and the one of them usually suspected already what the other one hadn't yet bothered to say. So she meant herself to testify to Donnie's own admirable features and declare her personal affection and regard for his regular unrejuvenated self, but she did not have any practice much in testifying and had never previously discovered cause to declare and so apprised Donnie Huff of her views and opinions after the only fashion to suit her, told him exclusively, "Oh Donnie," in a moderately wounded and throaty sort of voice, and she lay flat upon the spread so as to free herself to reach out her arms and draw Donnie Huff towards her with the aim of pressing at last his face flush against her GOBBLERS.

She wished him to know that, if not the girl with the disappointments and the couple with the dead boy, there were still troubled folks about he could see after maybe and relieve without running off to a monkey tent to seek them. She meant of course herself and meant of course their Delmon and meant of course Donnie's own buddies who probably needed every now and again uplifting, who could stand, she figured, some regular bucking up. She explained after a fashion to Donnie Huff how terribly fond she'd been of him before he'd grown preacherly, made anyhow assorted semiarticulate noises to that effect and prompted thereby shortly from her Donnie a variety of rejoinder, a meek and muffled piece of talk by which he intended to communicate to his wife Marie that assorted of his cartilages were being presently compressed after a fashion that he did not suspect he could long endure as it seemed to him that several of his more crucial airways had come to be persuaded to collapse, which he told in fact so lowly and so utterly flush against the GOBBLERS that his wife Marie mistook it for a semipreacherly piece of talk and grew consequently inclined to reorganize and freshen her embrace as a means of impressing further her opinion upon Donnie Huff who wriggled about sufficiently to speak plainly at last to his wife Marie and share earnestly with her, "Doll, you're breaking my nose."

So she came to be persuaded to relax her grip upon Donnie Huff who got allowed to sprawl again atop the spread, and he pinched between his fingers his noseridge and relocated his piece of air that his wife Marie permitted him to study for a time while she lay herself and listened to Opal her momma shutting off the tv and extinguishing the lights up in the front of the house where apparently the blind attorney had brought about the conviction and incarceration of what Godless flesh-peddling profiteers he'd been able to round up and prosecute. As had come to be her practice, Opal paused there at the niche and issued for the benefit of her grandbaby Delmon a blessing on his person and his prospects in the day to come. Marie could tell from atop the spread what her momma Opal was up to, her momma Opal who laid at length her lips to her grandbaby's forehead, stepped over to the front door, which she unbolted so as to make occasion to rebolt it herself, and then proceeded down the hallway to the bathroom where Marie could hear her fishing around in the vanity for her creams and her ointments.

And Marie shifted about on the spread and told to Donnie alongside her, "You know there's some people that can't be happy until everybody thinks what they think and everybody does what they do," which prompted Donnie to leave off for the moment with his piece of air and pay instead palpable regard to his wife Marie who repeated for him how it seemed to her some people were, which Donnie Huff did not offer to dispute or comment even upon but lay alongside his wife in silence and listened with her to Opal who beat about in the lavatory, turned on the watertaps and turned off the watertaps and flushed the toilet and dropped apparently her tub of face cream into the sink, which she could not manage to stifle an exclamation about that Marie and that Donnie heard her together at and eyed each other on account of like struck Marie as a suitable moment to open her mouth and inform her Donnie, "Her," which she did not see fit to enlarge straightaway upon and did not find even presently call to contribute to on account of how her Donnie looked upon her and snorted through his uncompressed passageways as a means of telling to his wife Marie what in fact he'd come himself to know and who in fact he'd come to know it about.

"There's things I can't do," Donnie Huff confessed in time. "There's people I can't help. I tried to tell her."

"Well, what did she say?" Marie Criner wanted to find out, and though Donnie Huff appeared to cast back and endeavored to recall he soon enough informed his wife Marie, "I don't know. Something."

"Yeah," she told to him. "Something."

And they lay again silently together and listened to Opal depart from the lavatory and enter into her bedroom across the hall where she drew out a bureau drawer and flung open her closet door so as to rattle a hanger or two before slipping soon enough into her nightdress and climbing in under the covers where Donnie and where Marie could hear her speaking to her dead Carl. They could not decipher precisely what it was she'd found fit to share with him but made out well enough the sound of her voice as she told probably where she'd been and told probably what she'd done there and confessed undoubtedly how fond of her Carl she continued still to be in advance of switching off her lamp and loosing her customary and altogether considerable end-of-the-day exhalation which served itself to further antagonize her girl Marie across the hallway where she wished her Donnie might listen if he would to that particular breath of air that Opal had seen fit to expel as if she'd lifted maybe a finger in the course of the day, as if she'd done a thing otherwise than sit upon her backside on the settee and in the Coronet and at the monkey tent and then back at last on the settee again. She just wished, Marie did, her Donnie might pay some mind to that Opal across the hallway breathing like she'd done a thing and made herself some use.

"If she's the Lord's own sort clean down to her toenails, then let Him leave me be," Marie declared and entertained from Donnie an ever so scant noise that sounded sufficiently encouraging so that Marie invited him to agree with her please that there were surely better ways to pass this life than in ceaseless worship of the Savior, which Donnie indicated with one noise further a willingness to allow.

"She did it to me too," Marie said. "You know how I was."

"Yeah," Donnie told to her, "I do."

And they lay again a time contemplating apparently a common piece of air, passed a few minutes in breathing and scratching and shifting about before Marie wondered of Donnie if he could recall how sometimes he used to slip up back of her while she was at the sink with her hands in the suds and wrap his arms around her at the waist and lay his nose against her neck and give her a jolt there when she'd not been looking for him and not probably been thinking of him and hadn't hardly been expecting an embrace. "You used to do that," Marie informed Donnie who confessed to recall that he'd been previously prone to it, told anyhow to his wife Marie, "I did, didn't I?"

"Yes sir," she said to him, "you did." And she raised herself upon her elbow and exhibited for her Donnie her sleek alluring frontside, her gray university t-shirt, and her flat stomach and her theme-park panties with the speckled waistband and the red piping and the feathery black duck which threw in and served to suggest together to Donnie Huff where it was probably salvation in fact resided, and he appeared inclined to say a thing but did not after all manage to speak and instead made available his cartilages and his airways that Marie Criner was quite pleased, with the aid of her breastbone, to warp and constrict.

iii

He didn't hardly look to her like he'd ever set foot in the woods, and she wanted straightaway to know of him where it was her dead Carl's braces had got to as she could not believe he had before him much prospect of seeming at all a lumberjack with just a belt alone. Plainly he'd given over as well his broadcloth trousers for a pair of unsuitable green twill ones of the variety that Opal guessed a plumber might favor. They did not anyhow begin to say "woodsman" to her, and she breathed at her Donald as a means of displaying her advancing exasperation and then settled her blue beaded bag with the sturdy clasp and the stout hinges upon the endtable so as to free herself to go forth and collect together for Donnie Huff a more appropriate outfit. And it did not appear that he would maybe muster up somehow the wherewithal to speak sternly to her, to advise her of what he'd in fact resolved to do and why he'd in fact resolved to do it, but Marie Criner from the kitchen doorway encouraged with a look her Donnie to go on ahead please and make to his loving wife's mother a forthright declaration, the identical forthright declaration they'd together formulated and devised there atop of the spread the night previous which Donnie Huff moved at last to issue and air, said that is to his loving wife's mother, "Opal," and wondered might she perch for a moment upon the settee as he had a thing he wished directly to speak to her of.

While Opal Criner was herself quite certain that Donnie Huff wouldn't change her mind as to the shortcomings of his ensemble, she indulged him nonetheless and lit upon the middle settee cushion from where she watched her Donald stride over towards the tv and back and then over towards the tv again with a vigor and a manly bustle that struck her together as ever so becoming, and she was harboring there intentions of complimenting her Donald upon his gait when he managed finally to deliver himself of the bulk of his declaration, made mention anyhow of what anymore he would do and what anymore he wouldn't, that he fairly much proclaimed as if he probably meant it, announced in very nearly the tone that him and that Marie had concocted together and honed. Now Opal Criner had in her years on this earth cultivated such a thoroughgoing distaste for the variety of disclosures that ran contrary to her plans and her wishes that she'd come in time to suffer from a species of hearing impairment, had apparently lost somehow the capacity to make sense of unwelcome revelations and was prone to look upon any bearer of bad tidings as if he'd spoken to her in some vagrant mongrel tongue with which she'd never had cause to come to be acquainted. Consequently, she did not make to Donnie Huff's declaration any manner of response but trained upon him merely an acutely quizzical expression as she waited for his opinion to shift and his intentions to transform.

From the kitchen doorway, however, Marie Criner pinched together for Donnie Huff's benefit her lips and inclined as a means of edification her head so as to prompt Donnie to go on and repeat if he might his highly resolved declaration that Donnie Huff mustered up the breath for and did in fact repeat with fairly palpable conviction, told that is sternly to Opal Criner what anymore he would do and what anymore he wouldn't and added beyond it where precisely he was shortly meaning to go and who precisely he was not intending to carry with him that

Opal Criner there on the settee entertained the news of and displayed exclusively her uncomprehending expression until Donnie Huff managed, with the further aid of his wife Marie's pinched lips in conjunction with an additional edifying nod, to intone for the benefit of his loving wife's mother the very item in fact he'd practiced atop the bedclothes and with precisely the emphasis and exactly the inflection him and his Marie had settled the night previous upon.

Naturally, in the face of such a fine and passionate performance, Opal Criner could not help but smile at last meekly upon her Donald and she managed to part her lips and show her teeth to her girl Marie off against the doorjamb before giving presently voice to the pitiful little noise that Marie had informed Donnie already her mother would give surely voice to and had instructed him to turn please upon her an altogether deaf ear which Donnie endeavored to do. But he wavered there in the face of superior execution, plumbed inadvertently such thoroughgoing woe in that lone little noise that Marie his wife was pressed to repinch and reincline and just altogether reedify as best she was able from the doorjamb and so managed to resurrect in her Donald his sense of resolve that had faltered plainly and flagged but returned to him in an adequate dose to allow him merely to withstand and merely to endure not just the initial pitiful noise but the eventual and subsequent pitiful noise as well that, with the aid of his wife Marie, he'd practiced atop the bedclothes enduring and withstanding both.

Opal Criner, who'd grown accustomed to the successful application of her pitiful noise, could not believe her Donald might muster up somehow the wherewithal to resist her own particular species of wounded lament. She guessed maybe she'd not rendered it with anguish enough to melt him and so she loosed upon her Donald a string of increasingly tormented discharges, inflicted upon him a veritable barrage of pitiful noises until Donnie Huff grew concerned that Opal was perhaps exposing herself to the threat of hyperventilation from her aggravated display of woe, and he consulted after a fashion with his wife Marie who merely pinched and inclined and edified from the jamb.

Delmon, who'd discovered out by the ditch a vein of clay to wallow in, had crossed lately the yard in the company of Sheba the wirehaired dog and had arrived at last upon the front slab from where he meant to display through the doorscreen an item he'd turned up with a stick, an item he suspected perhaps was a jewel of untold worth unless of course it was a piece of bottlebottom instead. Sheba herself, who'd not lately seen anybody much through the doorscreen and had not in a while enjoyed the pleasure of eying Delmon upright on the slab, commenced pretty directly to bark and blandish and carry on, but was obliged to take shortly instruction from Donnie Huff who made a wholly spontaneous and entirely unrehearsed manner of declaration that succeeded quite altogether as a curative for Sheba the wirehaired dog who lowered her backside onto the concrete and gazed with Delmon through the screenwire in the direction chiefly of Opal Criner on the settee who was demonstrating an advancing disposition to whimper which Donnie Huff had himself been forewarned about and so told her unedified and uninclined at one highly resolved thing further.

In a ploy that Marie Criner had not upon the bedclothes foreseen, Opal from the settee turned her attention to her grandbaby Delmon out on the slab and informed him of his daddy's newly minted opinions, wished Delmon would listen please to what it was she'd only just heard fall from the lips of that selfsame Donnie Huff, after which she concocted her own interpretive rendition of Donnie Huff's highly resolved declarations and assigned to Donnie Huff motives and intentions that she guessed could not help but seem even to a child unwholesome, and she wished might Delmon tell to her please if didn't it appear to him that his daddy was plainly a variety of sorry rascal that Delmon looked there on the slab to weigh and consider with some attention prior to wishing of his grandmomma back if she'd identify please for him the species of jewel he'd mined lately out at the ditch, which straightoff Opal informed him was trash.

Marie Criner and Donnie Huff had troubled themselves there atop the spread to reason out between them a fairly persuasive sort of an argument against Donnie Huff loving his

Jesus with the fiery ardor that Opal made out to love the Lord herself, and Donnie Huff, prompted by an edifying nod, set out to render up to Opal Criner what explanation precisely they'd cobbled together, but she proved of no mood to hear this evening talk further from her Donald and she made at him a motion with her hand, elevated slightly her fingers and exhibited them after a fashion that spoke plainly to Donnie Huff of how his loving wife's mother was not looking this night to learn how the Lord could do anymore without him. Instead she was hoping to be left to her thoughts and her musings, and she pinched together her own lips and inclined her own head as a means of suggesting her mood and her wishes to both her girl Marie, who retired to the dinette to lay an undercoat of varnish to her boltbox, and to her Donald as well who stepped himself onto the slab and grew pressed to suggest to Delmon his boy that he'd not probably scratched up an emerald.

Opal sat by herself in the front room and watched the shank-end of the national news show on the station in Bluefield, made anyhow to be looking at the tv as Donnie, who'd elected to carry Delmon with him, passed in the Coronet around the house and down the drive and over the culvert and on out into the road where he accelerated heedlessly and produced thereby one pitiful noise further, which Opal Criner from the settee vented and expelled before turning her attention to the tv screen where a man from Kentucky had plowed up in his cornfield a piece of a boat, a sizable portion of wheelhouse that he could not begin to account for as there wasn't any water much about. Delmon in the Coronet applied himself to tuning the radio, scanned up the dial and down the dial but returned pretty shortly to the Big Q-mix where he'd left in the first place from, and him and his daddy Donnie listened for a time together to a lilting duet with considerable fabricated violin accents and fairly intolerable spells of semiharmonious trilling and wailing, which they endured together in silence until Donnie saw fit to wonder of his child if he might extinguish for the moment the radio and listen instead to a declaration his daddy would find cause shortly to air in earnest, a declaration Donnie had cultivated and had honed with his Marie there atop the spread, a grave and sober sort of a sentiment that Donnie Huff intoned morosely across the carseat for the benefit of Delmon his boy who was truly no judge much of declarations and had gauged this one only ever so briefly before he saw fit to inform his daddy, "Ho!," thereby suggesting to Donnie Huff that he'd been perhaps insufficiently somber and inadequately morose.

So Donnie Huff passed the time to Gladesboro declaring and redeclaring his piece of talk and entertaining from Delmon his child assorted inappropriate exclamations, Delmon who gained permission to switch back on the Big Q-mix, where a fellow was telling through song the story of a saintly woman he'd known, a kindly, goodhearted, curvaceous manner of creature who'd perished some way or another from the face of this earth and had deprived thereby that fellow of her various qualities which he professed to miss and long for in a most palpably grievous and forlorn sort of a way which Donnie Huff found instructive, and he paid especially acute regard to the torment with which that fellow sang of his dead girlfriend's most comely parts that he'd grown pressed to do evermore without. Donnie Huff endeavored to manufacture on his own a similar sort of distress and applied to his pertinent declaration the species of anguished breathiness he guessed he might have call for if he were to come to be bereft of some handsome womanly features himself. He lacked of course the backbeat and the moody guitar strains that the fellow with the dead girlfriend enjoyed, but Donnie Huff could not help but feel that he'd rendered upon his declaration a noticeable improvement, which he invited his child Delmon to remark, encouraged him to turn down for the moment the Big Q-mix so as to hear from his daddy a piece of news which proved in fact to be the indentical piece of news Delmon had heard once already though in plainly a less respirated condition. And Delmon, not one to let a nuance and an alteration go unremarked, straightaway saw fit to inform his daddy, "Ho!"

Donnie Huff was late and the Reverend Mr. Dunbar had no tolerance much for a witness to the love and miraculous wonders of the Savior who on only his second night of testifying could not show up at the monkey tent on time. That Cotten, the reverend recalled, him with the hair and with the teeth and with the clefted chin had ceased firstoff to be prompt just ahead of becoming a fornicator on the road plainly to perdition, which the reverend figured maybe he'd speak of to Donnie Huff though he revised pretty shortly his intentions as he could not make ripe with hellfire the news that a boy of his acquaintance had suffered a willowy flaxen-haired woman to wrap her legs around his waist and squeeze the holiness from him. He guessed maybe instead he'd appeal to Donnie Huff's sense of professional decorum and let slip how poorly the brotherhood of healers looked as a group upon tardiness, and he was hoping he might be able to piece together as well a parable that addressed itself to the wages of an untimely arrival, but he spied the beige Coronet before he could get well under way, and he watched it pass between the fenceposts and down into the slop of the marshy bottom which was fairly filled already with vehicles. Donnie Huff endeavored, with the aid of the rearview mirror, to render himself suitably grievous and forlorn, which he hoped he might maintain as him and his child climbed from the Coronet and crossed towards the tent where the Reverend Mr. Dunbar stood hatless before the flap in his black suit and his string tie and awaited them with his arms crossed upon his chest, watched them skirt their way around an Electra and off between a Pinto and a Wagoneer before they angled directly towards him there at the tentflap, making their way with no detectable haste, which the reverend was intending to display his irritation about and had even already mustered up a peevish expression when he noticed the state of Donnie Huff's ensemble, failed that is to detect any discernible woodsy qualities, and regarded most especially the lack of braces as a serious omission which he guessed he might speak of instead but came straightaway to be prevented from it by Donnie Huff himself who told to the reverend an item of such exceeding breathiness and such unsurpassed torment that the reverend could not begin himself to make out the first word of it.

In the tent, the Reverend Mr. Dunbar's sister Sophia was fingering lightly her organ keys and swaying the way she was prone to on her stool as she offered up an airy devotional melody that fell sweetly upon the ears of Donnie Huff, who could not straightaway tell to the reverend how it was he'd expected to get taken for a timberman in a belt and a pair of green twill trousers, did not anyhow make much effort to speak to the matter and shared at last with the reverend instead the identical breathy and tormented item that he'd undertaken previously to share. But the Reverend Mr. Dunbar did not seem disposed to decipher at the moment in the respiration and the anguishment whatever grain of sense might lie there, and he made use of the lull on the far side of Donnie Huff's declaration to suggest to Donnie Huff how highly in fact the brotherhood of healers regarded among their members a prompt and timely fulfilment of their obligations like put the reverend in mind of a fellow he'd known who'd fallen into the ways of sloth and tardiness and had passed undoubtedly upon his death into the fiery nether regions where he'd become shortly baked goods. Consequently, it seemed to the reverend that if Donnie didn't wish to burn in hell he might in the future leave the house a little earlier which Donnie Huff rendered up a breathy tormented declaration about, the identical breathy tormented declaration he'd aired twice already and that he got for the third time ignored at by the Reverend Mr. Dunbar, who turned as if to lead Donnie Huff into the monkey tent proper and so heard straightoff from him one additional declaration further, was privy to a "Hey!" that Donnie Huff loosed with no dulcet respirational features to mute it.

The reverend swung around precipitously to discover just what in God's name the trouble might be, and Donnie Huff prepared himself to give once more voice to the piece of news him and his Marie had honed and had cultivated there atop the spread, but in looking at the reverend, in looking truly past the reverend and into the tent where folks sat and waited for what dispensation they could come by, Donnie detected in the congregation, in the way that they laid against their chairbacks and shifted heavily about to look every now and again upon each other, the origins of his complaint and the very seeds of the distress that him and his wife had attempted upon the spread to phrase and express with more delicacy truly and more grace than any of it called for and required. So Donnie Huff did not make again his declaration to the Reverend Mr. Dunbar who stood there at the tentflap just waiting to get declared at. Donnie Huff did not straightaway tell to the reverend anything at all, failed to make breathy mention of the couple with the dead boy and the girl with the soured prospects and the lady as well with the earbump alone, but only once he'd been bidden and once he'd been charged to go on if he meant to and speak did Donnie Huff announce in a clear and level voice, "I ain't going in there."

"Well son," the reverend told to him and demonstrated a native gift for lip pinching that quite altogether eclipsed the meager talents of Donnie Huff's wife and Donnie Huff's loving wife's mother.

"I can't do nothing for those people," Donnie Huff said, "and I don't want them thinking I can."

The reverend, from reflex chiefly, cited straightoff at Donnie Huff a scrap of verse that Donnie Huff was himself in no mood to plumb the sense of and he merely repeated for the Reverend Mr. Dunbar where it was he wouldn't go and what it was he couldn't do, and the reverend intoned again a portion of scripture on the topic largely of a frail and feeble faith.

"I just got to thinking about it," Donnie Huff told to the Reverend Mr. Dunbar, who failed to fly back at him with an additional piece of verse and encouraged thereby Donnie Huff to reveal as best he was able the various misgivings he'd lately entertained like had come with the laggards to a head but had been gnawing already upon him before the folks with the boy and the girl with the prospects and the people otherwise with the nameless distresses had stepped up to grip and hold to him. "I don't guess I've been square with you," Donnie Huff confessed. "I mean yeah I sunk to the creekbottom and they all of them tell me I was dead, tell me I went green all over, but I can't hardly swear to you what got vented and where to. Truth is," Donnie Huff said and leaned in towards the reverend so as to confide to him, "I don't much think I sailed and soared, got no recollection of the heavenly portal, hadn't ever run up on Jesus, and just don't guess I was meant somehow to make my way in this world by telling folks I have."

And the reverend said to Donnie Huff one time further, "Well son," and gazed for a moment rather aimlessly about as he endeavored to discover the words with which to inform politely Donnie Huff what a thoroughgoing fool he seemed to be. But Donnie Huff had no need to get even politely instructed and chastised, and he assured shortly the Reverend Mr. Dunbar, "I know I got killed like some people will, and I know I got over it like most people never do, and that might be maybe enough for the God-fearing sort who need just to clap eyes on a fellow who was dead once but isn't dead any longer. But what about the rest of them?" Donnie Huff wanted to know, "those ones with no talent much for thrashing and flapping around, them that won't pitch over, them that can't and never will. Is it enough for them that I got killed and come back, would it matter at all if Jesus Himself had took me up in His arms and kissed me flush on the mouth?"

And the reverend allowed how plainly on this earth there were hearts beyond the reach of even the grace of the Savior, souls that the very love of the Lord could hardly cause to quake and tremble, and the Reverend Mr. Dunbar dropped down a couple of octaves so as to recite for the benefit of Donnie Huff a piece of scripture on the topic of that last day and that last hour when that golden trumpet would sound to call the faithful home to the bosom of their keeper which served itself to stir Donnie Huff after a fashion and promoted in him a bout of genuine passion that he fairly completely vented and pretty thoroughly extinguished with one exclamation alone, suggested that is to the Reverend Mr. Dunbar, "Preacher, why don't you just put a lid on it."

And the reverend worked and shaped his features and got upon his face a look that Donnie Huff had been himself privy to before, that look that people who guessed they had breeding and thought they had charms were wont to work up and display once they'd come into the presence of the sort of pitiful, ignorant creatures that plainly didn't know their assends from the moon in the sky. The reverend exhibited baldly for Donnie Huff his thoroughgoing disdain and appeared inclined to tell to him, "Well," and tell to him, "Son," which Donnie Huff managed to head off by confessing to the Reverend Mr. Dunbar,

"Time was when I didn't believe in anything. Hell, I come from a whole string of people that got by believing in nothing, didn't ever have any blessings to count and didn't much care, there at the last, which way it was they went. Wasn't a one of them that loved his Jesus and here I was set to be the first just because I got dead and done in and that son-of-a-bitch Gaither beat me on back to life. I saw spots, preacher, little green ones and Opal tells me it was the Lord in heaven and damned if I don't get blessed straightaway with tits enough to make it seem maybe so. You're willing to figure it was Jesus yourself and the portal and the gates and the peaches and the nectarines, and all those folks that quiver and shake are making out surely like it's Jesus as well. But it's those ones that won't twitch," Donnie told to him, "those ones that can't flap around that tell to me plain enough who it was I lay dead and saw and who it was I didn't. And maybe if I can't go back and believe anymore in just nothing again I'll go ahead and believe in them instead. The thing of it is," Donnie Huff said and peered beyond the Reverend Mr. Dunbar and into the monkey tent proper, "I don't know anything about the Lord. I hadn't ever come across much sign of Him."

"Well," the reverend did say, "son," and he took upon his features a look of palpable sadness and remorse as if he was touched in fact deeply by the crisis of a brother healer and was sorrowful at the prospect of such a loss to the calling, and he appeared even likely to commiserate and console until he dropped his chin and reminded Donnie Huff, "I gave you your pay."

"Yeah," Donnie Huff told to him, "you did."

"I'll be wanting the most of it back," the reverend declared. "You haven't hardly done a thing to earn it."

"I witnessed for you."

"Just the once," the reverend said.

"And I stood out here and told all this to you," Donnie Huff informed him. "I could have stood in there and told it all to them."

"Yeah," the Reverend Mr. Dunbar informed him, "well," and he held out his right hand palm upwards towards Donnie

Huff and undertook to implore him with a look but Donnie Huff refused stoutly to be implored and suggested at length to the Reverend Mr. Dunbar, "There's money enough in there," and he indicated with his nose chiefly the monkey tent prior to dropping his head to indicate instead the fleshly miraculous thumbjoint before him. "Go on and beat it loose."

Delmon had discovered in a boggy place under a Buick a sliver of stone that it looked to him the Indians had shaped and sharpened and he clambered up out of the muck to show to his daddy his pointy rock which his daddy took up in his fingers and admired in advance of proposing to Delmon that they carry it home to show to his momma, which Delmon found straightoff to be a splendid idea and so drew on his daddy's hand to pull him away from the preacher and pull him away from the tent and retire with him in the direction of the Coronet, which the Reverend Mr. Dunbar watched them at for a moment in silence but determined presently to speak, guessed he was sorry himself to be the one to tell this evening to Donnie Huff where it was his flesh would get seared soon enough from his bones once his sins were tallied and his blasphemies revealed and his evils on this earth laid bare and made abundantly plain, where it was his soul would suffer ceaseless torments and neverending woes, would rot and would putrefy and would bring him no end of agony and regret, where it was the wages of his abundant foolishness and vice would get at last visited upon him in the wrath of the Savior Himself that the reverend was still speaking in fact of by the time Donnie Huff and Delmon his boy had gained the Coronet where they could hear anymore considerably less of what the reverend said and appreciably more of how he said it with his voice rising and falling by turns and mingling so with the lowly organ strains as to sound almost like Gospel.

Opal made like she didn't hear them. Once they'd pulled into the drive and crossed the culvert, Donnie Huff could see her through the doorscreen, spied her there sitting upon the settee showing to him the side of her head like she didn't hardly know they were about, hadn't seen the headlamps on the bushes or detected at all the tires upon the crushed stone, and she did

not swivel around and rise as they passed on up towards the
house and beyond the slab where Sheba the wirehaired dog
arrived from her hole in the crawlspace to make of Donnie
Huff vigorous inquiries as she followed the car through the
sideyard and across the backlot to the shed. Donnie Huff had
wadded Opal's green canvas tarp and jammed it up between
two wall studs off at the head of the shed where he sent his boy
Delmon to fetch it please back to him, and Donnie shortly and
Delmon together spread again that tarp upon the Coronet,
hooked it onto the front bumperends, drew it taut as best they
were able, and hooked it onto the back bumperends as well
before stepping out into the yard and showing each of them
their shoetoes to Sheba the wirehaired dog who'd seen fit to
blandish but demonstrated straightoff a willingness to engage
in other pursuits, and she allowed Delmon and allowed Donnie
to proceed around the house unblandished further at and step
together with no sendoff much in through the front doorway
where they entered into the presence of the side still of Opal
Criner's head, which came only at length and only in time to be
at last the front of it instead.

From the dinette in the kitchen Marie Criner heard the
doorscreen slap shut and so rose to take her place at the jamb
from where she watched her Delmon and her Donnie enjoy the
acknowledgment of Opal Criner who advised them to wipe
their shoebottoms please upon the mat prior to stepping onto
the rug proper, which she watched to see that they did in advance of returning her attention to the tv where a man in a gray
jacket and a blue striped tie was entertaining questions from the
audience in the studio and telling to them things they'd not
managed yet somehow to figure out for themselves. In the
interest of promoting a congenial exchange, Donnie Huff wondered of Opal Criner might she share with him please who it
was she was watching there on the set that Opal proved altogether delighted to oblige him in and informed Donnie Huff
back, "Just some fellow that thinks he's found out already every
little thing there is to know."

"Oh," Donnie Huff told to her, "him."

And Opal Criner showed to Donnie her pinched lips and

her sour expression and exposed at him as well the palm of her upturned hand as invitation to Donnie Huff to lay please and deposit her dead Carl's keys upon it, her dead Carl's keys that she dropped directly into her blue beaded bag, it with the grommets and it with the hinges and it with the clasp that shut like a gunshot.

Off beyond the planksaw in the bottom by the creek, little Gaither and Freeman MacAfee and even Buddy Isom too performed independently contortions and maneuvers and relinquished inadvertent semiagonized discharges as they listened together to Donnie Huff explain and describe and approximate the rigors of his ordeal, the stages of his decline into genuine and certifiable crisis, and the glories of his rejuvenation that had left him at last a happy and robust manner of fellow once again.

"It was like pissing walnuts," Donnie Huff declared and thereby prompted little Gaither into a wholly reflexive variety of squat that was itself the immediate result of the simultaneous tautening and puckering of his sinews and muscles in sympathy with Donnie Huff's tracts and ducts and byways that had been pressed to accommodate Donnie Huff's various sizable spiny stones. Freeman MacAfee was distressed to learn that Donnie Huff hadn't gone to the trouble to fish his stones from the bowl and make of them keepsakes like Freeman MacAfee had possessed himself the foresight to do and stored three of his own ones in a pimento jar in the cabinet over the refrigerator at home from where he took them out every now and again when he was feeling poorly so as to remind himself how poorly in fact he might feel.

Buddy Isom inquired of Donnie Huff if hadn't he said that one of his stones had been about the size of a butterbean which proved itself news enough to fairly reduce little Gaither to a puckering heap even before Donnie Huff had seen fit to expand upon Buddy Isom's inquiry and allow how he'd endured in fact a stone about the girth of a cocktail olive which little Gaither gave tongue to a squeaky sort of a noise about while Freeman MacAfee attempted himself to figure out how a fellow might pass such a stone which Donnie Huff was pleased to explain to him, revealed anyhow to Freeman MacAfee how there were men about with hose enough to pass some sizable nuggets and men about with no hose much to speak of that Freeman MacAfee ruminated upon prior to discovering at length cause to tell to Donnie Huff, "Hey!"

Alvis spied him straightoff, rounded the heap of lapwood, accelerated up out of the swale, and laid eyes immediately upon him there beyond the planksaw with Buddy and with Freeman and with Gaither in a heap. And the notion came to him that perhaps after all he could get somehow reinfused, could twitch again and palpitate and gain once more the balm that had soothed him and brought to him peace before it had dwindled and before it had waned and before it had left him to be like he'd been. He liked to figure maybe he'd not gripped with sufficient resolve, had been timid with his fingerends upon the downy patch, which he guessed had probably affected his personal dosage of balm, had reduced and diluted it and explained thereby how he'd felt upon Sunday renewed and altered and had remained throughout Monday more than a little transformed before he weakened plainly in his condition and had lapsed here by Thursday to pretty much his customary low-slung and unimproved state. He just wanted to tingle again and soar maybe a little if he might, and Donnie Huff, for his part, didn't offer to dodge him. Donnie didn't make to shift away but stayed just precisely where he'd come already to be as Alvis nosed his Ventura in alongside Buddy Isom's half-ton and left it straightaway for the clutch of them there off beyond the planksaw by the creek where Alvis endured a blessing apiece from Buddy Isom and from Freeman MacAfee and from little Gaither as well who lifted his fingers in a papal fashion and moved them devoutly about. And Donnie Huff offered to Alvis his hand on the arm with the downy patch upon it but did not appear much surprised at all when his knuckles went unsqueezed and his fingers went unshook and his forearm instead got gripped and held to by Alvis who waited to see if he'd tingle and waited to see if he'd find cause to lurch like he'd pretty much left off expecting he would but held nonetheless to the downy strip of flesh there by the planksaw along the bottom in the ruined woods with the trunks and the limbs and the lumber about but no faithful plainly to speak of.

Freeman MacAfee told of the sizable obstruction that Donnie Huff had claimed already hose enough to flush and invited Alvis Nevins to be with him please quite altogether skeptical as to the girth of the stone and ever so highly doubtful as to the wealth of the equipment which Freeman MacAfee recalled having caught once sight of previously there in the hand of Donnie Huff where he'd not himself been able hardly to tell it from a finger.

"A finger?" Donnie Huff said to him and disengaged his arm from Alvis Nevins's faltering grip so as to lift up his hand and display a lone digit for the benefit of Freeman MacAfee of whom Donnie Huff inquired, "Was it this finger here?" which Freeman MacAfee could not apparently say straightoff though he saw fit to grow mildly inflamed and told to Donnie Huff with some fabricated passion and some manufactured disdain, "And you a preacher."

"Well, go in peace," Donnie Huff told to him and left upright his solitary digit, "but just go," which Gaither saw fit to Amen and then wag and work devoutly assorted of his own uplifted fingers about that Buddy Isom proved disciple enough to throw in with while Alvis Nevins, for his part, stood there in the bottom between the planksaw and the creek and insinuated with his various features the merest beginnings of a sour, dyspeptic display.

Opal didn't let on to have heard them, made as if she'd come across enchantment on the network news, and so paid her mind exclusively to the set even once Donnie Huff had taken his leave of Buddy Isom, swung shut the truckdoor, and tossed his empty can into the bed, freeing him to show Sheba his potent leather upper. He lingered on the slab, peered in through the screenwire at his loving wife's mother there atop the settee from where she exposed at him strictly the side of her head even after he'd scuffed his bootbottoms on the cement and had snorted and had dredged so as to make himself plainly known to her, and he told her through the doorscreen, "Evening Opal," whereupon her jaw muscles tautened and grew defined, which she allowed to stand as comment and serve alone as rejoinder while she collected her beaded bag, rose from the settee, and retired in silence down the hallway towards her room where she figured plainly the residue of her Carl—his blazer on the maple butler, his oxfords on the closet floor, his handsome color portrait upon the bureau—would speak likely more to her of goodliness and grace than Donnie even in the very flesh.

And he didn't trouble himself to call to her but only watched her through the doorscreen retire prior to entering on into the house and depositing himself in his upholstered chair from where he shouted into the kitchen, "Hey doll," and spied on the tv the President scratch his spaniel.

Donnie's child Delmon was eating a confection as he slipped from the kitchen into the front room where he approached the upholstered chairarm and told to his daddy the thing he'd been charged to tell, but he was freighted as he told it with so awful much yellow cake and so awful much red filling as to obscure his declaration pretty completely, and so he chewed and he swallowed and he told in time to his daddy again, "Momma says she's at the sink," which Donnie Huff weighed and Donnie Huff considered prior to asking presently of Delmon his child, "What?"

"At the sink," Delmon told to him. "Momma says she's there."

And once he'd selected a piece of air to gaze if he might upon, Donnie Huff gazed in fact for a moment upon it before telling one time to himself, "Oh," and telling, "Oh," one time to Delmon his child as well in advance of and as preamble to gaining straightaway his feet and hauling his cartilages and transporting his airways out altogether from the front room where Delmon remained by the chairarm sculpting and shaping his confection and ingesting every now and again a portion of it while he watched on the tv somebody somewhere lying in the road under a sheet, a fellow sprawled face down beside a streak of pavement that he'd stained to the gutter where his fluids had drained and run off, and Delmon touched his tongue to his confection and dripped a drop of filling onto his shirtfront as he heard, above the sirens on the tv, above the vigorous lamentations of the kin, above the sober, measured baritone of the national correspondent, a lone girlish shriek of delight.